TITLES BY KAY HOOPER

Haven
The First Prophet

THE
FIRST
PROPHET

KAY HOOPER

JOVE BOOKS, NEW YORK

THE BERKLEY PUBLISHING GROUP
Published by the Penguin Group
Penguin Group (USA) Inc.
375 Hudson Street, New York, New York 10014, USA
Penguin Group (Canada), 90 Eglinton Avenue East, Suite 700, Toronto, Ontario M4P 2Y3, Canada
(a division of Pearson Penguin Canada Inc.) • Penguin Books Ltd, 80 Strand, London WC2R 0RL,
England • Penguin Ireland, 25 St Stephen's Green, Dublin 2, Ireland (a division of Penguin
Books Ltd) • Penguin Group (Australia), 707 Collins Street, Melbourne, Victoria 3008, Australia
(a division of Pearson Australia Group Pty Ltd) • Penguin Books India Pvt Ltd, 11 Community
Centre, Panchsheel Park, New Delhi—110 017, India • Penguin Group (NZ), 67 Apollo Drive,
Rosedale, Auckland 0632, New Zealand (a division of Pearson New Zealand Ltd) • Penguin Books,
Rosebank Office Park, 181 Jan Smuts Avenue, Parktown North 2193, South Africa • Penguin China,
B7 Jiaming Center, 27 East Third Ring Road North, Chaoyang District, Beijing 100020, China

Penguin Books Ltd., Registered Offices: 80 Strand, London WC2R 0RL, England

This is a work of fiction. Names, characters, places, and incidents either are the product of the author's
imagination or are used fictitiously, and any resemblance to actual persons, living or dead, business
establishments, events, or locales is entirely coincidental. The publisher does not have control over
and does not have any responsibility for author or third-party websites or their content.

THE FIRST PROPHET

A Jove Book / published by arrangement with the author

PUBLISHING HISTORY
Jove premium edition / December 2012

Copyright © 2012 by Kay Hooper.
Cover photograph copyright © Andy and Michelle Kerry / Trevillion Images.
Cover design by Rita Frangie.
Text design by Laura K. Corless.

ISBN: 978-0-515-15288-3

JOVE®
Jove Books are published by The Berkley Publishing Group,
a division of Penguin Group (USA) Inc.,
375 Hudson Street, New York, New York 10014.
JOVE® is a registered trademark of Penguin Group (USA) Inc.
The "J" design is a trademark of Penguin Group (USA) Inc.

PRINTED IN THE UNITED STATES OF AMERICA

10 9 8 7 6 5 4 3 2 1

ALWAYS LEARNING   **PEARSON**

THE
FIRST
PROPHET

Report
September 22

To Whom It May Concern:

I address this report as I have done because you and I agreed it would be best that your name not appear in any written form, for obvious reasons. Future reports will be submitted in the same format and manner, as requested.

As a brief preface, I will say that in my routine monitoring of various psychics in this country and elsewhere, active and latent, whom I considered candidates for either the Special Crimes Unit or Haven, I found myself becoming suspicious of certain events. I cannot say it was a situation I immediately understood; my understanding, as these reports will make clear, is ongoing as I—and others—slowly piece together the disparate bits of information and actions that are clearly a part of what is going on.

I will also repeat, as I told you when we met, that I intend to take no one else into my confidence unless

*and until it becomes necessary. Until then, only you
and Miranda will be privy to the information I am
able to collect.*

*I cannot say just why I believe something sinister
is going on within and around the largely underground psychic community; it is not a certainty I can
attribute to either my or my wife's precognitive abilities. Psychically, we are both . . . blocked . . . whenever
we turn our attention toward certain events and
actions—and people. That alone would have drawn
my attention, but there was more. Much more.*

*I therefore submit the following narrative, assem-
bled from among those involved in the situation that
transpired, and from my own firsthand observations
and senses as events unfolded. I have no doubt we are
a long way from learning the complete story, but
herein, I believe, is a good place to begin these reports,
detailing a situation that occurred several months
ago, and which I believe may prove to be the catalyst
that will begin to unlock at least some of the secrecy
surrounding these events.*

Respectfully submitted,
Noah Bishop, Unit Chief
Special Crimes Unit, FBI

PROLOGUE

They moved with the kind of stealth that came of long experience and grim purpose, and they didn't waste a motion or make a sound. They numbered no more than half a dozen, not counting the man who stood back from the isolated cabin they had encircled and watched them. He had extremely well-developed night vision.

Through his unobtrusive, almost invisible headset, a whisper reached him.

"She's not alone. Brodie's with her."

He barely hesitated before speaking softly into the microphone. "How long have they been here?"

"The vehicle is cold."

"Then he's had time to call in reinforcements."

"Maybe. But we have lookouts posted, and no one's

reported any movement toward this position. We may have hours yet."

"And we may not." Duran glanced back over his shoulder at what daylight would have shown was a cliff edge no more than a few feet behind him, and a sheer drop to a boulder-littered canyon below. "Brodie chose well; this is an easily defensible position. For him. I don't propose to be trapped here, and dawn is minutes away. I assume Brodie is armed."

An unamused chuckle came from the headset. "He usually is. To the teeth. And he'll go down fighting to protect this one."

"I know." Duran wondered absently whether his lieutenant had reached this conclusion because he knew the fragile young psychic inside the cabin very much resembled another young woman Brodie had nearly died trying to protect years before, but the next words he heard through his headset answered that question for him.

"She'd be as valuable to him as to us. If we're right about her potential, she's worth ten times her weight in gold."

"Yes. I need to know what's going on inside that cabin. Move closer. Carefully."

———

Not being psychic himself had its drawbacks, Brodie knew. Like now. How the hell could he tell her she was wrong when he wasn't sure?

"I have to try," she insisted, her face too gaunt for a young woman and her eyes far too strained.

"You can't." He kept his voice matter-of-fact, having learned at least that psychics as a rule loved a challenge—and young women could rarely resist one. "You're exhausted. You haven't slept for two days or eaten since yesterday. Besides that, it's new to you, not yet under control—"

Her soft laugh was hardly a sound. "If I don't at least try, it'll be under *their* control. They're here, Brodie. They're all around us. I can feel them."

Brodie didn't let her see the chill he felt crawling up and down his spine. "I can hold them off until our people get here. The sun'll be up in less than an hour, and the bastards aren't invisible. Until then, even if they could they wouldn't bust in with guns blazing, not with you here."

She was shaking her head, and her voice shook as well. "No, they want me badly. *He* wants me badly. They might take the risk of wounding me. I think they might. And they'd kill you for sure, you know that."

"Listen to me." He held his voice steady, held both her hands tightly, and tried his best to hold her gaze despite the way it darted around in building panic. "The windows are shuttered and, like the door, are made of steel-sheathed solid oak with iron hinges and locks. The walls are two feet thick. There's no chimney. This cabin is a fortress. They'd have to take it apart to get to us. That's one of the reasons I picked it."

She wasn't listening, wasn't hearing. "I have to . . . try. I have to stop them. What they'll do . . . You don't understand, Brodie, what they'll do to me. You can't understand."

"Jill, don't. Don't let them panic you into doing something that could destroy you."

She snatched her hands from his grasp and backed away from him. "I'm afraid of them, don't you know that? *Terrified*. I know what they'll do if they get me. *I know*. My dreams have shown me. Over and over again. They'll hurt me. They'll hurt me in ways you couldn't imagine in your worst nightmares."

"I won't let them hurt you—"

"You can't stop them. But I can. I know I can."

Brodie saw her eyes begin to darken and lose focus, saw her entire body tense as she called on all the energies she had left in a desperate attempt to form some kind of weapon that her panic demanded she try to use to save herself.

And even with only five senses to call his own, Brodie had a terrible premonition. "No! Jill, don't—"

———

Duran's headset crackled softly in his ear, and he pulled it off and stared at it. He was granted only that warning, and only scant seconds to understand what it portended. For him, it was enough.

Without putting the headset back on, he snapped into the microphone, "Remove the headsets. *Now*." And dropped his to the ground.

Before it had quite touched the pine needles underfoot, the elegant little electronic device emitted an ear-splitting shriek and burst into flames.

Duran looked toward the cabin and his men and saw

immediately that two of them had not been quick enough in obeying orders. One lay about thirty feet from the cabin, stretched out on his back as though napping. But from the neck up was little more than a lump of blackened, smoldering flesh.

The other who had hesitated just that instant too long was Duran's lieutenant. He had, clearly, managed to get the headset off quickly enough to prevent the worst from happening, since it burned a foot or so away from him, but not soon enough to save himself completely. He didn't make a sound but held his head with both hands and rolled around on the ground in a way that told Duran that at the very least his eardrums had certainly been destroyed.

The others were rushing to their fallen comrades. Duran didn't move. Instead, he stared at the cabin that was now more visible in the breaking dawn, and very quietly, he murmured, "You shouldn't have done that, Jill."

———

Her body was limp when Brodie picked her up and placed her gently on the couch. She was breathing. Her eyes were open. When he checked, her pulse was steady.

But Jill Harrison was gone.

And she was never coming back.

Brodie had been warned this could happen, but he'd never seen it. And hadn't believed it possible. Until he knelt there beside the couch in that quiet, quiet cabin and looked into eyes so empty it was like looking into the glassy black eyes of a doll.

Still kneeling at her side, he took out his handkerchief and carefully wiped away the trickles of blood from her nose and ears. He folded her hands in a peaceful pose over her stomach. Absently, he brushed a strand of her hair back from the wide, unlined brow. He closed her eyes.

Jill Harrison. Not dead, but gone.

She had been twenty-two.

After a long, long time, Brodie got to his feet. He felt stiff, and so tired it was beyond exhaustion. He felt old.

"God damn them," he said quietly.

———————

Duran was the last to leave, remaining there until his dead and wounded men had been taken away by the others. He was about to get into his car when he heard the cabin door open.

Brodie stood in the doorway.

Across the sixty or so feet separating them, through the morning chill, they stared at each other in silence.

Though he knew the other man couldn't hear him, Duran said softly, "This time, we both lost."

Then he got into his car and drove away, leaving behind him a young woman damaged beyond repair and a man who was his mortal enemy.

ONE

It had once been an excellent example of an updated Victorian, but now it was only a smoking ruin swarming with fire department personnel. As Tucker Mackenzie got out of his car, he heard the hissing and crackling of embers as they were soaked by the fire hoses, and the pounding of axes as smoldering wood was broken up, and he heard the brisk voices of the men working to make certain the fire would not flare up again. He also heard the whispers of the neighbors who were standing around in clumps, watching her while pretending their attention was focused on what was left of the house.

She stood alone. She looked alone. Her pretty dress was a bit too thin for the hint of cold that was creeping into late September, and she stood almost hugging herself, arms crossed beneath her breasts, hands rubbing up and down above her elbows as though to warm chilled flesh. Her dark, reddish hair was blowing in the fitful breeze that also snatched at the long skirt of her dress, and she appeared to notice that no more than she noticed she was standing in a muddy puddle left by the fire hoses.

Tucker hesitated, then walked over to her side. Before he could speak, she did.

"Are you the one who's been watching me?" she asked in a curiously remote voice.

"What?" He had no idea what she meant.

"Never mind," she said, as if it didn't really matter. She turned her head to look at him, scanning him upward from his black western boots to his windblown blond hair. Her pale brown eyes rested on his face, wide and startled. More than startled. She looked briefly shocked, even afraid, Tucker thought. But it was a fleeting expression, vanishing completely and leaving behind nothing except her earlier numb detachment. She returned her gaze to what had been her home.

"Someone's been watching you?" When she didn't reply or react in any way, he said, "I'm sorry about your home, Miss Gallagher. What started the fire?"

She glanced at the fire marshal, who was standing some distance away scowling at the ruin. "He thinks it's arson," she said.

"Is that what he told you?"

"No. He didn't have to tell me." She sent Tucker another brief look, this one mildly curious. "Haven't you heard about the local witch? That's me."

"I had heard that you were reputed to have psychic abilities," he confessed. "I wanted to talk to you—"

"Let me guess." Her voice went flat, something ground beneath a ruthless heel. "Someone you love has died, recently or a long time ago, and you want to communicate with them. Or you've lost something you need to find. You're suffering unrequited love and want a magic potion to solve that problem. You or someone you know has a horrible disease and you're searching for a cure. Your life has gone off track, and you don't know how to right it. Or you want to make a million bucks and need me to pick your lottery numbers . . ."

When her voice trailed into silence, Tucker said evenly, "No, it's nothing like that."

"You're searching for something. They're always searching for something."

"They?"

Her shoulders lifted and fell in a tired shrug. "The ones who come and knock on my door. The ones who call and write and stop me on the streets." Again, she turned her head to look at him, but this time it was a direct stare. "There are only two kinds of people, you know. Those who run toward a psychic, hands outstretched and pleading—and those who run away as fast as they can, frightened."

"I'm neither," he told her. "I'm just a man who wants to talk to you."

The breeze picked up, blowing a curtain of reddish hair across her cheek and veiling her mouth briefly. "Who are you?" she asked, again mildly curious.

"My name's Tucker Mackenzie. I'm a writer."

Her gaze was unblinking. "I've heard of you. What are you doing here?"

"As I said, I wanted to talk to you. I've been trying to call you for more than a week but couldn't get an answer. So I decided to take a chance and just come over here. Obviously, I—didn't know about the fire."

"You're a novelist. Is it research you're after?"

"Not . . . specifically."

"Then what? Specifically."

Tucker hadn't come prepared to deal with this. He had discovered very early in his career that people liked to talk about themselves, particularly to a novelist. Under the nebulous heading of "research" he had asked and listened to the eager answers to an astonishing variety of questions both professional and personal. It was obvious, however, that this taut woman would not accept vague explanations for his curiosity and his questions.

Problem was, he had no specifics to offer her. None he was willing to voice, at any rate. *I'm after answers. I need to know if you really can predict the future. I need to know if I can believe in you.*

Before Tucker could figure out something close enough to specifics to satisfy her, a plainclothes detective who had been talking to the fire marshal picked his way through the puddles to stand before Sarah Gallagher. He was tall and thin and looked to have dressed by guess in the dark, since his purplish tie definitely clashed with a shirt the color of putty, and the khaki pants hardly matched a jacket with the suggestion of a pinstripe. But for all his sartorial chaos, there was something in his dark eyes that warned the contents made a lot more sense than the package.

"I'm sorry, Miss Gallagher." His voice was deep and abrupt. "The house is a total loss. And since your car was in the garage, it's gone too."

"I can pretty much see that for myself, Sergeant Lewis." Her smile was hardly worth the effort.

He nodded. "There'll have to be an investigation, you realize that. Before you can put in an insurance claim. The fire marshal thinks—that is, evidence suggests this might not have been an accident."

It was her turn to nod. "I gathered that."

The detective seemed uncomfortable beneath her direct stare and shifted just a bit as though to escape it. "Yes. Well, I just wanted you to know that we'll be keeping an eye on the place. And since there's nothing you can do here, maybe it'd be best if you went to a hotel for the night. You've been standing out here for hours, and anybody can see the weather's taking a turn for the worse. I'm sure you could use a hot meal and— privacy. Time to collect your thoughts and make a few decisions. I'd be glad to drive you, explain things to the manager so there's no trouble while you wait until the banks open tomorrow and you can make arrange- ments . . ."

"I won't need to stay at a hotel. There's a small apart- ment above the shop. I can stay there for a few days at least."

He produced a notebook and consulted notes made

earlier. "That'd be the antiques shop? Two-oh-four Emerson?"

"Yes."

"You said your partner—Margo James—is out of town?"

"On a buying trip, yes."

He frowned slightly as he returned the notebook to his pocket. "Miss Gallagher, can you think of anyone who might . . . wish you harm?"

"No."

Lewis seemed dissatisfied with the terse response, and Tucker was surprised; why didn't she say something to the cop about being watched? If that was true, if someone was watching her, then surely she must have realized that whoever it was might wish her harm. But she didn't mention that, just continued to look at Lewis without much expression.

The cop said, "Several of your neighbors saw a strange man hanging around here not more than a few minutes before the flames were spotted. Does that surprise you?"

"That my neighbors watch my house? No."

This time, Lewis scowled. "The man, Miss Gallagher. Did you see anyone hanging around here today?"

"No. As I told you before, I was reading in the front room and didn't see or hear anything until I smelled smoke. None of the smoke alarms had gone off, so I had no warning. By the time I smelled smoke, the fire was so bad I barely had time to call 911 and get out. I couldn't even get to my car keys so I could move the car out of the garage." She drew a little breath to steady a voice that had begun to wobble just a bit, and finished evenly, "I wasn't cooking anything. I didn't have any candles burning. No fire in the fireplace. And all the wiring was inspected just ten months ago when I completed the renovation. It was no accident that my house burned. But I don't know of anyone who would want to hurt me by starting that fire."

"All right." Lewis lifted a hand as if he would have touched her, then let it awkwardly fall. It was obvious that he was wary of touching her, and equally obvious that Sarah Gallagher knew it.

How much of that sort of thing had she been forced to put up with? How many times had she seen people draw back in fear, or look at her as though they believed she wasn't normal? Mysterious watching strangers notwithstanding, Tucker couldn't help wondering whether one of her wary neighbors had decided to burn out the local witch.

Avoiding her steady gaze, the cop turned his own to Tucker and scowled. "Who're you?"

Rather surprised he hadn't been asked before now, Tucker gave his name and no further information, surprised again when Sarah Gallagher added a cool explanation.

"He's a friend, Sergeant. If you've finished with me, he's going to drive me to the shop."

"I'm finished—for now. But I might have more questions for you tomorrow, Miss Gallagher." Lewis sent Tucker another glowering look, then turned away.

"Do you mind?" Sarah was watching Lewis stalk toward the fire marshal; her voice was distant.

"Of course not. I'll be glad to drive you to your shop." Deliberately, Tucker reached out and took her arm in a light grip. "Why don't we go now, before it gets any colder. You must be frozen."

She looked down at his hand on her arm, then raised her gaze to his face. For a moment, her expression was . . . peculiar. To Tucker, she seemed both disturbed and resigned, as though she had no choice but to accept something she knew would bring only trouble. Bad trouble. He didn't like it.

"You can trust me," he said.

Matter-of-factly, she said, "It has nothing to do with trust."

He didn't know how to respond, either to that or to her oddly fatalistic smile. Opting to let it go for now, Tucker led her to his car and saw her in the passenger side, then went around and got in himself. As soon as he started the engine, he turned the heater on high, not because she was shivering but because she should have been.

"The shop's on Emerson?"

She nodded. "It's called Old Things."

"I think I know where it is." Tucker put the car in gear and pulled away from the curb, and as he did so he caught a glimpse of a tall man in a black leather jacket slipping around behind a wooden fence two houses down from the smoking remains of Sarah's house. His foot touched the brake, and Tucker tensed. He didn't know why, but every sense was instantly alert; he could feel the hairs on the back of his neck stirring. When he looked quickly at Sarah, he found her looking after the man, her face still.

"Did you see him?"

She nodded. "Probably just a curious neighbor embarrassed at being caught gawking."

The car was barely moving now, and Tucker hesitated either to stop completely or go on. "You don't really believe that."

"It's what the police would say." She shrugged.

She was probably right, he thought, especially since the man had seemingly vanished; when the car drew abreast of the wooden fence, there was no sign of him. Tucker took his foot off the brake and continued down the quiet residential street. But the hairs on his nape were still quivering a warning. "You asked me earlier if I was the one who'd been watching you. What makes you think somebody has been?"

"I know somebody has. For a week, maybe a little longer. I've caught a glimpse of him several times."

"That man back there? The one in the black jacket?"

"Maybe. I've never been close enough to get a good look at him. There could be more than one, for all I know. But always at least one."

"Why didn't you mention that to Lewis when he asked if you knew of anyone who might want to hurt you?"

Sarah shrugged again. "He never made a threatening move. Never came close. He just watched me."

"Stalkers *just watch*, Sarah, at least in the beginning."

"He isn't a stalker." She didn't react at all to Tucker's use of her first name. "He isn't obsessed. There's something very . . . businesslike about him. Something coldly methodical."

"As if watching you is his job? A private investigator, maybe?"

"Maybe. But I don't know who would have hired him, or why."

"You said you'd been getting a lot of unwanted attention lately. People who came to you for help."

"Yes. So?"

"So maybe you gave somebody the wrong advice and somehow made an enemy. An investigator could have been hired to look for something that could be used against you in court."

"Like what? That I use imported tea leaves instead of domestic?" Without waiting for a response to that dry question, she went on in the same tone. "I don't offer advice. I don't give readings. I don't take money from anybody unless they're buying a Regency table or a Colonial chair. I've never owned a crystal ball or a deck of tarot cards. I don't claim to be able to solve problems, or I would have started with my own. So I don't see how anyone could claim I'd wronged them."

"All right. But if you're being watched, and if he's a pro, then somebody had to hire him. There must be a reason."

"I suppose."

As he stopped the car to wait at a traffic light, Tucker

turned his head and looked at her. "Any trouble with an ex-husband or lover?"

She seemed almost to flinch, but her answer was steady enough. "No."

"You're sure?" he probed.

Sarah looked at him. "I've never been married. As for lovers, since you ask, I've had only two in my life. One was back in college; we broke up amicably and still send each other Christmas and birthday cards. The other decided back in April, a few weeks after I got out of the hospital, that he didn't want to live with a woman who freaked out every time he got near a railroad crossing. So he requested a transfer to the West Coast."

"And?" Tucker kept his gaze on her face, his attention caught by the thread of pain in her otherwise expressionless voice.

"And he was killed two weeks later. At a railroad crossing." She turned her head to look forward, adding, "The light's green."

Tucker tried to pay attention to his driving, but it wasn't easy. He got the car rolling forward and fixed his gaze on the car ahead of him. "Let me make sure I understand this. You told your lover that railroad crossings were dangerous to him, that he'd be killed at one? Because you'd seen it in his future?"

Softly, she said, "I hadn't yet learned that warnings were useless, that what I saw would happen no matter what. I thought I could save him. But I couldn't, of course. I couldn't change his destiny."

"Don't you believe in free will?"

"Not anymore."

Tucker digested that for several blocks in silence. "According to what I've read, even the best psychics don't claim to get a hundred percent right; haven't you ever been wrong?"

"No."

He sent her a quick look. "So what makes you so special?"

"I don't know." She took the question seriously, obviously thinking about it. "Maybe it's because I never go looking for the future. What I see comes to me without any desire on my part."

"You can't control it?"

"No."

"Can't block it out?"

"No."

"And you truly believe that what you see is the absolute truth, actual events that haven't yet taken place. You truly believe that you can see the future before it happens."

She was silent for a moment, then replied simply, "I truly believe that."

Tucker made two turns without comment, but then curiosity made him say, "But that isn't all, is it? I mean, you knew the fire marshal suspected arson. Did his face give away his thoughts, or can you also—pick up information from the people around you?"

He didn't think she was going to answer at first, but finally she did.

"Sometimes I know things. I look at a person's face . . . and I know things."

"Oh? Do you know anything about me?" He didn't mean to sound so challenging, but knew he did even as the words emerged. He started to take back the question, knowing from experience that nobody liked being backed into a corner and ordered to perform, particularly a self-proclaimed psychic. But she surprised him.

She really surprised him.

Without looking at him, and in a tone that was almost idle, she said quietly, "I know why you came to see me today, if that's what you mean. It was for the same reason you've spent your adult life chasing after anyone who claimed to have psychic abilities. Shall I tell you why, Tucker?"

"No." The refusal emerged harshly before he thought about it, but given a couple of minutes of silence to consider it, he wasn't tempted to change his response. If she did know the truth, there was time enough to find out later; if she was only guessing, there was time enough to find that out as well. Either way, he wasn't quite ready to put it—or her—to the test just yet.

Still, he couldn't quite let it go. "You asked me back there why I came to see you. If you already knew the answer—"

"I just wondered if you'd tell me the truth. Most don't. As if it's some kind of test. That was your reason. You've been waiting for a . . . real psychic. Someone who'll know without any hint from you. Someone you can really believe in."

Tucker was more shaken than he cared to admit, even to himself.

"Turn left here," she said in the same detached tone. "The shop's up ahead a couple of blocks."

He obeyed, telling himself silently that she was only making shrewd guesses and nothing more. She had not, after all, told him anything remarkable. She'd said herself that people came to her because they were looking for something they hoped she could help them find. And he didn't doubt that many of those seekers came to her with a chip on their shoulders, waiting for her to "see" them clearly and know without being told what they wanted.

Sarah didn't seem disturbed by his silence. "You can let me off at the front," she said.

Instead of doing that, Tucker pulled his car into one of the parking places at one side of the neat, two-story building that had once been a residential home but now joined others on the street as a small business. "If you don't mind," he said pleasantly, "I'd like to go in with you. I could use a cup of coffee, for one thing."

She turned her head and looked at him as he shut off the engine. "I don't need you to look in the closets for monsters. I don't mind being alone."

For the first time, Tucker felt he was getting a sense of her, and he thought she was lying. She did mind being alone. She minded it very much. Ignoring her protest, he said, "If there's no way to make coffee here, I can get some at that restaurant down the street and bring it back for us."

After a moment, Sarah nodded and reached for the door handle. "I can make coffee here."

He couldn't tell whether she wanted his company or

was merely resigned to it, and didn't ask. He was very good at getting his foot in the door, and for now that was all he wanted.

Sarah led the way around to the rear of the building, where a flight of stairs provided access to the second-floor apartment. They were greeted at the top by a large cat who was sitting on the railing. A large black cat.

Of course, it would have to be a black *cat.* Tucker reached out and scratched the cat under his lifted chin while Sarah got the door key from under a flowerpot also on the railing. "Yours?" he asked, reading the cat's name tag in surprise and with a vague sense of familiarity.

"He seems to think so. He showed up a few days ago, and so far no owner's come forward to claim him, so I've been feeding him." She unlocked and opened the door, stepping just over the threshold to reach inside and deactivate a security system using a keypad by the door. Then she looked back at the cat. "You want in, Pendragon?"

Pendragon did. He jumped down from the railing and preceded them into the apartment.

The place had the slightly stale smell of infrequent use, but it was cheerfully decorated and bright enough. The main room was a combination kitchen/dining area/living room, with low bookshelves separating the dining and sitting areas and a breakfast bar partitioning the kitchen from the rest. There were area rugs in muted colors on the polished hardwood floor, light and airy curtains hanging at the few windows, and overstuffed furniture chosen for comfort in light neutral shades, with plenty of colorful pillows scattered about. There was even a gas-log fireplace and compact entertainment center.

A doorway led to a short hallway, off which Tucker assumed was a bathroom and one or two bedrooms.

Sarah went first to the thermostat on the wall near the hallway and adjusted the temperature so that warm air began to chase away the slight chill of the room. Then she went into the kitchen and got coffee out of one cabinet and a small coffeemaker out of an appliance garage to one side of the refrigerator.

"I stocked the place with groceries just the other day," she said conversationally as she measured coffee. "And I have spare clothes here. When either Margo or me is out of town, the other one usually spends at least a few nights here. It gives us a chance to catch up on paperwork while we're keeping an eye on the place."

Tucker wondered whether she was talking just to fill the silence, or whether it was her way of keeping reality at bay. The numbness couldn't last forever; sooner or later, she would have to face the loss of her home and belongings, with all the shock and grief that would entail. But if her choice was later, it was, after all, her choice.

He sat down on one of the tall bar stools at the breakfast bar, watching her. "Have you had break-ins here?"

"No. Most burglars are looking for valuables they can put in a sack, or at least carry by themselves; our stock is made up mostly of furniture, with very few easily portable valuables. But Margo is paranoid about theft, which is why we have an excellent security system. And I don't mind spending time here when she's out of town."

"How long will she be gone this time?"

"Another week, maybe two." Sarah got a pet bowl out of the dish drainer beside the sink and filled it with kibble, then set it on the breakfast bar in front of the stool beside Tucker's. He watched in silence as Pendragon leaped up on the stool, sat down, and began eating delicately from his bowl, then looked at Sarah.

She met his quizzical gaze and smiled for the first time in genuine amusement. "I found out quickly that Pendragon likes to sit up and eat like people. I hope you don't mind."

"No. It's more his house than mine."

She nodded, the smile fading, then said, "I think I'll go change. If the coffee's ready before I come back, help yourself. Cups are in that cabinet, and the sugar and cream are already out on the counter."

"Thanks. Take your time. I'll be fine." He watched her leave the room, then absently reached over and scratched Pendragon behind one ear. The cat made a faintly disgusted sound, which Tucker took to mean he disliked being touched while eating. "Excuse me," he told the cat politely, drawing back his hand.

Pendragon murmured something in the back of his throat, the sound this time so obviously mollified that Tucker blinked in surprise.

Peculiar cat.

The coffee was still dripping down into the pot,

beginning to smell good but not quite ready to drink. Restless, Tucker left the bar stool to prowl around the room, studying the decorations and furniture without really seeing them. After only a slight hesitation, he turned on the gas-log fire, which immediately made the room seem more cheerful but didn't do much for the little ripple of coldness chasing up and down Tucker's spine.

That unnerving sensation drove him to one of the two narrow dormers that provided a view out the front side of the building, and he found himself cautiously drawing aside filmy curtains so he could see the street below without calling attention to himself.

But the caution was wasted, because the tall man in the black leather jacket seemed to have a sixth sense of his own, vanishing into the shadows of an alleyway across the street before Tucker could catch more than a glimpse of him.

———

"Shit." Brodie straightened from the crouch holding a piece of charred wood in his hand, his lean face as grim as the curse. He turned the wood in his hands—it had, once, been a piece of decorative porch railing—then dropped it and rubbed his hands together angrily.

"We don't know they did it," Cait Desmond reminded him.

"We don't know they didn't," he retorted. "I prefer to err on the side of past experience."

His partner looked at him for a moment, then looked back at the ruins of what had been Sarah Gallagher's home. It was nearly dark now, but the devastation was still obvious. A cold wind whined miserably past the chimney that still reared up in a stark silhouette above the dead house, and Cait shivered as she turned up her collar and thrust her hands into the pockets of her jacket.

"Did you find out anything?" Brodie asked her, the anger muted now in his brisk tone.

Cait moved closer to him and kept her voice low even though there seemed to be no one else about and certainly no one within earshot. "Yeah. I talked to one of the neighbors while she was out walking her dog a little while ago. Arson is definitely suspected; a couple of people reported a stranger hanging around today."

"Why doesn't that surprise me." It wasn't a question. Brodie sighed, his breath misting in the cold air. "Well, they didn't get her, or you would have said so by now. So where is she?"

"According to the neighbor, Sarah Gallagher left here with a tall blond man who 'looked vaguely familiar.' Not another neighbor, and not a cop. He was driving a late-model Mercedes."

Brodie whistled in surprise. "That doesn't sound like our guys. Their wheels tend to be very unobtrusive."

Cait nodded. "That's what I thought. Unfortunately, the neighbor didn't get a license plate, so that's no good. She did, however, say that she thought the cop in charge talked to both Sarah and the blond stranger before they left, so there's a solid chance the locals know where Sarah's supposed to be. Especially since she probably hasn't been ruled out as a suspect herself."

"Yeah, they will check the obvious first." Brodie nodded slowly.

"So we need eyes and ears inside the local police department," Cait said. "They probably wouldn't know me, so—"

Brodie was shaking his head. "I don't think so, Cait. We need to move too fast; planting someone on the inside takes time. But . . . I might know someone who already has eyes on the inside."

"Someone you can trust?"

He smiled faintly, as though he found the question amusing. "I don't deal with people I can't trust. Come on—we need to get out of here before that squad car makes its next scheduled pass by here. And let's find a landline; I don't want to use the cell for this call."

———

When Sarah came out of her bedroom wearing a bulky sweater and jeans, Tucker didn't mention the watcher outside. It was not out of some outdated—and no doubt unwanted—sense of chivalry that he kept silent, but simply because he was convinced Sarah would not be surprised by the knowledge. She knew she was being watched; he thought she knew why, or had some suspicion why—and it had nothing to do with frightened neighbors.

It was an answer he wanted.

Sarah glanced toward the fire without comment as she passed through the living room, then turned on a couple of lamps and went into the kitchen area.

"I didn't know how you took yours," Tucker said, lifting his coffee cup in a slight gesture.

She poured a cup of coffee for herself, taking it black. "No problem. Look, it's after six; I have some ready-made stew and bread in the freezer, if you're planning to stay for supper."

Tucker had to smile at the wording. "I'd hate to impose."

"No, you wouldn't," she said, either another shrewd guess or certain knowledge. Whichever, it was accompanied by a slight smile as Sarah began getting out a pot and the frozen stew, and turning on the oven for the bread.

Tucker reclaimed his stool at the breakfast bar, sitting beside a cat who was neatly washing his paws and face after his own meal. "Okay, so I wouldn't hate it. I've got the nerve of a burglar, according to most of my friends. But I was trained right; if you're going to do the cooking, I'll do the dishes."

"Suits me." She put the bagged stew into the microwave to thaw, then leaned back against the counter and sipped her coffee, looking at Tucker across the space separating them. "Are you planning to spend the night?"

That question would have bothered Tucker, except for the fact that she sounded totally uninterested in the subject. "That depends on you."

"I told you I didn't mind being alone. There are no

monsters in the closet or under my bed; I just checked."
She wasn't smiling.

Neither was Tucker when he said, "There's one outside. Watching. Wearing a black leather jacket."

Her eyes seemed to flicker slightly. "You saw him?"

"Yes. A few minutes ago, before it started getting
dark. Who is he, Sarah?"

"I don't know."

"Why is he watching you?"

"I don't know."

Tucker shook his head. "And yet you aren't worried
about it? I don't buy that."

"Why worry about something you can't change?" She
shrugged.

"Then you *do* know why he's watching."

Sarah hesitated, then shook her head. "No. I—I don't
know the *why* of any of it. Just the fact of it."

Baffled, Tucker frowned and watched her turn to get
the stew out of the microwave and put it in a pot on the
stove. "So what is the fact of it?" he asked her.

"He's watching me. He's waiting. And sooner or later,
he'll do what he came here to do."

"Which is?"

"I don't know."

After a moment, Tucker drew a deep breath. "Yeah,
I'm spending the night," he said flatly.

She looked back over her shoulder at him, her eyes
flickering again. "To guard the door? To keep the monster out? Don't bother. You can't save me from him."

Her fatalistic attitude irritated Tucker. "At least I'm

willing to try, which is more than I can say for you. Where's the phone? This is something Sergeant Lewis should know about."

"He can't save me either," she said softly, returning her attention to the stew.

"Why the hell not? He's a cop, isn't he? It's his job."

Sarah shook her head. "To protect and serve? No. There's nothing he can do—even if he believed me. Even if he believed you. And he wouldn't."

"You can't know that."

She turned toward him again, leaning back against the counter and picking up her coffee cup. She was smiling. "Can't I? Then you've wasted a trip, haven't you, Tucker?"

It silenced him, but only for a moment. "You're not going to do anything about that guy out there? Not even report to the police?"

"Not even report to the police. I've learned to accept what I can't change."

"You accepted me awfully easily," he said curiously. "Why? Was our meeting—meant to be?" The question wasn't nearly as mocking as he had intended it to sound.

"I recognized you," she replied with yet another shrug.

"Recognized me? From where?"

"I had seen you." There was an evasive note in her voice, something Tucker was quick to pick up on.

"Where had you seen me, Sarah?"

There was a moment of silence. She looked steadily down at her cup, a slight frown between her brows.

Then, finally, softly, she said, "I had seen you in my dreams. My . . . waking nightmares."

"You mean you had a vision and I was in it?"

Sarah almost flinched. "I hate that word. *Vision.* It makes me sound like some cheap carnival sideshow mystic. Pay your money and come into the tent, and Madam Sarah will look into her crystal ball and tell you your future. All filled with hope and dreams. Except that isn't what I do. I don't have a crystal ball. And I can't get answers on demand."

Patient, Tucker brought her back to the point. "All right, then. You had seen me in your—waking nightmares. You had seen me in your future. So you knew you could trust me?"

Her slight frown returned. "It has nothing to do with trust. I saw you. I knew you'd be there. When it happens. I knew you weren't involved in it. At least—I don't believe you are. But you're there. When it happens."

The writer in Tucker was going crazy with her tenses, but he thought he understood her. At least up to a point. "When what happens, Sarah?"

She looked at him, finally. Her gaze was steady and her voice matter-of-fact when she replied, "When they kill me."

TWO

"You bungled it," Duran said.

Varden stiffened, but there was no sign of anger in his voice when he said, "At the time, it seemed the best idea."

"A house fire? Guaranteed to draw law enforcement as well as numerous spectators? How did you expect to remove her from that situation without attracting further attention?"

"Obviously, I intended to remove her before the fire was noticed."

"Then why didn't you?"

"The fire spread faster than I bargained for."

Duran turned his head and looked at the other man. Gently, he said, "It was an old house. They tend to burn quickly."

Accepting that rebuke with what grace he could muster, Varden merely nodded without further attempts to defend himself.

Duran gazed at him a moment longer, then moved away from the window of the cramped hotel room and settled into a chair across from a long couch. "Sit down." It wasn't an invitation.

Taking a place on the couch, Varden said in a carefully explanatory tone, "I was under the impression that the judgment of the Council demanded quick action. Tyrell said—"

"Tyrell reports to me," Duran said with an edge to his quiet voice. "The decision is mine."

"You thought she could be salvaged?"

"What I thought is not your concern. You follow orders."

"Yes, sir."

Duran waited a moment, his gaze boring into Varden. Then, almost casually, he said, "I want Sarah Gallagher."

"Yes, sir."

"And you're going to get her for me, Varden. Aren't you?"

"Yes, sir."

"Good," Duran said. "That is good."

———

Tucker drew a long, slow breath, trying with calm and logic to keep the chill inside him from spreading. "When who kills you, Sarah?"

"I don't know who they are. Whenever I try to concentrate on them, to see them, all I see are shadows. Misshapen, sliding away whenever I try to focus on them, impossible to identify as anything except . . . shadows." She shook her head a little, helpless. "This is all new to me, in case you didn't know that. I was mugged last March, and a head injury put me in a coma. When I came out of it, I started having the waking nightmares."

He nodded, familiar with the facts because a newspaper story had reported them—and had brought him here. "I understand that. What I don't understand is what, exactly, makes you believe that someone is going to kill you. What did you see?"

The bell on the microwave dinged, and Sarah turned to set her coffee aside and get the stew out. "Haven't you ever had nightmares, Tucker? The surreal kind, full of frightening images?"

"Of course I have. They made zero sense. And they sure as hell didn't predict the future."

"My waking nightmares do." She was clearly unoffended by his skepticism.

"Okay, then, tell me what you saw. Why are you so convinced you're going to be killed?"

Sarah didn't respond for several minutes as she transferred the thawed stew to the pot on the stove and began stirring it as it heated. All her attention seemed to be fixed on the task. And when she did begin speaking, Tucker thought that her voice was very steady the way someone's was when they were telling you something that scared the living shit out of them.

"Because I saw my grave. Waiting for me."

"Sarah, that doesn't have to mean—"

She nodded jerkily. "There are other things I don't remember, images that terrified me. But the grave . . . that was all too clear. It has a tombstone, and the tombstone is already inscribed. It has my name on it. In the . . . waking nightmare . . . I'm falling toward it, into it, so fast I don't see the date of—of my death. But the month is October, and the year is this year. And just as the darkness of the grave closes over me, I hear them applauding. And I know they've won. I know they've killed me."

"They?"

"The shadows."

"Sarah, shadows can't hurt you."

She looked at him with old eyes. "These can. And will."

Tucker watched her as she turned to check on the steaming stew and put the thawing bread in the oven. There was a lot for him to think about. On the face of it, his first inclination was to ascribe her "waking nightmare" to something she'd eaten or a vivid imagination; as badly as he wanted to believe in precognitive abilities, he had yet to find a genuine psychic, and years of frustration had inured him to disillusionment.

He certainly had no proof that Sarah Gallagher was indeed psychic. The information he had gathered seemed to indicate that she was, and those witnesses who claimed to have heard her predictions prior to later events seemed both reliable and reputable. But there was no way to be sure that her "predictions" had not come from some as-yet-undiscovered means of foreknowledge that had nothing to do with so-called extrasensory perception.

Each of the "predictions" he knew of could, after all, be rationally explained, given a few reasonable possibilities. Months before, she had been mugged on her way home one night, and the resulting head injury had put her into a coma for sixteen days. She could have overheard information while in that coma, for instance, and—consciously, perhaps—forgotten where it had come from. That could explain her apparent foreknowledge of the early birth of a nurse's baby, which had been her first recorded prediction. Some doctor with a suspicion of what could happen might have mentioned it within Sarah's hearing. And though her prediction of a Chicago hotel fire that had killed forty people certainly seemed remarkable, Tucker had discovered that one of the men later arrested for arson had been treated for a minor traffic injury in the same Richmond hospital where Sarah had lain in a coma. It was a coincidence that bothered him.

Other minor predictions she had made could—with some ingenuity—also be linked to her stay in the hospital. Tucker had utilized quite a bit of ingenuity, so he knew it could be done. He hadn't yet been able to explain away her apparent foreknowledge of several murders apparently committed by a serial killer in California, but he was half-convinced he could, given enough time.

All of which, of course, raised the question of why he had bothered to seek out Sarah Gallagher at all.

"You want so badly to believe." Her voice was quiet, her gaze direct as she turned to look at him.

"Do I?" He wasn't quite as unsettled, this time, by her perception—extrasensory or otherwise.

Instead of directly answering that question, Sarah said, "I can't perform for you, Tucker. I can't go down that list of questions you have in your mind and answer them one by one as if it's some final exam. I can't convince you of something you need irrefutable proof to believe. That's not the way this works."

"You mean it's like believing in God?" His voice was carefully neutral. "It requires faith?"

"What it requires is admitting the possible. Believing the evidence of your eyes and ears without trying to explain it all away. Accepting that you'll never be able to cross every *t* and dot every *i*. And most of all, it requires a willingness to believe that science isn't the ultimate authority. Just because something can't be rationally explained on the basis of today's science doesn't mean it isn't real."

"That sounds like the party line," Tucker said dryly, having heard the same sort of "answers" for years.

She shook her head. "Look, I never believed in the paranormal, in psychics, myself. When I thought about it, which wasn't often, I just assumed it was either a con of some kind or else coincidence—anything that could somehow be explained away. Not only was I a skeptic, I simply didn't care; I had no interest in anything paranormal. It didn't matter to me."

"Until you found yourself looking into the future."

Sarah tilted her head a bit to one side as she considered him and his flat statement. Then, with a touch of wry humor, she said, "Well, when you're up to your ass in alligators, it's a bit difficult to pretend you aren't involved in the situation."

Tucker appreciated the humor, but what interested him most was a glint of something he thought he saw in her eyes. Slowly, he said, "So, are you involved in this? Or just along for the ride?"

"I don't know what you mean." She turned abruptly back to the stove to check the stew and bread, then busied herself getting plates and bowls out of the cabinets above the counter and silverware from a drawer.

"You know exactly what I mean, Sarah. Are you resigned to dying next month because you believe that's your fate? Because you believe your destiny is—literally—written in stone? Or do you have the guts to use what you've seen to change your fate, to take control of your destiny?"

She didn't answer right away, and when she did, her voice was almost inaudible. "Strange questions from a man who doesn't believe I could have seen my future—or anybody else's."

Tucker didn't hesitate. "I'm willing to suspend my disbelief—if *you're* willing to accept the possibility that what you saw—or at least the outcome—can be changed."

Again, Sarah took her time responding. She sliced bread and ladled out stew, setting his meal before him and then placing her own so that she was sitting at a right angle to him. She tasted her stew almost idly, then said,

"I saw a hotel fire that killed people, and I couldn't stop it. I saw the man I loved killed by a train, and I couldn't stop it. I saw a serial killer commit horrible acts, and I couldn't stop him. A week ago, I saw my house burn to the ground, and today it burned."

Tucker began eating to give himself time to marshal his arguments, and in the meantime asked a question he was curious about. "Why didn't you call the police when you saw your house burn?"

"Oh, right. Officer, somebody's going to burn down my house. How do I know? Well, I saw it in a nightmare. A nightmare I had while I was wide awake, not under the influence of drugs, and cold sober." She gave Tucker a twisted smile. "Been there, done that. And I'd really rather not become the poster child for the Psychic Early Warning Society."

Tucker shook his head. "Okay, so maybe nobody takes you seriously—at first. But sooner or later, that's bound to change."

"Is it?" She shrugged. "Maybe. But in my case, that's hardly relevant, is it? I have this . . . rendezvous with destiny next month."

Like most writers, Tucker had a head stuffed full of words, and a very apt quote sprang readily to mind. " 'I have a rendezvous with Death at some disputed barricade,' " he murmured.

"Who said that?" she wondered.

"Alan Seeger. It's always stayed with me."

Sarah nodded. "Appropriate."

"I think so. Think of the phrase he chose, Sarah . . .

some disputed barricade. Maybe there's always room for argument about where and when we die, even if there is such a thing as fate. Maybe we change our fate, minute by minute, with every decision we make. Maybe destiny becomes the sum of our choices."

She frowned. "Maybe."

"But you aren't convinced?"

"That I can choose to avoid the fate I know is in store for me?" She shook her head. "No."

"Sarah, you didn't see your death. You saw an image, a symbol of death. And symbols can't be interpreted literally."

"A grave is pretty hard to interpret any other way."

He shook his head. "In tarot, the death card can mean many things. A transition of some kind. The death of an idea or a way of life, for instance. A turning point. The grave you saw could mean something like that. A change in your life that you're thrown bodily into, maybe against your will—which would explain your fear. You never saw yourself dead, did you? You never saw your death occur literally, an accomplished *fact*."

"I never saw David's death as an accomplished fact either." Her voice was quiet. "But I knew he was going to die at that railroad crossing. And he did."

That stopped Tucker for only a moment. "But you saw the *means* of his death clearly. In your—nightmare—about your own fate, there's no weapon, no method by which you could be killed. So it *could* have been a symbolic grave, a symbolic death. At least it's possible."

Sarah pushed her plate away and leaned an elbow on

the bar, looking at him for the first time with her certainty wavering. "I suppose so. Possible, at least that I saw something other than a literal death for myself."

Tucker didn't make the mistake of hammering his point home. Instead, he said musingly, "I've always thought that if it *was* possible to see into the future, it would have to be with the understanding that what a psychic is actually seeing is only a possible future. Moment by moment, we make decisions and choices that change our path through infinite possibilities. And once a psychic 'sees' an event, that psychic becomes in some way involved in the event and so affects the outcome—which causes the 'future' event that he or she saw to change in unexpected and unpredicted ways."

She was frowning slightly, her gaze fixed on his face with what seemed an unconscious intensity. "Or—to actually happen. How do I know that if I hadn't warned David, if I hadn't been so insistent that he avoid railroad crossings, he might not have been killed since he wouldn't have gone to California to get away from me? How do I know that my—my prediction didn't cause that nurse to go into premature labor out of stress and worry? How do I know that any of it would have happened if I hadn't . . . interfered?"

Coolly, Tucker said, "You don't. If, as you believe, our fates are set, our destinies planned for us at birth, then every step you've taken, every action you thought was yours by choice was all just part of the pattern you had to follow."

"I . . . don't much like the sound of that."

"Then consider another possibility," he advised. "Maybe you aren't going to die next month after all. Maybe you can master your own fate. If you want to, that is."

Since they were both finished eating, he got up and began clearing up in the kitchen. It wasn't until then that he realized the big black cat had remained on the stool beside his during the meal and conversation without once calling attention to himself. It struck Tucker as odd and curiously uncatlike, though he couldn't have said why; he didn't know a great deal about cats.

Even as that thought occurred to him, Pendragon quite suddenly lifted a hind leg high in the air and began washing himself in a definitely catlike manner, and Tucker almost laughed aloud. His imagination was working overtime, as usual. Not that it was surprising; whether Sarah Gallagher was a genuine psychic or not, she was obviously in trouble, threatened by person or persons unknown, and his awareness of that had heightened all of Tucker's senses. Which explained why he got that creepy-crawly sensation near his spine each time he'd caught a glimpse of the watcher in the black leather jacket.

And why he was very conscious of Sarah sitting at the breakfast bar in silence, her gaze occasionally following him but more often turned inward.

He wished his awareness weren't quite so heightened where she was concerned. He was too aware of her physically, too conscious of her quiet breathing, her faint movements—even the oddly compelling scent that was her perfume overlaid by the acrid odor of smoke that clung to her hair.

Keep your mind on the subject at hand, Mackenzie.

"I wouldn't know where to start," she said finally as Tucker turned on the dishwasher and poured fresh coffee for them both.

Tucker felt a surge of triumph, but it was short-lived. He didn't know where to start either. But he was unwilling to allow her to slip back into her earlier numb resignation. "We can find a place to start."

"We?" She looked at him steadily.

"I never could resist a mystery." He kept his tone light. "Or a challenge. And, as you said—I want to believe. Maybe the mistake I made in the past was in not getting to know the . . . psychics . . . I met. Maybe it's not so much a question of faith as it is a question of trust. I have to trust you before I can believe in you, and trust demands knowledge."

"Quid pro quo? You'll help me try to change my fate in exchange for the opportunity to convince yourself I'm a genuine psychic?"

"It sounds workable to me."

"Tucker, that man watching outside is dangerous. I don't know if he burned down my house. I don't know if he came here to kill me. But I know that he's very, very dangerous."

"I can take care of myself. And I can help you, Sarah."

She shook her head, her eyes going momentarily unfocused in that inward-turned gaze. "No. You don't understand. Sometimes, when I know he's out there,

I can sense things about him. There's something . . . wrong with him. Something that isn't *normal*."

"In what way?"

"I don't know." Her eyes cleared. "It's like when I try to see who wants to kill me. All I see are shadows. Shadows all around me."

He couldn't deny the reality of that man who was probably still outside somewhere, probably still watching, but Tucker wasn't about to lose the ground he felt he had gained in the last couple of hours. "He's just another piece of the puzzle, Sarah, that's all. We can solve it."

"How?"

At the moment, it was an unanswerable question, so Tucker merely shrugged and said, "By putting the pieces together. But not tonight. You've had a long and tough day, and I'm a little tired myself. I know it's early, but why don't we turn in?"

Her expression was unreadable. "There's only one bedroom."

"That couch looks comfortable. I'll be fine out here, Sarah."

Without further comment, she left the breakfast bar and went to get a blanket and pillow from the storage closet across from the bedroom. She piled them on one end of the couch. "There are clean towels in the bathroom, and some men's toiletries in the linen cabinet; Margo has an occasional male guest stay up here, and she believes in being prepared. Help yourself to whatever you need."

"Thanks."

She didn't seem eager to leave. "Pendragon should be put out before you settle down to sleep; otherwise he'll wake you up at dawn."

"I'll take care of it." He didn't move away from his position near the bar. "Good night, Sarah."

"Good night." She turned abruptly toward the bedroom, pausing only when she reached the hallway. She stood there for a moment, as if in indecision, then looked back over her shoulder at him. Quietly, her expression quizzical, she said, "I'm sorry. She never wanted to be found, you know. That's why you couldn't." Then she went on into her bedroom and closed the door softly behind her.

Tucker wasn't sure he was breathing. He forced himself to draw air into his lungs, and it made him briefly dizzy. Or something did. He stood there staring after her, conscious of his heart thudding heavily inside his chest and cold sweat popping out of every pore.

"Jesus Christ," he muttered.

———

The witching hour, Brodie thought, studying the deserted street in front of his parked car. At three A.M. on this Thursday morning, the day after Sarah Gallagher's house had burned to the ground, the only lights were streetlights; in this part of Richmond, at least, all was quiet.

He caught the flicker of light in the rearview mirror and tensed just a bit, his hand sliding inside his jacket and closing over the reassuringly solid grip of the .45

ready in its holster. Even when the light flickered half a dozen more times in a definite signal, he didn't entirely relax, though his foot tapped the brake lightly in the expected response.

It wasn't until the passenger door of his car opened and a man slid in that Brodie relaxed and left his gun holstered. The dome light had not come on (since he had earlier removed the bulbs), but a faint whiff of a very expensive and even more exclusive men's cologne confirmed the identity of his companion for Brodie.

"You didn't have to come yourself," he said, surprised.

"I was in the neighborhood."

Brodie made a rude but soft sound of disbelief. "Yesterday, you were in Canada, at a board meeting still going on today. You're elusive as hell, Josh, but I'm very good at what I do."

"You don't have to tell me that." Josh Long, worldrenowned financier, philanthropist, and a dozen other things that made him very famous indeed, reached into his casual jacket and pulled out a large manila envelope. "This is a verbatim copy of the police report concerning Sarah Gallagher's house fire, including all notes made at the scene by the investigating officer. Also a copy of the fire marshal's report."

"What, you didn't get a fingerprint and ID of the culprit as well?" Brodie asked dryly.

"You'll have to forgive me—there was so little time."

Brodie let out a brief laugh, honestly amused, as he accepted the envelope. "Yeah, sorry about that. But

we're in a hurry, as usual. As I told you, we've lost track
of Gallagher. She left the ruins of her house after the fire
yesterday with a man—"

"Tucker Mackenzie."

After a moment of silence, Brodie said thoughtfully,
"The novelist?"

"According to my source inside the police department, yes. The investigating officer had no idea who he
was at the time; he's apparently no reader and Miss Gallagher introduced Mackenzie only as a friend."

"And is he one?"

Josh shrugged. "Hers? No evidence they'd met before
Wednesday. Ours? Your guess is as good as mine. We
managed to scare up a bit of data on Mackenzie; it's in
the envelope with the rest. Based on that, I'd have to say
he looks like a possible ally, but there's no way to know
that for sure. In going to her he obviously has some
agenda of his own, though what that might be I couldn't
find out. In any case, he appears to have elected himself
her watchdog, at least for the moment."

"He's still with her?"

"He was as of midnight tonight. In the apartment above
the antiques shop owned by Gallagher and her partner."

Brodie didn't ask the address, knowing that it would
be included in the envelope of information. He wasn't
someone who trusted easily, but he had learned to trust
in the man beside him—and in his information-gathering
capabilities. He had also learned to respect the strength
and fighting instincts apparent in the visitor's next restless words.

"I can take a more public role, you know. Make some noise. Get more people on our side. Be more of a help to you. Just providing information and equipment when you need it is nothing at all."

"You do more than enough."

"It doesn't feel that way."

Brodie tucked the envelope away inside his jacket and half turned to look at the other man, who was, in the darkness, virtually invisible to anyone who didn't have eyes like a cat. Brodie did.

"Josh, we don't have many advantages in this thing. They're bigger than we are, faster to react to a situation. They're better organized and they may even be smarter than we are. They're sure as hell more ruthless. So we need every edge we can get. Being able to call on you for assistance and information has been invaluable, so never think you aren't helping."

After a moment, Josh sighed and settled his shoulders in the gesture of a man resigned. "I don't much care for fighting in the dark, John."

"We need you in the dark. We need someone with your resources, your power, and your abilities—and we need you hidden in the dark, where they can't see you."

"I know the value of an ace in the hole. But I don't have to like it."

"We're grateful, Josh. We're all grateful."

Josh turned away the gratitude with a slight gesture, then fished inside his jacket for a cigarette and lighter. "Don't worry about anybody seeing this," he said absently as the lighter's flame illuminated his lean, aristocratic features and lent his rather hard eyes a fierce glitter. "Zach is watching."

"I thought he might be," Brodie said gently.

A faint grin was sent his way before Josh snapped the lighter shut and plunged them back into darkness. "*My* watchdog. Are you working with Cait again?"

"Yeah. She's at the hotel. And when I get back there, she'll pretend she isn't the least bit curious about who my mysterious source is—and it's killing her. Don't worry, though. She knows the score. She knows only what she needs to know, just like the rest of us."

"So if one falls, only a few more can be taken down at the same time," Josh murmured. "Like the Resistance cells in World War Two, protecting those at the core, the few who know the identity of all the fighters in every cell. The safest way, I know. But it makes it all the more difficult for you to work effectively as a team."

"What choice do we have?" It was a rhetorical question, and Brodie didn't wait for any attempt to answer it. "Thanks for the data, Josh."

"Let me know, any hour of the day or night, if you need anything else. And I mean anything, John."

"I will."

They didn't shake hands or say good-bye, though both knew it might easily be months before they saw each other again.

If they saw each other again.

Josh slid from the car with hardly a sound, and a few moments later Brodie saw headlights come on farther back along the street. An exceptionally quiet motor purred as the dark sedan passed his own car, turned a corner, and vanished into the night.

After a few minutes, Brodie started his own car and pulled away from the curb, his eyes automatically seeking any sign that the meeting had been noticed as he left the quiet neighborhood and headed back to the hotel and his impatiently waiting partner.

———

Tucker came abruptly out of a deep sleep, his first disoriented thought that Pendragon wanted out. The cat had mysteriously vanished by the time he had been ready to bunk down on the couch, and Tucker had been reluctant to knock on Sarah's closed door to find out whether he had somehow slipped in there with her.

So the faint scratching sound brought him upright on the couch, filled with the sense of something left unfinished. *The cat wants out. Damned cat.* He blinked at the morning brightness, automatically checking his watch to find that it was seven thirty, then pushed the blanket away and swung his feet to the floor.

It wasn't until then that he looked toward the door and saw the knob turning.

Even as he heard the security system beep a mild warning as the door was opened, Tucker was on his feet and moving swiftly in that direction. It occurred to him belatedly that he didn't have a damned thing handy with which to defend himself, but that didn't stop him.

He almost decked her.

Wide blue eyes took him in—fist raised, bare-chested,

beard-stubbled, and wearing only a pair of boxers decorated with cartoon characters—and she let out a rich chuckle.

"Well, I would say Sarah finally struck gold after way too much brass, but if you're sleeping on the couch, handsome, she's obviously still missing the train!"

THREE

Margo James was a redhead like Sarah, but all resemblance stopped there. She was tall and voluptuous, her gestures and movements were quick and almost birdlike, and she talked with blunt, brisk cheerfulness, contentedly misusing words and mixing metaphors right and left.

Tucker had plenty of time to observe all these traits when he had returned from his quick retreat to shower, shave, and dress, because Margo insisted on fixing breakfast, telling him that Sarah always slept till nine at least.

"I'm the early bird, and she's the bat."

Tucker stopped himself from wincing. "You mean the night owl?"

Margo waved a spatula. "Yeah, right. It's amazing that we get along so well. We're really as different as afternoon and morning. Take our antiques, for instance. Sarah has a real feeling for what's genuine but doesn't have a clue how things should be priced, whereas I know the value of a thing down to the penny—but can be fooled by a fake really easily."

"Sounds like you two are perfect partners," Tucker commented, cautiously sipping coffee that was very, very strong and had a shot at holding a spoon upright in the cup.

"Yeah, it's been great. Hey, I fed that cat she's adopted and let him out. He seemed to want out."

"I was supposed to let him out last night," Tucker admitted, "but he disappeared on me."

Margo shrugged. "Maybe he slept in Sarah's room. She told me he does that sometimes."

Tucker wondered when, in that case, Sarah had let the cat out of her room, but it didn't seem important enough to worry about.

In a lightning change of mood, Margo said with sudden gravity, "Jeez, I was sorry to hear about Sarah's house. She loved that place, poured her heart into restoring it."

"How did you hear about it?" he asked casually.

"On TV—the news last night. That's why I came back ahead of schedule, of course, even though she didn't call me. Maybe *especially* because she didn't call me. I know Sarah. She's as strong as bronze—"

"Steel," Tucker murmured, unable to stop himself.

"Yeah, steel. Strong as steel, thinks she can handle anything and everything on her own—but she's had a fairly bad year, and I just don't know how much more she can take. First that damned mugging, and then David—" Her gaze cut swiftly to Tucker. "You know about David?"

He nodded without comment.

Margo was obviously still trying to size up the relationship since Tucker had introduced himself only by name, and was clearly disappointed that he didn't react in some dramatic way to mention of the last man in Sarah's life.

"Yeah, well. First we find out the bastard was not one of your basic in-sickness-and-in-health guys when she got hurt; he could barely bring himself to visit her every couple of days, for Christ's sake, and made it screamingly obvious he wanted to be someplace else when he did show up. Then, when she finally comes out of the coma . . ."

"Able to see the future?" Tucker supplied when her voice trailed off.

She grimaced. "Yeah. I didn't know if you knew."

Again, he nodded without comment.

Margo flipped a fried egg—the fifth so far, with two more still in the pan—onto a plate on the counter beside the stove, and Tucker was mildly tempted to ask how many people she planned to feed. But he didn't want her to be distracted from the subject at hand.

"She really can do it," Margo said, defending her friend staunchly. "It scared the hell out of her at first— still does, I guess. Well, wouldn't it you?"

"Definitely."

Margo nodded. "Yeah, me too. In fact—Well, never

mind that. The point is that Sarah's life has been hell this year. And now the house . . . jeez. The news said the cops suspected arson?"

"So I understand." He didn't mention the stranger who might still be outside watching; he hadn't been able to casually look out a window without drawing her attention, and he wasn't sure how much—if anything—Margo knew.

"That means the insurance won't pay off for ages," she said in a practical spirit. "Damn. She can stay here as long as necessary, of course—this place is half hers—but it would be a lot better if she could concentrate on rebuilding right away. With everything at fives and sixes like this, she'll have way too much time to think about . . . stuff."

Tucker didn't bother to correct her. "About what happened to David . . . ?" he probed, wondering whether she knew that Sarah's latest prediction supposedly concerned her own death.

Margo's exotic face darkened. "That son of a bitch. I know you aren't supposed to speak ill of the dead, but if you ask me, he got what he deserved. If he'd treated Sarah with a modem of respect, things might have been different."

Tucker cast about in his mind and settled on *modicum*. Yeah—a modicum of respect.

"But he didn't," Margo continued, oblivious of having misspoken. "Oh, he was charming enough—Sarah's a sucker for charm—but he sure as hell backed off fast enough when she got hurt. He made a pass at me while she was in the hospital. Can you believe that?" She shot Tucker a fierce look. "Poor Sarah, lying there with a head injury and the doctors shaking *their* heads because they don't know if she'll ever come out of it, and that bastard's leering and pinching me on the ass!"

Tucker just stopped himself from commenting that he could understand that other man's urge, base though it had certainly been; as complimentary as he meant the words to be, he was both old enough and wise enough to know she wouldn't appreciate them. "But things really changed when Sarah got out of the hospital?" he asked instead.

"With David, you mean?" Margo nodded. "Oh, yeah. Well, before that, really. When she predicted the nurse would have her baby. And the hotel fire, she predicted that in front of a bunch of us, David included. He thought she was crazy when she said it'd happen. Then, when it did—he *really* thought she was crazy."

"And it scared him?"

"I'll say. But before he could come up with a halfway decent excuse to break it off with her, she saw his future. He lasted about a week with Sarah worrying about rail- road crossings, then bolted for California so fast you'd have thought his ass was on fire."

"And died out there—at a railroad crossing."

"I didn't grieve for him. But Sarah nearly fell apart. For weeks, she wouldn't even leave her house, wouldn't talk to anybody except me—and hardly to me." Margo frowned a little as she finished the eighth and final egg and turned the burner off, then plugged in the toaster and reached for the loaf of bread on the counter. "I don't know if she would have come out of it, except that the visions—I mean the waking nightmares—stopped for a while. It gave her a chance to get her bearings, I guess."

"And when the—waking nightmares came back?"

Margo shook her head. "Well, either they didn't come very often, or she didn't tell me about all of them, because I only know about a few. Mostly minor things—except for that serial killer out in San Francisco. That one really freaked her out." She paused for a moment or so, then added soberly, "But she's been awfully quiet these last months. Awfully quiet."

Tucker drew a breath and said, "You're afraid of her too. Aren't you?"

She looked at him, those brilliant eyes darkened, and said shakily, "Oh, I'm afraid. But not of *her*. I'm afraid of what she can see. Because she saw my future. And she won't tell me what it is."

The morning sun was halfway to its noon position, and long shadows stretched from the west side of the building in downtown Richmond. A tall woman with short and rather spiky blond hair stood motionless on the balcony, virtually invisible in the shadows and among tall potted plants. She cursed absently as a palm frond stirred by the breeze waved in front of her binoculars, shifted her weight just a bit, then went still again as her field of vision cleared. Her attention was fixed on the rather shabby hotel across the street, and a particular room a floor below her own fifth-floor vantage point.

The drapes at that window had not been drawn, and a generous percentage of the room was visible to her.

Careless. Duran must be losing his touch.

Two men were in the room. She would have given a lot to know what they discussed as they sat so casually across from each other. But there had been no time to plant listening devices, and from her angle, it was impossible even to make an attempt at lip-reading—a skill she had worked very hard to acquire.

She lowered the binoculars, lips pressed so tightly together there was no hint of softness there, and vivid green eyes furious. "Damn," she whispered. "Damn, damn, damn."

She eased back through the balcony doors into the apartment she had—so to speak—sublet and bent over a lovely Regency desk. The former occupant's work had been unceremoniously shoved aside, and an open laptop sat in the center of the pretty floral blotter.

"Jeez, enough with the plant motif," she muttered, momentarily distracted as she glanced around at the very pretty, very feminine, and very floral bedroom in which she stood. Frilly was hardly Murphy's style. Barely suppressing a shudder, she fixed her attention on the screen of the laptop.

A section of a city map, brilliantly colored, met her intent gaze. She studied it for a long moment, frowning, then tapped a few keys to produce a close-up of the section.

Her index finger traced the distance from a square repre-
senting the hotel across the street to a quieter street where
former residences had been turned into small businesses.

"Too close. Dammit, they have to know where she
is." Murphy wasn't even conscious of speaking aloud, so
accustomed to working alone that talking to herself had
become a habit.

The words had barely left her mouth when the very
faint sound of a key in the lock of the apartment's front
door brought her head up alertly, and this time the curse
that left her lips was a mere whisper.

*Just my luck that Ms. Bank Vice President went off this
morning and left her damned lunch on the kitchen counter!*

Swiftly, unwilling to wait and find out whether the
apartment's legal occupant would choose to come into
the bedroom for some reason, she closed the laptop and
dropped it into the pouch hanging against her hip. Without a wasted motion, she backed out onto the balcony
and slid the door closed.

There was a fire escape, which was good, but leaving
the shelter of the greenery meant she was too visible,
even in the shadows, for her peace of mind. Still, being
seen by the wrong person was infinitely preferable to
being arrested for breaking and entering, which was what
likely would happen if she remained on the balcony.

She moved quickly and quietly down to street level
and, once there, paused only long enough to stow the binoculars in their pocket of the pouch containing the computer.

The pouch was not conspicuous, resembling nothing

so much as a large, if bulky, shoulder bag, but someone might well have taken notice of the binoculars.

A quick glance around told her that none of the few people about seemed interested in her. She was just about to relax when a carefully casual glance up at the window across the street brought her to a dead stop just two steps away from the fire escape.

Duran was at the window, and he saw her.

He was too far away for her to recognize his face, but she knew it was him. She knew he was looking at her. And she knew he recognized her. She could feel it. Like some night animal caught unexpectedly in the light, she stood frozen, not breathing, a panicky sensation stirring deep inside her. It was not a feeling she was willing to define to herself, though if asked she would have said angrily that it was hatred. Pure hatred.

If asked, Duran would have said the same thing.

The moment seemed to last forever, and if a car horn had not rudely shattered the quiet of the morning, there was no telling how long she would have stood there staring up at the man in the window. But the horn brought her to her senses, and with a soft little sound more violent than a curse, she hurried to the corner and around it, taking herself out of his field of vision.

———————

He turned away from the window and looked across the room at the other man.

"What is it?" Varden asked, instantly alert.

"We've run out of time," Duran said.

———

Sarah?

She was struggling up out of the depths of an exhausted sleep, frantic to wake up and get control, to be able to shut out the whisper in her mind.

Sarah, you must—

Her eyes snapped open, and Sarah was awake. Her heart was pounding, and she could hear her own shuddery breathing. As always, once she was awake and aware, the voice fell silent.

That voice. God, that voice.

It had begun only a few days before, creeping into her awareness during both waking and sleeping dreams, during vulnerable or unguarded moments. A whisper without identity, eerily insistent. She didn't even know whether it came from inside her . . . or somewhere else. It felt alien to her, yet she couldn't be sure it *was*— because all of this felt alien. The dreams. These frightening new abilities. The feelings she couldn't explain even to herself.

All she really knew was that all of it terrified her.

She pulled herself out of bed and went to take a shower, heavy-eyed after lying awake for most of the night. It wasn't until she came back into her bedroom and began dressing that she heard a loud laugh and the cheerful notes of Margo's voice.

Margo. Dear God.

Sarah knew she should have called her, of course. Last night. She should have called her and reassured her that it was okay, that she didn't have to come charging back home to support her partner and friend. Anything to keep Margo safely away from here. But Sarah's thoughts last night had been fixed on her own troubles—and on Tucker Mackenzie.

Real. He was real. Not a figment of her imagination. Not a face in a half-remembered nightmare, probably formed out of random features drifting like flotsam in her subconscious. Real. One more indication to her that the prediction of her own future was going to come true. One more sign that it was useless to fight what had to be.

That was what she would have said—had, in fact, said—yesterday. But Tucker hadn't merely presented himself as a sign or a symbol or an indication. He was a real man, and being a real man, he had his own thoughts and opinions and his own agenda. He wanted to believe.

He wanted to believe in her.

Sarah had seen something similar more times than she could count these last months. People with anxious voices and eager eyes and desperate smiles. Asking her, begging her, for answers. The difference was, those people hadn't wanted the truth. No, they wanted answers, but only those answers that would make them feel good, or at least better, about their problems, their lives. They wanted reassurance, comfort, hope. They hadn't been able to find it within their own belief system, whether that be religion or something else. So they had come to her.

Tell me my husband forgave me before he died.

Tell me my runaway daughter isn't walking the streets somewhere, or lying dead in a gutter.

Tell me I'm right to choose my lover.

Tell me my mother didn't suffer.

Tell me there's no hell.

Tell me there is a heaven.

Tell me I have a future.

Tell me life doesn't just end.

Tell me . . . please tell me . . .

Sarah had discovered for herself that hope was a fragile thing, difficult to hold on to in the harsh face of day-to-day living. She blamed no one for trying to hold on to it, or reach for it again after it had been lost or driven away. But she was helpless to offer hope to others when all she saw was bleak and dark and violent—and without promise.

She had expected Tucker to ask her for hope. But that wasn't what he wanted from her. He wanted the truth. He didn't care whether it proved to be a dark and bleak truth. He didn't care whether it caused him pain. He just had to know the truth.

She could have given him most of what he wanted of her within the first hour of knowing him. That she had not was due to several reasons. Though he would doubtless disagree with her assessment, she knew he was not yet ready to hear the truth he needed to hear. Not yet ready to listen and understand. Proof of that had been his shocked reaction to the tiny glimpse of the truth she had shown him just after they said good night.

And then there was his part in the sequence of events

that all these new instincts of hers told her had already begun. His arrival told her that the countdown had started. With his truth revealed to him, he would no doubt turn away from her, and she knew it wasn't yet time for him to do that. There was another reason for him to be here with her. They had . . . some place to go together. Some place where it was cold and . . . bleak.

Her rendezvous with death.

And that was the final reason why she had not offered him his truth. Because he had intrigued her with his challenge. With the possibilities of what he saw. He was so sure. So sure that fate could be changed. That destiny was merely the sum of one's choices.

Sarah needed his certainty. She didn't want to die. There were things she hadn't done yet, places she hadn't seen, experiences that eluded her. She was not ready to leave life, at least not willingly. But she had no hope of her own left, no certainty that her path could be chosen by her.

All she saw was darkness.

If he was right—if there was even a small chance he was right—then Sarah needed his help to attempt to change her destiny. She needed his certainty to keep her going, his hope to replace the hope she had lost.

It was thoughts such as these that kept Sarah awake long into the night, but when she heard Margo's buoyant voice in the other room, thoughts of her own dim future were cast aside.

Margo was home. In Richmond.

The last place on earth she needed to be today.

When Sarah came out of the bedroom to greet the other two, her first glance and tentative smile at Tucker met a somewhat guarded response. She knew why, of course. Even a brief glimpse into someone else's soul left that soul feeling disturbingly naked.

Psychic eyes aren't so fascinating when they're aimed at your soul, are they, Tucker?

It hurt, though.

"Good morning," she said, impartially to both but shifting her gaze immediately to Margo. "You didn't have to come running back here, Margo. You shouldn't have."

"I was worried about you, kid. I didn't want you to be alone." Margo grinned suddenly, a pleased look that belied the anxiety in her expressive eyes. "Didn't know about Tucker, obviously, or I wouldn't have barreled back here to be a sixth wheel."

"Third," Sarah corrected automatically. She looked at Tucker, caught the flicker of a laugh in his green eyes, and they shared a brief moment of silent amusement.

"Oh, right, third." As always, Margo accepted the correction amiably. "Breakfast, Sarah?"

"Just coffee." The pot was almost empty, and Sarah used that as an excuse to make fresh. Margo made the worst coffee in creation, and repeated instructions had done nothing to change that.

"You should eat," Margo protested. "Look, at least some toast, and maybe the bacon Tucker didn't finish—"

"All right, toast." Her head was pounding, and Sarah

really didn't feel like arguing. Conscious of Tucker's silent scrutiny as she moved past him on the other side of the breakfast bar, she tried not to think about him, something that required a disturbing amount of effort. Instead, she tried to think of a way to get Margo to leave as soon as possible. She didn't want to frighten her friend, but even less did she want to lose her. For good.

Unbidden, the image that had haunted her for weeks rose starkly in her mind, all too clear and without ambiguity. Tomorrow's newspaper, with a headline that turned Sarah's blood to ice . . .

"Are you all right?" Tucker asked quietly.

Sarah looked blankly at him for a moment before she realized she had been standing immobile with one hand on the breadbox for just that instant too long. "I'm fine." She wondered idly what her expression looked like to make him look so doubtful. "Really."

She busied herself making toast, while Margo leaned back against the counter sipping her coffee and Tucker sat at the bar drinking his, and both watched her. She had no idea what they had discussed before she had gotten up, no idea whether either had confided in the other.

Some psychic I am! I can't even get this cursed thing to work for me when I need it to!

Before she could think of something casual to say, the silence was broken by the distant sound of a bell ringing below in the shop.

"I forgot to turn the bell on up here," Sarah said. "It's past opening time. I'll—"

"No, I'll go down and see who it is." Margo set her cup on the counter and headed for the door. "Whether we stay open today—well, we'll see. In the meantime, you relax and eat your breakfast. Talk to Tucker. See you two later."

Sarah actually opened her mouth to warn her friend, then closed it even as the door closed behind Margo. *What should I do?* She had tried to warn David and had only gotten him killed. None of her other warnings had made the slightest difference. But this, this was so damned specific, maybe it was different . . .

"Sarah?"

She looked at him.

"What did you see in Margo's future?"

She didn't mean to tell him but heard her own frightened voice respond without hesitation. "Death."

Tucker didn't look surprised, and his voice remained quiet. "Are you sure?"

Sarah drew a breath. "I saw a Richmond newspaper with tomorrow's date. The front page. Below the headline, there was a picture of Margo. The headline read, *Local Antiques Dealer Killed.* The first line began, *Local businesswoman Margo James was killed yesterday afternoon in a bizarre accident that took place in her antiques shop.*"

Drawing another breath to steady a voice that shook uncontrollably, Sarah added bitterly, "Now you tell me if there's any way to misinterpret *that*."

He was silent for a moment. "Which is why she's supposed to be out of town now?"

Sarah nodded. "I shouldn't even have let her go down to the shop just now, but . . . I don't know what to do. If I try to keep her out of the shop, if I warn her, I'm afraid I'll bring about the accident I want to prevent. Like I did with David."

"You don't know that you brought that about. He might have been killed at a railroad crossing if he had stayed here."

"Yes—or he might not have. And Margo . . . I made sure she'd be away, didn't call her about the house burning hoping to *keep* her away, but now she's come back. As if she's fated to be here, today. It was very clear, what I saw. An accident, this afternoon, in the shop. But I don't know exactly when it's supposed to happen, or what happens."

"A bizarre accident," Tucker mused.

"I couldn't see what that meant, what actually happened." Sarah went to pour herself a cup of the fresh coffee, absently noting that the toast had popped up without her awareness and was now undoubtedly cold. Leaving it, she fixed her coffee and then turned back to face Tucker. "It isn't afternoon yet, and newspapers try to be precise . . . but it could happen at any time."

Tucker frowned. "Wait a minute. Margo is supposed to be out of town, which means you're supposed to be the one in the shop. Right?"

She nodded. "It's just her and me, no other full-time staff. A couple of guys from the health club nearby help us out moving large pieces of furniture when we need to, but we do all the rest. Why?"

"Maybe it's my writer's imagination at work, but think about this, Sarah. Somebody's been watching you recently. You, not Margo. Yesterday your house burns down, probably due to arson. Today, you're here—which is where you'd logically be after losing your house. It's even logical that you'd probably be downstairs working, to occupy your mind if nothing else. I mean, if Margo hadn't showed up, wouldn't you be down there now, in answer to that bell?"

"Of course."

He waited, watching her.

Sarah was a bit slow getting it, maybe because of her pounding head or because her mind was filled with fears for Margo. But, slowly, the possibility he offered came into focus. "You mean, me? Somebody could be trying to kill me, and got—gets—Margo by mistake?"

"She's a redhead too. Hard to mistake one of you for the other close up, but at a distance it wouldn't be so unlikely. Especially if you're likely to be down in the shop and Margo is supposed to be out of town. Maybe that *bizarre accident* you saw was a deliberate act intended to look accidental."

Sarah didn't bother to ask him whether he actually believed she had seen the future; he was, as he'd said, suspending his disbelief, but only time and proof would convince Tucker that she could predict events that had not yet occurred. In any case, she was thinking more painful thoughts.

"I told you—there's no reason anybody would want to hurt me."

"And yet you predict your own death—at the hands of some mysterious *them* you can't identify." His voice was not in the least sarcastic.

It had not occurred to Sarah either to connect Margo's death with her own future or to consider her shadowy enemies apart from the ending she felt sure they planned for her. But now, thinking about it, she had to admit that Tucker had made a number of points. Looked at objectively, as he clearly could, it was obvious that Sarah was the target of whatever was happening.

"But why?" Like any human being, she found it extremely difficult to even imagine that someone else might want to put a period to her existence, despite her own predictions. "I don't understand why anyone would want me dead."

"The reasons people kill are usually simple," Tucker offered. "Desperation. Greed. Jealousy. Rage. Fear."

Sarah shook her head, unable to connect any of those powerful emotions to her life. "I'm not . . . I'm not even close enough to anyone to inspire anything like that. My friends are casual—except for Margo; I have no family to speak of, just cousins who aren't even a part of my life. How could I have roused those kinds of emotions in someone without knowing it?"

"Even fear?" He looked at her steadily. "Sarah, your life changed dramatically six months ago. You became psychic. And as you said yourself, there are people out there who are terrified of the very idea of precognition. People very afraid of psychics—maybe even to the point of trying to start a witch hunt."

They burned my house. Witches were burned.

"It wouldn't be the first time someone perceived as different became a target of intimidation tactics," he reminded her, and echoed her own thoughts when he added, "Suspected witches were burned; nearly the first thing you said to me was that you were the neighborhood witch."

"But there would have been warnings, wouldn't there? Nasty phone calls, notes—or something worse—left in my mailbox. Isn't that how it works? They wouldn't have *started* by setting my house on fire. Would they?"

Tucker shrugged. "I wouldn't have said so. But in these days of stalkers and serial killers, the extreme gets more common every day."

Sarah accepted that reluctantly. "So it's possible somebody wants me dead because I'm psychic." She shied away from anyone hating and fearing that much to focus on her friend's safety. "Then . . . then if I'm the target, Margo should be out of danger if I send her away. Right? If she's nowhere near me, she won't be an accidental target."

"That seems reasonable to suppose," Tucker agreed.

Sarah looked at her watch. "It's after ten. I should go downstairs and try to talk her into leaving Richmond before lunch. Will . . . will you help me convince her?"

"I'll try." He hesitated, then added, "If you'll take my advice, I think you should tell her the truth. She knows you've seen something, Sarah. It's worrying her."

"Yes, I know." Sarah turned the coffeepot off, then looked around in sudden awareness. "Where's Pendragon?"

"Margo fed him his breakfast and let him out, she said." He hesitated, then said, "I never did let him out last night; he disappeared on me. Was he with you?"

"No, not unless he decided to sleep under the bed." She shrugged. "Which he might have done. This is the first time I've spent the night here over the shop since he showed up, so I'm not sure about his nighttime habits."

"He's been altered, right? So not as likely to want to wander at night like intact toms do."

Absently, Sarah said, "I thought you didn't know much about cats."

There was a brief silence, and then Tucker said, "I guess most people know that much."

"I guess. Yeah, I made sure he'd been neutered, otherwise I would have taken him to a vet. Too many stray cats around for my peace of mind. They live dangerous lives, poor things." With a shrug, she added, "He probably belongs to someone in the area, given his condition and that collar. He's been somebody's cat, obviously cared for."

"Then maybe he went home after his breakfast."

"Maybe so."

"Ready to go down to the shop?"

"As ready as I'll ever be."

They left the apartment and went downstairs to the shop, finding Margo occupied with a customer.

"I had something a little more . . . economical in mind," the attractive young woman was saying somewhat wryly as she studied the price tag of a beautiful early Victorian writing desk.

Margo chuckled. "Antiques are always economical, especially if you're looking at long-term investment, Miss Desmond. Just think of having something this beautiful to pass down to your children."

"You mean instead of the cash?" Miss Desmond grinned.

Sarah recognized from Margo's happy expression that she expected to make a sale, so she didn't try to interrupt. Instead, she led Tucker through the maze of gleaming furniture to a back corner, where a stunning ormolu-mounted boulle bureau plat of Regency design acted as a desk where Sarah and Margo did the necessary paperwork for the shop.

"Nice place," Tucker commented.

"Thanks. It's taken us almost eight years to get the kind of stock and clientele we dreamed about when we started. A lot of long hours and hard work went into Old Things, to say nothing of every penny Margo and I could come up with." She said it matter-of-factly but with a trace of wistfulness, filled with the conviction that this part of her life was ending. She didn't know whether her prediction of a bleak future would be fulfilled, but she was sure, utterly sure, that her partnership with Margo was ending.

One way or another.

Sarah glanced back across the shop at Margo and the customer, then looked at her watch uneasily. It was still well before noon, but she wouldn't feel that her friend was out of danger until she was out of Richmond and far away from this shop.

"I think I'll wander around a bit," Tucker told her. "I've always been interested in antiques." He nodded toward Margo, adding, "Sing out when you need me."

"Okay." Sarah sat down at the chair behind the desk and opened a file to go over several shipping invoices. It was busywork and nothing more; the clock in her head was ticking away minutes, and all she could think about was talking to Margo and getting her out of here.

With that tense part of her awareness, she was conscious of Margo talking to the customer, leading her from piece to piece but always returning to that Victorian writing desk she clearly intended to sell the woman.

"Let me just sit here and think about it," the customer finally said, sitting down somewhat gingerly in a George III mahogany-framed dining chair.

"It's a tough decision, I know," Margo said sympathetically.

"I'll say. I do love that desk, though."

"We have a layaway plan. Ten percent down, and you can take a year or more to pay the balance."

The customer groaned. "You're an evil woman. Tempting me."

Margo laughed. "It's something I've been accused of before. But what can I say? I like people to have beautiful things."

That, Sarah reflected absently, was true. Sales techniques aside, Margo did genuinely enjoy the thought of the beautiful things she valued giving pleasure to others.

"My husband will shoot me," the customer said with another groan. "He expects me to come home with a plain old desk, not an antique. I just stopped by here on impulse."

"Sometimes," Margo said, "impulse is the best way to find the nice surprises in life."

"Yeah." The customer frowned. "Look, give me a few minutes, will you, please? I want to think about this."

Her meaning was clear, and Margo smiled brightly. "No problem. Just call me when you're ready."

"Okay. Thanks."

Margo turned and headed toward the back of the shop where Sarah waited.

Sarah rose to her feet, anxious to warn Margo and get her out of the shop as soon as possible—sale or no sale. But before she could leave the desk, the phone rang.

"Good morning, Old Things, this is Sarah," she said as she answered automatically.

Without preamble, a man said, "I was in your shop the other day looking at an Irish mahogany breakfront wardrobe, and I think I absentmindedly left a small black notebook inside. At least, I hope I did. Could you look for it, please?"

"Sure. Hang on just a minute." She put him on hold, then winced as the phone immediately rang again. Answering the second line, she found one of their shippers upset because he couldn't find the armoire he was supposed to be picking up. Sarah put him on hold as well, then began searching through the folders on the desk.

"Need a hand?" Margo asked cheerfully.

Sarah found the relevant folder. "Oh, you noticed?" She smiled at her partner. "Guy on the other line lost a small black notebook here the other day. He says maybe inside that Irish breakfront. Could you check, please?"

"You bet."

Sarah turned her attention back to the aggravated shipper, relating the address where he was supposed to be and soothing him when it developed that the mistake had been his. She listened to his sheepish apologies, her gaze absently following Margo across the shop to the huge wardrobe, one of their most massive pieces.

"No problem, Mike," she murmured, hanging up the phone just as Margo reached the wardrobe and swung open the heavy doors.

All Sarah remembered thinking afterward was, *That candelabra on top shouldn't be wobbling like that.* And then, in a terrifying instant, she realized why it was.

"Margo! It's falling!"

Sarah was too far away to help, and the wardrobe was so huge and heavy that even though Margo was reacting to the warning, turning, her face white with shock, there was simply no way she could get out from under the thing in time.

Sarah knew that. There was nothing she could do but watch, totally helpless, the scant few seconds that passed stretching into a lifetime she lived paralyzed with dread.

Then she saw Tucker lunge from between two tallboys

and grab Margo's arm, both of them now in the path of the toppling wardrobe.

It was the last thing she saw, her eyes closing instinctively, as the wardrobe crashed to the floor with a force that shook the entire building.

FOUR

"I keep telling you, it wasn't at all unusual. Customers leave things in here often and call us in a panic. I didn't think twice about it." Sarah kept her voice even with an effort. "I didn't notice anything in particular about his voice. Just a man, that's all. Very polite and worried about the notebook he'd lost. I thought."

"But you believe his call was designed purely to cause you to go to the wardrobe and open it?"

"Isn't that obvious?"

"Not to me, Miss Gallagher. It could have been a simple coincidence." Sergeant Lewis frowned at her. "But even if the call was placed with such an intention, what do you expect us to do about it?"

"Find him," she said, with a very faint snap to the words.

"Miss Gallagher, according to the Call Return on your phone, the call came from a pay phone near here—one of the very few left—at a busy service station where at least a dozen people and quite likely more have made a call today. Nobody working there noticed anything or anyone unusual. There are no prints on what's left of that wardrobe, except the prints that should be there. Your security system was active until Miss James came in here this morning, and shows no signs of tampering, so how anyone could have gotten in here and rigged this, leaving no evidence behind—"

"Are you saying we imagined it?" For the first time in all this, Sarah's overpowering emotion was anger. It felt good.

"I'm saying . . . maybe the wardrobe just fell. It's an old piece with a shallow depth, and the doors are heavy. Maybe it was just unbalanced."

Sarah drew a breath. "That wardrobe, Sergeant Lewis, has been in this shop for nearly a year. I've opened both doors countless times, and so has Margo. So have numerous customers. It never fell before."

He glanced back over his shoulder at a couple of his men who were standing near the overturned and seriously damaged wardrobe, and from both he received faint shrugs. Sighing, he looked back at Sarah. "There are no signs that anyone tampered with it, Miss Gallagher."

"In other words, you're not going to do a thing about this."

"There's nothing I *can* do." He sighed again. "Look, Miss James wasn't hurt—"

"I wouldn't go that far," Margo said. She was sitting near Sarah with an ice pack pressed to the back of one shoulder, which had been dealt a glancing blow from the falling wardrobe. She was still rather pale, but composed—and uncharacteristically quiet. "But at least I wasn't smashed flat as a waffle. Thanks to Tucker."

Lewis looked mildly troubled for a moment but didn't comment on Margo's unusual simile. "I'm not discounting what happened to you, Miss James, believe me. But it could have been—probably was—an accident. That's all I'm saying."

Tucker spoke up for the first time. "What about the customer?"

Lewis looked at him, frowning slightly as he took in the other man's lounging position in a very fine George I walnut wing armchair, also near Sarah. Lewis didn't like Tucker, and it showed. "What about her?"

Tucker, who had been curiously expressionless since the police had arrived and hadn't said much before then, shrugged. "She vanished pretty quickly. Didn't even say good-bye. But then—maybe she just doesn't like loud noises." His sarcasm wasn't blatant, but it was there.

With a clear air of humoring him, Lewis held his pencil poised. "Okay, did anybody get her name?"

"Desmond," Margo said. "Cait Desmond. I called her a miss, but she mentioned a husband later, so she's a missus."

Quietly, Tucker said, "She wasn't wearing a wedding ring."

"Wasn't she?" Margo frowned at him.

"Some men notice. I do. No rings at all."

Margo looked back at Lewis. "Okay, then either she was a wife who likes bare fingers or she lied about the husband. Although I don't know why she would have."

Still quiet, Tucker said, "When you left her alone and started back here, she got up and moved toward the wardrobe. I was on the other side of the shop, but I saw her. A piece of furniture blocked my view for a moment, and by the time I moved to get a better look at what she might be doing, she was returning to that chair where you'd left her. And if I had to come up with a word to describe her attitude, it would have to be—surreptitious."

"You are a novelist, are you not, Mr. Mackenzie?"

The implication was clear, but Tucker didn't rise to the bait. "I am. But I'm not in the habit of imagining things unless I'm getting paid to do so."

"Funny that you're just now mentioning what you . . . saw," Lewis said coldly.

Without offering an excuse, Tucker merely said, "I started toward the wardrobe then, no more than vaguely concerned, but Margo got there before me. She and I were both knocked off our feet when the thing fell; by the time I got up, the customer was already out of the shop. It seemed more important to make sure Margo was okay, so I didn't take the time to rush outside and see where the woman went after she bolted out the door."

"A gesture of courtesy I very much appreciated," Margo told him.

Tucker inclined his head gravely, but his gaze remained fixed on Lewis. "I'll buy that she was startled—the whole building shook—but there was no reason why your average customer would run away without even stopping to find out if everybody was all right. Or returning to check after the first panic might have driven her outside. Goes against human nature. Unless, of course, she had something to do with the . . . accident."

Lewis drew a breath and let it out slowly, the picture of a man holding on to his patience. "As I keep telling you, Mr. Mackenzie—as I keep telling all of you—there is no sign the wardrobe was tampered with. And since none of you claim this customer was standing behind it pushing, I fail to see how she could have had anything to do with the *accident*."

"And you're so sure that's what it was. Even though Sarah's house burned down yesterday, probably due to arson. Even though she was supposed to be alone in the shop today. Even though there's no logical reason why that wardrobe would have fallen on its own. You don't find that to be at all suspicious."

"Surprising, maybe. Coincidence, certainly."

Tucker's eyes narrowed. "Every cop I've ever met in my life believes there's no such thing as coincidence. Funny that you do."

"Not funny at all." Lewis was visibly stiff now. "The world is full of strange things, Mr. Mackenzie. This is just one more strange thing."

After a moment, Tucker looked silently at Sarah, and she said immediately, "Then we won't keep you any longer, Sergeant Lewis. Thank you for listening." She neither rose nor offered to shake hands.

He hesitated, his notebook still open, then closed it with a snap. "I'll be in touch, Miss Gallagher. About your house. We're still investigating that, of course." He gestured briefly to his men, and all three left the shop.

Margo got up, went to the front door and locked it, and turned over the sign so that it read CLOSED. Then she returned to her chair. "Okay. You two want to let me in on this? What's happening here?"

Tucker said nothing.

Sighing, Sarah turned a bit in her chair so that she faced the other two more squarely. "I knew there was going to be an accident—a bizarre accident—here in the shop today," she told Margo. "But I thought it would happen later today, in the afternoon. And . . . it was supposed to be fatal."

Margo blinked. "I was supposed to be . . . dead?"

Mildly, Tucker said, "As a writer always in search of the right words, I take issue with the phrase 'supposed to be.' Let's just say that Sarah saw a future event that didn't turn out quite as she expected it to." He was looking at her steadily.

Sarah met his gaze, her own startled.

He smiled. "Somehow, you managed to change Margo's destiny."

She wasn't at all sure he was right, because she had an unnerving feeling that everything today had happened just as it was supposed to, despite the headline she had seen. But all she said was, "Not me. You. You pulled her away from the wardrobe."

"I wouldn't have been here if you hadn't allowed me to be. And I wouldn't have been wary, watching for anything unusual, if you hadn't told me about your prediction." He shrugged. "In any case, the point is that what should have happened—didn't. At least, not the way you saw it happen. Fate was averted."

Somewhat uneasily, Margo said, "The afternoon isn't over yet. Maybe we'd better leave."

Tucker immediately rose. "I agree. Not that I expect another bizarre *accident* to take place, but better to be safe. If you ladies will allow me, I'll buy you a late lunch."

"And then maybe a movie?" Margo suggested as she got up. "I don't think I want to come back here until the afternoon is definitely past."

———

Douglas Knox glanced at his watch for the third time and sighed as he returned his gaze to the impressive view of San Francisco visible through the hotel window. Dammit, where was she? It wasn't like her to be late, especially since she'd asked him to be early.

He was still a little surprised that she'd wanted him here an hour earlier than usual, but he certainly hadn't complained; it was rare that they could spend more than a couple of hours together without taking too big a risk. If her husband found out, or even suspected, then Amy would suffer for it—losing her daughter at the very least.

Douglas moved away from the window, frowning a little. He didn't want her to lose the kid, but sneaking around like this was getting old. It took too much energy to do it, for one thing. And he wasn't one of those guys who got off on taking risks, not when it came to his love life.

Unfortunately, Amy's husband was both possessive and a vengeful son of a bitch; he had *punished* her more than once in the ten years they'd been married. She still had the scars.

"Wonder if I could give the bastard a nice little heart attack," Douglas murmured aloud.

No. Probably not. He didn't know enough about the heart, where to push or . . . squeeze.

Sitting down in a deep chair beside the desk, he held his hand out and watched dispassionately as a pen on the desk began to roll across the polished surface toward him. It picked up speed as it rolled, and when it reached the edge of the desk it seemed to launch itself through the air to land neatly in Douglas's palm.

A nice little party trick. He closed his fingers around the pen and swore under his breath. Amy said if he went to Vegas he could make a fortune, especially at craps. But Douglas had the superstitious notion that to misuse his ability to move things would be to lose it. And he liked having it.

He liked being different.

But what use was this ability of his if he couldn't do anything meaningful with it? Oh, sure, he could pluck a pen off a desk when he was three feet away, or get a book off a shelf without getting up, or even move furniture with a lot less sweat and effort than most people expended. And he could open locked doors by just *thinking* them open. And once, just a week before, he had stopped a car when the idiot driver had left it parked incorrectly on a hill and it had started to roll.

He'd probably saved at least one life that time, since the car had been rolling toward an oblivious window-shopper. The newspapers had blathered on about the "inexplicable" way the car had just stopped right in the middle of the hill like that, and he had enjoyed being the secret savior.

"Not bad," he murmured, turning the pen in his fingers briefly and then tossing it toward the desk. So maybe he had done something useful, after all. And maybe, if he could get close enough to see the bastard at just the right moment, maybe he could give Amy's husband a secret little shove down a long flight of stairs . . .

The hairs on the back of his neck stood straight up.

Douglas frowned and let his gaze track slowly around the room. Nobody was there, of course. Still—something wasn't right. He could feel it. It seemed difficult to breathe all of a sudden, as if the air had grown heavy. And he could have sworn it was darker than it had been a moment before, even though the drapes were open and two lamps burned brightly. It just somehow *felt* darker.

He looked at his watch. Twenty minutes after two. The sun was shining in a cloudless sky out there. It was the middle of the day. And he hadn't turned out a light in here. So why was it getting darker?

"Okay, so maybe I won't push him down the stairs," he said aloud, hearing in his own shaky voice the worry that he might have opened up a box of troubles by even thinking about using his abilities to do something bad.

It was getting darker. And when he tried to move, terror shot through him, because he couldn't. He reached out desperately with his mind, but the door didn't open. The little pen on the desk didn't even move.

It just got darker.

Until he couldn't see anything at all.

When Amy Richards opened the door of the hotel room, it was two thirty. She was early for their usual three o'clock meeting, so she wasn't surprised he wasn't here yet. She *was* surprised to find an envelope on the desk with her name on it. From Doug.

She was stunned and heartbroken to read that he had quit his job and moved back east, that he never wanted to see her again. She didn't believe it even when she went to his apartment and found all his things gone. Or when she checked with his boss and found he'd quit the day before, without even giving notice. But she had to believe it eventually.

Because she never saw him again.

———

"I'd just feel much better if you went back to Alexandria and finished the buying trip," Sarah said seriously, sitting down on the edge of Margo's bed as she watched her friend repacking a suitcase she had unpacked only that morning. They were at Margo's house, where Tucker had dropped them off less than an hour before.

"It's after three; the afternoon is pretty much shot." Margo was still protesting, but she was packing. Her bruised shoulder didn't appear to be bothering her, though Sarah didn't doubt it would ache tomorrow.

It bothered Sarah. It bothered her a lot. If Tucker was right, that so-called accident had been meant for her, and Margo had simply gotten in the way. Sarah didn't want her to get in the way again.

"I know, but . . . well, humor me."

Straightening abruptly, Margo directed a sharp look at her friend. "Have you seen something else? About me?"

Sarah shook her head. "No. Not about you, I swear."

"About you, then?" When Sarah remained silent and avoided her friend's gaze, Margo bent once again to her packing but went on, "You and Tucker were talking pretty intently when I came out of the restroom and back to our table; you two are planning something, aren't you?"

Vaguely, Sarah said, "Nothing unusual about dinner plans."

"Is that all it was? Fancy that. When he dropped us off here, he said he wouldn't be long, so I assumed you had plans for the evening. After you crate me back to Alexandria, that is."

"Ship. You need to finish the buying trip, you know that."

"Uh-huh. And what do you need to finish? And don't say dinner, because I'm not buying it. The story, I mean."

Sarah began to protest, but instead said, "Look, Margo, with everything that's happened lately, I just don't want to worry about a friend if I don't have to. So, you go to Alexandria, and finish the buying trip. I'll be fine. Tucker seems determined to . . . to hang around, and the police are going to find out who burned down my house—and I'm okay."

Frowning, Margo said bluntly, "You look like a stiff breeze would blow you away."

Sarah shrugged, but she wasn't happy at being told she looked that fragile. "I admit, things have been a strain. The last six months have been a strain. Hey, maybe I'll close the shop for a few days and get away, take that vacation you've been after me to take for years now. Maybe I'll go house hunting and find another fixer-upper instead of rebuilding. But I'll be okay, Margo."

Margo was silent for several minutes while she finished packing and closed her suitcase, then straightened, still frowning. "I know you've seen something. Something bad."

Steadily, Sarah said, "Whatever I've seen, today taught me something very . . . hopeful. It taught me that I'm not always right. That there's . . . that there may be . . . room to change what I see." She didn't believe that, but for Margo's sake she tried to sound convincing.

"That's what you and Tucker are planning to do, isn't it? Change some future disaster you've seen."

"How could we do that?"

"You tell me."

"There's nothing to tell." As she had explained to Tucker earlier, telling Margo of the bleak fate she had seen for herself would accomplish nothing except to alarm her friend and quite probably convince Margo that she should stick close and watch over Sarah.

Neither Sarah nor Tucker thought that would be a good idea; if being mistaken for Sarah had put Margo in danger today, there was always a chance it could happen again.

"So you're not going to tell me what's going on?"

Sarah hesitated, then said, "I have to learn to live with this, Margo. With what I've become."

"Don't say *what* as if you'd turned into a monster." Margo's voice was irritated.

"Okay. But I do have to learn to live with the changes in my life. I don't know—yet—how I can do that, but I have to figure out a way. Tucker thinks he can help me. I think I should let him try. And that's all."

Margo looked as though she wanted to continue pushing but finally swung her suitcase off the bed with a sound that in anyone less feminine would have been a snort of disgust. "All right, all right. But I think you're both full of cold cuts."

"Baloney. Full of baloney." Surprising herself, Sarah began to laugh. It felt as good as her earlier anger had felt.

Margo stared balefully at her for a moment, then joined in.

They had sobered considerably by the time they stood outside Margo's neatly landscaped Queen Anne–style house. She put her suitcase in the backseat of her ten-year-old sedan, then hugged Sarah hard and said, "I don't want to hear about the next disaster on the news, pal. Call me if anything happens. Or even if it doesn't."

"I will. And don't worry—I'll lock up before we leave."

"Just remember—don't hesitate to stay here if you get tired of the shop's apartment. Or for any other reason."

"Thanks. Have a good trip."

"I will. And you kiss Tucker for me." Margo winked, then got in her car and backed it out of the driveway.

Sarah watched her friend drive out of sight, and it was only when the dark car was gone that she became aware of the chill of the late September afternoon. Feeling abruptly alone and too vulnerable, she quickly went back up the walkway to the house, conscious of her heart suddenly pounding. As if a door had opened to allow a chill breeze into her mind, she knew there were eyes on her. Watching.

Waiting.

Sarah . . .

She hurried inside and turned to close the front door, and caught a glimpse of a tall man in a black leather jacket moving away between two houses across the street. Just a glimpse, and then he was gone.

Colder than before, Sarah closed and locked the door. But she didn't feel safe. She didn't feel safe at all.

————

"You want what?" Marc Westbrook's black brows rose, and his gray eyes were suddenly uncomfortably searching.

"I'd like to borrow your gun. That forty-five you got

from your father." Tucker kept his voice casual and did his best to meet the level gaze of his childhood friend with total innocence.

Apparently, innocent wasn't his best face.

"What're you up to, Tucker?"

"Look, you know I won't shoot myself in the foot; I can handle guns as well as you, if not better. I learned when I wrote the one where the mystery hinged on a marksman—"

"I know you can handle guns." Marc leaned back in the leather chair behind his big, cluttered desk, his frown deepening. "I also know you make a damned good living and can easily afford to buy a gun if you want—or need—one. So why borrow mine?"

"I don't need a gun to *keep*, just to . . . use for a while. To have for a while. A few days, maybe a couple of weeks. You know I don't approve of guns in the house, so—"

"So why do you need one, even temporarily? Last I heard, you had a dandy security system and a damn big dog."

"The security system is fine. The dog belonged to my sister and she came and claimed him when she got back from England."

"Tucker, why a gun?"

"Hey, do I ask you nosy questions?"

"Frequently." Marc smiled, but it was fleeting and left him looking unusually serious. "Out with it. Why do you need a gun? And why do I have this uneasy feeling that you came to me simply because you're in a hurry and don't want to sit out the waiting period?"

Tucker would have liked to confide in his friend. He thought a great deal of Marc. They had played cops and robbers as boys, had competed for and fought over girls as teenagers, and still managed to get together once a week or so even though both had demanding careers and Marc was now happily married and about to become a father. But Marc was a solidly—not to say rigidly—law-abiding man, and Tucker had no doubt that, once told of the situation, he would strongly disagree with the plan forming in his friend's fertile and not always cautious mind.

It was a potentially dangerous situation, he would say, and he would be right. From that point of agreement, they would immediately diverge. Marc thought the police should handle dangerous situations, that most cops were good cops and could be trusted. Tucker was beginning to have his doubts, especially after today's interview with Sergeant Lewis.

Slowly, Tucker said, "I'm asking for a favor, Marc. I need to borrow your gun for a little while. No questions asked."

"That's a fine thing to say to a criminal lawyer."

"Yeah, I know. But I'm saying it. You still keep the gun here, don't you? In your desk?"

Marc nodded.

"Well, then?"

"You aren't going to rob a bank, right?"

"Very funny."

"Well, how the hell should I know what you've got in mind? When you were writing the one about a terrorist group, you damn near ended up with a working bomb, and that one set on a runaway train got you blacklisted by Amtrak. I shudder to think what's next."

Tucker had no qualms in allowing his friend to believe he needed the gun for some reason associated with his latest novel. Lightly, he said, "You'll find out when you read all about it. The gun?"

Marc hesitated, but they had been friends a long time, and so he unlocked a lower drawer of his desk and produced the holstered gun. Handing it across, he said, "I just cleaned it the other day. The clip's full, chamber's empty."

"Gotcha. Thanks, Marc. I really appreciate this."

When Tucker stood up to leave, Marc said only, "I don't know what's going on, Tucker, but watch yourself."

"You bet. Say hello to Josie for me."

"I will."

They didn't shake hands, though later Tucker wished they had.

———

He continued with his meal even after he felt more than heard someone slide into the booth behind him. He heard the waitress come and brightly recommend this week's chicken dish, heard a low voice order the chicken with a slight indifference that seemed to miff the waitress. Either that, or she was upset that her charms had no effect on this particular customer.

Save it, sweetheart. He's made of ice.

When she'd gone away, he leaned back, making a

show of sipping his coffee and looking around casually, a satisfied diner relaxing after his meal. He spoke in a low voice without turning. "It's no good. Mackenzie's suspicious. He won't buy another accident, especially if Gallagher disappears."

"You're sure?" The answering voice was also low.

"Absolutely. And she's looking to him for help, that's clear, so he's going to be with her. I don't know what he'll do next, but if I were in his place . . . I'd get her out of Richmond. Fast."

"And go where?"

"I don't know."

"We need better information."

"I'm aware of that." He heard his voice stiffen and strove to make it once more calm and casual. There were some men it just didn't pay to get angry at, and this man headed the list. "Mackenzie's been all over the country in the last ten years, researching and promoting his novels. Believes in immersing himself in a subject if he needs it for one of his books—and some of those subjects have been fairly esoteric."

"For example?"

"Explosives—the kind you can put together from ingredients in most kitchens. Computer hacking. Survival training. Weapons. Defensive driving. He's taken courses through the FBI on topics ranging from antiterrorism to psychological profiling. He has a degree in electronics, and a measured IQ of over one-eighty, which puts him solidly in the genius range. And he was a fucking Boy Scout. Probably thinks he's MacGyver. Oh, and one last thing. From what I've been able to gather, he's always been interested in the paranormal. You should see all the books on his shelves."

The ice man's voice was grim. "In other words, the perfect person to keep Sarah Gallagher safe."

"I'd feel safe in his keeping, and I don't like the bastard."

"Why wasn't I told of this before?"

"I didn't know before." He forced the irritation from his voice. "Even with my resources and all the social networking out there, it takes a good twenty-four hours to search deep background on somebody unless that person is a criminal. Mackenzie isn't. And despite being famous in his field, he has a surprisingly small online presence, and that's almost entirely about his books." He fell silent as the waitress returned and served the chicken dish to the ice man. Once again she tried flirting, and once again her customer was indifferent.

Wave your boobs in my face, sweetheart, and we'll talk. Hell, we'll do a lot more than talk. But she wouldn't, of course. They never did.

When she'd flounced away, he spoke again. "If Mackenzie didn't have a certain amount of celebrity, I wouldn't have been able to find out as much as I did this quickly."

But you won't thank me, will you, you icy son of a bitch. Oh no.

"What else do you know?"

Oh no, no trouble at all. Don't mention it, really.

"Tax records, voting record, credit report, school records—"

"What do you know about him that will help us?"

He was silent for a minute or two, pushing aside his dangerous anger as he considered all the varied information about Tucker Mackenzie that had been dumped into his retentive brain. When he spoke, it was slowly. "He's a puzzle solver. Creative, of course. Intuitive. Stubborn. Highly loyal to friends. Athletic; hiking, climbing, and swimming are some of the ways he keeps in shape. He knows how to get information. He knows how to work alone. He knows how to think ahead. Plays a mean game of chess. Grand master."

"What are his weaknesses?"

"He might not take Gallagher's predictions as seriously as she does."

"Why not?" Interest quickened in that low voice.

"It's just a hunch, but I don't think he believes. He's debunked a few psychics in the past, and I hear he's so good at it he might have made a career out of it. In fact, I'm surprised you don't know more about him than I do."

"We can't be everywhere."

"Could've fooled me," he muttered.

Ignoring that, the ice man asked, "What else? Weaknesses?"

"Hell, I don't know. He could be reckless. Cocky maybe, at least until he figures out what he's up against. He'll underestimate you in the beginning, I'd bet money on that. I'd say he likes to believe himself in control of any given situation; the kind of guy who never loses his temper if he's losing a game, and smiles while he's already planning how to kick your ass next time. And—I don't know if he could kill someone up close and personal. I don't know if he's got that in him."

"Maybe he doesn't. But she does."

He was tempted to glance back over his shoulder but didn't. Instead, he lit a cigarette despite the NO SMOKING signs posted and blew a lazy smoke ring. "Whatever you say." Quite deliberately, he didn't ask what he was supposed to do next. He hated that shit, he really did.

Not that the ice man waited for him to ask.

"All right, maintain the surveillance until you hear from me."

"If he's going to move, he'll move quickly."

"I know. So be ready."

"Me? What comes next is up to you people. I'm just here to watch, report—and clean up the mess."

"You're here to do whatever we need you to do." The ice man's voice was silky.

"I'm not your fucking hired thug."

"You're my dog if that's what I need you to be. Shall I order you to sit up and bark?"

He smoked furiously, hating the bastard. And hating himself. He glared at the waitress, who had started toward him the instant he lit his cigarette but now decided instead to clear off a couple of tables.

"Be ready. Understand?"

"Yes."

A moment later, he was alone in the back of the restaurant. He didn't see the ice man leave. Hell, he didn't even hear him leave. And he should have. He really should have.

A few moments later, the flirty waitress came back to the ice man's table, bewildered by his absence but clearly pleased by the size of the tip left on the table. Even so, she glanced at the man in the next booth and said rather mildly, "Sir, there's no smoking inside."

He pulled his ID from his pocket and laid it on the table, open long enough for her to see the badge.

She left without another word.

When Sergeant Lewis lifted his cigarette to his lips, he saw that his hand was shaking.

FIVE

Sarah drew a breath of relief when Tucker returned to Margo's house, not realizing until that moment how tense she had been while waiting for him. As for Tucker, he too seemed on edge and a bit preoccupied, and she wondered whether he was having second thoughts about even temporarily hitching his fate to hers.

Not that she blamed him for that. No man in his right mind would want to be saddled with her.

"Every light in the house is on," he said mildly as he came in.

She blinked and looked around, surprised to find it true. She had been restless, and she had wandered from room to room, her skin crawling with that now-familiar creepy sense of being watched. Her subconscious had obviously felt at least a bit safer with lots of light.

She had very carefully not thought about the voice in her head.

"He was outside," she said.

Tucker stood in the small entrance hall, ignoring her automatic gesture indicating they could go into the living room. He didn't have to ask who she was talking about. "When did you see him?"

"Right after Margo left. Across the street, moving between two houses. I didn't see him again after that, even though I looked." *But he's still there. Still watching. Still waiting.*

"I didn't see him when I pulled up, but it's getting dark." Tucker frowned.

She tried to think of something reassuring. "Maybe he's just watching. Maybe he didn't have anything to do with the fire. Or with the wardrobe falling."

"I hope you're wrong about that."

"Why?"

"Bad enough to be looking back over our shoulders for a guy in a black leather jacket; if he isn't the only one watching you—if he isn't the only threat—then we have no idea what the other threat looks like."

Sarah half-consciously wrapped her arms around herself in an attempt to ward off the chill.

Tucker reached out and touched her shoulder lightly, but said only, "I'm going to go turn off some of these lights, okay?"

She nodded and wandered into the living room to wait for him. The plan, agreed upon earlier in a hasty discussion in the restaurant after Margo had excused herself, was to return to the apartment over the shop tonight—and to leave Richmond in the morning.

Sarah wasn't sure how she felt about that. There was a small, almost distant part of her that was alarmed by the hurried decision and bewildered by her willingness to just up and leave everything she had known, yet a larger part of her consciousness was convinced it was the right thing to do.

Yes. Walk away from your friends, your business, and the ashes of your home, because you're afraid. Put your trust in a man you met yesterday because he says he thinks you can change fate . . . even though he doesn't believe you can see the future . . .

As wrong as it sounded, it felt right. This was what she was supposed to do. This was her fate. A fate Tucker was somehow part of; she knew that too. And that was what frightened her the most, because she knew it meant she was already walking the path that led to her destiny.

Toward the death she had seen.

"I already checked all the doors and windows," she told him when he joined her in the living room. "That is what you were doing, isn't it?"

He didn't try to deny it. "All locked. Drapes are drawn." He paused, then added, "There were automatic timers on a couple of the upstairs lamps."

"Yes, Margo always sets them when she goes out of town. The living room lamps have timers as well."

Tucker didn't say why the subject interested him, but he seemed even more preoccupied after they locked up

Margo's house and drove back to the apartment over the shop.

"Why don't you go ahead and pack tonight," he suggested, almost as soon as they arrived. "We might decide to leave pretty early."

Sarah might have asked him why, but she was actually relieved to have something to do. It was very quiet in the apartment, neither she nor Tucker seemed inclined toward conversation, and her nerves were very much on edge. Something was going to happen. Soon. And she didn't want to think about what it might be. So she packed.

It didn't take long. Both she and Margo kept a few extra things in the apartment, including a packed overnight bag in case either had to go out of town for an unexpected estate auction or something like that, so it was a simple matter to take the bag from the closet and add in the rest of the clothing she had here. All the clothing she had left, as a matter of fact.

All the anything she had left.

That realization, late in coming but devastating, made her sit on the bed and cry. Gone. It was all gone. All her things, from the furniture she had lovingly collected over the years to the strand of pearls that had been all she had left of her mother. The few family pictures she had. The pictures of David. The few gifts he'd given her. Gone.

And the work, all that hard work to restore the house, it was all gone. The hours spent covered in sawdust and plaster dust and paint spatters, wasted. The bruised knuckles and fingers sore from using unfamiliar tools, wasted. The shopping for just the right moldings, the right wallpaper, the right curtains and rugs and fixtures, wasted.

Her life wasted.

She didn't make a sound, unable even in that moment of intense grief to forget the man waiting for her in the next room. She didn't want him to hear her and come in here. Whether he offered comfort or bracing common sense (losing a house wasn't so much when compared to one's life, after all), she didn't think she'd be able to accept either. And she didn't want him to see her crumpled on the bed, red-eyed and weepy, because . . .

She just didn't want him to see her like that.

It wasn't a very satisfying bout of tears and left her weary rather than relieved, but it did seem to take the edge off her nerves at least.

And it seemed to leave her mind clearer than it had been in days. She sat there on the bed and stared at the packed bag and suddenly couldn't believe what she was doing. What was she doing? Running off to God knew where with a man she didn't know, abandoning her business and just bolting without a word to her partner and best friend, when what she ought to be doing was locking her doors and pulling up the drawbridge, guarding her own life as she had always done . . .

She started to rise, bent on going out into the other room and telling Tucker she couldn't go with him—and that was when it happened.

The room around her vanished. There was nothing but darkness, so black and impenetrable it was a solid mass around her. She couldn't feel her legs beneath her. She couldn't move. She couldn't hear anything. And all she knew was cold fear.

Out of the black silence, gradually, the sound and sensation of air rushing past filled her senses. She was moving, she knew that, moving through space . . . and time. Moving into the future. She didn't want to go, struggled against it, but she was given no choice. She had to go.

Had to see.

At first, the vivid images exploded out of the darkness with such bright intensity that she was blinded and couldn't see them, in a confusion of sound so loud and garbled it hurt her ears. But slowly, her eyes and ears or her mind adjusted until what she saw and heard began to make sense. Or at least, as much sense as a waking nightmare ever made.

There was a low hum, the sound of many voices murmuring, like a carrier wave permeating everything. And then a male voice, one she suddenly remembered from that other waking nightmare, said calmly above the hum, "Even if you run, we'll find you. We'll always find you."

She tried desperately to see his face, but all she could see was his silhouette, like a featureless shadow on a wall. Then he was gone.

It was getting colder.

The antiques shop. It was late, very late, and dark. Two cars crept up to the curb, their lights out. Men got out of the cars in an eerie silence and moved toward the shop. She couldn't see who they were. But they carried things, things she knew were deadly. Not just guns but . . . other things,

things that made her skin crawl. She wanted to scream out a warning, to alert the neighborhood and signal those inside the shop that danger approached. Then she realized that the men were going to the apartment above the shop, and she knew whom they were after.

"They're after you, Sarah."

"No." She didn't want to listen to this voice, the insistent one she'd heard in her head before.

"They'll get you. You have to leave. You have to run."

"But where? Where should I go?"

The background hum of many voices whispering grew louder, drowning out the voice the way electrical interference drowned out a radio signal, and Sarah wasn't even sure she heard, ". . . north . . ."

"Who are you?" she asked desperately. "What are you?"

This time, there was no answer at all, just the now quieter whispers she couldn't quite make out.

It was getting colder.

Blackness swept over her abruptly, and lasted what seemed to Sarah to be forever. And the background rustle of those wordless whispers became louder and louder until she wanted to clap her hands over her ears to shut out the awful noise that made her head ache.

It was so cold.

So cold . . .

Sarah blinked dazedly and looked around her. She was sitting on the floor by the bed, her arms wrapped tightly around her upraised knees. Shivering. According to the clock on the nightstand, no more than a minute or two had elapsed.

It felt like a lifetime.

She sat there for several more minutes, until the shivering gradually stopped as her body temperature began to return to normal. She didn't know why it always dropped when the waking nightmares came, but it always did, leaving her chilled for a long time afterward. Even her skin was cold to the touch, and she rubbed her hands together slowly to try to warm them. Her body obeyed when she tried to get up, but it was stiff and sore, as if she had endured some kind of physical trial.

But for the first time, she came out of it with a sudden, bitter self-awareness. Waking nightmares. Bullshit. Why did she keep calling them that? Who was she trying to deceive? Herself. They were visions, and what was the use of calling them something else? A different definition didn't make them any less real. Any less frightening.

Visions. I have visions. And let's not forget the voices in my head, at least two different ones.

Visions urging her, driving her through fear. One voice insisting she couldn't escape even as another one insisted that she run. And over it all, permeating everything, was her numbing certainty that no matter what she did, no matter where she went, that yawning grave was waiting for her at journey's end.

She left the packed bag on the bed and went out into the living room, where Tucker was watching a news program. He immediately turned off the set and got up when she came in, his eyes narrowing as they searched her face intently.

Probably look like I've seen a ghost. Ha-ha.

"Sarah? Are you all right?"

"Not really, no."

"Has something happened?"

He didn't want to ask her whether she'd had a vision, but it was obvious that was what he meant. Sarah realized she was still rubbing her hands together when he briefly looked at them, and she started to tell him it was because she was still so cold. But that would take too long to explain, so instead, she said simply, "We should leave now."

"Why?"

"Because they'll come tonight. Come for me."

"How do you know that? Did you see it? In one of your waking nightmares?"

He was good, she thought dimly. His voice hardly gave away his disbelief. Hardly at all.

"I had a vision," she said starkly. "Just now. They will come tonight, Tucker. And if we're here . . ."

In an abrupt gesture, he nodded. "Then we'd better leave."

But in the end, he had another idea.

––––––––

The security system guarding Mackenzie's house was a good one. It took Murphy almost three minutes to bypass the alarm and get inside. She didn't turn on any lights, depending on the narrow beam of her pencil flashlight to find her way around. She didn't waste any time, moving from room to room in a quick, methodical search.

Within ten minutes, she was in his office and had the wall safe behind his desk open. She ignored some stock certificates, leafed uninterestedly through a couple of contracts with his publisher, and swore softly when the safe offered nothing else.

She kept searching, paying close attention to what she found on the cluttered desk. A folded map held her interest the longest; she spent several minutes bent over the desk studying it, and when she straightened at last, she slipped it into the leather pouch at her side.

"Not quite as smart as you think you are," she murmured.

Her cell phone vibrated, and she pulled it out of the leather pouch with a scowl. "Yeah, what?"

"Find anything?" His voice was, as always, almost preternaturally composed.

"If I do," she responded with equal calm, "I'll report. As agreed."

"We're running out of time, Murphy."

"You don't have to tell me that."

There was a brief silence, and then he said somewhat dryly, "You might at least reassure me that we have the same goal in mind."

"I might." She smiled in the darkness of Tucker Mackenzie's office and did not add the requested assurances.

He knew her too well to push, though the almost inaudible sound of a sigh reached her intently listening ears. His voice was carefully matter-of-fact when he said, "I need information, Murphy."

"Yes, I know. Give me a chance to do my job."

"Very well. I'll wait for your report."

"Do that." She turned off the phone decisively without waiting for him to sign off first. She was willing to bet she was one of very few who would dare to hang up on him. She liked that. The cell was a burner, intended to be used only once and then discarded; she'd toss it into the nearest Dumpster before moving on; it was too easy to track cell phones these days. She'd have another burner in an hour, and he'd have to wait for her to call him next time. She liked that too.

She stood there in the dark and silent office for several more minutes, thoughtfully fingering the folded map in her leather pouch. Finally, she left the office and made her way from the house, pausing only long enough to lock up behind herself and put the security system back online.

The neighborhood was dark and quiet in the hours past midnight, and Murphy went on her way without attracting any notice, not even disturbing the few sleeping watchdogs with her softly whistled rendition of "Stormy Weather."

In perfect pitch.

———

"But why?" Sarah asked much later.

"We know they— We know somebody is watching you." Tucker's voice was patient. "What we don't know is whether the guy in the black jacket is all we have to worry about. I want to know that, Sarah. I think we need to know that. Before we leave."

His car was parked near the shop as before, but in the dense shadows of a spreading oak tree. There was, he'd explained to Sarah, a clear path of retreat here, with little chance of the car's being hemmed in by other cars.

Assuming, of course, that no one realized they were sitting in the car.

They had eaten and then returned to the apartment above the shop as if they intended to spend the night there. Then they had slipped out and made their way cautiously—and hopefully unseen—around behind several houses and back to the car. Timers on the lights inside the apartment made it look as if they had settled down for the night around eleven thirty. It was now after midnight.

Sarah had realized only gradually that Tucker had had something like this in mind even before she'd had her vision. For one thing, he had left Margo's house with two of her automatic timers in his pocket. For another, he had brought from his own house a couple of thick blankets and comfortable pillows. Sarah was using the blankets and pillows now, reclining in the backseat and wrapped snugly against the chill of the night. Tucker was in the front, sipping hot coffee. And watching.

He'd had the foresight to remove the lightbulbs from the car's interior lights so they wouldn't give away their return, but there was still, he'd told her dispassionately, at least a fifty percent chance that if the man in the black jacket was watching, he had seen them.

In the dark quiet of the night, Sarah was wide awake and almost unbearably edgy. It was horrible, waiting to see whether someone would come as she had seen. Horrible waiting to find out whether she was meant to die tonight. *Do they want to kill me? I don't know. All I know is that I'm afraid of them. Terribly afraid.*

"I won't let anything happen to you, Sarah." His voice was low.

After a moment, she said, "You're a touch psychic yourself."

"No. It doesn't require psychic abilities to know you're frightened. Anybody would be. But I am not going to let anything happen to you. I promise."

"Promises can get you in trouble." *They have before.*

"That one won't."

Still edgy, she asked, "Why are you doing this, Tucker? Why are you getting involved in my problems?"

"We've already discussed that, remember?"

"Because you want to keep me alive long enough to find out if I'm for real?"

When he answered, it was slowly. "I know you're for real, Sarah. I know you're not . . . a charlatan, not faking psychic ability for some reason of your own. I know that you genuinely believe you can see the future."

"You just don't believe I *can*. Which is one reason why we're out here, right? So you can see if they come the way I saw them." She tried not to sound defensive.

Again, he hesitated before responding. "That's one reason. To see something that hasn't happened yet . . . of all the psychic abilities, that's the one I find most difficult to believe. How can you see what doesn't yet exist? How can the human mind possibly do that?"

Sarah closed her eyes. "Do you think it's any easier, any more believable, to see . . . a place you've never been, even though it exists? To see something that happened long ago in the past, when you weren't there? To have someone touch your hand and know something about them, something so secret they don't even tell themselves?"

"I don't know. I suppose not." He sounded a bit wary.

Doesn't like the idea that I might know all his secrets. "You don't believe in those things either. You always think there must be some logical explanation, some . . . deception involved."

"I know you aren't trying to deceive anyone."

"Ah. Then I'm either crazy, or I'm telling the truth."

"The truth as you believe it to be."

"Which is just another way of saying I'm crazy. Thanks." *I hear voices in my head. You'd really think I was crazy if I told you about them.*

"No, that's not what I'm saying. Hell, I don't know what I'm saying. I just . . . I can't blindly accept the party line, Sarah. I can't tell myself I could see a unicorn if I only believed they were real. It's not the way I'm wired."

Quietly, she said, "And yet I've never met anyone who wanted so desperately to believe."

To that, he said nothing.

Sarah lay there in silence for a while, her eyes closed. She heard his occasional faint movements, smelled the coffee he drank, and mentally looked at his face.

It was a good face, but it puzzled her a great deal and made her feel more than a little apprehensive. What made a man like Tucker? He had achieved unusual success in his chosen field, penning bestseller after bestseller that enjoyed critical as well as commercial success. She had read several of his novels, though she hadn't mentioned that to him. They were clever, those stories, not only entertaining but intelligent and well researched, peopled with vividly alive characters, and left a reader satisfied.

He was one of those semifamous authors who had not quite crossed the line into mainstream celebrity; his name was very well-known, but his face was unlikely to be recognized on the street. At least two of his novels had been made into films, but Sarah had read that he wanted nothing to do with that interpretation of his work—he wrote books, other people made films—and so had taken no part in the process.

So. He was wealthy enough that he probably wouldn't have to write another word for the rest of his life if that was his choice. Successful enough to have reached the peak of a difficult and demanding profession while still in his thirties. He was single. Did he have family, friends he cared about?

Behind her closed lids another face appeared, clear as if it were a color photograph, and she studied it for several seconds. A pretty face. A face she didn't know—and yet did. She knew the face, the woman. She knew her name. Lydia. She knew what Lydia was to Tucker. She knew what had happened to her.

It was no vision, no dramatic sequence of images and sounds. It was simply a knowing, a certainty of facts she should not have known. It had happened to her before since the mugging, but infrequently, and only with people she had known well.

Never before with a stranger, until Tucker.

Sarah opened her eyes as the face faded into darkness, and for a moment she was tempted to tell him what she had seen, what she knew. But she didn't. In the last few months, she had learned too well the costly lesson that even the people who wanted to hear the truth all too often hated the truthsayer for telling them. So he was going to have to ask her. When he was ready, when he stopped doubting her, then he would ask her. Only then would she tell him what he so desperately needed to know.

Unable to bear the silence any longer, she said, "All this isn't interrupting your work, is it?"

"No. I'd only just started a new book, and it wasn't coming together very well. A break will do me good."

"Just a little break to go on the run with a hunted psychic."

"You never know—maybe I'll get a book out of it."

And maybe you'll get dead. But she didn't say it, of course. Instead, she said, "Where will we go?"

"I have a feeling that once we get moving, you'll know which way to go," he said with more confidence than she thought he had any right to feel.

North. I think we have to go north. But I don't know how far. Or why we have to . . .

But all she said was, "And until I know that— assuming I do?"

"Away from Richmond is the first priority, I think.

Unless you disagree, our first stop will be a place near Arlington."

"Why Arlington?" *Heading north. And I didn't even have to tell him we're supposed to. Fate again.*

"Because a friend owns a cabin near there. A place to rest our weary heads and plan the next stage of the trip."

"Plan?"

"We'll come up with something, Sarah."

"You just want an adventure. A road trip. That's it, isn't it?"

He chuckled. "Yeah, that's it."

She was silent for several minutes, then said abruptly, "I should have gone to the bank. I don't have any money." It had just occurred to her that this was likely to be an expensive trip.

Tucker responded promptly. "I stopped by my bank this afternoon and got some cash. Enough, I think. We'll need to avoid plastic, avoid using ATMs because of the cameras, cell phones because they can be pinged—which is why I left mine at the shop and asked you not to bring yours—or anything else that might give them a way to track us as we move. Cash is the way to go."

"I can't let you—"

"Sarah, it's not a problem."

"Yes, it is. I can't let you pay my way."

"Look, if it really bothers you, we'll settle up later. Until then, don't worry about it."

She was silenced, but not happy. It went against the grain for her to depend on anyone else, particularly financially. She hadn't even allowed David to bring in an occasional bag of groceries, and he'd practically lived at her place. Something Margo had scolded her for.

"He eats like a goat, Sarah! Why the hell shouldn't he kick in some for groceries? He's got you cooking for him practically every night!"

Sarah frowned, a little startled to realize that the memory had roused resentment rather than pain. He *had* usually suggested they eat at her house. And he hadn't been able to cook, so she always had. Sometimes he'd helped her clean up afterward, but many times he'd had to "eat and run" because of business calls he needed to make from his own apartment. Or something like that.

Now that she thought about it, he had bought dinner once or twice a week—when they ended up having sex.

Jesus, he was paying for it!

"Sarah?"

"Hmm?" *Dinner out—sex. A little quid pro for his quo. Wonderful. Why didn't I see it before?*

"Don't be upset about the money."

She wrenched her mind back to the present and drew a breath. "Okay. But I expect you to keep track. This is my little adventure more than yours, and I'll be damned if I'll let you pay for it."

"Gotcha."

"As long as we understand that."

"We do."

They fell silent again. Sarah shifted a bit. Mercedes or not, the backseat wasn't a terribly comfortable bed. Then again, she was probably too edgy to sleep. Like last night.

If this kept up, she'd really be a bundle of raw nerve endings. "What time is it?"

"After one."

It felt like dawn at least, to Sarah. She was so tired.

"Why don't you try to sleep?" he suggested.

"If you watch all night, you'll be exhausted."

"I can lose a night or two without it bothering me too much. Probably comes from a habit of all-night writing marathons. Try to sleep, Sarah."

She didn't think there was a chance in hell of her actually sleeping, but she once again closed eyes that kept drifting open, and this time she did her best to stop thinking. Following directions from a relaxation tape she'd listened to, she concentrated on letting all her muscles go limp and imagined lying peacefully on a beach listening to soothing ocean waves.

That was the last thing she remembered.

"Sarah."

She came awake instantly, her scratchy eyes and heavy head telling her she hadn't slept more than an hour or two, if that. "Hmm?"

"Look."

She sat up carefully, fighting her hands free of the covers so she could rub her eyes. It took her a moment to focus, and to look where Tucker was looking, but as soon as she did, she saw them.

"Oh God," she whispered.

The two cars, lights extinguished, were coming down the street toward the shop from the opposite direction.

In an eerie quiet that didn't even seem to contain the
faint sounds of engines, the cars pulled into parking
places at the shop. Doors opened—no interior lights
betrayed them either—and men got out of the cars.

Sarah numbly counted eight men, four from each car.
"So many," she whispered.

Tucker nodded, silently watching.

The men slipped toward the building, some going
around to the sides and back. They all seemed to be
wearing black, or at least dark colors, and Sarah strained
to see whether the tall watcher was among them.

"Do you see him?" she asked Tucker, still whispering.

"No."

"Neither do—Oh. That isn't . . . that can't be . . ."

"But it is," Tucker responded grimly.

One of the men had paused for a moment at the end
of the walkway, and the light from a nearby streetlamp
shone full on his face. Then he was moving with two
others toward the stairs that led to the apartment.

"I don't understand," Sarah said. "Why would he be
here? Why would he be doing this?"

"I don't think we want to stick around and ask right
now." Tucker released the emergency brake, and since
the car was out of gear and only the brake held it station-
ary on the slight incline where he had deliberately parked,
it immediately began to roll forward silently.

They were well down the street when Tucker finally
started the engine, but even then Sarah couldn't help
looking back over her shoulder. Already, the shop was
lost to sight, and no screaming engines followed them as

Tucker turned a corner and headed for the highway. But what Sarah had seen was branded in her mind.

How could she trust anyone when even cops came sneaking in the middle of the night to kill her?

———————

"Son of a bitch." Sergeant Lewis stood at the foot of the stairs and watched his breath mist with the curse. He was vaguely aware of one of the men coolly disabling the shop's security system and going inside, but he didn't bother to follow.

They wouldn't be there. They were long gone.

And he was anxious to get out of here. If one of the neighbors happened to wake up and look out a window, he'd have to answer some very uncomfortable questions in the morning.

His cell phone rang just then, and he swiftly drew it out of an inner pocket and answered before it could ring again. "Yeah?" Of course, he knew who it would be. Who else would it be at four o'clock in the fucking morning?

"Well?"

"We missed them."

"I know that."

Lewis looked around at darkness and shadows and felt his heart thud a bit faster. *You bastard—where are you?*

"What I want to know," the cool voice continued, "is how you intend to find them now that you've lost them."

Lewis gritted his teeth and spoke between them. "I'm sure you have a suggestion."

"I have several. You won't like any of them."

So what else is new.

"Meet me in one hour. The usual place."

Lewis opened his mouth to object, but the line went dead. Slowly, he closed the phone and returned it to his pocket. He had a hollow feeling about the coming meeting.

A very hollow feeling.

S I X

"Very clever, our Mr. Mackenzie." Brodie lowered the infrared binoculars and glanced aside to meet Cait's gaze. "He kept Gallagher out of harm's way and still managed to take a look at the presumed enemy."

Cait sniffed and then rubbed her nose. It was cold on the roof of the building across from the antiques shop, and they had been up here for hours. Her nose was beginning to run. "He was too close, if you ask me. If he knew they were coming, why not just take her and run?"

"Maybe he didn't know they were coming, just thought they might. Or maybe she knew and he wasn't sure."

"Even so, they could have been seen sneaking back to the car. We saw them."

"Umm. But the others didn't, did they." Brodie

frowned. "Odd, that. They're usually Johnny-on-the-spot whenever something like this goes down. Wonder who fell asleep at the switch."

"Maybe that cop. Jeez, how many does that make?"

"Too many. At the local *and* state levels so far. And impossible to guess who'll show their face next. Be a lot easier on us if they'd just wear a sign. But at least we have one more name to add to the list."

Cait rested her chin on her hand as she peered across the street and watched silent men getting silently into weirdly silent cars. "Think he's a major player?"

"Hell, I don't know. I've never seen him before, but this was our first case in Richmond, so that doesn't mean much. I'd give a lot to know who called him just now. He didn't look very happy about it."

"You think he removed the evidence I couldn't find from the shop yesterday, don't you?"

"I'd bet money on it. Nobody'd expect a cop—probably the first at the scene—to pocket a piece of evidence. At least, nobody but a suspicious bastard like me."

"Think he did the same thing at Sarah Gallagher's house? The fire marshal suspected arson, but so far he can't find any proof."

Brodie nodded, lifting the binoculars to gaze once more across the street. "Makes sense. They do tend to clean up after themselves whenever possible—and suspicious fires make for uncomfortably public headlines."

"Okay, so what do we do now? Stick with the cop or go after Mackenzie and Gallagher?"

He hesitated only an instant before lowering the binoculars and easing back away from the edge. "I'd love to go after the cop, but we'll leave that to someone else. We have to get our hands on Sarah Gallagher. And it'll be a lot harder now. You can bet they saw Lewis just as clearly as we did, and you can bet it scared the hell out of both of them. We're taught to trust cops, to depend on them for safety. Hell of a thing when we find out that's a luxury we can no longer afford."

"Amen," Cait agreed soberly.

Neither made a sound as they crossed the roof and took an exterior stairway down to the ground. Their car was parked nearby, and neither spoke again until they were in it and moving.

"We don't know where they're going. Do we?" Cait asked as Brodie drove toward the highway.

"No. Get on the cell. Call it in."

Immediately, Cait drew a specially modified cell phone from a bag on the floorboard and punched in a familiar number.

————

Sarah watched the sun come up from the front seat of Tucker's Mercedes and wondered idly why it looked no different from the last sunrise she had seen, only a few weeks before. It should look different, she thought. The whole world had changed since then. It had gotten darker. And grimmer. And as terrifying as any nightmare.

She could still feel them. Out there somewhere.

Somewhere near. Looming over her like the shadow of something vast and far-reaching. It was like feeling breath on the back of her neck, the cold, fetid breath of an ancient predator.

Where are you? Who are you?

But she was afraid to look too hard, to reach into that place inside herself where the voices—at least one of the voices—might have the answers. She was afraid to willingly open that door.

Afraid of the answers she might get. Afraid they would see her before she could see them.

"We're about two hours away from the cabin," Tucker said finally. "We'll stop for groceries when we get closer; there's never anything in Pat's refrigerator but beer, and we might be there a few days." His voice was matter-of-fact but didn't quite hide the fact that Lewis's presence in that hit squad had shaken him almost as much as it had her.

"Does this friend of yours know you're—we're—coming?"

"He doesn't live in the cabin, just spends summers there. I called him from my bank, and he said I was welcome to spend a few days there. Polishing the latest novel. Most people assume that requires peace and quiet."

Sarah was suddenly uneasy, her instincts jangling. "Will he tell anyone you're there?" After seeing a police officer coming stealthily by night to get her, paranoia was stronger in her than it had ever been before. Except that it wasn't paranoia, of course.

"No, he won't breathe a word. Don't worry, Sarah."

"Right."

He glanced over at her. "I'm sorry. That sounds facile, doesn't it?"

"A bit."

"It wasn't meant to. I'm not kidding myself, and I won't kid you. What we saw last night makes this a whole new ball game. It means we can't trust the cops."

"Any of them? They can't all be . . . be in on this? Can they?"

Tucker shook his head. "I can't imagine some mysterious conspiracy that large. But how can we possibly know who to trust? Unless you find some special insight along the way, I think we'd better not take chances. You trusted Lewis, didn't you?"

"Yes. Until . . ."

"Right. Until he showed up outside your apartment in the dead of night, intending to kill you. That *is* what you believe?"

Sarah hesitated, then nodded. "I know they came for me. I don't know if they were going to kill me, but I know they wanted to . . . hurt me."

Tucker sent her another glance. "But you still don't know why Lewis—why anyone—would want to hurt you?"

"No. But . . . it isn't just him. He wasn't the man who was watching me. And . . ." She hesitated, then said slowly, "When I had the vision about them coming for me, I heard a voice—a man's voice, but not Lewis's— saying, 'Even if you run, we will find you. We will always find you.'"

Tucker looked at her sharply. "You didn't tell me that."

"Those men coming to the apartment were the immediate threat. That's all I thought about until we got away."

"But you heard a voice saying they'd find you?"

"Yes. And a low hum of . . . murmuring and whispering. Tucker . . . I think there are a lot of them. Like an army. I didn't see them, but I heard them. Soft murmuring voices all around me. And they weren't friendly voices."

Tucker was silent for a moment, then said quietly, "My name is Legion: for we are many."

"That's from the Bible."

He nodded. "As I recall, it refers to the devil and his minions."

"Evil." Sarah shivered. "I . . . feel that about them, in a way. Darkness, shadows. Threatening, always threatening. And all around me. Reaching out for me. They want me, and I don't know why."

"But you do know that your life was perfectly normal until you were mugged—and woke up psychic."

She tried to think, to force her fears to the back of her consciousness. "Yes. So it has to have something to do with that."

"Somehow," he mused, "being psychic, having visions, makes you valuable to someone. Or a threat to someone. Why? Did you—have you made a prediction that hasn't yet come true? I mean, one involving someone else?"

"No. The only threat I saw was aimed at me."

"That serial killer out in California; you predicted something about him, didn't you?"

"Just that he'd strike again. Which he has. But he's still out there killing. And he's just one man."

"You don't feel a threat from him?"

"To myself? No. He doesn't even know I exist."

Tucker glanced at her. "Okay, tell me this. Are we heading in the right direction?"

"We aren't heading in the wrong one," she said slowly.

He let out a faint sound of humor. "Well, that's something."

"I'm sorry." She felt a bit stiff, very conscious of the things she had not been able to bring herself to tell him. Like those other voices. But he didn't need to know about them. Not really.

"You're doing fine. Tell me this. Do you know *why* we need to head in the right direction? Are we looking for something? Someone? Or is the point simply to get away from Richmond and the threat back there?"

"I . . . don't know." Then, suddenly, she did know, and blurted, "Someone. I think there's someone we have to find. Someone we have to look for."

"Who?"

The moment of clarity was gone as abruptly as it had come, and Sarah slumped in the seat. "I don't know. I don't *know*."

"All right, Sarah. Don't force it. You're exhausted anyway; it's a miracle you were able to come up with anything at all. Look, I think we could both use some coffee and a couple of breakfast biscuits. I'll get off at the next exit and find a place."

She looked down at her hands and rubbed them together because they felt so cold.

"Sarah?"

"I'm okay. But I could use some coffee." She didn't want him to know how fragile she felt right now. How unutterably tired. How frightened.

This is my fate. My destiny. All this has to happen.

"You'll be safe at the cabin, Sarah. You'll be able to rest."

"At least for a while?"

He hesitated, then nodded. "At least for a while."

Staring through the windshield now, she said idly, "They will find us, you know. They're very, very good at that. They've been good at that for a long time. A long time."

"How do you know that?"

"I just do." It was like catching a glimpse of something from the corner of her eye, Sarah realized. There was knowledge there, off to the side, just out of sight. Waiting for her to pay attention. She could see it if she looked.

She didn't want to look.

After a moment, Tucker said, "A long time. Then maybe you're not the first psychic they've gone after."

She turned the possibility over in her mind. "Maybe. Maybe there are others. Or were."

Almost to himself, Tucker muttered, "That might explain a few things in my life."

"What do you mean?"

"There have been a few psychics I heard about and went looking for, but was unable to find. They just seemed to have . . . dropped off the face of the earth. I always assumed they changed their names and ducked out of sight because one scam too many had brought the cops sniffing after them. Or disgruntled customers."

"Maybe it wasn't that at all."

Tucker fell silent, frowning a little as he guided the car onto an exit ramp where signs promised several fast-food restaurants. He didn't speak again until they had collected coffee, orange juice, and several sausage biscuits from a drive-through and were once again on the highway heading north.

"So . . . what we know or think we know is that there's someone after you. Possibly because you're psychic, but we don't really know that. We think they want to kill you—but we don't really know *that*. And we think we should head north, maybe to look for somebody, but we don't know who or why."

"We don't know a hell of a lot, actually." She bit into a second biscuit with more determination than appetite.

"No, but it ought to be an interesting trip." He laughed a little.

She looked over at him, more wary than reassured by his humor. "Tucker's excellent adventure."

He met her gaze briefly, then returned his to the road as he began unwrapping another biscuit. "Don't run away with the idea that I think this is just a game, Sarah. In games, you don't end up dead. In this . . . well, it's a definite possibility."

But you don't understand what that really means, I think. You don't know just how brutal real bad guys can be. But all she said was, "Then why are you getting such a damned kick out of it?"

"Not a kick—just a certain amount of . . . intellectual enjoyment. What can I say? I love puzzles. And I'm good at them."

Sarah finished her juice and then started on the coffee, brooding. She was too tired to think and she knew it, but it was impossible to turn off her mind. She felt curiously adrift, caught up in a current that was carrying her along in a direction she hadn't chosen and didn't want, and since it was not her nature to be so helpless, it bothered her.

But this is my fate. My destiny.

She was here with Tucker because she was supposed to be. Heading north because she was supposed to be, because there was someone waiting for her and because it would end in the north. Running for her life because that, too, was part of the plan. Letting Tucker set the pace and make decisions because she was supposed to.

She wasn't supposed to think. To question. She was just supposed to accept.

Because it's my destiny.

Even as that litany echoed in her mind, Sarah frowned. Somewhere in the dim recesses of her consciousness, rebellion stirred, and resistance. Why did that statement rise in answer to so many of her questions? For the first time, she wondered whether that was simply another of the voices in her head, not a beckoning future she couldn't escape but someone—or something—intent on shaping her destiny to suit some shadowy purpose.

I'm being led somewhere. Pushed. Guided. And how do I know it isn't them? How do I know they aren't defining my fate, controlling my destiny? How can I trust even my own mind not to betray me?

She couldn't. That was the most terrifying thing of all.

Near Arlington, Tucker turned off the highway toward the west, which made Sarah vaguely uneasy. She tried to pay attention, to listen to whatever was tugging at her, but the sensation was just tenuous and uncomfortable, impossible to define, and only faded some time later with another change of direction.

They turned again off the main road and onto a winding secondary road and, quietly, Sarah said, "We're heading north again."

He looked at her quickly. "Still not the wrong direction?"

"I think . . . definitely the right one. I don't know where we're going, but it's somewhere to the north."

Tucker turned onto an even more winding secondary road, and said, "Just a few more miles now. The cabin's on a small lake, quite isolated. There isn't much of a town nearby, but there is a small general store. Sort of."

That last wry comment was explained some ten minutes later, when Sarah found herself sitting in the car and staring bemusedly at a sign cheerfully proclaiming WANDA'S BAIT AND PARTY SHOPPE. It looked like the kind of small gas-station-cum-general-store found in many small towns, selling everything from gas to groceries. And, apparently, bait.

Tucker went in alone to get the groceries, after telling Sarah it might be best if he appeared to be traveling alone. If anyone was searching for them—and they had to expect someone was—then they would be looking for and asking questions about a man and a woman, not a man alone. It was a logical caution.

So Sarah sat in the car and waited. She didn't have to wait long. Tucker returned in about fifteen minutes, carrying several small plastic bags, which he put in the backseat.

When he slid into the driver's seat, Sarah asked mildly, "Who's Wanda?"

"Beats me. Every time I've stopped by here— admittedly just a few times over several years—the only one inside has been an old man watching television while one of his relatives runs the cash register. Today it was a nephew."

His voice had been light, but Sarah heard something else and looked at him intently. "What is it?"

He started the car but paused with his hand on the gearshift and looked at her with grim eyes. "There was a news program on. And a report about something that happened in Richmond."

"What?"

"They found a man's body early this morning near an abandoned building. Shot through the head. The city's up in arms. He was a cop."

Sarah felt a chill. "Not . . . Lewis?"

"Lewis. Nobody saw anything. Nobody heard anything. There are no suspects, at least as far as the media knows. Just one very dead cop—who must have been killed not long at all after we saw him at the apartment." He paused, then added, "Unlike the late sergeant, I don't really believe in coincidence. So I'd say that, for Lewis, failure was not an acceptable option."

Sarah didn't say a word.

———

Inside Wanda's Bait and Party Shoppe, the old man looked toward the front counter and spoke querulously. "You ain't supposed to leave the desk!"

"It's all right, Uncle," the younger man said, in the loud voice one used to speak to the hard of hearing. "No customers."

The old man grumbled but returned his attention to the television and a morning game show.

The younger man moved to the front window and gazed out at the Mercedes only now pulling away. He watched it until it moved out of his sight, then returned to his place behind the counter. He glanced at the absorbed old man, then reached for the phone and punched in a long number.

"Yeah, it's me," he said when the call was answered. "They're on their way to the lake."

———

It was nearly four that afternoon when Sarah came out of the cabin's single bedroom. It was a rustic cabin only in the sense that it was constructed of logs and river rock; it had all the modern conveniences, including plenty of hot water Sarah had used in her shower, and a television connected to a small satellite dish on the roof.

The television was on, turned down low and tuned to MSNBC. But Tucker was watching another screen. He had his laptop set up on the coffee table and was obviously working on something. But he immediately looked up when Sarah came into the room.

"Working on the book you're going to get out of this?"

"No, something else. You look much better."

"A few hours' sleep and a shower can do wonders," she agreed. "Did you manage to get any rest?"

"A little." He didn't elaborate. "You should eat something."

"You're always trying to feed me," she said, nevertheless heading for the corner of the great room devoted to the kitchen.

"Well, aside from the fact that the fit of your clothes says you've lost some weight recently—weight you didn't need to lose—it's also a good idea for people on the run to follow the soldier's maxim. Eat when you can, because you never know when you'll get another chance. Goes for sleep too. Basic survival training."

Sarah didn't reply to his comment about her weight; the too-loose fit of her clothing *was* obvious, and she knew it. Instead, she poured herself a cup of coffee and said, "I'm not really hungry, so I think I'll wait awhile. If you got stuff for a salad we can have later, I'll fix that."

"I did." He smiled slightly. "Need to keep busy?"

"Don't you? What *are* you doing?" She came around the breakfast bar dividing the kitchen from the rest of the room and perched on the arm of an overstuffed chair at a right angle to the couch where he sat.

"Sleuthing."

"Ah. And what are you sleuthing?"

Tucker smiled again. "The case of the missing psychics."

Sarah thought about that, her gaze on the laptop's screen. "There's wireless Internet out here?"

"Via the satellite dish, so it's not the fastest, unfortunately. But it gives us some access. You can find out almost anything if you know where and how to look, and I don't mean just using Google. The real trick is having enough firewalls and other protection to ensure nobody else catches you looking."

"Which you have." It wasn't a question.

"In these days of highly visible social networking, it pays to be at least a little paranoid, especially if you create intellectual property vulnerable to theft. I protect my work as best I can, and that includes whatever I happen to be researching."

"So, have you found out anything?"

He leaned back on the couch and linked his hands together over his flat middle, frowning now. "So far, I have more questions than answers. I've been checking newspapers in major cities, looking for missing persons believed to have some kind of psychic ability. I've gone back more than ten years, so far, and checked half a dozen cities."

"And?"

"Come see for yourself."

Sarah moved over to sit beside him on the couch, keeping a careful few inches of space between them. She held her coffee cup in both hands, and looked at the laptop's screen. There was what looked like a brief newspaper article accompanied by a photo of a young woman. She had to lean forward to read the article. It was dated March 17, 2008.

> Carol Randolph, 16, vanished from her Phoenix home yesterday. She had apparently returned safely from school, since her backpack and other articles were found in her room, and the remains of her usual afternoon snack were in the kitchen. There were no signs of a disturbance, no indication that a stranger had forcibly entered the house. No ransom note has been found.
>
> Police are asking that anyone with any knowledge of Carol and her movements yesterday please come forward. Carol is five feet seven inches tall, with long blond hair usually worn tied at the nape of her neck. She was last seen wearing a blue sweater and jeans.

Sarah looked at Tucker, very conscious of his nearness. "What makes you think she was psychic?"

"The program I've set up cross-references missing-person and accident reports with available police reports. They had added her school records to their files, and in those records were comments from several teachers about the girl's 'unusual abilities.' Also a few highlights from a psychological profile I shouldn't have been able to access; her parents took her to a shrink just before she vanished because they were worried about her, and had been since she was small. She 'knew things' she wasn't supposed to know. Sound familiar?"

"Very."

"Yeah. Anyway, the shrink believed she was a genuine psychic, recommended the parents take her to be evaluated at Duke University or one of the other legitimate programs set up to study parapsychology. They never got the chance."

"Are you supposed to be able to access police reports?"

He smiled. "No."

She decided not to ask. "I see. So—you did find a missing psychic."

"Not just one." Tucker leaned forward, his shoulder brushing hers, and tapped a few keys, then leaned back again so that Sarah could see the screen. Another article appeared, this one dated September 12, 2009.

Thomas Kipp, 30, has been missing from his Miami home since last Thursday. A popular teacher at Eastside High School, Kipp had been recently reprimanded by the school board for unconventional teaching methods after parents complained that he was spending too much time on New Age topics as well as such controversial subjects as parapsychology.

His students claim that Kipp had a "knack" for predicting the future, though no evidence exists to support this.

Police have no leads in the disappearance.

Sarah nodded slowly. "Another missing psychic."

"There's more," Tucker said, and reached past her to tap a few keys briskly. On the screen appeared another newspaper article, this one dated August 12, 2006.

A Nashville man was killed yesterday when his car went out of control and crashed into a concrete embankment. Due to the resulting fire, tentative identification was confirmed by dental records. The deceased was Simon Norville, 28, a part-time carpenter who claimed to be a psychic and frequently augmented his income by reading tarot cards for tourists.

Alcohol is suspected as the cause of the accident.

"But he was killed," Sarah said. "He isn't missing."

Silently, Tucker leaned forward and tapped keys again. This time, the article was dated April 24, 2007.

Philip Landers, 34, was killed Saturday when a friend's twin-engine Cessna he was piloting crashed moments after takeoff near Kansas City. Landers, a struggling artist, earned extra income in carnival work, proclaiming himself to be a mind reader.

Alcohol is suspected as the cause of the crash.

"They're eerily similar," Sarah admitted, "but—"

Still silent, Tucker keyed up yet another article, this one dated July 2, 2010.

Beverly Duffy, 40, was killed yesterday when her Los Angeles home caught fire and burned to the ground. Ms. Duffy, locally famous for reading tea leaves and selling "love potions," had recently and correctly predicted the San Jose earthquake, which had garnered her considerable media attention.

Friends say the attention upset her.

Investigators suspect a careless cigarette for the fire.

"A house fire," Sarah murmured, shivering as she thought of her own gutted home.

"One more body burned beyond recognition," Tucker said.

She leaned a little away from him. "What are you saying?"

"I'm saying that either you psychics are peculiarly accident-prone, or else something very suspicious is going on. You're dropping like flies."

He reached out to the computer again, this time hold-ing a key down so that Sarah could watch article after article scroll slowly past. She couldn't read the individual articles, but words and phrases jumped out at her.

Car crash ... accidental electrocution ... lost while skiing ... drowning ... house fire ... a fall from a lad-der ... robbery ... plane crash ... apparently struck by lightning ... fell while mountain climbing ... vanished while hiking ... body burned beyond recognition ... no body found ... no body recovered ...

The deaths and disappearances ranged back more than ten years and were spread over dozens of different cities in states from coast to coast. And there were so many of them.

"All psychic?" Sarah whispered.

"So they—or those closest to them—claimed."

She looked at him mutely.

Tucker raised a hand as if he would have touched her, but let it fall and leaned back on the couch. "I wanted to see if it hit you the same way it did me. Obviously, it did." His voice was dispassionate.

"All . . . accidents. Manufactured accidents?"

"I'd say it was a good bet."

"Then someone *is* killing some psychics—and taking others."

"I'm afraid so. They all look like accidents or simple disappearances, Sarah, nothing overtly suspicious about any of them—until you start tying them together. You saw a fraction of the number of articles I've found so far. In every major city I've checked, at least a dozen psychics have been killed or turned up missing in the last ten years. Now, I don't know a lot about the law of averages, but assuming the psychic population of this country is as small as I think it is, there seem to be a disproportionate number of them dying or vanishing."

"And nobody's noticed?"

"Why would they? Like I said, the deaths all look accidental—or at least explainable. Nothing to alert law enforcement or catch anything more than the momentary attention of the public. And scattered over years. The way people always die in big cities, and with depressing regularity. Nothing to send up a flag or make anybody look closer, especially given the huge territory and sheer number of law enforcement jurisdictions involved. I was looking for a pattern, but I knew what that pattern was supposed to be. And I found it—no natural deaths. No heart attacks or strokes or cancer. Most of these psychics were young, under fifty, and all of the ones who died, died violently."

Sarah drew a breath and got to her feet in a slightly jerky motion. Avoiding his intent gaze, she carried her cold coffee back to the kitchen area and poured it into the sink. Chilled, she refilled the cup with hot coffee. Still not looking at Tucker, she said, "What about the disappearances?"

"Well, bear in mind that I'm just getting started on this. Given a few days or, better yet, weeks, I bet I could really turn up something. So far, what I'm finding is that the psychics who've disappeared tend to be younger than the ones killed—I'm talking kids and teenagers in many cases. For those under eighteen, the police end up calling some of them runaways and most of the rest unsolved abductions. No witnesses, no good suspects . . . and no bodies ever found. And, let's face it—those kinds of cases, unless the kid is famous, just don't linger in the headlines. They're too damned common these days, even with Amber Alerts keeping them in the news for a while."

"I know. Pictures on milk cartons."

He nodded soberly. "Exactly. Unsolved and, after a while, with no leads, little hope, and precious little manpower to devote to them, pretty much going cold. Most of the families try to keep the searches going, keep the public aware, but . . . other people move on. And those kids are just plain gone."

––––––––––

Donny Grant was big for his age, which is why the other members of his Richmond neighborhood baseball team had elected him to be center fielder. He threw too wildly to be a pitcher, but his long legs could cover a remarkable amount of ground quickly, which, as any true baseball fan could tell you, counted for a lot.

Still, he didn't really like to run, so maybe he didn't move fast enough when his best bud, Gabe Matthews, hit a rocket to deadaway center field. The vacant lot wasn't big enough to hold it.

"Go get it, Donny," their pitcher Joe Singer yelled disgustedly as he watched Gabe happily kick the half-full cement bag that was second base as he passed. "I ain't got another ball, you know!"

"I thought you had at least two," Gabe shouted, and cackled at his own wit as he jumped on home plate with both feet.

"Fuck you!" Joe turned and put his hands on his hips as he watched Donny pick his way gingerly through the gap in the old board fence as he went after the home-run ball. "Shake a leg, Donny!"

Donny needed very little encouragement to move faster. He didn't much like the adjoining vacant lot, overgrown with weeds and brambles and rumored to be the site of drug deals and the occasional gang brawl.

So he moved quickly, bent over as he swiped at the ground with his glove in a wide arcing motion. Where the hell was the thing? It couldn't have gone much farther, surely—

"For Christ's sake, Donny!" Joe yelled again.

Donny half turned in order to yell back a choice insult he'd just thought up, and promptly tripped and fell flat on his ass.

Jeez, this place has more roots and vines than a jungle. He put his ungloved hand down to boost himself up, and froze for an instant before instinctively jerking his hand up. That wasn't a vine, and it sure as hell didn't feel like a root.

He looked down and for a moment had no idea what he was looking at. Then he got it.

Oh. A woman's hand.

He knew it was a woman's hand because the nails were painted a pretty pink color. And there was a ring on one finger, a delicate little rose; it was caked with dirt now, of course, but still pretty.

She seemed to be almost pointing up at him, her pointer finger extended while the others were gently curled. Pointing at him, almost beckoning him to come closer. Without thinking, he bent closer.

That was when he realized that her wrist ended at the ground because the rest of her was under it. That was when he realized she was dead.

That was when Donny Grant wet his pants and began to scream.

SEVEN

Slowly, Sarah said, "Then . . . we *are* talking about a conspiracy."

"I hate to admit it, and I can't even begin to imagine why it's happening, but I think so. It would take more than one person to cover up any murder or disappearance, and by definition that makes it a conspiracy. I can't think of another explanation."

"Who?"

Tucker let his breath out in a long sigh. "I don't know. But if this is an organized effort, we're talking something so big and complex that it almost defies belief. It does defy belief. Think of the cost. Think of the manpower. I mean, they have to be . . . monitoring the media, for one thing."

"What do you mean?"

"Sarah, how do you think they found out about you? Six months ago, you were mugged, but there was no mention in the papers of psychic ability. It was just later, weeks ago, that the Richmond papers picked up the story. And what happens soon after? You realize you're being watched. And your house burns down. And somebody comes in the night to kill you."

"You mean they've got people just . . . reading the papers looking for mention of psychics?"

He nodded toward his computer. "The high-tech version. Using computers and keywords, you can search through a hell of a lot of newspapers, blogs, and other social media even in a single day. Could be an automated system. But even so, you need people to monitor, to weigh and consider what they find—and do something about it. A lot of people, assuming they don't go after one psychic at a time. It would have to represent a huge investment."

"So what's the payoff?" she realized.

"Exactly. Why are they taking some psychics—and killing others? What are they doing with the ones they take? What is the threat, or the reward, that makes these actions necessary? In other words—what the bloody hell is going on?"

To Sarah, the possibilities were terrifying. It was one thing to believe that an anonymous *someone* was after her, but to suspect that her enemy was organized on a national scale, ruthless and frighteningly efficient, and had been taking and killing psychics for more than a decade, was the most chilling thing she had ever even imagined.

She avoided his steady gaze and looked into her coffee cup instead, and said the first thing that came into her head. "Lewis was a cop. If even cops are involved in this . . . if even cops are expendable . . . then how can we begin to fight them?"

"We begin with information," he answered promptly. "We gather the pieces and put them together until we have a complete picture, until we understand what's going on."

"While we're on the run from them?"

Tucker shrugged. "We may be running from them— or running toward something that might help us understand who they are and what they're doing. We won't know until we get there."

"I still think . . . I'm still afraid that the end of this journey for me will be death."

"I know," he said. "I think that's why you can't see where it is we're supposed to end up. You don't want to see, because you're afraid you'll die there. But you won't, Sarah. Margo's fate as you saw it was changed. Your own fate as you saw it will not happen the way you saw it. We're going to change it."

"You're so sure of that."

"Positive."

But I'm not. I think this is all part of the plan. We're like rats in a maze, pleased we're finding our way and unaware that at the center there's a trap instead of cheese . . .

———

Melissa Scanlan picked up the phone before it rang, and said absently, "Hi, Sue. What's up?"

"Don't do that!" Susan Devries ordered in a harassed voice. "I hate it when you do that. Let the phone ring at least once before you pick it up, dammit!"

"Sorry," Melissa said ruefully. "I usually remember, but . . . never mind. We can't go to the dance tonight, Sue. There's weather moving in, and we have a cow out and ready to calve. Joe wants me to help him look for her. It'll probably take us hours to find her."

"You might at least wait for me to ask," Sue said, mild now. "Bad weather?"

"Snow. I think."

"You're usually right about that. Okay, I'll tell Tom. Be careful out there, Melissa."

"Always. Bye." Melissa glanced out the kitchen window as she pulled on her gloves. It was still calm out there. Too calm. The weather service said it'd stay that way, but she knew better. It was one of the things she could predict with near-one-hundred-percent accuracy— the Wyoming weather.

She went outside in the cold late-September air and joined her husband in the main barn, where he already had their horses saddled.

"Still sure?" he asked, always a man of few words.

Melissa nodded. "Should start about dark. We only have a couple of hours to find her, Joe."

"Then let's move."

She swung herself into the saddle, reflecting with pleasure that Joe never disbelieved her. And he never made her feel like a freak. His grandmother had had the Sight, and Joe considered himself fortunate to have married a woman who also had it.

They split up not far from the house, with Joe heading off to the east and Melissa going west. With bad weather coming, they couldn't spare any of the hands to help in the search; the men were already working hard to get the other stock into safer areas. Unfortunately, the particular cow that was about to calve had a habit of hiding herself away for the duration, and she was both very valuable and a favorite of Melissa's.

It took Melissa half an hour to work her way out to the place where the cow had hidden last time. It was a low-lying area, thick with brush, and the worst kind of place for a cow and calf to be during a snowstorm. It was also an extremely difficult area for a horse to pick its way through.

At first, that was why Melissa thought her horse was edgy. Because this was a bad place to be stuck with a storm coming, and animals often seemed to know when trouble loomed in their simple lives. So when her gelding shied nervously when the increasing wind rustled bushes nearby, she didn't worry too much about it. Especially since she heard a cow bleat mournfully at about the same moment.

It took her ten more minutes to home in on the cow, and when she reached her she was relieved that no calf was present yet. She reached for her rope and dismounted, and in a soothing voice said, "You idiot cow, what's the matter with you? You should be close to the house, not way out here with a calf and snow coming—"

Belatedly, she realized two things. That the gelding was backing away nervously, trailing the reins that should have made him stand still as per his rigid and reliable training, and that the cow was tied.

"What the hell?" Melissa took a hesitant step toward the cow, staring at the thick rope that bound her to a tree. She very obviously was not about to calve, and the scuffed ground all around her testified to her restless attempts to move away from the tree.

Bait. Bait for you.

She didn't know where that inner voice came from, but Melissa instantly dropped her rope and turned back toward her horse, one hand reaching for her rifle and the other for the walkie-talkie hanging from the saddle horn.

She never touched either one.

Her horse came back to his stable just minutes before the storm hit, wild-eyed and lathered. The missing cow also returned.

But Melissa Scanlan didn't.

———

When Tucker woke abruptly, his internal clock told him it was still well before dawn, probably three or four A.M. He had been asleep since just after midnight and had no idea what had awakened him. He listened intently for several minutes, one hand under his pillow grasping the .45 just in case, but heard nothing to alarm him.

He finally relaxed a bit—though not completely. He

had the idea he'd never be able to relax completely again. What he had discovered so far about the seeming conspiracy to kill and kidnap psychics had shaken him far more than he had allowed Sarah to see. At least, he hoped she hadn't seen. Or sensed. She needed him to be sure of himself, he thought. Her belief in fate was so strong that he had to be equally strong in insisting they could avert the future she had seen for herself.

Even if he wasn't sure.

How in hell were they supposed to fight an enemy that was organized on a national scale? An enemy with resources they couldn't begin to match, with more manpower and undoubtedly some kind of uber-efficient communications network. An enemy ruthless enough to murder a cop—and smart enough to get away with it. How could that enemy be fought? How?

The fire he'd built the night before was no more than glowing embers in the rock fireplace, and he lay there on the couch watching them dim and brighten. Once awake, his mind refused to shut itself off again.

He wondered whether Sarah was sleeping. After seeing all those news clippings, she hadn't had much to say. And she had kept a careful distance between them. Physically, emotionally, and mentally.

Or maybe the mental distance he felt was due to his own wariness. The more convinced he grew that Sarah was a genuine psychic, the more he could feel himself getting . . . still inside. And watchful. He didn't want to withdraw from her but couldn't seem to help himself.

Pushing that out of his mind for the moment, Tucker

thought of all the charlatans he had met over the years, so many of whom cheerfully plied their trade in carnivals and malls and psychic "fairs" around the country, and knew those people were not threatened by anything but the occasional suspicious police officer. He was certain, however, that if he had been able to meet any of the people on the growing list of dead and missing, he would have found them genuine. The fakes and phonies stood in no danger from this; people with true psychic abilities were the targets.

Which meant, he thought, that the people behind this had some way of determining the genuine from the fake. Or . . . did they simply watch and wait, as they had apparently watched Sarah, until they could decide? That was possible, maybe even likely. He thought of watchers all over the country observing potential psychics, checking off items on a list until the total added up to "genuine," and felt a spreading chill.

Jesus Christ—the *enormity* of the thing.

And it was so damned inexplicable. Why psychics? Were they a threat to someone, or did their abilities make them somehow valuable? That was the question he felt needed to be answered, and it was the most elusive— because dead or missing psychics offered no answers, and as far as he could tell, nobody else had bothered to ask.

He could remember reading of long-ago experiments in this country and others, when it had been theorized that psychics could be used in some fashion as weapons or deterrents to weapons, but those experiments—as far as he knew—had proved worse than useless. Only a handful of genuine psychics had been able to control their abilities in any real sense, and nobody had really known what to do with them. They could not, after all, stop bullets or prevent bombs from blowing up. And their predictions had been erratic at best.

But that had been back during the Cold War, when paranoia and suspicion had compelled more than one government to attempt unconventional means of attaining and maintaining power over others. Things were different now.

Weren't they?

Tucker shifted restlessly on the couch. Whoever was killing and taking them, the list of psychics was turning into a long one. No wonder Sarah had grown so quiet. In his research so far, she was one of a much smaller list made up of psychics who had lived normal lives well into adulthood before some trauma—usually a head injury—had left them struggling to understand new and baffling abilities. That alone would have been enough of a strain for anybody without finding out she was also a target of some mysterious conspiracy.

And on that smaller list of new and untried psychics, most had wound up dead in some "accident" within months of the birth of their new abilities.

Tucker turned over onto his back and stared at the dark, beamed ceiling. Sarah was in deadly danger. And the only thing standing between her and the people who would kidnap or kill her was him.

"So how're you gonna stop them, Mackenzie?" he muttered aloud.

He didn't know.

Realizing suddenly that sleep was not going to return, he sighed and sat up. Glancing toward the bedroom door automatically, he stiffened when he realized it was open. He was on his feet before he decided to be, gun in hand and senses flaring.

If they had snatched her right out from under his god-damned nose—

A moment later he relaxed. One step away from the couch had brought the sliding glass doors into view, and through them he saw the moonlit deck and Sarah standing at the railing gazing out over the lake.

Tucker hesitated, then stuck the automatic into the waistband of his jeans at the small of his back and shrugged into the flannel shirt he'd earlier removed. His boots were nearby, and he put those on as well before heading for the glass doors.

He paused there, his hand on the handle, and for several moments studied her through the glass. She stood much as she had the first time he'd seen her, with her arms crossed over her breasts and hands moving slowly up and down her upper arms as though to warm chilled flesh. But she hadn't been cold then, not from the weather. From something inside her. And it was the same inner chill now, he realized. Sarah wasn't cold.

She was alone.

For the first time, he realized that for all her passive acceptance of his company, Sarah had never stopped being alone.

She was as shut in herself as she had been that first day,

isolated within walls of wariness, remote in a way he didn't really understand. And inside her were thoughts and feelings and terrors she had not put into words. Perhaps had not dared put into words. But they were there. Buried deeply. Locked away from him and anyone else who wanted to be close to her. Looking at her, he had the sense of things moving slowly and with terrible deliberation underneath a frozen stillness, like an ocean under ice.

Tucker drew a breath and opened the door, wondering how he could reach her. Wondering whether he could reach her.

It was chilly out on the deck, but not actually cold here at the end of September. In fact, it seemed warmer here than it had been in Richmond, and Tucker didn't bother to button his shirt as he joined Sarah at the railing.

Before he could speak, she did, almost idly. "I knew when you woke up. Isn't that strange?"

"Maybe not," he said slowly. "Maybe not for you."

She was fully dressed in jeans and a sweater, and definitely wide awake as she glanced at him. "That makes you uneasy."

It did, as a matter of fact, but he denied it. "Of course not."

Her smile, clear in the moonlight, held a twist of bitter certainty. "Oh, no? Then what about this: I'm changing, Tucker."

"Changing how?" He was cautious, not only because of what she was saying, but because he realized he had caught her at a raw moment when she might reveal more than she wanted to.

She turned her gaze back to the lake and put her hands on the deck railing as if she needed something to hold on to. But her voice remained steady. "Whatever was born in me six months ago is . . . growing. Bigger. More powerful. Affecting my other senses and even the way I think. I . . . know things I shouldn't know. Not because I have a vision, but just because. I feel things I don't understand and can't explain."

"Sarah—"

"I'm changing. I don't know how to stop it. And I don't know what I'll be when it's over."

Tucker had always assumed it would be a cool thing to see the future, and God knew it would be helpful and less painful to see one's mistakes ahead of time and have a shot at not making them. At least that was what he had always thought. But he was beginning to realize that the future might not be such a cool thing to see after all. Not when monsters lurked there. Not when all you saw was death, and danger, and frightening things. He had never seen anybody with haunted eyes until he had looked into Sarah's the night she'd had a vision of men coming to kill her.

"She never wanted to be found, you know. That's why you couldn't."

That was when he had started to believe in Sarah Gallagher.

He drew a breath and kept his own voice quiet. "Maybe that's natural, Sarah. For you."

"You mean for what I've become."

"I mean for *who* you've become. Who you're becoming. How could you not change after what's happened to you?"

"Words," she said softly. "Just words. They don't mean a lot to me these days."

"Then tell me what I can do to help you."

"I told you the day we met. You can't help me."

"Sarah, I thought we had gotten past that."

"Then you were wrong." She turned her head once more to look at him, and something hard and bright glittered in her eyes. "You think we're safe here? We're not. They're everywhere. All around us. *All the time.* We're never going to be safe until it's over. And it won't be over until they get me. That's one of the things I know now. One of the things I can't explain knowing."

"You were wrong about Margo," he reminded her, still holding on to that evidence of fallibility.

"Strike one. Do I get three before I'm out?" Her voice was tight and brittle.

Tucker frowned suddenly as his own instincts and senses stirred and began talking to him. Flatly, he said, "I'm not going anywhere, Sarah."

She sent him a quick glance, then returned her gaze to the lake. Her profile was immobile, unrevealing.

"I'm not going to run away from this," he went on steadily. "From you. I don't believe you're some kind of freak. I'm not afraid of you, or of anything you might see."

"You're lying," she whispered. "You are afraid of what I might see. If I look inside you."

He had never really been faced with a genuine psychic

before, not one like Sarah, so Tucker had not realized, in all the years of his search, that he would in fact be wary of one. But he was. And the only thing he knew for certain was that he couldn't lie to her about it.

"This is new to me too," he reminded her quietly. "Give me a little time to get used to it."

"Time is something we don't have a lot of."

"Maybe. But you might at least stop trying to scare me off. I don't scare so easily."

Almost inaudibly, she said, "What I know would scare you. What I've seen."

Tucker reached out and turned her to face him, keeping his hands on her shoulders. She felt very slight to him, and there was a tremor running through her tense body.

Is she strong enough to make it through this?

"Sarah, we're going to survive this. Both of us."

"Are we?" She refused to meet his eyes, keeping her gaze fixed on his chest. She sounded very tired all of a sudden, and there was something hollow in her tone that told him she was alone once more.

He wondered whether she had finished grieving for her David, the dead lover Margo had been so scornful of. Had she? Was he just a memory now, or would she torment herself for the rest of her life because she hadn't been able to save him?

Are we both haunted by what we didn't do?

That thought almost made him obey the urge to protect himself and pull away from her, but instead, giving in to some compulsion he didn't question, he pulled her into his arms and held her.

Sarah was stiff for only a moment before she relaxed and leaned into him. Her head tucked perfectly into the curve of his neck, and her warm breath against his skin sparked a tiny flare of heat deep inside him. She felt good in his arms. Almost terrifyingly delicate, but very good.

Her arms slid inside the flannel shirt and around his waist, and he knew the moment when she touched the gun.

She didn't react at all except to say, "You have a gun."

Belatedly, he remembered she was an army brat; guns undoubtedly were familiar to her. "I thought it might come in handy," he said.

"You're probably right."

One of his hands lifted to touch her hair, winding the silky strands around his fingers. "Can you handle guns?"

"Yes. But I never liked them much."

"It's just another precaution, Sarah."

"I know." She drew back just enough to look up at him.

He hadn't intended this to go any further than comfort, but the next thing Tucker knew, her warm, soft lips were beneath his.

It was a careful, tentative kiss, without force and yet tense with a hunger he could feel growing stronger and stronger inside him. A hunger he felt in her as well. It was held rigidly under control in both of them, something he was very aware of, and that restraint made the kiss curiously more erotic.

He raised his head finally, reluctant but all too aware of both her vulnerability and a bad situation that was only going to get worse. "Sarah . . ."

She reached up and touched his mouth lightly, her fingers gently stopping whatever he would have said. "I don't think either of us is going back to sleep. Why don't I go get the coffee started?" Her voice was a little husky and nakedly defenseless.

After a moment, he nodded and let her go. He wanted to say something, to reassure now in a different way, but the words wouldn't come.

Left alone on the deck, he stood for a few more minutes gazing out over the lake. It was quiet and calm and peaceful. He wished he could say the same about himself. Finally, he turned and went into the cabin, where Sarah had turned on the lights and was making coffee.

"You're so cautious," Cait said with a sigh.

"When you've been at this a little longer, you will be too," Brodie told her as he peered through the infrared binoculars.

"You're also made of iron," she grumbled. "What, you only sleep on odd Thursdays? I'm beat."

Brodie smiled slightly but kept the glasses trained on the small cabin on the other side of the lake.

She shifted, trying to find some comfortable position on a hard and chilly ground, and sighed. "Look, we've got to approach them sooner or later, or Gallagher's going to slip right through our fingers again."

"Not in the dark," Brodie said flatly. "Never trust anybody who comes to you in the dark, Cait."

She glanced at him curiously, but said only, "Lesson number one thousand and one?"

"If you like." He met her gaze, his own a little impatient. "Dammit, I'm trying to keep you alive."

"I realize that," she said with some dignity. "Just stop treating me like a child."

He looked at her a moment longer, then shook his head and returned his gaze to the cabin. "It'll be light soon."

"What're we going to do about Mackenzie?"

Brodie's mouth tightened. "Not much we can do."

"He won't let us get at her without a fight."

"I know that."

"So? If she's made him part of the package—"

"Then he's part of the package. I doubt the world would notice the disappearance of one writer more or less."

Cait opened her mouth to respond, but before she could, Brodie spoke again. "Pack up."

"Yes, sir," she muttered with a small salute.

Brodie didn't notice.

———

Tucker came into the great room after showering and shaving, feeling better physically but still more than a little rattled emotionally. He didn't really know what to say to Sarah, except to follow her lead and just not mention those unsettling few minutes on the deck.

They had both retreated, quickly and cautiously, as if from the edge of a precipice.

She was frying bacon in the kitchen, and as he came to fix a cup of coffee, she said, "Tucker?"

"Hmm?"

"What we found on your computer last night . . . all those dead and missing people . . . Who could be doing it? I mean, the whole thing is so huge. Do you think . . . it might be the government?"

He understood her wary suggestion. "I know it's a pet theory of the people who believe there's a conspiracy under every bush."

"I know. But . . ."

Tucker nodded. "Yeah. But. It's hard not to wonder. The kind of manpower this has to involve, the cost, the sheer scope of the thing—how many organizations could handle it? Not many, I'd guess."

"But the government could."

He smiled faintly as she turned her head to look at him. "I'm one of those people who believe our beloved government couldn't keep a secret for more than ten minutes no matter what it involved. However . . . I also believe that's the Our Government entity—the entire unwieldy mass of bureaucrats stabbing each other in the back while they try to run the country. Or not, as the case may be. Within that mess, there could well be considerably smaller groups a bit better organized and a lot better at keeping secrets. The CIA's supposed to be dandy, and the FBI not half bad. And we can't discount the various branches of the military."

"But why would they?"

"That's the question we need to answer. Somehow I doubt we'll be able to figure out who's doing this until we understand why it's being done."

She was silent for a moment or two, then said absently, "Your computer beeped a little while ago."

"Um. Must be finished with the search." Before they had gone to bed, he had set up his laptop to search a number of data banks for some of the information they sought, and then had simply closed the lid and allowed the machine to work, hoping the satellite wouldn't cut the search short; reception up here tended to be spotty at times.

Now, he carried his coffee with him to the couch and sat down to open the laptop. What he saw surprised him.

"E-mail? What the hell . . ."

Sarah turned off the stove and came to look over his shoulder at the computer. "Is something wrong? You have an e-mail address, don't you? Everybody seems to, these days."

"Yeah."

"Then it's probably one of your friends."

Tucker shook his head. "Sarah, this message isn't coming through a server into an e-mail account. It's being sent directly into my system via the satellite dish and my wireless connection, even though I set the program to disconnect from the Internet as soon as it had completed its task. A message being sent straight into the laptop's operating system . . . that is not supposed to be possible. Not only does it mean my firewall has been breached, it also means whoever did it knows where I am."

After a moment, she said steadily, "Then maybe we'd better see what the note says."

Tucker opened the note. And it was brief.

> Leave the cabin now.
> They're coming.

"It could be a trick," Sarah whispered.

"To drive us into a trap?" Tucker knew his voice was grim. "We're trapped now, with our backs against the lake. God, how stupid can I be? Grab your bag, Sarah." He was typing rapidly.

"What are you doing?"

"Trying to find out where the note came from. Grab your bag, we're leaving."

She obeyed, returning to the great room only a couple of minutes later. "I'm ready. I have your bag too."

"Thanks. Dammit, they've routed the call through so many proxy servers, it'd take me a week to trace it."

"We don't have a week."

He hesitated only an instant, then swore and quickly closed his computer, flipped it over, and removed the battery, severing whatever connection there was between his laptop and whoever had contacted it. Sarah was right; they were out of time. It took only a minute more to pack up the computer in its case, grab it and his other bag, and kill the lights.

They slipped from the darkened cabin as quietly as possible. The car was parked nearby, and it took only seconds to stow the luggage and get moving. Tucker didn't turn on the car's lights.

"I know these roads," he told Sarah as she sat tensely beside him. "They're like rabbit trails around here. If I can get far enough back into the woods, we may be able to slip past them." He was assuming that, as at the apartment, the enemy would come in force, possibly from several different directions at once. He thought it was poor strategy to make any kind of assumption, but knew it would be far safer to overestimate the enemy rather than underestimate them.

The Mercedes purred quietly through the woods, shocks efficiently absorbing most of the bumps from a narrow and badly rutted road. But they were forced to go slowly without headlights as Tucker picked his way cautiously around curves and between looming trees.

And they were no more than half a mile from the cabin when suddenly, ahead of them, lights stabbed blindingly through the darkness.

Tucker didn't hesitate. He hit his own lights and turned the wheel hard to the right in almost the same movement. "Hang on," he told Sarah.

It was in all reality hardly more than a rabbit trail, an old road so narrow that brush scraped along the sides of the Mercedes, and so uneven that the shocks didn't have a chance—especially since Tucker was driving at a reckless speed. But, somehow, he was able to keep the heavy car on the road around one hairpin curve after another, even at this speed and with the roar of a pursuing car behind them.

Unlike all the car chases in television and the movies, no shots came from the car behind them. Hardly any sound at all, in fact. There was just that grim, steady pursuit, unceasing and unrelenting. But there was only one car behind them—as far as they could tell.

"There have to be more," Sarah said.

"Bet on it. If I were them, I'd take one or two more cars and circle around, try to get ahead of us. They have to figure these roads all lead to the main one, where we have to end up eventually."

"Are they right?" she asked, hanging on for dear life to keep from being tossed around inside the hurtling car.

"No. This road goes on for miles, all the way to the highway—and it doesn't cross another road along the way."

Sarah looked back over her shoulder. "I think they're gaining on us." Her voice was remarkably calm, especially considering that she could hardly breathe for the fear clogging her throat.

"In just a minute," Tucker said tensely, "I'll see what I can do about that. If memory serves—and I hope to God it does—our friends back there are about to get a little surprise."

Memory served. It was a very easy turn to miss, because it was sharp and totally unexpected; a deceptively gentle rise kept even a wary driver from realizing that there were only two choices once you reached the top—take a punishingly sharp turn to the right, or do a swan dive into a small pond.

Tucker made the turn.

The car behind them didn't.

———

Duran stood behind the cabin looking out over the lake. With the sun up now, it sparkled invitingly. He thought briefly of swimming or fishing or just drifting on a boat, but the thoughts didn't last. They never did.

"Report," he said as almost silent footsteps approached behind him.

"They didn't leave anything behind but a half-cooked breakfast. No sign of where they're headed next. No sign of their ultimate goal."

Duran glanced over his shoulder briefly. "I imagine the ultimate goal is to escape."

"Yes, sir."

"Tell the others it's time we were going."

"Yes, sir."

Footsteps retreated.

Duran returned his attention to the lake, but this time his gaze scanned beyond it. Eventually, he focused on a spot directly across from the cabin. Misty in the early morning. A couple of fallen trees, thick shrubs. A very peaceful scene. A perfect place from which to . . . observe.

He smiled slightly as he studied that perfect place. Then, still smiling, he turned and went unhurriedly toward the cabin.

———————

"Tell me that bastard didn't know we were here," Cait pleaded.

Watching several dark cars leaving the cabin across the lake, Brodie laughed shortly. "He knew."

Cait was still visibly upset. "What's he doing here? Why is *he* leading the hunt for Sarah Gallagher?"

"She must have more potential than we realized."

"But they tried to kill her."

Brodie sat back and began stowing the binoculars, frowning. "Maybe not. That fire could have been an attempt to get her rather than kill her. A house burns down, a female body is conveniently found inside burned beyond recognition—who's to say it isn't Gallagher?"

Cait looked a little sick. "Kill some poor woman just to provide a body for something like that?"

"It's been done before," Brodie replied without emotion.

After a moment, Cait drew a deep breath. "So you think Duran wants her?"

"I think he wouldn't be here on the front lines unless he had something more in mind than Gallagher's death."

Cait nodded slowly. "What now?"

"Now," Brodie said grimly, "we find some way of getting our car out of that fucking pond."

EIGHT

"I am guilty of criminal stupidity."

Sarah turned her head quickly to look at Tucker, startled by the grim anger in his voice. "Why? You couldn't know they'd find us back there so quickly—"

"That's just it. I should have known. I should have *realized*."

"Realized what?"

"How they could find us. Wasn't there a sign back there for a rest stop coming up?"

"I think so. But—"

Tucker shook his head. "Let's see if I'm right about this. Ah . . ." He took the exit for the rest stop, and minutes later he was pulling into a parking space slightly apart from several other cars. "There should be a flashlight in the glove compartment; could you get it for me, please?"

She did, and handed it across. "Tucker—"

"It'll just take me a minute to check something. Stay here, Sarah."

He left the car running, and she watched in puzzlement as he got out and promptly dropped to the pavement to check underneath the car. He hadn't been there more than a couple of minutes when another motorist paused on his way past and called sympathetically, "Hit something?"

Tucker's response was cheerful, "Yeah, a hell of a pothole back there. No damage, though." He climbed to his feet and brushed at his jeans.

"Your lucky day," the man responded, and continued on his way.

Tucker slid into the car and closed the door. "No damage at all," he muttered, his face grim once more as he reached across Sarah to return the flashlight to the glove compartment.

"What is it?"

"A bug," he said bitterly. "A damned electronic device used to track things. In this case—us. They didn't have any trouble finding us because they knew exactly where we were."

It shouldn't have surprised Sarah since they had already agreed that their enemy had to be both smart and organized. But it did surprise her. And it gave her a creepy feeling, even worse than being watched. Someone knew every place they had been, every stop they had made. It was as if a ghostly companion had come along in the backseat, smiling derisively because they'd thought they were alone.

"Did you remove it?" she asked him, trying to keep her voice steady.

"No." He looked at her intently. "Let's make it work for us."

"How?"

"By leading them on a wild-goose chase while we head in another direction. How do you feel about a quick but roundabout trip to Chicago?"

Her first impulse was to say that was the wrong direction, but she thought she had some idea of what he had in mind. "Then we'd double back?"

"Later. After we get rid of this car."

Sarah thought about that, then said, "Wouldn't it be easier to just put the bug somewhere else—maybe on a bus or something? You shouldn't have to lose your car because of this."

He shook his head. "This bug has a magnetic seal, and I'm betting they'd know it if we tried to switch it to another vehicle. But if *we* switch vehicles, they won't know. And by the time they find out, we should be well on our way back . . . to wherever it is we're going. And I was about ready to trade this car in anyway. We need something more rugged, maybe a Jeep or some other four-wheel-drive utility. Our romp through the woods proved that."

"We couldn't just switch vehicles here?"

"We could. But if we want to throw them off the track

for any time at all, we should head in a direction other than north for a while. Besides, I have a friend in Chicago in the car business who'll let me trade this car and conveniently lose the paperwork for at least a few days, which might give us a little more time."

Paperwork could be traced, Sarah knew. And the DMV could almost certainly be accessed with a computer and the right codes, so they had to assume the enemy could do just that. At least that. But she still felt profoundly uneasy. So much time and distance would be lost. "If you have to wait until Monday to trade the car . . ."

Tucker started to reach for her hand but stopped himself before he touched her—and both of them were aware of that reluctance. "Chicago's only ten or twelve hours from here, Sarah. We won't lose much time. We can take a more direct route east as soon as the trade's made, and be heading north again by Monday night."

"With only a few days of September left."

"It's a risk, I know. We could just tear the bug off and leave it in the trash can out there. But if we do that, there's a good chance they'd still be able to find us. This car is fairly visible, and they know we're driving it. They could guess we'd still be heading north. If they have the right connections in law enforcement or just the right equipment, they could track this car's GPS. Or they could even have all the major highways covered somehow, have people on the lookout for us. But even more, we can't be sure they didn't plant something else in this car. Something I wouldn't recognize as dangerous to us. And that's a chance we *can't* take."

Slowly, Sarah nodded. But in her mind was the panicked awareness of delay and time lost.

It was almost October.

———

Murphy's third burner cell phone of the week rang, and she answered it with a frown. "Yeah?"

"What the hell happened?"

She didn't allow his anger to spark her own. "I was doing my job. Did you enjoy your swim?"

"Goddammit, Murphy. Did you put them on alert?"

"Duran was coming."

"Why the hell didn't you warn *me*? Five minutes earlier and I wouldn't have ended up looking like a jackass."

"You'll have to forgive me. I was more concerned with them than you."

He drew a breath and let it out slowly. But the words were still snapped out when he said, "This is what happens when the right hand doesn't know what the left one is doing. I've warned you, Murphy."

"I work alone."

"And I have no problem with that. But when I'm working the other side of the street, I expect you to alert me before you act."

"Noted." Her voice was level.

"Are you on them now?" He had the wisdom not to sound triumphant.

"Not exactly."

"Murphy—"

"You worry too much, Brodie."

"Do you understand how much time we have left?" His voice was tight. "Are you aware that it's probably just a matter of days now?"

"I am aware of that, yes." It was her turn to draw a breath in an attempt to hold on to patience.

"Then do your job."

He hung up on her.

Murphy closed the burner phone and removed the battery for good measure, tossing it into a trash can as she passed while the phone itself was drop-kicked into the gutter. "But that's what I'm doing, Brodie," she murmured to herself. "My job."

She pulled yet another disposable phone from the leather pouch hanging against her hip, turned it on, and punched in a familiar number. As soon as the call was answered, she spoke briskly.

"I kept him from making contact. And he's pissed."

"Never mind him. He'll get over it."

"Easy for you to say," Murphy muttered. "He has a mean right hook. I've seen him use it. I'd rather not be on the receiving end, thanks all the same."

"With a little luck, you won't be anywhere near Brodie for a while, so relax."

"Yeah, right. And in the meantime?"

"Chicago."

———

Sarah didn't say much after they turned back onto the highway, grappling with the growing certainty of just how far-reaching and complex this situation obviously was. And how terrifying.

The lake had seemed like a safe place, a place where they could rest and regroup, make plans. Then that warning had come, presumably from a friend or ally and, again in the middle of the night, they had run for their lives.

Where had the warning come from? A friend? Another psychic? How had it been sent to Tucker's computer when he, a computer expert, insisted that was next to impossible?

Their car bugged, their every action apparently monitored by the enemy, and now it was beginning to look like there was someone else out there watching them, someone who might be on their side . . .

And Sarah had no idea who they could trust.

She wasn't able to brood about it for too long, because Tucker turned the car toward the west about fifteen minutes later. And it required all her self-control to keep from reaching over and jerking the wheel to turn them north once more.

It was an actual physical sensation, a tugging deep inside her that almost hurt. This was the wrong way. *The wrong way!* She had to close her eyes and consciously argue with whatever was tugging at her. *We'll go the right way. We will. In a day or two, we will.*

It has to be north.

I know.

The answer is north.

What answer is that?

North.

Right. We'll go north. Soon.

After a few minutes of the continued silence between her and Tucker, she reached and turned on the radio, needing to listen to something besides the faint, anxious echo in her head.

———

"So she's just a friend, huh?" Keith Hayden grinned at Tucker as they sat in his office at the car lot. "How come all your friends look like her and all my friends look like you?"

"Because there is a God." Tucker was signing his name on a multitude of papers and didn't look up.

Keith snorted. "Listen, Tuck—"

"*Please* don't call me that," Tucker interrupted. "It doesn't sound any better now than it did in college. And it especially sounds bad when I've just let you rob me blind."

"Who, me?" Keith was deeply injured. "Can I help it if you're in too big a hurry to insist on a better price for that tank of yours? By the way, you didn't tell me why you were in such a hurry."

"Because we have places to go and people to see." Tucker hesitated and looked at his old friend. "You won't get into any trouble misfiling the papers on the Jeep for a few days, right?"

Keith shrugged. "It's my business, I can do what I like. And I'm lousy at filing things promptly. Just remember, you're still using your own tag, and it'll be listed in the DMV as belonging on a Mercedes. If you get stopped or pulled over, they might ask questions. But you'll have your copies of the papers, so it should be all right, at least for a few days. I still say you ought to switch the insurance, though."

"I have a special policy that covers me no matter what I'm driving. It'll have to do." Changing his insurance would reveal the make and model of the Jeep in all the necessary records, and Tucker wasn't prepared to risk that.

"Then for God's sake, drive carefully."

"I intend to." Tucker nodded. "So we've taken care of my end. But on your end . . . Keith, if anybody shows up asking questions about Sarah and me, tell them you sold me a Corvette or something and don't have a clue where we're headed."

"Is somebody likely to show up?"

Shrugging, Tucker finished signing and pushed the papers back across Keith's desk.

"In trouble, old buddy?"

"Sarah's ex isn't too happy about us," Tucker said lightly, ever inventive. "Let's just say he knows some pretty ugly customers and we'll both be better off if the trail ends here."

"No problem." Keith looked through the glass half wall of his office where he could see Sarah standing outside in the showroom apparently watching traffic pass the car lot. "I thought she looked a little ragged. You too, buddy. And now coming all the way to Chicago to trade your car in is starting to make a little more sense."

"I want Sarah to have some peace finally, that's all," Tucker said in one of the few utterly truthful statements he'd made today.

"Yeah, I imagine you'd do most anything for a pretty lady like her." Keith grinned, then added, "My guys are switching your stuff from the Mercedes to the Jeep, including the tag. While they're doing that, I'll have our bank transfer the balance I owe you to a branch of your bank here in Chicago."

"Tell them I'll be by for the cash within an hour," Tucker said.

Keith raised his brows. "Is the ex that close? I was hoping I could buy you two lunch."

"We need to be on our way, Keith, but thanks." Tucker glanced back over his shoulder, and added, "I'll wait with Sarah while you finish up in here, okay?"

"Okay."

Tucker came up behind Sarah as she stood looking out at traffic, approaching her warily. He couldn't help wondering how on earth Keith had mistaken them for lovers; two more guarded and isolated people would be hard to imagine.

She had withdrawn from him almost completely during the journey to Chicago. They had gotten motel rooms both Saturday night and last night but had spent less than six hours in them each night. Tucker, for one, had barely closed his eyes since they had left the cabin on the lake, and on Sunday morning Sarah had come to breakfast hollow-eyed and strained, saying in answer to his insistent questions that she'd had another vision. The yawning grave again, and the whisper of voice she couldn't quite understand, but this time accompanied by the sounds of bells—"like church bells"—and the sight of a Celtic cross.

Neither of them had said much after that.

"Sarah?"

She looked at him, unsurprised by his approach but with distant eyes, as if she returned from someplace else.

"Keith's taking care of the final details, so we'll be out of here in just a few minutes."

She nodded, but said only, "Did you notice it?"

"Notice what?"

"That." She pointed toward the passing traffic.

He looked in the direction she indicated, but it took him several moments to realize what she meant. Across the street, at a slight angle to the car lot where they stood, was one of those places that sold stonework. There were all kinds of things outside the building advertising the business: birdbaths, statuary, columns, benches and tables—even tombstones. Off to one side, curiously isolated and leaning a bit, was a Celtic cross. A big one.

"I saw a Celtic cross, canted to one side."

"Is that—?"

"It's the one I saw in the vision." She turned her head to look up at him again, her expression still. "A part of the journey. We were meant to come here all along. Do you still believe it was all your idea?"

"Sarah, there must be other crosses like that one, especially in the northeast where so many Irish settled. We'll probably see dozens of them once we head north again." He questioned her certainty not because he doubted her, but because he didn't like to think that his decision to come here had been less his own idea than the dictate of fate.

"There may be thousands of crosses for all I know. But that one is the one I saw."

He gazed into pale brown eyes that were distant and wary and very sure, and sighed. "Okay. But it still doesn't mean your life will end the way the vision did. That is not going to happen."

Slowly, she said, "Switching cars like this . . . it'll give us a head start maybe. A few days' grace, if we're lucky. But they will find us eventually. They want me too badly to just give up."

"We're going to use the time we have," Tucker told her. "I'll disable the GPS in the Jeep so nobody can track us that way. Hopefully they'll believe the trail ends here, at least for a while. In the meantime, while we're heading north toward whatever it is you feel is so important, we'll use the computer every chance we get and keep gathering information until the pieces start to come together."

"Couldn't they trace that? If we connect to the Internet even wirelessly?"

"Don't worry; I'll run it through so many proxy servers they'll never be able to trace us. Sarah, we'll make sense out of this. And then we'll find a way to deal with these people."

"You're so sure we can deal with them." She shook her head a little. "How? How can you *deal* with people willing to kill a cop? How can you deal with people who bug cars? Who abduct *children*? Who kill people only because they're . . . different? How are we going to deal with people like that, Tucker?"

He didn't have a ready answer, and admitted that reluctantly. "I don't know. But we'll find a way."

Still looking at him, she nodded slowly, but her voice was remote when she said, "Don't underestimate them, Tucker. Whatever you do . . . don't do that."

"No, I won't. Not again." He hesitated, and then, needing to regain the sense of control her questions had shaken, said, "I've been thinking. It'll probably be smarter to avoid staying any place where either of us has stayed before. Even at the places I have no traceable tie to, I probably used credit cards in local stores, or talked to people who might remember. We have to assume somebody asking the right questions could find out about those places. And find us."

"So we stick to anonymous hotels and motels?"

"I think it'll be safer, and not just because it'll be harder to find us. If we're surrounded by other people and not isolated, it won't be easy for them to move against us."

Sarah nodded again, but said, "Unless they have another Sergeant Lewis on the payroll. People usually don't interfere with the police."

"That's a cheerful thought." He managed a smile. "Look, everything they've done so far has either been designed to look accidental or scheduled for the dead of night with no witnesses. Lewis didn't come to 'arrest' us openly, and I'm betting no other cop will. They don't want to be that visible, Sarah. What they're doing is secret, and they want to keep it that way. That's our ace."

"Our only ace."

Deliberately, he said, "No. You're our ace too. One vision warned us to move. You could have others."

"Don't count on me, Tucker." Her pale eyes were completely unreadable, her voice matter-of-fact. "I can't control what I see. Or when I see it. Don't forget—I never saw them coming to the lake."

He frowned slightly. "But somebody did. Somebody knew, and warned us."

"Using technology in a way you said was impossible."

"Next to impossible, given the safeguards in my system and the fact that I wasn't even connected to the Internet at the time. I know what you mean, though. If they can manipulate technology with that kind of expertise, then maybe we have some nameless friends who *do* know how to deal with our enemy."

"So how do we ask for help?"

"We don't. Not until they surface, at any rate."

Sarah nodded, and said, "So we're still on our own. And we can't count on another warning—either from our nameless friends or from me."

"True. But I think the enemy will be more cautious now; they didn't catch us off guard when they expected to, and that has to give them pause. They can't know how much you see. I think that's one reason they move at night."

A flicker of interest narrowed her eyes. "Because I'm presumably asleep?"

"Yeah. It's just a hunch, but . . . Sarah, the day we met, the day your house burned, I watched Lewis when he talked to you. I noticed that he started to touch you—and then drew back."

"A lot of people are that way about psychics." She shrugged. "Or so-called witches. They're afraid their darkest secrets will be revealed to me if I come into contact with them. I've noticed quite a few friends and acquaintances doing the same thing."

She looked briefly at the careful foot of space between them and added, "It surprised me when you touched me so calmly that day."

Tucker refused to let himself get sidetracked. "But Lewis wanted to touch you, I could see that. He didn't stop because he was afraid. It was more like he . . . remembered something he wasn't supposed to do. Sarah, what if they *know* their darkest secrets will be revealed to you if you touch them? What if that's the reason they keep their distance except at night when you should be sleeping? Because if they get too close or linger too long when you're awake and aware, you'll recognize them for what they are."

"Lewis was close, even if I didn't touch him."

"Yeah, but he was also a cop. You had no reason to be wary of him, you thought. Trust dulled your sense of self-preservation—and all your other senses as well. Plus, he may not be one of *them* in the strictest sense, but rather a tool they use when necessary."

Sarah thought about that, her gaze returning to the cross on the other side of the street. "You are good with puzzles, aren't you," she murmured at last. "That makes sense."

"It makes sense, but it's still only a guess. Plus, even if I'm right, this is still new to you, so I can't see how we can use the theory, make it work for your protection. As you said yourself, it's something you haven't yet learned to control; they may very well be wary of you but we don't yet know how to use that."

"So . . . half an ace?" She offered him a faintly twisted smile.

"Better than nothing."

Her smile faded, and Sarah said, "If only there were others like me I could talk to. Psychics with more experience than me. People who know how to control this, how to use it."

"Maybe there are."

"Still alive?"

"It's possible. According to the research, there have been psychics in the news recently for reasons other than death or disappearance. Names we've ignored because they didn't fit our search criteria."

"Psychics who aren't targets? But why isn't the . . . the other side interested in them? If they've killed and taken so many, if they're after me now, why ignore others?"

Tucker frowned. "Maybe there's some common denominator among some psychics that makes them less valuable, or less of a threat. That has to be it. A particular kind of ability, maybe, or the strength of their abilities. Hell, maybe it's something so subtle we could be looking right at it, something as simple as eye color or background, something like that. The only way we're going to find out is to get more information, and then . . ."

"And then . . . approach another psychic?"

"It's a possibility. Another psychic, one more experienced, could probably help you, Sarah. Help you learn to use your abilities."

"Have you considered that it's also possible those psychics aren't targets because they already belong to the other side?" she asked steadily.

Tucker had not considered that, and the possibility chilled him.

Down to the bone.

NINE

It was fairly late when they got to Cleveland, nearly nine o'clock that evening. They found a hotel with rooms available, and Tucker got them a small suite on the tenth floor.

"I think we should stay together," he told Sarah. "But at least in these suites, there's a separate bedroom to give you a little privacy."

Sarah didn't argue. She was slightly surprised that he wanted them to be together now when, presumably, they had a bit of breathing room; when things had been a lot more tense en route to Chicago, he had gotten them separate rooms. Keeping a careful distance, she'd assumed. She didn't know what his reasoning was now and was too tired to think much about it.

The hotel had an underground garage, which was one

reason Tucker had chosen it; their Jeep would have a bit more security than if it were parked out in the open, and it would certainly be less visible to passersby. It was also a fairly busy hotel, with people coming and going; it was hosting some kind of business convention, and that made it a virtual certainty that there would be people about at all hours.

The suite turned out to be a nice one, with a spacious sitting room that had a sleeper sofa (which Tucker matter-of-factly claimed for his bed), a couple of good chairs, a desk, and a comfortable bedroom with a king-sized bed.

Sarah barely noticed. Travel-weary and just plain tired, all she wanted was to take a long, hot shower and get ready for bed. Tucker told her to go ahead while he plugged his laptop in to charge the battery while his system continued gathering the information that might help them.

"Aren't you tired?"

"Yeah, but too wound up to sleep just yet. I need to wind down, and I'll sleep better if I work on this for a while." He looked at her searchingly. "It's been hours since we stopped for supper; I think I'll order some soup and sandwiches from room service. Okay?"

"Fine." She was surprised to find herself a little hungry. Tucker had been feeding her at regular intervals, and she was beginning to get used to it.

Leaving him in the sitting room, she went and took a luxuriously long and hot shower. It felt wonderful. She washed her hair with shampoo thoughtfully provided by the hotel, and as she stood at the vanity drying it with the dryer also provided, she reflected with a bit of rueful humor that someone really should publish a self-help book on what to pack for an indeterminate journey on the run for one's life.

Moisturizer, for example, should go into every woman's survival kit. You couldn't always count on a hotel to provide it, after all. When you could even stay at a hotel, of course. And a nice bottle of bubble bath for those rare occasions when a few precious minutes could be spent soothing a travel-weary body. And a small makeup bag and a bottle of pleasing perfume would certainly come in handy when you were traveling with a man. A nice man.

A sexy man.

Idiot. Get him out of your head.

The only sleepwear Sarah had brought with her was something styled like a man's button-up, cuffed-sleeve shirt. It was fairly short, reaching just below the middle of her thighs, and rather sheer.

She looked at her reflection on the back of the bathroom door and sighed. Too pale and still too thin despite Tucker's regular meals, she looked almost anemic. And the stark white sleep shirt didn't help.

My kingdom for some blush and lipstick. A touch of foundation. Something.

The faint spurt of self-derisive humor faded. She leaned her forehead against the cool mirror for a moment and closed her eyes. Her head was hurting, throbbing. It was almost like a sinus headache, an aching pressure behind her eyes, but she knew it wasn't sinus. It was this thing inside her, this thing that had been born in violence six months before.

It was growing.

Tucker hadn't understood when she'd told him that; she knew he hadn't. How could he? How could anyone know what it felt like to have something alien inside you, something that was part of you and yet not under your control? Not . . . normal.

"Go away," she whispered.

For a moment, she could have sworn the pressure inside her head increased, as if in protest, and far back in her mind she thought she heard the echo of a whisper.

Sarah . . .

Fate. Destiny.

Sarah lifted her head away from the mirror and opened her eyes. They looked very bright and shiny, and felt hot. But she refused to let the tears fall. She locked them inside her and angrily wished they'd drown that thing that kept growing, that thing that wouldn't go away and leave her in peace.

Then she squared her shoulders and left the bathroom. Reluctant to let Tucker see her looking so damned ghostlike and . . . insubstantial, Sarah put on one of the bulky terry-cloth robes also provided by the hotel. It was also white, which hardly lent her any color, but at least it made her look less in need of care and feeding.

Even so, he looked at her for an unnervingly long moment when Sarah went back into the sitting room just a couple of minutes after room service had arrived. But all he said, lightly, was, "Feeling better?"

"Much."

"Good. Here, I had the waiter leave the cart in the room so we can use it as our table . . ."

The food occupied them for some time, but finally Sarah nodded toward the laptop set up on the desk and asked, "Find anything yet?"

"More of the same, so far." He leaned back in his chair and frowned slightly. "I'm still sorting through all the information the computer gathered while we were at the lake. Every news item just seems to confirm what we believe—that someone is abducting young psychics and killing older ones. There are some exceptions, of course. I've read articles on at least a couple of very young psychics who seem to be doing fine, and a number of articles about older psychics who've been in the news more than once."

"So what does that tell us?"

"I'm damned if I know. Unless it's a question of genuine versus phony. Maybe all the ones still alive and kicking just didn't satisfy whatever criteria the other side is using to determine the real from the fake."

Sarah thought about it. "Can you set up your computer to look for a pattern? I mean, in case there's something we're just not seeing?"

Tucker nodded. "When we have more information, sure. I'll probably have to write the program, but that won't take too long. In the meantime, I'm also starting a list of psychics who don't appear to be under any kind of threat. And I'll narrow that list to those living in the northeast."

"You still believe we should approach one?"

"I think we have to try, Sarah. We'll be as careful as we can in choosing who to approach and how we approach them."

"How do we know we're being careful?"

"Good question," he said ruefully. "The only answer I have is—we do the best we can. Maybe the computer will provide us with something useful. Maybe your senses and instincts will kick in. Or maybe, in the end, we'll just have to wing it."

Sarah sipped her decaf for a moment, then said slowly, "We can only gather information about those people who've been in the news or some kind of official report. Tucker . . . don't you think there are probably people out there who've successfully hidden their abilities? I mean, I would have, if it hadn't hit me so suddenly and so hard at first that I blurted things out without caring who was listening. If I'd had my druthers, nobody would ever have found out about me."

"I'm sure there are others out there who think that way," he agreed. "And maybe they've escaped notice. But it means the same thing to us as it does to the other side: those psychics will be virtually impossible to find."

"Unless the other side has ways of finding them besides the media and official reports."

"Right."

She nodded. "I can't help wondering about them, though. The ones that might be hiding out there. What if they're so quiet because they know what's going on?"

"That could be."

She felt a little chill and unconsciously drew the lapels of the robe more closely together. The throbbing behind her eyes intensified. "I just . . . I just have this unsettling feeling that there are people moving all around us, and that *they* know what the hell's going on. That if we only knew who to ask, it would all start to make some kind of sense."

Tucker smiled slightly, his gaze intent on her face. "I have a lot of faith in your feelings. Maybe . . ." He hesitated, then said, "Sarah, maybe if you concentrate on those feelings, if you . . . open yourself to them . . . you'll be able to sense some information the computer could never provide."

Sarah set her cup down on the table and stared at it. Lovely pattern. Roses. Unusual, since most hotels stuck with utilitarian white . . .

"Sarah?"

"I don't know how to do that." Her head throbbed.

"I think you do. Now, I think you do."

Softly, starkly, she said, "I'm afraid to do that."

"I know."

Her gaze lifted to meet his, and she realized that he did know. But he didn't understand, not really. He still didn't understand. She managed a faint smile. "Can't help being a coward, you know. It's the way I'm made."

"You aren't a coward."

"Sure I am. Do you think I'd be doing all this if you weren't with me? I'm leaning on your strength, Tucker. And your confidence. And your belief that, somehow, we can change a future burned into my mind. Left alone, I'd still be back in Richmond. Waiting to die."

Tucker shook his head. "You are not a coward, Sarah. You were blindsided by all this and it shook you off your balance, but there's nothing fainthearted in you. A coward would never have left Richmond, with me or anyone else. A coward wouldn't have survived—with astonishing calm, by the way—seeing men come to kill her on two separate occasions."

She didn't believe him but shrugged slightly. "If you say so. But I know what's inside me, and right now there's little but fear."

"Fear can help you. Every soldier knows that, Sarah. It can keep your instincts and your senses sharp, keep you alert to danger. And it doesn't make you a coward."

"It does if it keeps you from acting. I'm *afraid* to open myself up, to deliberately try to look into dark places I'd rather not see." She got up abruptly and went over to the window. The curtains were partially drawn, but through the narrow opening, she looked out on city lights. It looked very cold out there, and she felt very alone.

Softly, she added, "I'm really afraid to do that."

"Sarah . . ."

He was behind her, too close, but there was nowhere she could go. She was trapped. *Trapped*. The hot throbbing behind her eyes was like an alien heartbeat. In a voice that was suddenly harsh and angry, she said, "You have no idea how it feels, none at all. I told you once, at the lake, but you didn't *listen*. There's something inside me, Tucker, something alien. And it's growing. It whispers to me, telling me what I should do and how I should feel—and I don't trust it."

"Sarah—"

"You think it's just another tool, like your laptop, something you can use to get information. Push the right button and get what you want." She did turn and look at him then, through hot eyes, and her voice was low and strained. "But it's not that easy. It's like claws inside me, do you understand *that*? Something alive and struggling—and hurting me. Every bit of information I manage to tear free leaves bloody wounds behind it. How long do you think it'll be before I bleed to death?"

"Sarah."

"Leave me alone." She avoided his intent gaze and tried to move around him, but he was too close.

"You've been alone too damned long." He put his hands on her shoulders to keep her still. "Sarah, you're right, I can't even imagine what it's like—and I make my living imagining things." His voice was low, steady. "But I can understand fear. And the only thing I know for sure about fear is that we have to face what frightens us. We have to. Otherwise it can cripple us."

"Then I'm crippled."

"Not yet. You're only crippled if you let yourself be."

She looked up at him, feeling so nakedly vulnerable that it actually hurt. "Everything I've seen has been . . . darkness. Violence. Death. I don't want to see that anymore, Tucker."

His hands tightened. "Then don't look for death or violence. Try to control it, Sarah. Ask yourself a specific mental question and concentrate on finding the answer to only that. I don't know if it'll work—I'm not psychic, so I can't know that. But I know the mind is an incredible instrument, one that can be focused and fine-tuned. One that can be controlled. I believe you can do that. If you try."

Sarah didn't know if she could try. What she did know was that she didn't want to. And she knew she was too weary to be standing here this close to Tucker. She knew that tonight it would be all too easy to make a mistake. She wanted him to put his arms around her and hold her. She wanted him to kiss her again. She wanted him to hold the darkness at bay.

She wanted him.

But Tucker had made it clear to her that he considered their brief kiss at the lake a mistake. He had avoided even the most casual touch since then, and he had withdrawn so completely from her that Sarah found it difficult to gauge even his mood, much less his thoughts. Even now, with his hands on her, all she sensed from him was wariness and reserve.

And even knowing that, even being painfully sure that he didn't want her, she still wanted him.

Before she started clinging to him like an idiot and made a total fool of herself, she carefully drew back away from him until his hands released her. "I'm really tired," she said. "I think I'll turn in."

She was at the door of the sitting room before it occurred to her that he would have to go through the bedroom in order to get to the bathroom. She paused and looked back at him. "Don't worry about disturbing me when you need to use the bathroom. I always . . . I sleep like the dead."

Still standing at the window, Tucker merely nodded. "Good night, Sarah."

"Good night."

Sarah tried not to think very much after that. She pushed the bedroom door to but didn't completely close it. She thoughtfully left a light on in the bathroom when she was finished in there so that Tucker would be able to see his way. Then she shed the robe, climbed into the huge bed, and turned off the lamp.

She wanted to sleep, to just close her eyes and let everything stop for a while. She needed that. But when she closed her eyes, the worries and questions and thoughts refused to stop.

Who are they?

Try to control the thing inside you. Try to see something to help us.

Why are psychics so important—or such a threat—to them?

There isn't much time left. I feel that.

Why did this have to happen to me?

All I see is death.

Tucker needs to find Lydia.

Am I going to die?

Am I going mad?

Finally, even though she knew she was too tired and afraid to make the attempt, Sarah concentrated on closing out everything except one single, vitally important question. *Who are they?* She fixed it in her mind until it was so clear she could see the letters of each word.

Then, hesitantly and very afraid, she tried to open up her mind, her senses, and invite the answer to come.

At first, all Sarah saw was the question, bright as neon. Gradually, though, the question dimmed and all around it the blackness lightened. She saw a large, featureless building very briefly, just the flash of the image, but it made her skin crawl, as if she stood briefly at the mouth of a dark cave where something unspeakably brutish dwelled. Then she heard the low murmur of many voices, what they were saying indistinguishable but rousing in her another powerful primitive response as the hairs on the back of her neck stirred a warning.

Wrong. It was all wrong, worse than bad . . .

Then she saw the shadows. They were many, all shapes and sizes, tall and thin, short and squat, manlike and bestial. Nightmare shapes. They moved rapidly, flitting across her inner field of vision with an energy and purpose that was chilling. Arms reaching out. Hands grasping . . . something. She couldn't see what they were doing. Couldn't see what it was they caught and held so avidly. She couldn't see their faces.

She couldn't see their faces.

Panicked, Sarah wrenched herself out of it without even realizing she was going to. When her eyes opened, she found herself sitting up in bed, her heart pounding and breathing rapid and shallow, as if she had awakened from a nightmare. Was that it? Had her psychic abilities actually shown her something that was real, or had her fears and worries simply been given frightening shape by her anxious mind?

She didn't have the same sense that a vision left her with, that what she had seen was real. There was no feeling in her of inevitability. Instead, what she felt was a profound but wordless and nameless uneasiness. A fear that was purely instinctive, like the primal response to snakes and spiders and noises in the night.

Sarah wanted badly to get out of bed and go into the sitting room. To Tucker. She wanted to tell him what she thought she had seen and how it made her feel. She wanted to hear him tell her that there was nothing to be afraid of, and everything would be all right.

But she didn't, of course. Instead, she lay back on the pillow and tried to reassure herself. *You're a grown-up and hardly as weak as you've been acting. You've got to stop leaning on him—even if you survive this, he won't always be around. Think about it. Figure it out.*

It had, likely, only been the frightened musings of her mind. And even if it hadn't been, even if she had actually been able to tap into some kind of psychic awareness, what had she seen? Nothing really. A building. Some shadows, distorted as shadows always were, without a clear shape or texture and scaring her because . . . She didn't know why. Because shadows scared her. Because her world had been turned upside down, and everything seemed to scare her these days.

Her head was throbbing, the pressure behind her eyes building.

That alien thing in her head was growing.

———

Tucker pushed the room service cart out into the hallway, then settled down at the desk with coffee and his laptop.

But he didn't turn his attention to the computer immediately. Instead, he brooded.

Here he was in a hotel suite with a woman he hadn't
known a week, on the run possibly for his life and hers,
grappling with a puzzle the enormity of which was the
stuff of paranoid fantasies . . . and he had hardly bothered to stop a moment and ask himself why.

The simple answer, of course, was that he wanted her
to tell him about Lydia. And that was certainly the reason he had first sought her out. But from the moment he
had elected to spend the night on the couch outside her
bedroom because a watcher with unknown motives lurked
in the dark night, he had turned a corner, and from that
point there had really been no going back.

None of his friends, he thought, would be surprised
to find him involved in something so bizarre. He had a
reputation for getting hip-deep in things purely out of
intellectual curiosity and the love of challenge, which was
undoubtedly one of his motivations in this case. It was a
puzzle to end all puzzles, that was for sure.

But it was more than that. Much more. During the
past days, he had realized that he was with Sarah because
he wanted to protect her and knew that he could. He had
been certain of that.

What he hadn't known was whether he could save her.

Now, especially, he was conscious of doubts he'd never
felt before. This thing was so big, so bizarre—and so
clearly deadly. Sarah was already in more pain than he
had bargained for, pain that promised to get worse before
it got better. If it got better.

And there was an added complication now. No matter how wary her abilities made him, the undeniable fact was that Tucker was having a tough time keeping his distance. He was so aware of her all the time, so conscious of her every movement, of the sound of her voice and the fleeting expressions that crossed her face. He wanted to touch her.

He wanted to wake up next to her.

But he couldn't deny that he hadn't come to terms with her abilities; after so many years of charlatans, the real thing had definitely thrown him off balance. And he also couldn't deny that even if Sarah felt something for him—and he had no idea whether she did—she was in no shape physically or emotionally to take a lover.

He didn't think she was quite so fragile as she had been days ago, but at times, especially when she was tired, she still seemed to him too frail and shut in herself to be able to go on much longer. When he looked at her, he had the sense of something almost ethereal. Unreal. As if some delicate creature of myth and legend had drifted out of the mist and into his life.

That's the Celt in me.

Or maybe just the writer, steeped in mythology and legend, shaping daydreams in the mind and giving them form on paper. That man could easily imagine Sarah as an elf or faerie, native to some dreamy betweenworld and just visiting this one, vulnerable to danger, terrifyingly fragile and lovely. Enchanting him because, in ancient times, the current of love between humans and faeries had run deep and strong, even though the price demanded for such joy had all too often been death . . .

Definitely the Celt in me.

Her abilities might make her seem otherworldly, but Sarah was all too human, Tucker knew. Human enough to be very afraid of what she could see and the fact that she could see it. Human enough to be in pain, to want to withdraw even more when she was afraid, to push him further away.

Especially when he pushed her.

He didn't want to push her. He didn't want to hurt her. Didn't want to see her fear and dread at the thought of deliberately trying to open doors she would much rather keep closed. And he definitely didn't like seeing her draw even further away from him when he suggested she try. But Tucker was all too aware of time passing, and even more conscious of how damnably little they knew.

They needed to—had to—use their only real ace, and that was Sarah.

If the other side was after her with such grim determination because they either feared her or valued her, then Tucker thought the chances were very good that Sarah could use whatever it was they feared or desired against them. The question, of course, was whether she could do it. Whether she could even try to do it.

As much as he had learned over the years about psychic abilities and the paranormal, Tucker still felt very unsure about what to tell Sarah, about how to advise her. He was not psychic, and as he'd told her, he couldn't begin to feel what she felt. Not even his vivid writer's imagination could help him to help her.

Until he had met her, he had seen in the world of the paranormal very little he'd believed to be genuine. And even the few psychics who had impressed him with their abilities had been erratic not only in what they had been able to do but in their interpretations of what they had seen and sensed. That was why he had, in the beginning at least, questioned Sarah's interpretations. But she seemed—so far—less erratic than those psychics had been, and far, far less likely to try to "fill in the blanks" of what she saw with hunches and outright guesses.

Maybe that would come in time. Maybe every genuine psychic learned to create a patchwork of vision and guess and interpretation in order to present something complete and understandable to those inquiring. Maybe it was simple human nature.

And then there were those things not so easily explained.

"She never wanted to be found, you know. That's why you couldn't."

A quiet statement, offered in a quiet moment, as if it had simply come to Sarah without her bidding. A reluctant glimpse inside the mind of someone she did not know, had never known. Someone who had been gone for a very long time.

Sarah had simply known.

Her abilities, Tucker believed, were still new and raw. Unformed, in a sense. Unrestrained by the checks and guards and filters her mind would no doubt struggle in time to erect. They might at this point be beyond her ability to control, but they were also undoubtedly powerful, and the force of them was undiluted by her conscious mind. Where an experienced psychic might try to interpret what was seen, Sarah merely reported it.

This is what I see. This is what I know.

When she looked—even absently without her full attention—she saw.

He had to make her look. No matter what it cost her.

No matter what it cost him.

The usual crowd populated Venice Beach, but it had been a slow day for Daisy Novak. Plenty of curious looks were directed toward her kiosk, but not many seemed eager to pay twenty bucks to get their fortunes told.

Absently, she polished her crystal ball with her sleeve and watched the people wander past. It was nearly dark, but there were plenty of lights around, and still plenty of people, and Daisy hesitated. She was stiff after sitting here so long. Damned arthritis. But just another twenty bucks or so would mean she probably wouldn't have to work on Saturday. Another hour, then. But no longer; her cat, Moses, would be waiting for his supper.

She reached under the draped table and flipped the switch that turned on the light under her crystal ball. A nice effect, if she did say so herself. Especially since her kiosk was in one of the dimmer areas of the boardwalk. The light shone upward through the crystal, and she knew it made her face look nicely spooky and unearthly.

And it was effective too. Within minutes, a customer sat down on the other side of the table.

"Twenty dollars for ten minutes?" She pushed a bill across the table.

Daisy smiled and slid the bill into her voluminous blouse. "Yes, indeed. Do you have a preference, Megan? Tarot, palm reading, crystal ball?"

Megan blinked, then smiled. "You're pretty good." She was young, in her twenties, and pretty, dressed as casually as everyone around her in shorts and a skimpy top, and she had that I-dare-you expression that Daisy easily recognized. "Let's try out the ball."

Automatically, Daisy cupped her hands around the base of the crystal and peered at it intently. Now she regretted turning on the light; the damn thing made her eyes water. "Past, present, or future?" she murmured. "The crystal shows all."

"Suit yourself," Megan said.

Daisy glanced at her, noted the challenging expression, and felt irritated enough to reach a bit deeper than usual. So this one was a skeptic, was she? Well, then, Daisy would just give her her money's worth.

Briskly, Daisy said, "I see buildings, with young people walking all around—ah. You're a graduate student. Economics." She sneaked a glance up and saw Megan blink again. Good. A direct hit. "Single, but you have a boyfriend who is . . . a musician. You spend weekends with him. Hmmm. Doesn't like the missionary position much, does he? Wants you to do all the work whenever possible. And he just bought a book with more positions illustrated for next weekend—"

"All right, that's enough about that." Megan's face was flushed. But there was an eager light in her eyes now. "My future. What's my future?"

Daisy peered more intently, but she wasn't looking into the crystal. She was looking inward. "I see . . . a man. He's . . . he's in the shadows. He's giving you something. Money. He's paying you." Daisy felt a chill spread through her and was only half-aware that her voice had grown anxious. "Don't, Megan. Don't go to him for your money. He's . . . there's something wrong with him. With all of them. Don't become a part of their plans. He—they—want you to do something bad. Helping them is a bad thing. Don't do it—"

She reached across the table instinctively to grasp Megan's hand and only then realized that the girl had fled.

More than a little unnerved herself, Daisy turned off the crystal's light and packed up to go home. Jeez, what had she seen? A guy in the shadows, a guy she'd felt was somehow not normal. This was California, for Christ's sake—nobody was *normal* here. So why had it scared her so much?

Daisy tried to push it out of her mind, but she was still nervous as she walked home, jumping at shadows and noises. She told herself to calm down, reminded herself that this was a safe route home and always had been. But that reading bothered her.

She was half a block from home when a shadow loomed out at her from an alleyway, and she didn't jump quite fast enough. A hand like iron grabbed her arm and pulled her into the alley.

Daisy should have screamed. But the moment he touched her, coldly terrifying images flooded her mind so vividly that they stole her breath.

"Hello, Daisy," he said gently.

She looked up at his shadowy face, and in the moment granted to her for understanding, she suddenly knew what he was.

"Oh, my God," she whispered.

She never saw the knife.

———

By noon the next day, Tucker's laptop was sorting through the most recent download of media information and official reports, which left him and Sarah with nothing to do. They had both awakened early, breakfasted quietly, and said little to each other during the hours since. It had been agreed that they would remain here until early afternoon, leaving this hotel and continuing their journey to the next stop. Syracuse.

That destination was not so arbitrary as it might seem; one of Tucker's tasks this morning had been to begin putting together a list of psychics living in the northeast, and the first name on that list belonged to a man who lived in Syracuse. Since that city was along their general route northward, they had decided to make that their next stop.

Whether they contacted the psychic would be decided later.

"Why don't we go downstairs and have lunch in one of the restaurants?" Tucker suggested as his laptop hummed quietly. "You must be more than ready to get out of this room."

Sarah, who had occupied herself by restlessly watching the news and mostly not watching one old movie on television, was definitely ready. "That sounds good."

They left the DO NOT DISTURB sign on the door to prevent housekeeping from cleaning the room while they were gone; Tucker didn't want his laptop disturbed.

Sarah found herself looking around warily as they crossed the vast lobby to one of the restaurants, but nothing awoke suspicion. Everybody around them looked and acted normal and unthreatening.

But so did Sergeant Lewis.

"You're very quiet," Tucker said, after they'd given their order to the waiter.

"Am I? Sorry." Her head no longer hurt, but that unsettling pulsing sensation was still present, that heartbeat throb behind her eyes.

"You don't have to apologize for it, Sarah."

"Okay," she said absently.

"Is anything bothering you? I mean, anything in particular?"

She looked at him for a moment, then smiled impersonally and allowed her gaze to slide away and roam idly past the low wall defining the restaurant and out into the lobby. "No, not really."

The restaurant was fairly busy and the lobby more so. She watched people moving about, many of them wearing business suits and name tags as they clustered in the various seating areas and walked briskly toward whatever seminars they were due to attend in the nearby meeting rooms.

"Are you sure? You seem a bit . . . preoccupied today."

"Do I?" One man caught her attention, and it didn't surprise her that he would have. He was extraordinarily handsome, for one thing—and despite what she thought was a scar down his left cheek. Very distinctively, his black hair sported both a widow's peak and a streak of pure white at the left temple.

He was clearly powerful physically, broad-shouldered and athletic, and more than one passing woman did a double take. He was sitting alone in a seating area designed for two, the second glass on his table mute indication that he was not as alone as he appeared.

He was looking around idly much as Sarah was, and for an instant she caught his gaze. His eyes were very pale in that almost coldly handsome face, and though they flickered very briefly with interest when they rested on her, Sarah's reaction was more ambivalent.

One of these things is not like the others.

"Sarah?"

She looked at Tucker, trying to ride out the fleeting surge of panic. She was not afraid of the stranger, she realized. She didn't recognize him as an enemy. No, her reaction had been more nebulous than that. He was just . . . wrong. Out of place somehow.

"Goddammit, will you talk to me?"

"About what?" It wasn't until Tucker sat back and stared across the table at her with a certain amount of frustration that Sarah realized how she was acting. She shook her head. "I'm sorry. Really, Tucker. I'm just . . . unsettled today."

"Do you know why?"

"It's nothing I can put my finger on." She glanced back toward the dark stranger to find that an equally handsome female companion had joined him and had his full attention. To Tucker, she added, "Just jumpy, I guess. I didn't sleep very well."

He was silent for a few moments while the waiter returned with their drinks, then frowned and said, "Have you tried to focus on the jumpiness?"

"I'm just tired, that's all."

"Sarah." He leaned toward her, resting his forearms on the table and holding her gaze steadily. "I read somewhere that using psychic abilities is like listening. Have you tried that?"

Lightly, she said, "All I hear is a fairly noisy hotel lobby. And somebody just dropped a dish back in the kitchen."

Since that crash had been evident to everyone in the restaurant, Tucker barely wasted a nod. "Shut out all the sounds. Listen for what's underneath."

She broke the hold of his gaze and looked down to find that she'd unconsciously crumbled half a bread stick. Brushing the crumbs into a neat pile, she said, "I can't hear anything."

"You aren't trying."

"I told you. I'm tired."

"You can't afford to be tired," Tucker said, his voice suddenly hard. "If listening will help keep you alive, you have to listen."

Sarah refused to look at him. "I've told you. It *hurts*. Can't you understand that?"

Very quietly, Tucker said, "I think you have a choice. Hurt a little now to save your life, or avoid the pain now—and die the death you saw for yourself."

"Then that's my choice to make, isn't it?" She drew a breath and let it out slowly. *Destiny. Fate. Is it really my choice?*

Whatever Tucker might have said in response was prevented by the return of their waiter with the meal, but when they were alone again, he said, "I'm in this now too, Sarah. Don't forget that."

He didn't say anything else, and neither did Sarah. And she didn't taste the meal she ate, though she ate as much as she could of what was on her plate. The pressure behind her eyes throbbed.

They didn't linger in the restaurant, and they both remained silent as they crossed the huge lobby to the bank of elevators. Sarah noted absently that the handsome dark man seemed even more enthralled by his lovely companion, since he was smiling at her in a way that would cause any woman's heart to stop. She envied them their simple closeness.

Tucker unlocked the door to their room and went in

first, automatically cautious. But it was Sarah who saw what was different.

On the desk beside the still-humming laptop was a lovely vase of cut flowers.

Sarah found a card among the blooms and studied it in silence for a moment before handing it to Tucker. The message was simple.

WELCOME TO CLEVELAND

TEN

Duran sent his people on to the next destination, but did not immediately go himself. Nobody questioned him, of course. His methods might be unorthodox and occasionally paradoxical, but he got results. Not even Varden, the most treacherous lieutenant Duran had ever been forced to work with, had been able to undermine his authority—despite several subtle and creative attempts.

Duran drove himself out of the city of Cleveland and to a remote warehouse being used for storage. The place was locked up and deserted, but the key Duran had been provided got him inside, and once inside he found that the dirty windows allowed in enough light to see by.

He walked through shoulder-high stacks of boxes with no interest in their contents, working his way gradually toward the center of the building. When he reached his goal, he saw that a skylight directly above his position threw light down around him in a neat circle. He wondered whether she had chosen this spot for that reason.

"You're late," she told him, stepping out of the shadows.

"No," he said coolly, "you're early."

She shrugged. "I was brought up right. How about you, Duran? Military training?"

He ignored the question. "Do you have it?"

If anything, she seemed amused by his refusal to reply to her seemingly innocent question. "I wouldn't be here if I didn't." She took a step toward him and pulled a large manila envelope from inside her jacket, handing it across the space between them.

He took it but didn't open it. Instead, looking at her, he said, "Any trouble getting this?"

"Other than risking everything, you mean?" Her smile was sardonic. "No, no trouble."

"How long do I have?"

She shrugged again, patently unconcerned. "I would say that depends on the current . . . situation. If everything hits the fan right on schedule, you'll have a week at the outside. From today. After that, you might as well burn it for all the good it'll do you."

"I need more time." His tone was measured, his expression carefully neutral.

"Sorry. It isn't my fault you've set things up this way."

"I had no choice," he reminded her.

"Maybe. Or maybe you just got too ambitious. In any case, it's your problem. Not mine."

Pleasantly, he said, "You really don't like me very much, do you?"

"No," she replied, equally pleasant. "I really don't."

She didn't say good-bye. She just backed away until the shadows swallowed her.

Duran tapped the edge of the envelope against his hand for a moment, then sighed and slid it into his coat pocket, still without opening it. Then he turned and left the warehouse, not forgetting to lock the door behind him.

And went to join his people.

———

Hurry, Sarah.

No matter how far you run, we'll find you. We'll always find you.

Destiny. Meant to be.

"If it was them," Tucker said as the Jeep sped along the interstate highway toward Syracuse, "what the hell are they up to?"

"Maybe they wanted to remind us—me—that it's no use running," Sarah offered quietly, shutting out the whispers in her head.

Tucker, who had taken a roundabout route from the hotel to the interstate and convinced himself they weren't being followed, said, "The hotel must have sent the flowers."

"They said not."

"Yeah, but they couldn't find any paperwork on the delivery. I bet somebody just screwed up."

"And put the flowers in our room despite the DO NOT DISTURB sign? I've never heard of a hotel doing that."

He sent her a quick look. "They couldn't possibly have found us so quickly, not after we ditched the car in Chicago."

"No. Logically, they couldn't have. Unless they were much closer than we thought, saw us drive away in this Jeep, and followed us to Cleveland."

"You believe that's what they did?"

"I believe we'd better assume it's what they did. That someone is following, and closely."

Tucker was silent for some miles, then spoke abruptly. "What are your feelings telling you?"

Sarah half-turned in the seat to look at him. "Not much. Nothing, really. But . . ."

"But what?"

She hesitated, then said, "For days now, I've felt a . . . pressure building inside me. In my head. Behind my eyes, like a sinus headache. The whole time we were at the hotel, it really bothered me. As soon as we left, the pressure eased a bit. I can barely feel it now."

"You think you were reacting to their nearness?"

"I don't know. I'm just telling you what I felt."

He frowned. "You said you didn't sleep well. Because of the pressure?"

"I guess."

"Do you remember your dreams?"

"No. But I kept waking up, and whenever I did, I felt restless and uneasy."

"Not frightened?"

Being frightened was such a constant state that Sarah had to think about his question, had to ask herself whether she had awakened with more fear than usual. She thought about it and shook her head. "No, not especially frightened. Just uneasy. Anxious. The way you feel when—oh, when you hear a faint sound you can't immediately identify. Tense, sort of listening. Then I'd relax and, eventually, go back to sleep. That happened over and over all night."

Tucker was silent for a few more miles, then said, "If we suppose they were back there at the hotel, watching us, the question becomes—why didn't they make a move? Maybe the answer is what I guessed before. Maybe you're becoming aware of them on some level, even if it's unconsciously. And maybe they know that."

"How would they know, supposing it's true?"

"Experience, maybe. Look, from what we've been able to find out, these people have been after psychics for years. Decades. Along the way, they must have . . . oh, hell, learned their trade, for want of a better phrase. Learned what worked for them. Suppose they found out through trial and error that they have only a relatively small window of opportunity during which they can move boldly to grab a psychic?"

"Until the psychic starts to react to their presence?"

"Why not? An enemy as large in number as you feel they are must give off a hell of a lot of negative energy. From the research I've done about psychics, that seems to be the thing: energy. Psychics tune into it at various . . . frequencies. React to it when there's a lot around, like during a storm."

Slowly, she said, "Storms have bothered me since I came out of that coma."

"It's not uncommon, or so I've been told. Say that's it, say whatever you can do, the basis of any psychic ability is energy. And in the beginning, whenever a psychic becomes psychic, or wakes up to it—whatever—the energy has to be almost overpowering."

Sarah nodded silently.

"So the mind learns to protect itself. It learns to build walls or some other kind of protection against that overwhelming energy. Maybe it learns to filter through all the static and focus on certain frequencies."

"Makes sense," she said.

"And it works, to varying degrees. But when these dangerous people are close by, this enemy, they must give off a different kind of energy. Dark, negative. A threat. Even if it's unconscious, I'm willing to bet that out of sheer self-preservation, any good psychic would catch on pretty quick and be able to start tuning in on them. On that particular frequency. It would naturally make those psychics a lot more wary. It might even cause them to wake up in the night feeling uneasy."

"But why would that keep the other side at a distance?" Sarah wondered. "Even if they assume I can feel them near me—so what? They outnumber us, we know that. They burned down my house, and we're reasonably sure they killed a cop as well as some psychics, so they're clearly not hesitant to use violence."

"No, but maybe they're afraid of attention. Grabbing somebody in a crowded hotel could be a noisy proposition.

It could draw too many innocent bystanders. Too many policemen not on the payroll. That could be another reason they seem to make their moves at night."

"So they're just watching and waiting? Looking for an opportunity to get me when it won't be noticed? When I can be caught off guard so I'm not likely to make too much noise?"

"It makes sense. As much as anything in this makes sense."

"Then why leave those flowers? Why make it obvious?"

"A terrorist tactic is my bet," Tucker said slowly. "Nobody can be wary twenty-four hours a day; if they can keep you rattled, frightened, they stand a better chance of either driving you to make a mistake or just plain exhausting you so you can't see them coming."

It was working, Sarah thought. In spades. She looked at him for a moment longer, then turned her gaze forward. The highway was busy on this Tuesday afternoon, and as she watched the cars ahead of them, she couldn't help wondering whether they were as innocent as they seemed. Maybe there were watchers in that van up ahead, or that racy-looking Corvette. Maybe the truck that had passed them a mile back had done so only to avoid suspicion, the watcher inside handing the duty off to someone else along the way.

Or maybe not.

When an enemy lurked all around, it was easy to become paranoid.

Uneasily, she said, "Has it occurred to you that an

accident staged on the highway would be a dandy way to get us?"

"Yes, it has." Tucker's voice was grim. "If they mean to kill us, that'd be the quickest way to at least try."

"If?"

"I have my doubts about that, Sarah."

She returned her attention to his profile. "Why?"

"So far, virtually everything they've done—with the possible exception of burning down your house, and we can't be absolutely positive that was their doing—could have been an attempt to get their hands on you rather than kill you. Even your own feelings are confused on that point; you know they're after you, but the major reason you think they want you dead is because of your vision. Right?"

"Well, what about that? I saw my death."

"You've seen a lot of things that could easily be symbolic. The bells, the open grave, and the headstone. Even the murmur of many voices. All of them are or could be symbols of death; the trappings of a funeral and burial."

"So?"

"So . . . maybe that's what you were really seeing, Sarah. The trappings. The *appearance* of death—of your death."

"I still don't—"

"Okay, suppose with me for a minute. Suppose that fire at your house was intended to be a—pardon the pun—smoke screen. Suppose the plan was to get you out before police and firemen arrived, to just take you. Officials arrive, find your house burning, maybe even find a female body in the ruins and, presto, Sarah Gallagher is dead—and nobody's looking for her."

"Then why didn't it work out that way?"

"I don't know. The fire spread too fast, maybe. The neighbors gathered too quickly. The dream—vision—you had before the fire made you too wary to be caught. Whatever the reason, they failed. But maybe what they failed at was taking you rather than killing you."

"That's a pretty big leap," she said slowly.

"Yeah, I know. But it bothers me that they haven't tried to arrange a little car crash for us—especially if they really did send those damned flowers. If they did, they pretty much had to be following us all the way from Chicago; we know damned well they were on us all the way *to* Chicago. That's a lot of miles, and faking an accident wouldn't have been hard. At these speeds, just bumping another car can be a one-way ticket to the morgue. So why haven't they at least tried?"

"Unless they don't want me dead," she finished.

Tucker nodded. "Unless they don't want you dead."

Sarah thought about it, then shook her head. "But what about Margo? That little *accident* was meant to be deadly, and you said they were probably after me."

"I haven't quite figured that out yet," he admitted. "But that's just one instance where it appears that death was clearly the intent—all the rest of the evidence is going the other way."

She tried to get her thoughts organized, something that was getting harder to do. Whether it was her interrupted sleep last night, the hasty flight from the hotel, or just stress and exhaustion over the whole frightening business, Sarah was having a difficult time thinking clearly.

"Are you saying you think some of the psychics who were supposedly killed really weren't?"

"When some of the newer information came in this morning, I noticed that in at least a third of those cases, either no body was found or else what was found was . . . pretty messed up. A lot of burn victims from house fires, car and plane crashes, things like that. Drownings where the body had . . . been in the water a long time. Identification was sketchy and often depended on the location of the bodies or the fact that nobody asked questions. If a man or woman lives alone and a body is found in their house or car; if that person is missing; if the body is the right sex, roughly the right size and age, wearing the missing person's clothing or jewelry—in a lot of cases, the assumption is made. And even when identification was made through so-called positive means, as in dental records or even DNA . . . well, records can be switched. I'd say that would probably be child's play for people with police officers in their pockets."

"You mean . . . innocent people might have been killed just to provide bodies?" That belated realization hit her hard.

"If the stakes are high enough, why not?"

"My God."

Tucker looked at her quickly. "I'm sorry."

She wondered vaguely what he'd heard in her voice,

but all she said was, "Do you think that if we checked the Richmond newspapers for the days after the fire, we might read that the body of a woman was found dumped somewhere? A woman about thirty, five four, a hundred and five pounds, maybe with dark, reddish hair? A woman who might have been mistaken for me in the right circumstances?"

"I don't know."

"Can we check?"

He sent her another quick glance. "Sarah, it isn't your fault. If some other woman died . . . blame them, not yourself."

"I'd like to know," she said steadily. "I need to know."

"Why? What good would it do?"

Sarah couldn't tell him that. She only knew that it was a question she had to have answered. But all she said was, "It would be another piece of information, wouldn't it? Another bit of evidence that—that we're guessing right. You said yourself we need to know all we can."

"I don't think that's your reason."

"It's reason enough." She waited through several moments of silence, then prompted, "Tucker?"

"All right. When we get to Syracuse, I'll see what I can find out. Just remember that Richmond is a big city. People die there. None of those deaths has to be connected to you."

She didn't respond to that, but said instead, "If the other side really is taking some of the psychics reported dead as well as those reported missing, what are they doing with them? What do they want with me?"

"If the object was to kill you, then you might pose a threat to them. If getting their hands on you and other psychics is the object, then obviously you have some kind of value to them. They want or need to use you somehow."

"How? To buy lottery tickets? To predict how the stock market's going to go in the months and years ahead?"

"Maybe. But among the supposedly dead and definitely missing psychics I've listed so far are those who can't predict the future any more than I can. Psychics whose gifts are along other lines. People with telepathy, telekinesis, the ability to supposedly channel the dead or sense spirits or start fires, or take pictures with the mind. It really runs the gamut."

"Then I can't see how there could be a single answer to this." Sarah rubbed her forehead fretfully. "It doesn't make any sense."

He was watching her more closely than she had realized. "Is the pressure building again?"

She thought about it, then shook her head. "No, not really. I'm just . . . having a little trouble thinking clearly." *And, of course, I'm scared half out of my mind.*

Tucker frowned, but said, "They must think they can gain something. I can think of a dozen scams where a medium or fire starter would come in handy."

She was surprised. "Scams?"

"Sure. A good medium can do a pretty brisk business, and arson can be immensely profitable."

"Yes, but . . . A fake medium could probably do okay,

especially given the apparent resources of the other side. And as for fire starters, all it takes to start a fire is a match."

"A match can also leave evidence of arson. Even so, to be honest, this doesn't feel like a for-profit thing to me. It's just too damned big, too complicated. And too costly. The payoff has to be big, maybe bigger than we can imagine. I just don't see that coming from sideshow mediums or burning buildings."

"So we still don't know what's going on."

He glanced at her. "We know what. Or part of what. We just don't know why."

"And all we can do is talk in circles." Sarah resisted the urge to rub her forehead again. *You must think you're going to get a pretty good book out of all this, Tucker, to stick with me this long.*

"We're putting the pieces together, Sarah. You have to admit, we know—or think we know—a lot more than we did a week ago."

"For all the good it does us."

"You're tired." His voice gentled. "It's hard for you to see that we are making progress. But we are. And we'll do even better once we make contact with another psychic."

I can't afford to be tired. You said it yourself. But all she said aloud was, "Assuming we pick the right psychic, and not one who belongs to the other side."

"You'll know if we're right."

"Will I?"

"I believe you will."

"Suppose I don't. Suppose I can't tell an enemy from a friend. What then?" As hard as she tried, she couldn't steady her shaking voice.

"Then we'll think of something else." His voice was calm, but there was an underlying note of tension.

"And keep running."

"We can run as long as it takes."

Sarah rubbed her cold hands together. They always seemed to be cold now. Nerves, she supposed. "How long are you prepared to put your life on hold, Tucker?"

"I told you. As long as it takes."

Only until October. One way or another, we'll stop running then.

But all she said was, "Whether they want me dead or not, we know they can kill; if you get in their way . . ."

"I intend to get in their way. And I'm betting you're stronger than they suspect you are. I'm betting on you."

"Are you willing to bet your life on me?"

Without looking at her, Tucker replied flatly, "I already have, Sarah."

There was really nothing she could say to that.

———

Beyond the window where he stood, Duran could see most of downtown Syracuse. He didn't think much of it. Not that he considered the matter with any undue interest. His attention was directed toward a specific building barely a block away, another hotel. It was almost nine o'clock on Tuesday night, and the hotel was flooded with light.

The footsteps behind him were inaudible, but he heard them. "Well? Have they checked in?"

"Yes, sir. Same as before, a junior suite. The door opens into the parlor, where Mackenzie will be."

"Where we assume Mackenzie will be," Duran corrected gently.

"Yes, sir."

Duran turned away from the window. "What does Astrid say?"

"That Gallagher is blocking—probably unconsciously."

"I wonder if she's telling the truth," Duran mused, not a question so much as thoughtful speculation.

Varden did not venture a response, though a faint frown pulled at his brows.

Duran saw it. "You think she wouldn't lie to us?"

"She was brought over ten years ago. If we can't trust her . . ."

"Yes. If we can't trust her." Duran smiled, something ironic in the expression.

Varden waited a moment, then said, "It is Astrid's opinion that Gallagher is on the edge of understanding at least some of what she's capable of."

"I can see that for myself without benefit of a psychic's abilities," Duran said, dry now.

"Yes, sir." This time, Varden waited patiently in silence.

Duran looked absently back toward the window for a moment, his pale eyes distant. When he returned his attention to his lieutenant, his voice became brisk. "Is Mason ready for them?"

"Yes, sir."

"He understands what I want him to do?"

"Yes, sir."

"Good." Duran made a slight gesture of dismissal. "See that he follows his instructions precisely."

Varden nodded a reply and left the room.

Duran returned to the window. This time, his gaze roved, studying the lights of various buildings as if searching for a particular one. Following the neatly laid-out streets, scanning the dark patches of parks and woods. Softly, as if to someone he expected to hear his voice, he said, "I feel you out there. Nearby. You think you can save her. You think you can save them all. Sometimes . . . you even think you can save me."

After a moment, he laughed very quietly, a sound that held little amusement.

————————

Sarah came awake suddenly, heart pounding. She was sitting up in bed, her hands reaching out for . . . something. Someone. She tried to recall her dreams, but all she remembered was the uneasy sensation of something missing. Something wrong.

A glance at the bright display of the clock radio on her nightstand told her it was just after midnight, which meant she had been asleep only a couple of hours. The pressure inside her head was . . . different. And she didn't have a clue what that meant.

The almost-closed connecting door to the parlor showed a sliver of light, so Tucker was obviously still up. Feeling too restless to attempt sleep again so soon after waking, Sarah slid out of the big bed. She turned on the lamp and blinked a moment in the light, then found and shrugged into the thick robe provided by the hotel.

When she went into the parlor, it was to find Tucker seated at the small desk frowning at his laptop. But he looked up alertly as soon as she came in.

"What is it?"

Sarah shook her head and sat down on the couch. "Nothing. I just can't sleep. Have you found anything?"

He hesitated and then, reluctantly, said, "There was a woman's body found in Richmond a couple of days after the fire."

Sarah felt her throat tighten up, but said steadily, "A body that could have been mistaken for me?"

"The police description is of a white female, age thirty, five foot four, about a hundred and five pounds, dark hair, brown eyes. The ME thinks she died sometime last Wednesday. The day of the fire."

"How was she killed?"

Again, Tucker hesitated. "Sarah—"

"How was she killed?"

"Smoke inhalation—though there were no burns on her body and she was found in a shallow grave in an empty lot. Some kids playing baseball found her there."

Sarah swallowed to fight the queasy sensation rising in her throat. "Kids. Great. What do the police think?"

"Reading between the lines of the reports, they don't know what to think. The woman lived alone; her neighbors claim nothing unusual happened around the time she must have died. The man she was dating has a solid alibi, and nobody thinks he did it anyway; he was, according to everyone who knew them, devoted to her. So far, they haven't found any enemies. She was not sexually assaulted, and was apparently laid out in the grave with some care, identification by her side. No sign that she fought or even struggled; the ME thinks she may have been asleep when the smoke got her; he found slight traces of a sedative in her body."

If Tucker thought Sarah found that last a comfort, he was wrong.

"What was her name?"

"Sarah, let it go."

She drew a breath. "What was her name?"

"Jennifer Healy."

Sarah repeated the name in a whisper, committing it to memory. She was reasonably sure the police would never solve the murder of Jennifer Healy. Reasonably sure that the media would accord the crime scant attention. Reasonably sure that in time the boyfriend would get on with his life and the friends would think of her less and less. Reasonably sure that the people responsible for her death had already wiped her from their minds.

But Sarah was certain that she, at least, would never forget.

"There's no way to be sure they intended to use her body," Tucker pointed out reasonably. "She could have been the victim of a garden-variety killer who was motivated by reasons we'll never know and wouldn't understand if we did."

"Right."

"And even if she did die just to give them a body they could use, it isn't your fault. There's nothing you could have done to prevent her death."

Sarah leaned her head back and closed her eyes, a weariness far more emotional than physical washing over her. "You know, when all this started, I thought it just affected me, that I was the target, the only one in danger. It never occurred to me that anyone else might get hurt because of me. But then there was Margo, in the wrong place at the wrong time. And now this poor woman, this woman I never even met. This woman who'll never marry, never have children, never grow old. Because of me. Who else is going to be killed or threatened with death because I got hit on the head and turned into a valuable freak?"

Tucker hesitated for only a moment before leaving the desk and coming to sit beside her on the couch. She was alone again, locked inside herself where it was cold and bleak, and he couldn't just leave her there.

"Sarah, you are not a freak." He reached over to cover the restless fingers knotted together in her lap. They were cold and stiff. "And this is not your fault."

"No?" Her eyes remained closed, her face still. "I keep thinking . . . there must have been a point somewhere along the way where I could have—should have—made a different choice. A different decision. And that would have changed everything. But then I remember that all this is fate. Destiny."

She opened her eyes then, raised her head and turned

it to look at him. Her eyes were darker than eyes should ever be, the pupils wide and black and empty. And her voice was curiously toneless, dull. "This is where I have to be. Where I'm supposed to be. You're who I'm supposed to be with. And everything that has happened was meant to happen just as it did. It was all . . . planned out for me a long time ago. So why don't I just accept that?"

"I don't believe our lives are mapped out for us," he reminded her quietly.

She looked at him a moment longer, those great dark eyes unblinking. "Then maybe I could have saved Jennifer Healy."

"No. That was a choice *they* made—not you. There was nothing you could have done, Sarah."

"All right." She didn't sound convinced so much as weary, and turned her head away to look vaguely across the room. "Do you— Have you found any new or useful information about them or what they've been doing? Anything helpful?"

For an instant, Tucker considered not letting her change the subject, but in the end he accepted the new one. He could only push so much, insist so often, before she would withdraw into some place where he'd never be able to reach her. He dared not risk that.

Deliberately, he took his hand off hers and leaned back away from her just a bit. "More of the same. Supposedly dead and missing psychics in two more major cities."

"Then . . . there's no safe place?"

"Doesn't look like it. Not in the major cities. Not in this country anyway."

Surprised, and more unnerved than she had yet been, she said, "You don't think this is worldwide?"

Tucker shrugged. "There's no way to know, really. I can tap into a few data sources worldwide, but nothing specific enough to answer that question, at least not without drawing attention to myself. It's difficult enough to stay under the radar here; the government is always looking for computer hackers, as threats *and* as assets. They monitor us a lot more closely than the average citizen realizes."

"Great. Something else to be paranoid about."

"We live in dangerous times. And . . . there were some pretty damned intrusive laws passed after the towers fell."

It was clear he took exception to at least some of those laws, and Sarah hoped they'd have a chance to sit and discuss it all. She really did hope they'd have that time.

But for now, there were more imperative things to discuss.

"So you don't know if this thing could be worldwide. If it is . . ."

"If it is," he said steadily, "we'll find out eventually. For now, we've got all we can handle."

"More than we can handle."

"We're doing okay. We're still alive and on the loose." He tried to sound positive and wasn't at all sure he'd pulled it off.

"Are we? Or are we just rats in a maze?"

He frowned slightly. "Is that what you feel?"

"Stop asking me what I feel."

"I can't do that, Sarah. Your feelings can guide us." Without giving her a chance to argue with him, he repeated, "Do you feel we're rats in a maze? Honestly feel that? Or is it frustration talking?"

Sarah got up from the couch and went over to the window, where the partially drawn drapes offered only a narrow piece of the night. She stood there looking out, and for a long time she didn't say anything.

Tucker waited patiently.

Finally, tensely, she said, "What you don't seem to understand is that sometimes . . . usually . . . I can't tell the difference. A vision is a very clear-cut thing, no matter how you choose to interpret it. But impulses, hunches, feelings . . . these damned voices in my head . . . how do I know what they mean? How can I tell? Is it just my fears talking to me? My imagination working overtime? Or is there a truer voice I should be listening to?"

"You won't know unless you listen."

"That's easy for you to say."

"Yes, it is," he agreed. "I'm not the one who has to sort through all the background noise you'll hear. But I'll help all I can, Sarah. Just tell me how to do that."

"I don't know how. I don't even know that."

After a moment, Tucker got up and joined her at the window. "Maybe we're both demanding too much too fast from you. Sarah, I would never do anything to hurt you. I hope you know that."

"I know you have only the best of intentions," she murmured.

There was no particular emotion in her voice, but Tucker nevertheless felt there was something ironic in her remark, and it made him defensive. "No matter what they say about the road to hell, we're not moving in that direction, Sarah, I promise you."

"You should stop making promises." She turned her head suddenly to look at him out of those too-dark eyes. "Your track record with them isn't very good."

He stiffened. "No?"

"No. Lydia would know that, wouldn't she?"

He felt a chill that went clear down to his bones, and gazing into her eyes he had the abrupt and incredibly unsettling sense of something alien. Something . . . unnatural.

She knew. She knew it all.

ELEVEN

Sarah's mouth curved in a faint, curiously mocking smile. "So we're not moving toward hell, huh? Then why do you look at me as though I might have been spawned there?"

"Sarah—"

"Oh, don't worry about it, Tucker. I'm not evil. I'm just not normal."

He knew—he *knew*—she had deliberately reached into his head and his nightmares in order to keep him at a distance. As coolly as any surgeon, she had slipped her scalpel into him with full knowledge of the effect it would cause, and now she studied him with calm assessment, her eyes distant.

This was what he got for pushing her. Sarah was

pushing back. And she was a lot stronger than either of them had given her credit for.

"I don't believe you're evil. And normal is what you get used to," he managed.

"Right."

He watched her move away from the window toward the doorway to the bedroom and made no effort to stop her. He wanted to. He wanted to call her back or go after her, to try to close the very real distance between them. But he couldn't.

Sarah had discovered his Achilles' heel, and if only to protect herself when he pushed and keep him out, she had learned how to use the knowledge against him. Until he could bring himself to face his demons, he had no defense against that tactic.

She paused at the door and looked back at him. As if nothing had happened, she said, "The psychic we're going to try to approach tomorrow—what did you say his name was?"

"Mason," Tucker replied automatically. "Neil Mason."

She nodded. "Good night, Tucker."

"Good night, Sarah."

———

Patty Lowell looked out her kitchen window for the fourth time in half an hour, just to reassure herself that Brandon was still out there playing in the sandbox with his dinosaurs, safe in their fenced backyard. He was, and she stood there for a few moments watching him before returning to her baking. It wasn't like her to be a nervous mother, but this was the third morning in a row that her five-year-old had awakened asking her anxiously if they could hide from the bad men.

Adam thought she was crazy, but Patty was convinced that Brandon had a special gift. He had always been an intensely sensitive child, filled with wordless terrors and worries, but now that his language skills were better developed, he was able to communicate his thoughts and fears more clearly than he had as an anxious toddler.

Poor little Brandon was frequently afraid. He didn't like the dark, or closets, or scary movies, and there was one place in the upstairs hallway of their old house that upset him terribly. *"There's a lady, Mommy. She keeps crying."* That was all Patty could get out of him. She'd never believed in ghosts, but she now gave that particular spot a wide berth.

Brandon had also startled her more than once by carrying on casual conversations with "the people." The people were not, apparently, connected to this house, since he talked to them on the playground and at his cousins' house and even at the Atlanta church where she took him to Sunday school. And they didn't seem to be threatening people, since Brandon displayed no anxiety at all about them.

But the flesh-and-blood people around him were beginning to notice. Her sister had made a remark just the other day about Brandon and his imaginary friends. And some of his little friends were beginning to tease him. Brandon, always a shy child with a mostly solitary nature, was becoming reluctant to get out of sight of his mother.

Adam said she was spoiling him, catering to his "childish fears and overactive imagination" by sticking close to him, but Patty didn't care. She was worried. Brandon was convinced that the "bad men" were coming to take him away, and it frightened him so much that it frightened her even more.

He could never tell her who these bad men were or even what they looked like, and since Patty's questions had only upset him further, she had stopped asking. Just bad men, was all he knew or could say. Bad men in the dark.

That thought sent Patty back to the window. And as soon as she looked out, her throat closed up and shards of ice stabbed at her heart.

"Brandon?"

She rushed out the back door, staring at the empty sandbox and then looking wildly around the backyard. The gate was still closed; she could see the lock still fastened. But Brandon was nowhere to be seen.

"Brandon!"

———

Sarah gazed out the car window and murmured, "A nice, normal little house in a nice, normal little neighborhood. I guess Neil Mason's neighbors don't know he's psychic."

"Or don't care," Tucker said.

"If they know—they care," Sarah said out of bitter experience.

The Jeep was parked across the street and half a block down, where they could look at the house without attracting undue attention. The neighborhood was quiet on this Wednesday morning, and so far they had seen no sign of life at Neil Mason's house.

"Anything?" Tucker asked, even more wary after their tense standoff of the night before.

Sarah wanted to snap at him to stop pushing her, but she was all too aware that this time he was right to do so. She studied the rather plain but pleasant two-story house, and hesitantly tried to "listen" to what her senses might attempt to tell her.

She felt . . . odd. The pressure she had been so conscious of was all but gone, only a whisper of it remaining. And what she heard was only a whisper, so quiet and distant that focusing on it was like straining to hear someone breathing on the other side of a vast room.

. . . he knows . . . he knows . . . he knows you're coming. He knows what they want of you. He has the answers you need. He knows . . .

"He knows." Sarah was hardly aware of speaking aloud.

"Knows what?"

The whisper faded to silence, and Sarah turned her head to meet Tucker's guarded gaze. "He knows we're coming."

"Is he on our side? Or with them?"

"I don't know."

After a moment, Tucker nodded. He opened the storage compartment between the Jeep's bucket seats, took out his automatic, and leaned forward to place it inside his belt at the small of his back. His jacket covered the gun so that its presence was hidden.

"Okay. Let's go find out."

Sarah was reluctant to leave the vehicle, where there was at least the illusion of safety, but she knew they had no choice. She got out and walked with Tucker across the street. All the way across and up the walkway, she tried to listen, but heard nothing. She was dimly surprised, when they reached the porch, that Tucker had to ring the bell. It bothered her somehow, though the feeling was no more than vague disturbance.

The man who opened the door was big. That was the first impression. Easily six and a half feet tall with shoulders to match, he had the appearance of a man of immense physical strength, even though approaching middle age had given him a belly that his belt rode beneath and the fleshy look of indulgence around the once-clean jawline of his rugged face.

The second impression Sarah got was that he wasn't nearly as happy to see them as his smile indicated.

"Hello." His eyes tracked past Tucker and fixed on Sarah. They were blue and very bright. "Hello, Sarah."

"Hello, Neil." Sarah drew a breath, and added, "I recognize you."

"Yes, of course you do," he said matter-of-factly. He stepped back and opened the door wider. "Come in, come in."

Tucker caught Sarah's arm when she would have moved forward. "Recognize him?"

She nodded. "Bits and pieces of my vision keep coming back to me. There were faces. His is one of the faces I saw."

Without letting go of her arm, Tucker looked narrow-eyed at Mason, who stood patiently, smiling, waiting for them to come in. "Do you trust him, Sarah?"

Her smile reminded him oddly of Mason's—the tolerant amusement of a parent for a child. He didn't like it.

"Of course not, Tucker."

"Then we'll find someone else."

"It's all right," she said. "We're safe here. For now."

Tucker released her arm when she started forward again. He didn't like this—all his instincts were screaming at him—but he followed her into the house nevertheless. In this situation, he felt he had to defer to Sarah, to accept her lead. She was the psychic, not him.

Still, he was uneasily aware that her belief in fate was strong enough to place them both in danger; Sarah was, he thought, perfectly capable of walking into a house she knew was dangerous only because she was utterly sure fate intended her to be there. That was one reason he continued to try to convince her that her choices could determine her own future—though he didn't flatter himself that he'd made much headway.

Sarah's blind spot was her belief in destiny, and until she could see past that, she was so vulnerable it was terrifying.

So Tucker walked into Neil Mason's house with all his senses wide open, as alert to possible danger as he'd ever been in his life. Even so, the first few minutes seemed to be designed to put him at his ease. Mason showed them into a pleasant living room and invited them to sit down, then went away briskly to fetch coffee. Music played softly in the background, unobtrusive but soothing. A fire crackled brightly in the rock fireplace, dispelling the chill of the morning here at the end of September.

It was all very . . . pleasant. Very ordinary.

It made Tucker extremely wary.

"If you don't trust him," he said to Sarah, "then why are we here? There are other psychics we can try, including two more right here in Syracuse." He stood near the leather couch watching her move restlessly around the room.

Sarah paused to scan the titles of some books on shelves near the fireplace and answered him in an absent tone. "It's important that we talk to him."

"Why?"

"Because he knows."

Tucker drew a breath and held on to his patience. He thought that Sarah was being deliberately vague and uninformative, and it bothered him. She claimed that trust was not an issue with them, yet ever since the lake he'd had the feeling that she knew more about this situation than she was willing to say; if it wasn't a lack of trust that kept her silent, then what?

"Knows what, Sarah? You said he knew we were coming here. Is that all?"

"No." She moved back to the fireplace and looked at the flames for a moment, then lifted her gaze to meet his. "He knows why they're after me."

Tucker refused to get too excited. "Will he tell us?"

She tilted her head a little as though listening to a

distant voice. "I don't know. Probably not." Her reply was matter-of-fact.

"And you still don't know if he's with the other side?"

"No. But leave this to me, Tucker. I have to handle him my own way. It's important."

Before Tucker could say anything else, Mason returned with a tray and the opportunity was lost. But Sarah had told him nothing to reassure him, so Tucker refused coffee and remained on his feet when Sarah came over to sit on a chair across from the couch. He moved to where she had been standing at the fireplace and turned his back to the flames so he could keep an eye on Mason as well as have a clear view of the door and windows.

"He's very cautious," Mason said to Sarah, handing her a cup of coffee and sitting down on the couch.

"He has reason to be. We both do."

"I imagine so. But I'm harmless. You might reassure him of that."

Sarah smiled. "Today, he's a guard. And a guard should always be wary."

Tucker elected to remain silent, as much as he disliked being discussed as though he'd left the room. He leaned his shoulders back against the mantel, crossed his arms, and watched them. And within a very few minutes, it occurred to him that what he was seeing was a performance where each word and gesture was both meticulous and deliberate. A dance where each knew the steps and the music, and where only one would remain standing when it was all over.

"How did you choose me?" Mason sipped his coffee.

Sarah set her cup on the coffee table untasted. "We have a list of surviving psychics in this general area. You were at the top."

Mason smiled at her, that curiously tolerant smile of a parent for a child, a master for a neophyte. "Ah. Then you didn't hear me calling to you?"

"No." Sarah appeared undisturbed by this. "Was I supposed to?"

"Well . . . if your abilities are genuine, I would have thought . . . However, it's no matter. You're here. Where you were supposed to be."

This time, Tucker had to bite his tongue to remain silent.

"Was I supposed to be here?" Sarah was innocently surprised.

Mason's smile widened. "Of course. You must know that. The visions and dreams, the voices in your head—they must have told you."

"Destiny." Sarah nodded thoughtfully.

"Exactly."

"So those are the voices I should listen to? The ones whispering that what must be—is?"

Sober now, Mason nodded. "Those are the truest voices, Sarah. It's why you—we—hear them the clearest."

"Then I can change nothing I foresee?"

He hesitated, those bright blue eyes searching her face. Then he shrugged almost offhandedly. "There is a difference between prediction and prophecy. When you see what is fated to happen, it will. No matter what you or anyone does to try and change it. That is prophecy. But you may also see a possible outcome in a given situation, and that may be influenced by the actions and choices of yourself and those around you. That is prediction."

"How can I tell the difference?"

"With practice. They feel different."

Sarah didn't appear to find that response inadequate; she merely nodded and changed the subject. Abruptly. "So which is of the greatest value—prediction or prophecy?"

For the first time, Mason seemed caught off guard. "I—don't understand, Sarah."

"Of course you do." Sarah smiled. "It's a simple question. With a very simple answer. Why are my abilities important, Neil? Because I can make predictions? Or prophecies?"

His smile was gone and his eyes were not nearly so bright. But he replied readily enough. "Each has its own sort of value."

"Ah. And they have a use for both?"

Mason leaned back in his chair suddenly, and Tucker had the distinct feeling it was because he needed to put distance between himself and Sarah. And there was, now, something wary in his eyes.

"They? Who are you talking about, Sarah?"

"The other side." Her voice was casual, almost indifferent.

"Other side? You talk as if there's a battle going on."

"Isn't there? Isn't it very simply a battle—between good and evil?"

Mason frowned. "Nothing is simple. And nothing is purely good, or purely bad."

"I think some things are simple. Some truths."

"For instance?" He was a bit impatient now.

"For instance, the truth that children abducted from their families is an evil thing. Wouldn't you agree with that?"

"I suppose so."

"And the truth that anything done to protect them—anything at all—is a good thing."

Slowly, Mason said, "There are always limits."

"In protecting children? I don't think so."

"Life always gives us limits," he insisted. "We can only do . . . so much. Be responsible for so much."

"So where do we draw the line?" She looked at Mason with an unblinking intensity that disturbed Tucker, and he was standing several feet away; he could only imagine how fierce those too-dark eyes appeared to Mason. But the older man didn't flinch or look away from her.

"What do you mean?"

"I mean, when do we decide we've done enough? When we've saved one child? Two? All of them? When we've defeated the people who take them?"

"Shouldn't we leave that to the police?" he suggested. "They're the best equipped to deal with . . . crimes."

"Not crimes against humanity."

Mason smiled. "Is that what we're talking about?"

"Oh, I'd say so. Children abducted, disappearing never to return. Adults killed—or supposedly killed. Because what they can do is important to someone. So they're taken away from their homes and families, from the people who love them. From their lives."

"Taken? Taken where?"

"You tell me."

"I?" He laughed quietly. "How would I know?"

"Because you were taken. Once." Her head tilted to one side in that listening posture. "A long time ago, I think."

Tucker felt his fingers close over the gun at the small of his back before he was even aware of moving. But he remained still, gripping the pistol but not drawing it. His eyes never left Mason's slowly whitening face.

Mason drew a breath as if he needed one, then said lightly, "I don't know what you're talking about, Sarah."

"Yes, you do. What is it they want you to do to me, Neil? Why are you trying so hard to crawl inside my head?"

Tucker glanced at her quickly, realizing for the first time that something else had been going on far beneath— or above—the level of his own awareness. Something deadly. Sarah's face was as pale as Mason's and held the taut look of someone concentrating intensely. Or some- one in pain.

"I only want to help you, Sarah," Mason said softly.

"You want to help them. You have to help them."

"I don't know who you're talking about."

"Them. The other side."

"There is no mysterious enemy, Sarah. Do you hear me? No battle. Just your imagination. Your fears. Your inexperience."

"Stop it," Tucker said.

Neither of them looked at him.

In a gentle tone, Mason said, "I can help you. I can teach you how to use your abilities, how to protect yourself."

"I'm protecting myself now." Her voice was strained but steady.

"But look what it's taking out of you. I can show you a better way, Sarah. I can make it less painful for you."

"Is that what *they* taught you?"

"What does it matter who taught me? I can teach you. I can make the pain go away."

"And keep me alive?"

"Of course."

"And what's the price, Neil? What did you sell them to keep yourself alive?"

"Isn't life worth any price?"

"No. Not any price."

"That's what you think now. But one day—soon— you'll discover you're wrong. Life is worth whatever you have to pay for it, Sarah. Life is worth any price."

"What did it cost you?"

He smiled suddenly. "What if I said my soul?"

"Then I'd say you paid too much," she whispered.

"I said *stop* it." Tucker crossed to Sarah's chair in two long steps and grasped her arm, holding the pistol pointed at Mason with his other hand. "Sarah, we're leaving."

She rose to her feet readily enough, but her gaze remained locked with Mason's and she was trembling.

In a conversational tone, Mason said, "Go on running if you have to. But it's no use, Sarah, you know that. They'll win. They always win."

"You mean the mysterious enemy that doesn't exist?" Her voice was still only a whisper.

His mouth twisted. "Yeah. Them."

"I'm sorry," she said.

Mason looked away suddenly. "So am I. Oh, put the gun away, Mackenzie. You have nothing to fear from me. Go on, get her out of here."

Tucker got her out of there. But he didn't take Mason's word for it that he was no threat, keeping the gun in hand until he and Sarah safely reached the street. He was wary even then, half-expecting long black cars to be waiting for them out there. But the neighborhood looked as quiet as before.

He put Sarah in the passenger side of the Jeep, one glance at her face telling him that she was in bad shape. She was so pale that her skin had a bluish cast, and her too-dark eyes were enormous and unseeing, the pupils so dilated that only a rim of gold showed around them. He got a blanket from the backseat and covered her because she was shaking so violently, then quickly got in the driver's seat and got the engine and heat going. He also didn't waste any time in driving away from Mason's house.

"Sarah, are you all right?"

She didn't move, didn't look at him.

"Sarah? Goddammit, say something or I'm taking you straight to the nearest hospital."

As if the effort demanded was almost too much, she turned her head and looked at him then, and her voice was whispery when she said, "They couldn't help me. The doctors. They wouldn't know what was wrong. I just need . . . to rest. Sleep. I'll be fine after I sleep."

He wasn't so sure about that, but in any case he had to ask, "What the hell went on back there?"

"It was . . . a skirmish."

"A *skirmish*? Jesus, Sarah . . ."

"Just a skirmish," she insisted wearily. "He wasn't even one of them, really. He was a tool they tried to use against me. A . . . pale echo of what they are. And even so, as ineffective as he is compared to them . . . look what it did to me to fight him. Look what it cost me just to hold my own with one of their tools."

"It was your first . . . skirmish," he reminded her. "You'll be better at it next time."

A little sound escaped Sarah, not a laugh or a cry but something in between. "No, I won't. I can't do that again."

"Sarah—"

"I can't. You don't know what it's like. You don't know what it does to me."

Tucker was beginning to understand but nevertheless said, "What was all that about kids?"

"I wanted to find out if he knew," she murmured.

"Knew what?"

"That they'd taken another child. Early this morning."

"How do you know?"

Starkly, her voice full of horror, Sarah said, "I heard him scream. In my mind."

Tucker nearly pulled off the road, every instinct urging him to put his arms around Sarah and offer some kind of comfort. But he kept driving. For one thing, something in her posture warned him that right now she didn't want to be touched by anyone. And since she had kept from him this knowledge of another abducted child, he was even more sure that she especially didn't want to be touched by him.

But he could, and did, change the subject to what he thought was a lesser horror. "You said that Mason was trying to get into your head—why?"

"To . . . convert me. To try to make me think the way they want me to."

"Which is?"

"That I can't fight them and win. That they'll always be stronger. That I already belong to them. That I'm . . . destined to lose."

Tucker glanced at her quickly, then turned his attention back to the road ahead of them. "But he failed."

"He didn't get inside my head."

"Did you get inside his?"

Sarah was quiet for a moment, then said, "Not enough to help us."

Tucker sent her another glance, this one a bit hard. More secrets. "What are you not telling me?"

"Nothing that matters."

"On a need-to-know basis, I think I need to know."

Again, she was silent, minutes passing before she finally said, in a curiously hollow voice, "It only matters to me. I know something I didn't know before. I know what it will cost me to survive if they get their hands on me. And it's not a price I want to pay."

"What do you mean?"

"I mean that I looked inside Mason's head, inside *him*, and there was nothing there."

"I don't—"

"He was telling the truth, Tucker. He did pay a high price for life. He paid with his soul."

———

Neil Mason sat there on the couch for some time after Gallagher and Mackenzie left and gazed at nothing. He was a little tired. More than a little, if the truth be told. He lifted one hand, holding it out in front of him and, dispassionately, watched it shake.

I'm getting too old for this. Hell, I was always too old for this.

His hand fell to rest on his thigh, and he looked around the living room almost curiously. Had it been worth it? Funny that he hadn't asked himself before. Hadn't been able to, maybe. Afraid of the answer, probably.

The phone rang, and Mason rose to get the portable from its place out in the hall. "Hello?" Idly, he walked back into the living room.

"Report."

That cool, incongruously pleasant voice had the usual

effect of removing the solid bone and cartilage from his knees, and Mason sat down abruptly in the chair Sarah Gallagher had occupied. *God, how did I let him do this to me?*

"I have nothing to report," he said formally.

"Then you have something to explain."

"She's stronger than I was told. Much stronger." *Maybe stronger than you knew, you son of a bitch.* "And smarter. She managed to block me very effectively."

"And the drug?"

"She never touched the coffee."

"You should have put it in something else."

Mason smiled, glad he was not visible to the other man. "When I offered coffee, she accepted. Took the cup—and set it down. She wouldn't have tasted anything I gave her."

"What made her suspicious of you?"

"Oh, I don't know. Unless it was the fact that her abilities are just about the best I've ever encountered. Lots of raw talent there."

There was a short silence. Mason waited patiently.

"I see. Is she aware of her own potential?"

"I'd say not. Still scared of it. And that says something, you know. Even scared, she did pretty damn good. When she gets her feet under her, she won't be a tool you can use. She'll be a weapon. If, that is, she's brought over by then."

"And how long do you estimate we have before she . . . gets her feet under her?"

"Hard to say. If the status remains quo, maybe a week

or two. If you keep her rattled and off balance, maybe longer. On the other hand, she's awfully close to the edge now. Push her the wrong way and that weapon won't be yours—it'll be hers. And she'll be out of your reach for good."

There was a soft click, and then the dial tone.

Mason turned off his portable phone and set it on the coffee table. Half to himself, he muttered, "Don't ask if you don't want to know."

Then he sat there looking absently around his pleasant living room and waited for them to come for him.

———

"A tool may fail even in the hand of a master," Varden said.

Duran turned from the window and gave him a look that warned him not to bother sucking up, but all he said was, "Bring Mason in."

"Yes, sir." Not making a second mistake, Varden left.

———

She had gone to sleep with the suddenness of an exhausted child just moments after telling him that Mason had sold his soul for life, and Tucker let her sleep. He needed to concentrate on getting them out of Syracuse, and he needed to think.

There was a lot to think about, not the least of which was Sarah's clearly expanding abilities. She had begun by having visions of the future, but unlike any precognitive psychic Tucker had ever heard of, she was also, at the very least, telepathic to some extent. And that was becoming more obvious as time passed. Last night she had accused him of failing to keep his promises and had cited a broken promise to Lydia—which she could only have known by looking into his own mind telepathically. Or reaching across distance and possibly time to look into Lydia's mind, as she had appeared to do once before.

Lydia. Jesus Christ.

He pushed that away, concentrating on what Sarah had done this morning. She had, she said, heard the mental scream of a child being abducted—and she had managed to hide her shock and distress from him. And as for Neil Mason, she had somehow managed to block his efforts to influence her telepathically. And she had looked inside him to find nothing.

He did pay a high price for life. He paid with his soul.

Tucker hoped she hadn't meant that literally. He really hoped so. He wasn't at all sure he believed that some evil entity could capture a soul—or even take one in payment for . . . anything.

No, surely she hadn't meant it literally. She'd meant it the way anyone would, using the phrase as a yardstick to measure how badly someone could want something. Mason willing to sell his soul for life meant simply that he was willing to give up just about everything else that mattered to him in order to live.

That was what she'd meant.

Except that Tucker had a crawly feeling it wasn't. Because the look on Sarah's face when she'd said it wasn't a price she was willing to pay had spoke of something truly terrible. More than the loss of possessions or even a way of life. The loss of a soul.

Literally the loss of a soul.

Which means—what? That we're fighting the devil?

No. No, there was nothing supernatural about the other side. So far, nothing that had been done by them could not be explained logically and rationally. In fact, everything he'd found out about this conspiracy—with the exception of its bizarre focus on psychics—smacked of all-too-human violence, and felonious intentions rather than mystical behavior.

Sure, the other side was or appeared to be all around them—though that perception was probably more paranoid than real. And they did seem to have vast, even limitless resources. But Tucker was still convinced that what lay at the heart of this conspiracy was a very ordinary and even unimaginative (if presently inexplicable) plan to profit in some way. To gain something—power, perhaps.

Even as those thoughts took form in his mind, Tucker was reminded of crossing a graveyard at night as a young boy. Whistling, as boys would, to prove to himself there was nothing wrong. Not looking to the left or the right, and surely to God not looking back, but only straight ahead. Marching briskly. Because there was nothing hiding in the graveyard, nothing about to jump out at him from behind a headstone.

Nothing was going to get him.

Half-consciously, Tucker turned up the Jeep's heater.

They had been on the road about an hour when Sarah

stirred and opened her eyes drowsily. Tucker had been waiting for her to wake and spoke immediately, hoping to use the unexpectedness of the question to tap into that odd well of knowledge she couldn't seem to reach into deliberately—or, at least didn't admit she could.

"Sarah, where are we going?"

"Hmm?" she murmured.

"Where are we going?"

"Holcomb. It's a little town northwest of Bangor."

The answer surprised him, but he tried to keep his voice calm and without any particular inflection. "Why there?"

"Because that's where it ended."

"Ended? Past tense?"

Sarah's eyes opened wider and she turned her head to look at him. For a moment she looked a little lost and more than a little puzzled, the pupils of her eyes wide like a cat's in the dark as they always seemed to be now. Then she shrugged and half-closed her eyes. "I don't know what I meant. A slip of the tongue, probably."

Tucker didn't think so. Her too-dark eyes were veiled against him, and her voice held an evasive note. He wanted to push, to insist that she tell him whatever it was she was holding back. But he couldn't quite bring himself to, not now. She was still exhausted, strained, and even in the delicate bones of her face was the finely honed look of unspeakable stress and pressure; he was afraid that if he pushed her now, forced her now, she would simply break.

So he forced himself to be patient. For now.

"But it is Holcomb we're headed for?"

"I— Yes. Yes, I think so."

Tucker thought about it, then shook his head. "The only city of any size roughly between here and Bangor is Portland."

"But that's on the coast."

"Yeah . . . but from there it'll be less than a hundred and fifty miles to Bangor. We can be in Portland in a few hours, spend the night there. Then go on to Holcomb tomorrow."

"On the last day of September," Sarah said.

"We're safer in large cities, and you're in no shape to drive straight through to Bangor."

"I'm fine."

"No, you're not. You need to sleep about twelve hours."

"I don't want to sleep that long. It wouldn't help anyway."

He glanced at her, then turned his gaze forward once again. "All right. But you do need to rest. And we need to decide if we want to look up another psychic. There are three on the list who presently live in Portland."

"I don't know." Her voice was evasive again. "We're running out of time."

"Maybe we should risk spending a few extra hours in Portland, Sarah. Visit at least one more psychic. If we go on to Holcomb with no idea of what to expect there . . ."

"What if the next psychic is . . . another of their tools? What if they all are?"

That hadn't occurred to Tucker, and he felt a chill. "They can't all be on the other side. Surely . . ."

"No?" Sarah closed her eyes again, and added softly, "But what if they are, Tucker? What if they are?"

TWELVE

Duran glanced back over his shoulder when Varden came into the room, then turned and faced the other man. "I've decided to deal with Mason myself."

"Yes, sir."

"Which means you'll be continuing on to Portland without me."

Varden nodded. "I understand."

"Do you? Then don't fail me, Varden. I want Sarah Gallagher."

"I will get her for you, sir," Varden said coolly.

"Will you? We'll see, Varden. We will see. In the meantime, I'll rejoin you at the next stage of the operation."

"Yes, sir." Alone at last, Varden went to the window for a moment and looked out. But there was nothing much to look at, and he turned back into the room with a faintly irritated shrug.

He was pleased, though. It had worked out better than he could have hoped for. He had time now, and a chance to run the operation the way he wanted, the way it needed to be run.

He picked up the phone and placed a call to a number he knew well. "Astrid. I want you in Portland, immediately."

"You want me?" Her voice was, just faintly, mocking. "Does Duran know about this?"

Varden kept a rein on his temper. "Of course."

"Well, in that case, I'm on my way." Definite mockery now.

Varden allowed the disrespect to pass unchallenged. It hardly mattered, after all. When his plan worked, Astrid would have no doubt at all who was her superior.

And neither would Duran.

———

By four o'clock that afternoon, they were checked into yet another chain hotel in another small suite. Sarah, who had said nothing else after their brief conversation and had at least appeared to sleep all the way to Portland, agreed only reluctantly to eat something before retreating to the bedroom and going to sleep once again. Despite what she'd said about sleep not helping, it seemed her body or mind demanded it.

Tucker checked on her several times during the next few hours, only to find her so deeply asleep that she never even changed position on the bed. That the depth of her sleep bordered on unconsciousness disturbed him, but he was reluctant to force her awake before she was ready. Especially given what lay ahead of them.

He was left with far too many hours alone in which to brood. He tried to occupy himself in searching for and gathering more information about the conspiracy surrounding them, but everything he found was more nebulous confirmation of his beliefs and theories—but no proof whatsoever. He finally turned off the laptop and slouched back in the uncomfortable chair at the desk near the window, staring across the room at the muted MSNBC on television without noticing what had gone on in the world today.

It was maddening that he'd been unable to find a shred of solid proof to confirm what they suspected. Yes, psychics had seemingly died or disappeared, all over the country and for years, yet each instance appeared accidental or at least explicable. There had even been people convicted in abduction cases and put away—and in at least a couple of cases executed—for murders, despite the absence of bodies. As far as the legal system was concerned, each was an isolated incident. Despite all the various databases beginning to connect diverse law enforcement agencies across the country, none had, apparently, noticed any kind of pattern.

There was no evidence of a conspiracy. No evidence, that is, that anyone not involved in this would believe.

Tucker began to feel some sympathy for the conspiracy "nuts" he'd heard about for years, those who insisted that someone else had fired at JFK from the grassy knoll, or that the government was hiding the existence of extra-terrestrials, or that Elvis was alive and well and living in Topeka.

The very idea of yet another vast, inexplicable, and secretive conspiracy sounded so absurd that the tendency was to laugh or shrug it off, or at the very least greet each new conspiracy theory with a roll of the eyes and patent disbelief. You could pile the facts one on top of the other, list a long string of events too similar to be coincidence, and come up with a neat (if bizarre) theory to explain it all—and there was absolutely no concrete evidence to back up your claims.

Even more, there was no explanation, no *reason* you could offer to add weight to the theory. Psychics were being taken. Why? Who was taking them? Where were they being taken?

And—oh, by the way—how come nobody but you noticed them being taken?

For something so vast and long-lived, this thing had left few tracks for anyone to follow and no fingerprints at all. There was no clue as to who was behind it. No clue as to the reasoning or purpose behind it. No evidence other than speculation, and precious little of that.

There was just this growing list of dead and vanished people whose only connection to one another was the fact that each was reputed to have some sort of psychic ability. And in most cases, even that connection was very nebulous for the simple reason that psychic ability was difficult, if not impossible, to prove.

Tucker was also just beginning to realize that, one way or another, he and Sarah were nearing journey's end. September was all but over. Whatever Sarah had foreseen for herself, it seemed clear that the conclusion was due to take place sometime in October, possibly in the first few days of the month.

And in, apparently, a little town called Holcomb. A town where something had ended, or would end.

Sarah's life?

Tucker rubbed his forehead with the tips of his fingers, vaguely conscious of the dull ache there. He felt damned helpless, and it wasn't a feeling he was accustomed to. In most areas of his life, success was a frequent if not constant companion, but he had one very bad failure haunting him, and he was beginning to fear that Sarah would be another.

Why the hell did he always fail the women in his life?

The question was too painful, and he pushed it away. God knew there were plenty of other questions just as pressing. Like the question of what awaited them in Holcomb. A face-to-face confrontation with the other side? The ending Sarah had foreseen, her own death?

Tucker leaned his head back and closed his eyes. Sarah. Too much depended on her. Too much weight lay across shoulders too frail and inexperienced to carry the burden. In the next room, she lay virtually unconscious, drained by the effort of holding her own with another psychic. and when she woke he would have to push her

gain.

rry, Sarah. I thought I could keep you safe, that I

*could find out who's behind this, but it's beyond my ken. I'm
not sure I can protect you anymore. I don't even know how to
help you. All I know how to do is watch . . . and wait . . . and
push you toward some ending I'm terrified will be final . . .*

The sound of the bedroom door opening brought his
head up, and he looked at Sarah as she stood blinking
drowsily in the doorway. For once, she had not put on a
robe, and the white sleep shirt she wore made her look
very small, very young, and almost ethereal.

"What?" she asked.

He shook his head slightly and only then realized
what had happened.

"Didn't you call me?" Her eyes were no longer as dark
as they had been, the pupils normal, and her voice was
slowly losing the sleepiness.

"No." He drew a breath. "But I was thinking about
you."

She frowned for a puzzled moment, and then her gaze
slid away from his and she came a bit farther into the
room to sit down on one end of the couch. "Oh. Then
obviously, I was just . . . dreaming."

"I don't think so."

She sat bolt upright, her fingers tangled but still in her
lap, her head bent. "Don't you?"

"No."

Sarah shook her head just a little. "No. Neither do I.
It's getting even stronger. It doesn't go . . . dormant . . .
when I sleep anymore. I was asleep, not even dreaming,
and . . . and I heard your voice very clearly. You said, 'I'm
sorry, Sarah.' It woke me up."

Tucker wanted to go to her but held himself still. "I'm sorry I woke you up."

She looked at him, expressionless, but didn't allow him to change the focus. "I'm sorry this bothers you so much."

"What?"

"This situation. Me. You aren't responsible for me, Tucker. There's no reason to feel guilty if . . . if I don't make it."

"You're going to make it."

She ignored that. "And I don't mind that I make you uncomfortable. Really, I don't. It's unnerving for me to find your thoughts in my head; it must be horrible for you to find them there."

"Sarah, you don't make me uncomfortable. I've been . . . caught off guard more than once, but if I gave you the impression—"

"You keep forgetting." Her smile was twisted. "You're talking to a psychic, Tucker. You've been very good at—at guarding yourself these last days, but I know damned well that you've seen or sensed this alien thing in me. This thing that's getting stronger and doesn't sleep now."

"There's nothing alien in you. Unusual, sure. But your abilities are a part of you now, Sarah. We both know that."

She shrugged. "If you say so. All I know is that I've made you uncomfortable. And will again. And I want you to know that I really don't mind if you need to keep some distance between us. I even—" She broke off abruptly.

"Want me to," he finished.

"Expect you to." Her gaze was steady. "I don't want my life or . . . or my soul on your conscience, Tucker. I don't want you to believe you could have done more, or something different, to change what's going to happen. I don't want you to carry that burden."

"What have you seen?" he asked slowly.

"Nothing new. Except . . . a kind of clarity. The struggle with Neil Mason seems to have stripped something away. It all seems so clear to me now, so inevitable. I know that what's going to happen is going to happen soon. Very soon. And I know that you're going to blame yourself for what happens. You'll think it was because of some choice you made, some decision that you could have made differently. But you'll be wrong, Tucker. There's nothing you can do to change what's going to happen to me. Nothing."

"Because of destiny." His voice was flat.

"Because a sequence of events was set in motion months ago, long before I met you. The sequence has to play itself out. You can't stop it."

"I can damned well try. And so can you."

"No, I can't. I know that now."

"Goddammit, Sarah, don't you give up on me. Not now. We've come too far for that. You said you needed my confidence, my belief that we could change the future. I still believe that."

"I don't think so." She hesitated, then added quietly, "How can you even look to the future when you've spent your entire adult life chasing the past? How can you face one when you haven't finished with the other?"

———

"Where are they?"

"Next door."

"You don't ask for much, do you?"

"This is as close as I could get. Can you do it, or not?"

"Yes. But it's going to take some time."

"Then go ahead."

———

Tucker wanted to deny her accusation. He wanted to change the subject, to once more avoid the painful memories and painful admissions he would have to reveal to her. To push it away, turn away, as he had so many times since he had met Sarah. But somehow, in this quiet room in the quiet hours before midnight, with so much uncertainty and possible violence lying just ahead of them, somehow he could avoid it no longer.

"You want me to ask you about Lydia," he said.

"I want you to tell me about her. You need to, Tucker."

She was right. He needed to. He had never told anyone the truth, not his family, not his best friend, and it had all been dammed up inside him for nearly twenty years. Once he began, the words poured out of him in a fast, jerky stream.

"We were high school sweethearts. Went steady all during our senior year. Lydia had been raised by her mother and an aunt; her father had died when she was just a baby. Her mother had invested the insurance money wisely, so there was plenty for college; we were both planning to go to UVA. We . . . made a lot of plans.

"A few months before graduation, her mother became ill. Very ill. Lydia was spending a lot of time at the hospital, but her mother insisted she stay in school and graduate with the class. With finals coming up, I helped her all I could. She'd go to school, then to visit at the hospital, and every night we were together at my house or hers, studying. Or trying to. We were both under a lot of stress and we . . . weren't as careful as we should have been."

"She got pregnant."

Tucker barely heard Sarah's quiet voice, but nodded slowly. "She told me right after graduation. And she was . . . so happy about it. So full of plans. We'd get married right away. She'd put off college, use the money to get a little apartment near UVA, furnish it, bank the rest for living expenses. And medical expenses. I could go on to college, maybe change my major to something a little more practical than English lit and, anyway, maybe that book I was working on would sell. Her mother might live long enough to see her first grandchild and her aunt would surely help out . . . Christ, she was so happy."

"And how did you feel about it?" Sarah asked.

He looked at her and, as vividly as if it had been yesterday, felt the shock and panic, the wild urge to run. Resentment and anger rising in him like bile, choking him . . .

"I felt . . . trapped. As rosy as she painted the picture,

I knew reality would be different. Neither of us had medical insurance and babies are expensive, so the money wouldn't last long at all. I'd have to get a job before long, and even if I managed to finish college, I'd have to take some practical courses, just like she'd said, aim for a job that would support a family right away. Everybody knew writers didn't make much money, and a degree in literature isn't much good for anything. I could see my life laid out all neat and tidy ahead of me, a job I hated, a wife I resented, a child I didn't want . . . and all my dreams in pieces behind me."

"And Lydia knew. Saw it in your face."

He nodded. "It had never occurred to her that I wouldn't be as happy about it as she was. All she'd ever really wanted was to be a wife and mother, to have a little house she could take care of. She'd planned on college mostly because of me, because I wanted it, figured she'd major in child psychology or development, something like that. She didn't want to teach. She just wanted to be a good mother."

Tucker drew a deep breath. "I'll never forget the shock on her face, the way she backed away from me as if I'd turned into a stranger."

"You couldn't let her go thinking that."

"No. I . . . told her it was just surprise, that she'd imagined the rest. She believed me. She wanted to believe me." He focused on Sarah's face and was vaguely surprised to find no condemnation there. But she hadn't heard the worst, of course.

Then, gazing into her eyes, he realized that she didn't need to hear him say it. She knew. She knew what he'd done. Sarah had known for a long time. And there was still no condemnation in her face.

Hoarsely, forcing the words out because he needed to, he said, "We made plans to elope the next week. Nobody'd be surprised, with her mother so ill. We'd just do it and then come back and tell everyone." He swallowed. "I told her everything would be fine. I promised her I wouldn't let her down."

Sarah waited silently.

"I meant what I said. I had every intention of meeting her at her house as planned, and going to get married." He looked away from Sarah and fixed his unseeing gaze on a lamp. It was so hard to say the rest, admit the rest, but he had to. "Then the days passed and . . . and it was suddenly time to do that. And somehow, instead of packing to meet Lydia, I packed to head to Florida with a buddy for a couple of weeks of sand and sun. I didn't tell Lydia I wasn't going to marry her. I just didn't show up."

"You were eighteen," Sarah said, not in an excusing tone, but matter-of-factly.

"Yeah, well, my father was eighteen when he married my mother, and nineteen when I was born. He was responsible, worked his ass off, and as far as I can see, never regretted any of it. I was old enough to be a father, so I was damned sure old enough to be responsible for the child I'd helped create. Some things can't be excused by youth. I was a cruel, selfish bastard to run out on her like that. And without a word, without even telling her I was sorry or that I'd help with the baby even if I couldn't marry her. Nothing."

"You came back a few days later," Sarah said.

He nodded. "I wasn't having much fun down in Florida; all I could think about was the way I'd run out on her. Finally I couldn't stand it anymore and came home. But it was too late. Lydia was gone. She'd left a note for her aunt, taken her college money and her car. Her mother was in a coma by then, and never knew what had happened. Her aunt was devastated. She showed me the note. Lydia hadn't mentioned the baby, or blamed me in any way. She just said she couldn't watch her mother die, that she had to get away, start a new life somewhere else. And to tell me . . . she was sorry, but that I'd be better off without her."

Tucker returned his gaze to Sarah's face. "Her mother died a few weeks later, her aunt less than a year afterward. Lydia didn't come home for the funerals. She never came home again. I started looking for her that summer, and kept on every chance I had. I hired a couple of private detectives in those first years, but they got nowhere, so I taught myself how to search. But I got nowhere myself. It was as if she'd dropped off the face of the earth the day she left Richmond. I spent endless hours searching birth and . . . death records, newspapers, tax rolls, every kind of public record I could access, beginning in Virginia and working north and south, then west. But I never found a single hint of her existence. By the time I left college the first time, I'd realized that I wasn't going to find her that way."

"The first time?"

"Yeah, I ended up going back. Picking up a couple more degrees in subjects that interested me." He shrugged jerkily. "Not that any of them helped me find Lydia."

"So you began looking for a psychic who could tell you where Lydia was."

"I'd always been interested in the paranormal. And I had to know. What had happened to her, to the baby. I had to know they were all right. But the so-called psychics I found couldn't tell me anything useful. It was mostly garbage, the standard you've-lost-your-love kind of crap they told every other customer. And even the few people I believed had genuine ability couldn't seem to tap into anything other than my need to find her."

"But you kept searching."

He nodded. "More than eighteen years now. Not a day goes by that I don't think about Lydia. About our child. Lydia thought it was a boy, from the very first, when she told me. He'd probably be in his junior or senior year of high school now, planning for college—"

Sarah looked away.

Tucker swallowed hard, a dull, cold ache spreading through him. "Except he isn't, is he?"

"No." Sarah's voice was almost inaudible. "He isn't."

Tucker closed his eyes for a moment, then opened them. Steadily, he said, "Tell me. Tell me what happened to them."

With obvious reluctance, she said, "I think . . . I know . . . the baby died very soon after birth. He just . . . went to sleep and didn't wake up. Crib death, I think."

Tucker thought of all the years spent searching. And the daydreams, sometimes reluctant but always vivid and detailed, of his child growing up somewhere. The first steps. The first baseball glove. The first bike. First day in school. First lost tooth. First kiss. First date.

All the firsts he had imagined missing. And now, to know that none of it had happened at all.

He was somehow surprised that it hurt so much, but he wasn't surprised by the guilt. If he hadn't run out on Lydia, would it have been different? Would their child have lived?

"It wouldn't have ended differently," Sarah said, still without looking at him. "If you and Lydia had married. If you had been the most wonderful husband and father possible. It would have ended the same way. I know you don't want to believe that, but it's true. Some things really are meant to happen just the way they happen."

He didn't have the emotional energy to argue with her about destiny. Not again. In any case, the idea that he could not have made a difference in his child's short life didn't offer much comfort.

"What about Lydia?" he asked.

Sarah shook her head slightly. "She . . . she's gone too. But later, I think. A few years ago."

Tucker never doubted that Sarah was telling him facts. There was no question in his mind. Just an overwhelming weariness and the echoes of that cold, dull pain deep inside him. And regret.

"So I'll never even be able to tell her I'm sorry." He

leaned his head back against the hard chair and closed his eyes. "Christ."

"She knew you were sorry."

"Not everybody is psychic, Sarah. How the hell could she know that? There was no sign of it from me."

"She knew you. The kind of person you were. She even knew you'd come back in a few days."

Tucker raised his head and opened his eyes, staring at her. "Trying to make me feel better?"

Sarah was looking at him now, her eyes once more darkened and her expression intent. "No. I'm telling you what I know. Lydia knew you'd come back. She knew you'd marry her, even if you didn't know that yourself. She knew that all she had to do was wait for you to work it out."

"Then why the hell didn't she?"

Sarah tilted her head a bit in that listening posture, and spoke slowly. "She realized what she was asking you to do. Give up your dreams of writing, or at the very least put them aside for a long time. She realized that what she wanted in life was not what you wanted, at least not then. She was sure she could make it on her own, raise her child alone. And she really couldn't bear to watch her mother die. So she left."

After a moment, Tucker rose from his chair and crossed the room to sit down on the couch beside Sarah. "How can you know all that, Sarah? What is it you're tapping into?"

"I don't know." She frowned a little, looking at him

and yet somehow beyond him. "It's a . . . place. A sort of crossroads where everything meets. Past, present, future. A place we all pass through. We leave a . . . an imprint behind, a sense of what we feel and think and are. I know what Lydia left there, so I know her. Who she was, what she thought and felt. It's all there, and I can see it."

Tucker knew there was a theory of a universal consciousness, a kind of energy field made up of all the thoughts and knowledge accumulated by humankind in all its history, a field some people claimed to be able to tap into. Thinking of that theory was as close as he could come to understanding what Sarah was talking about. Even so, in all his study of the paranormal, he had never—ever—read or heard of any psychic with the abilities Sarah was beginning to display.

He had the feeling that if the other side really knew what she was capable of, they'd be breaking down doors to get to her, and to hell with being sneaky about it.

Sarah blinked and suddenly focused on his face. Her pupils were still enormous, but a smile played about her mouth. "Everything that was, and is, and will be is there. We're there."

"We are?"

She nodded. "We're going to be lovers, you know."

Tucker's first response to that was purely physical and immediate, but he rode out the surge of desire as if it were an unruly bronc and did his best to control it. He hadn't realized just how badly he wanted her until that moment. "Are we?"

Sarah nodded again. "It's our destiny."

Even as he watched, her pupils were returning to normal, and it was the most fascinating thing he'd ever seen. Hypnotic. He couldn't stop staring at her, and his voice was almost absentminded. "Destiny. We've talked about that, Sarah. I don't believe our lives are planned for us."

"Not our lives. Just some things. We will be lovers."

"And what if I don't want to play along with destiny?" he asked, even as he wondered why on earth he was objecting.

"You don't have a choice. Not about this. Don't you know? Haven't you always known?"

His mind flashed back to the first time he'd seen her, standing before the ruins of her home in her pretty dress, and he thought he had known, even then, that they belonged together. Why else had he so instantly involved himself in her life? And why had he been so wary of her, if not because he had known immediately and instinctively what she could be to him—and he hadn't been ready to face that?

He hadn't been prepared to fall in love with the most complex woman he'd ever met in his life.

Tucker drew a breath. "I thought you were probably still grieving for David, but . . . I wanted you from the moment I set eyes on you."

"David is dead," Sarah said quietly. "Like Lydia. I couldn't have saved him any more than you could have saved her."

Tucker reached out to touch her cheek. "Maybe I couldn't have saved Lydia, but I failed her. I don't want to fail you, Sarah."

She didn't argue with him or reassure him, she just went into his arms and lifted her face with mute need.

"Sarah . . ."

"It's destiny," she whispered, just before his lips covered hers.

————

"Anything?" Varden asked.

Astrid frowned but didn't open her eyes or remove the fingers pressed tightly to her temples. "If you'd stop asking me that, maybe I could make some progress."

"It's taking too much time."

"You didn't ask me how long it would take. You just asked me if I could do it."

"And you said you could."

She opened icy blue eyes and glared at him. "I can. But this isn't easy, you know. No—you don't know, do you? That's sort of the point." A mocking note entered her voice.

Coldly, Varden said, "Don't forget the other point. *You* know only because we allow you to. Stop being helpful, and . . ."

He didn't have to finish that sentence. Her boldness seeped away, and she closed her eyes once more. "All right, all right. Are you sure Duran okayed this? He must be getting desperate, if he did."

"Don't you know that he did?" Varden asked dryly.

"Of course not. Nobody can read Duran. Now shut up and let me concentrate . . ."

Sarah woke with a slight start, though she had no idea what had startled her. The bedroom was quiet, lamplit. Even as she began to relax, Tucker pushed himself up on an elbow beside her and smiled down at her.

"That was a short nap," he noted.

She couldn't see the clock, but an inner sense told her it was still before midnight. "I slept most of the day, remember?" And it was difficult, now, for her to sleep more than an hour or two without waking, uneasy and anxious.

Even, it seemed, in Tucker's bed.

"Mmm." He leaned down and kissed her, briefly but not lightly.

She reached up to push a heavy lock of fair hair off his forehead, then let her fingers glide through more of the silky stuff until her hand finally wound up at his nape. How long did they have? A few hours? This night? What would happen when tomorrow came?

Time was passing so relentlessly, pushing them inexorably toward the future. Her future.

That yawning grave.

"Sarah? What's wrong?"

"Nothing." She pushed the whispering little fears out of her mind, determined not to spoil tonight.

It might well be all she ever had of him.

"Are you sure?"

She nodded. "It's just . . . I'm surprised, that's all."

"Why?"

Sarah felt her cheeks warm, which was, she told her-self, ridiculous. "I've never— That is . . ."

"Haven't you?" His hand slid to her inner thigh and stroked her sensitive flesh lightly.

The warmth was spreading through her rapidly, but Sarah tried to concentrate. "No. I mean . . . like I said, it surprised me. To feel like that. I didn't expect it."

"What did you expect?" He leaned down, nuzzling the sheet aside as his lips trailed over her upper breast.

"Pleasure. But not like that." Her fingers tangled in his hair and she shifted a bit to better feel the hard length of his body against hers. "Not like this."

"I'm glad I could surprise you." His eyes gleamed at her in a fleeting glance. "It's obviously something I won't be able to do very often."

She wanted to tell him he was more right than he knew but had a hunch that this was not the best time to explain that the passion between them had sparked yet another aspect of her peculiar abilities.

I'm not alone anymore. You're with me.

Something inside her had opened up to him, had flung itself wide and invited him in, and whether he knew it or not, Tucker had accepted the invitation. It was not some-thing she had expected, or even wanted consciously, yet it was what she had needed. It was the most amazing sense of closeness Sarah had ever known, an inner warmth that seemed to wrap gently—and protectively—around her soul.

It wasn't that she knew what he was thinking or feeling. It was more than that. Deeper than that. She knew him better than she would ever know herself, and far, far better than he would ever know himself.

What that would mean, to him and to her, Sarah didn't know. The door that had opened so abruptly and shown her the "crossroads" where she had found the intimate knowledge of Lydia and the certainty that she and Tucker would become lovers on this night had closed just as abruptly. And since she had no idea how she had managed to tap into that place at all, she doubted the door would open again anytime soon.

"Sarah . . ."

"Hmmm?"

"Dammit, pay attention to me."

She couldn't help but smile when he lifted his head to show her a glare that was only half-feigned. "I'm paying strict attention to you."

"You were thinking. This is not the moment to be thinking."

"Even if I was thinking about you?"

There was a glitter of amusement in his eyes, but he frowned and held on to the playful role of sulky male. "Well, even so, if you're able to think about anything at all, I've obviously lost my touch."

His touch roamed up her inner thigh just then, and Sarah had to struggle for a silent moment to find the breath to murmur, "Perish the thought."

"Literally? You can't think anymore?" He had pushed the sheet down, and his lips teased her breast with single-minded intensity.

"Tucker . . ."

"Don't think about anything, not even me. Just feel."

She didn't have a choice. He had quickly learned just how to please her, and he used all that knowledge now to keep her mindless. It was a gift, a glorious escape from fears and worries and dread of a future that loomed all too near and much too dark, and Sarah accepted it gratefully.

And just as before, it surprised her that he could make her feel so much, surprised her that she was even capable of feeling so much.

But when he came inside her, when her body surrounded him and they moved together, everything that had gone before seemed merely a prelude, a pale imitation of what they were truly capable of. The pleasure built and built and built toward some impossible peak Sarah couldn't even imagine, and when they reached it at last it was together.

One body. One soul.

THIRTEEN

Murphy wasn't happy and it showed; she had never been known to hide her feelings. About anything. "This is not a good idea," she said.

"You're ideal for the job I need you for, we both know that. You have a natural shield, and it's the strongest I've ever encountered. They'll never know you're sharing information with me."

"You're trusting I won't tell them."

"I know you won't." His voice was calm. "You've given over your entire life, all that you are, to this war."

After a moment, she said, "Interesting that you call it a war."

"Don't you?"

"Yeah. And it's one we have to win."

"I agree. Which is why I need someone on the inside

to keep me, as much as possible, in the loop. Some information I'll find myself, the way I found you, but there are way too many puzzle pieces still missing."

"Just how did you find me?" That was bugging her, and it showed.

"I don't believe in coincidence as a rule, but you happened to cross paths with one of my team whose ability is detecting other psychics. She was probing because we were on a case. She picked up on you. With a little luck and a lot of effort, I was able to find you, obviously. You aren't completely off the grid, just mostly."

"Yeah? And what about you and your team? You've got a good shield yourself, Bishop, but that doesn't mean one of your people or one of the bad guys you go after might not pick up on more than either one of us can live with. Literally."

"I'll make sure that doesn't happen. Aside from myself, the only other team member who knows anything about what's going on is Miranda, my wife."

"And I'm supposed to trust you on that?"

"Yes. You are." He paused, then added, "It's a two-way street. I can be a source for you, especially when it comes to information you might need on various . . . factions . . . of the government. I can get information for you more quickly than you could ever get it on your own."

"And all I have to do in return is keep you informed."

"I need to know what you know, Murphy. If for no other reason than I need to be sure that my team is safe, that Haven operatives are safe. I have to be certain none of them are targets, and that means I need all the information you can give me."

She drew a breath and blew it out impatiently. "That's sort of the point of this setup, you know; the fewer people who know everything, the less damage done if somebody goes down. I'm not planning to go down, but let's just say I do. Now I've got knowledge about you and your teams."

"No more knowledge than you could find tapping into any law enforcement database. The other side has to know about the SCU and Haven. That's why I need more information from you and the people you're working with. As far as I can tell, none of my psychic agents or operatives have been targeted. Yet. There must be a reason for that."

"Yeah, I imagine there is. But I can't give it to you."

"Not directly, no. But over time the information you can provide me will be pieces of the puzzle. Until I can put it all together."

She scowled. "Look, my source says you can be trusted, but *my* trust has to be earned."

"I understand that. Ours is a relationship I hope to build on."

"It may take a while," she warned.

"That's all right," Bishop said. "I'm a very patient man."

———

It was several hours later when Tucker woke. He propped his head on one raised hand, the better to watch Sarah as she slept, but otherwise didn't move. He still felt a bit shaky, and it wasn't only because his muscles had been pushed to their limits tonight. Something else had been pushed to its limits, maybe beyond them. He wasn't sure what it was, but he knew he'd never be the same again.

He gazed at Sarah's sleeping face, and a wave of aching tenderness swept over him. It was stronger than anything he'd ever felt before, so intense it was more than a little terrifying. He had known her hardly more than a week, yet he couldn't imagine his life now without her in it. The wariness he had so often felt around her no longer troubled him. He had never felt so close to another human being, so . . . wrapped up in her.

And so afraid for her.

How could he protect her from the other side? How could he keep her safe?

That agonizing question had barely risen in his mind when a sudden realization struck. Jesus, not only was the pistol in the other room, but he wasn't at all sure he'd used the dead bolt and night latch on the door after he'd pushed the room service cart back out into the hallway hours ago.

Careful not to wake Sarah, he slid from the bed and found his shorts and jeans. He would much rather have remained in bed with her, absorbing her warmth and her scent, watching her sleep and waiting patiently for her to wake so they could make love again. But things left undone nagged at him.

It was after three A.M. but since he was wide awake now and Sarah seemed to be sleeping deeply, he figured he might as well try to get something accomplished while she got the rest she undoubtedly needed. He was hardly in the mood to wade through more statistics of dead and vanished psychics, but he could try to refine the program he'd written to look for some kind of pattern in the morass of facts and speculation.

Somewhere, there had to be a pattern, something he was missing. There had to be. Nothing this extraordinary and far-reaching could have existed for so many years without leaving evidence of its existence. Surely . . .

He opened and turned on his laptop first, then looked around for the gun.

And didn't find it.

He couldn't believe he'd left it in the Jeep, but the longer he thought about it the more convinced he became that he had done just that. He remembered shoving the pistol into the storage compartment between the Jeep's front seats just after they'd left Neil Mason's house. He'd been so worried about Sarah, he didn't think he'd given the gun another thought.

"Shit. Some hero I am," he muttered aloud. How the hell was he going to protect Sarah without the damned gun? Throw rocks at them? Oh, yeah, that would be just great.

Before he even realized he was going to, he had pulled on a sweatshirt and sat down to put on his socks and boots. He paused then, frowning, because there was something else nagging at him. But it was a distant thing, out of reach and only vaguely troubling, and he shrugged it away.

The important thing, the only thing that mattered,

was to protect Sarah. He had to go and get the gun, so he could protect her.

He remembered to take the door keycard, and the keys to the Jeep. He remembered to test the door carefully after he closed it, to make sure they couldn't get in and hurt Sarah while he was gone. He remembered to be cautious as he walked down the hallway, to be alert, and to check the elevator warily before getting in.

He even remembered to lock the elevator open on the right garage level, so it would be there waiting for him and he wouldn't waste time. Because he had to get the gun and get back upstairs so he could protect Sarah.

The garage, like most of its kind in the wee small hours of the morning, was badly lit and filled with shadows as well as eerily silent and cavernous, so that Tucker's normally quiet footsteps echoed hollowly off the concrete and metallic surfaces. The Jeep was parked not too far from the elevator, so it didn't take long to walk to it, but he was nevertheless aware of a growing anxiety by the time he reached it.

He had to protect Sarah.

He was straining to listen but heard nothing. His head was throbbing oddly, and it was getting difficult to think, as if a fog crept into his brain. For a moment, as he stood beside the Jeep, he couldn't even remember what he was doing there.

The gun. That was it. He had to get the gun and protect Sarah.

It took him several minutes to figure out how to use

the keyless entry gadget to unlock the Jeep doors, and he shook his head in bafflement when he finally got the driver's door open.

Christ, what's wrong with me?

He leaned in and opened the compartment between the seats. The usual vehicle clutter met his puzzled stare. A couple of folded maps, some paper napkins and two paper-wrapped straws, the sunglasses he hadn't needed today. Yesterday. A flashlight. And in the bottom, when he pushed the rest aside and searched all the way down, a tangled and gritty nest of coins, gum wrappers, and general Jeep lint.

But no gun.

Tucker stood there, leaning across the driver's seat, and scowled. Where the hell was the gun? He'd left it right here—

Then, abruptly, with the suddenness of a soap bubble, the fog vanished from his brain, and he realized why the gun wasn't here.

Because it was upstairs in their room.

He remembered. He remembered looking right at it when he'd gone back into the sitting room. It was on the desk, beside his laptop. Where he had placed it, as soon as they had settled into the room, so it would be within easy reach while he worked at the computer and Sarah slept. Where he had left it hours ago.

Where it had always been.

He knew then. Knew in a terrible moment of absolute clarity what they had done to him. He had underestimated them, badly underestimated them. Because they had used the one tool he had never expected them to use, the one tool he hadn't even imagined they could use.

His own mind.

They'd crawled inside his head. They hadn't been able to get inside Sarah's, so they had turned to him. Somehow, they had crawled inside his head and made him think the gun was here, made him believe he had to come down here and get it, leaving Sarah alone upstairs . . .

"Sarah. Oh, Jesus, Sarah—"

He never heard them behind him. He only had time to realize that, once again, he had failed the woman he loved. He felt the agony of that even before the shock of the blow, the blinding pain in his head. And then nothing.

———

"Tucker?"

Sarah found herself sitting up in bed, the sheet clutched to her breasts and her own voice loud in her ears. There had been a dream, a warmly reassuring dream of Tucker fretting about protecting her. Then he had seemed to fade away for a long time, until a sudden burst of agony shot through her head, a terrible pain that was in his head and his heart and his voice.

"Sarah. Oh, Jesus, Sarah—"

And now . . . nothing.

Terror and panic were ice water in her veins, and she couldn't breathe, couldn't think about anything but him. Desperately, she reached out, closing her eyes and concentrating as hard as she could, harder than she ever had before, as she tried to find Tucker.

Instantly, a cacophony beat inside her mind like the wings of a hundred birds, the chatter of a hundred voices, and she heard her own voice cry out in surprise and fear even as her eyes shot open and she instinctively slammed shut what her desperation to find Tucker had wrenched open.

It took her several moments to calm down, and longer to realize what had happened. She had reached out wildly and without any kind of focus, and what had rushed into her open mind had been the mental voices and dreams of all the people around her.

Sarah shivered, afraid to try again—and more afraid not to. The sensation of all those thoughts and dreams and nightmares was the closest she ever wanted to get to actual chaos, the most unsettling thing she had ever experienced, and she did not want to experience it again, so this time she focused her mind as narrowly as she could before opening herself up.

Tucker. Just Tucker, he was the only one she wanted to find, the only one she wanted to hear.

At first, there was nothing. Silence. Darkness. She reached further out warily, like feeling her way through an unfamiliar room without lights, probing the darkness. And finally, dimly, on the very edge of her awareness, was a sense of Tucker's presence. No thoughts, no inner voice telling her where he was and what had happened to him, just his quiet presence. No matter how hard she tried, she couldn't bring him any closer, couldn't see him clearly, but at least he was there.

That certainty that he was still alive quieted some of the panic racing through her. Not much of it, but some. She slid out of bed, dragging the top sheet with her instead of pausing to find something to put on, and wrapped it around her. She went into the sitting room and stood looking slowly around. All her senses flared, but carefully now, reaching out warily.

It was one of the still-strange, new senses that sent her to the desk where the laptop lay open. She glanced once at the pistol lying in its holster beside it, but her attention was on the computer's screen. The machine had been off earlier, she remembered, so obviously Tucker had gotten up sometime in the last hour or so and decided to do some work. The open program on the screen, she saw, appeared to be sifting through information already acquired, so apparently he had judged it too dangerous to leave his computer tethered in any way to the Internet when he was not present to monitor it. He was being as cautious as possible in how he went about gathering more information.

So why had he left so abruptly and without a word to her? She couldn't believe he could have been taken from this room without her awareness, so he must have left on his own. But to go where? And why?

She frowned down at the laptop. As she watched, the program running appeared to pause, and then the screen went dark. No working program visible, no screen saver. Just a black screen.

And then, slowly, words began to appear, brilliantly white against the darkness.

> If you want him,
> Come get him.

Sarah sank down in the desk chair and stared at the screen until the words burned themselves into her brain.

"Oh, my God," she whispered.

———

The first psychic on the list was one of them; this time, Sarah knew it even without getting out of the Jeep. The second psychic was not one of them, but she was also not a genuine psychic—though it took Sarah a good ten minutes of intense concentration to be sure of that.

Fifteen minutes later, she pulled the Jeep into the driveway of a small, neat house set back from the road among tall trees. She kept the vehicle in gear and the engine running as she stared at the house and tilted her head to one side to listen intently.

Hello, Sarah.

She caught her breath, and her hand on the gearshift tightened. Friend or foe? This time, she couldn't tell. But a genuine psychic, definitely, and there was something hauntingly familiar about that voice . . .

I can help you, Sarah.

She was trying very hard to keep her own mind quiet and still and closed, unwilling to give anything away when she was unsure who was trying to get inside her head. Except that this voice wasn't probing or pushing or trying to break through her guards. It was just there, gentle and calm.

And it had been there before.

Please, Sarah. Come in.

She hesitated but finally put the Jeep in park and turned off the engine. This could be the biggest mistake she'd made yet, but she wasn't willing to run away without trying to find out who the placid, compassionate inner voice belonged to.

She was aware of no particular sense of danger as she went up the walkway to the front door. Wind chimes hung beside it, tinkling softly in the slight breeze, and hanging baskets and pots of flowers decorated the porch—an awful lot of flowers for the end of September, Sarah thought.

Before she could knock on the door, it swung open. A woman stood there smiling at her. She was about Sarah's height or a little less, very slender, with delicate bone structure and long black hair, and looked about sixteen years old. Except in her eyes. They were dark and fathoms deep and old as time.

"Hello, Sarah. I'm Leigh."

Sarah drew a breath. "You've been . . . trying to talk to me for a long time now."

"Yes. I have."

Leigh Munroe led the way into a comfortable living room filled with overstuffed furniture and glowing lamps, where a fire burned and hot coffee waited, and this time Sarah didn't hesitate to accept a cup. The need to find

Tucker was clawing at her, but she forced herself to be patient. She had to do this first.

Her sense of the other woman was mostly positive—but oddly . . . incomplete. She knew she was in the presence of power, yet the power was muted and controlled and curiously distant. There was no strong impression of a personality as she felt with Tucker, of emotions and thoughts shifting like quicksilver beneath the surface; there was just a peaceful surface and what seemed to be utter calm underneath. There was goodness, but also the feeling of something dark lurking, and it made Sarah wary.

"You haven't eaten anything today," Leigh said gently, pushing a small plate of cheese and crackers across the coffee table to her guest. "You have to eat, Sarah. The more you use your abilities, the more energy you'll need."

Vaguely, Sarah wondered whether that was why her abilities had gotten so much stronger in the last week, because Tucker had made sure she'd eaten on a regular basis; before that, she had been very prone to skipping meals.

"He took care of you by instinct," Leigh agreed, her tone casual as though part of the conversation had not happened silently. "That's rare, you know. He values what you can do, even if he's still adjusting to it. He'll never ask you to be less than you are. And—he's a bit psychic himself, though he isn't aware of it. You couldn't have chosen a better champion."

Champion. An old word, used the way Leigh used it,

but Sarah knew it fit. She ate a cracker absently and said aloud, "I didn't choose him. I just . . . accepted him when he came."

Leigh smiled. "Is that what you did?"

"It's what I thought I did. I thought I was just . . . following the path I had to follow."

"But that was your choice, wasn't it? To follow the path?"

"I suppose. Except . . . I always had the feeling that even if I tried to do just the opposite, I'd still end up on the path somehow."

"You might have. Fate has a way of being insistent about some things, no matter what we do. In any case, you haven't followed blindly, Sarah. You've struggled and questioned. That's important. We do control our own destinies, you know. In the end. Often imperfectly, but our lives and our fates are what we make of them."

Sarah frowned. "Then what I saw, my vision . . ."

"Was a possible future. But not the only one."

"Someone told me that there was a difference between prediction and prophecy. That one might come true— but the other always does."

"An arguable point, I suppose. But it's been my experience that the future is a series of infinite possibilities. Each step we take toward it, each choice and decision, alters the possibilities. This journey is important for you. We all have at least one in our lives, a path that leads us to a crossroads where we have to make the decisions that will determine our future. It's a path you have to follow."

Sarah felt a stab of uneasiness. The other woman was

smiling, but there was still that darkness lurking and this talk of destiny . . . "But you said we controlled our destinies."

Leigh laughed softly. "Sarah, hasn't it occurred to you that what you foresaw was your future as you decided it would be?"

She blinked. "What?"

"Think about it. You saw a series of images, of symbols. You saw a journey culminating in—what?"

"Death. My death."

Leigh didn't seem surprised. "It's quite likely that was purely symbolic. In visions, the death of the seer often represents a sudden and drastic change in one's life. A crossroads where a choice must be made. The end of a *way* of life, of a way of thinking."

That didn't reassure Sarah terribly since she had some idea of what would happen if the other side got their hands on her.

The end of a way of life, indeed.

"All right. But you said—it was my future as I decided it would be?"

"Sarah, even the best and strongest of psychics must see through intensely subjective eyes. You might be objective when seeing someone else's future but never when it's your own. You know yourself, know your thoughts and wishes and hopes and dreams, and everything you see is filtered through that knowledge even if only subconsciously. So when your mind leaps through time to peek at the future, it's with the total awareness of your own nature."

"I still don't . . ."

"All right. Think about Tucker. Do you really believe that you accepted him and his help because destiny insisted you should? Or had your mind looked ahead, seen him, known how it was in your nature to respond to him—and offered you a future possibility in which you did just that?"

Sarah thought about that for a long time, turning it over in her mind. She was hardly aware of Leigh's steady gaze, or of absently eating two more crackers and finishing her coffee.

Finally, she said slowly, "That's . . . a lot more complex than I thought it was. And confusing. How can I trust any of what I see if it's all so subjective? What's the good of being able to see the future if there are so many possible interpretations of what I see?"

Leigh smiled faintly. "Did you really think this was a good thing?"

Sarah gazed into those old, old eyes and slowly shook her head. "No. No, I didn't."

"It's neither good nor bad," Leigh told her. "It's just another sense, like sight or hearing; your eyes and your ears can be fooled. So can this. You can mistake what you see or hear; you can mistake what this sense tells you as well. You can strain your eyes in bad light or too much light, or hurt your ears listening to loud noises; you can injure this sense too."

"How?"

"By overworking it. By misusing it. By not allowing it the time and quiet to develop properly."

Sarah heard a warning and shook her head. "I don't have time. You know that."

"You have to find Tucker."

"Yes."

"He's alive," Leigh said.

"Yes. But they have him." It was the first time that the other side had been mentioned, and Sarah watched Leigh intently to judge her reaction.

She wasn't sure what that reaction was. Those old eyes met hers squarely, but the quiet that lay behind them gave nothing away.

"They, Sarah?"

"Don't pretend you don't know who I'm talking about."

"All right. I won't. And I won't pretend that I believe you can confront them on your own. That won't get Tucker away from them. They'll just kill him and take you."

Sarah drew a breath. "Who are they?"

"I don't know."

"Don't you?" Tentatively, Sarah tried to reach in past those quiet dark eyes.

Without a word aloud, Leigh let her in.

The pain was nearest the surface and came first, the awful, tearing pain of friends and loved ones lost, of tragedy and failure. It was dark and vast, an emptiness that ached and would never be filled. Then the emotional struggle of being different, the sense of isolation, the shame and loneliness. The battle for understanding, for control. For acceptance.

The years were there, many more years than Sarah had imagined, and they were filled with conflict and secrets and commitment. People coming here briefly with desperate faces and frightened eyes, and then passing on out of her hands. Other people coming here and talking with quiet courage and utter dedication. Plans discussed, arrangements made. Clandestine lines of communication formed and broken and altered.

And finally, deep, deep inside, there were the shadows, lurking like the worst nightmare her mind could conjure. They loomed and flitted and filled all the dark corners. They brought terror with them and left destruction as they passed, and they were many, so many . . .

Slowly, Sarah opened her eyes. She felt utterly exhausted with the effort of looking inside Leigh's mind and with the trauma of what she had found there. "My God."

"That's all we see," Leigh said. "Shadows. Even the strongest psychics we know have been unable to learn anything about them, not who they are, or where they're based, or what's behind their actions. We don't know how they're able to block us, but somehow they can—possibly by using the psychics they've already taken. But we can sense that shadowy part of them, and sometimes it helps us identify them; if you come into physical contact with one, you'll see or sense the shadows. But as you've already found out, they also use tools, other psychics and ordinary people, and those are not so easy to identify.

"And touching them is usually not a very good idea." Leigh's smile was twisted. "By that point, it tends to be too late to escape them."

Sarah drew a deep breath. She understood, now, where the darkness inside Leigh Munroe came from. "You keep saying 'we.' Who are you talking about?"

"You aren't alone, Sarah. We aren't alone. There are people, psychics and nonpsychics, who are trying very hard to find a way to fight and defeat the other side." She shook her head slightly, and her voice gentled. "We'll talk about that. But right now, you need to rest."

"I can't rest. Tucker—"

"Sarah, you can't help Tucker if you're exhausted. You need to sleep, for a few hours at least, and then you need to eat. Then we'll talk about what to do."

Bitterly, Sarah said, "I obviously can't do very much at all if two minutes of effort costs me this much." She was almost swaying with weariness.

"Those two minutes were rather remarkable, if you only knew." Leigh came over to take her arm and urge her gently to her feet. "Come on. I have a very comfortable bed upstairs."

Sarah didn't want to go to sleep. She needed to find Tucker. But just getting to her feet, even with Leigh's help, was almost more than she could manage, and the stairs left her weak and shaking.

She was asleep even before Leigh could cover her with a blanket.

———

Leigh stood gazing down at her sleeping guest for a long moment, then went slowly downstairs, frowning. She gathered the tray from the living room and took it to the kitchen. A glance at the clock made her frown deepen, and she reached for the phone on the breakfast bar. The number she punched in was a familiar one.

"Hello."

"It's Leigh. She's here."

"At last. Were we right?"

"She looked into my mind as if through an open door, all the way to the center. And she has no idea what she did. She may well be the one we've been waiting for."

"Good. I'll send them immediately."

"Tell them to hurry. She won't sleep long."

The first thing Tucker was aware of was a pounding headache. Next came the thought that someone had filled his mouth and ears with cotton. He was awake yet couldn't seem to get his eyes open or hear anything at all, even his own breathing. He thought he was lying on his side on something marginally softer than the floor, and he had the sense of a lot of space around him.

And someone was watching him.

Playing possum seemed like a good idea, at least until his head stopped pounding and he could think clearly. In any case, pretending he couldn't move wasn't a problem. He couldn't move. He didn't think he was tied up, but his body felt cold and leaden. Pretending he was still asleep was harder; the temptation to try to look around and find out where he was was almost overpowering.

Gradually, as he concentrated on feigning sleep and waited for life to return to his limbs, his ears began working again. He heard his breathing, soft and even. He heard, faintly, a dripping sound. He heard a peculiar low rustling sound, almost as if . . . as if many people somewhere nearby spoke together in whispers.

"I hear voices, many voices all around me, all talking at once, but almost whispering, so quiet that I can't tell what they're saying."

Because he had to, Tucker allowed his eyes to open just a slit. At first, he thought even those tiny muscles were refusing to obey him, but then he realized the truth. His eyes were open. And he couldn't see a god-damned thing.

Either it was very, very dark in this place—or he was blind.

And someone was still nearby, watching him.

FOURTEEN

It was cold and dark, and somebody was watching him.

Like a nightmare holding her in its grip, Sarah could feel Tucker's waking realizations, and they chilled her to the bone. She wanted desperately to be there with him, to offer comfort, and reached out instinctively in the effort to touch him. She thought she managed it, thought he was suddenly aware of her—and then there was a sharp jab in his arm and his awareness faded rapidly, leaving her alone once more.

She swam up out of the depths of sleep, still tired enough that the emergence was slow and gradual, her heart aching because for an instant Tucker had seemed close enough to touch.

She couldn't seem to get her eyes open, but her ears were working, and she heard, dimly, voices speaking downstairs. Without even deciding to, she listened with that other sense.

"Will she trust us?"

"I think so. What choice does she have?"

"What about Mackenzie?"

"She wants to go after him."

"When they're holding him as bait? That's insane. In another week or two, maybe, but—"

"He'll probably be dead in another week or two, Brodie. You know that. She came out of the coma in early April; this is the last day of September."

"I know, I know. Six months, max, and they miss their chance. If we can keep her alive and out of their hands for just a couple more weeks, Duran will back off."

"Maybe they won't kill Mackenzie."

"And maybe the sun won't rise tomorrow morning. But I wouldn't bet against the probability."

"Dammit, Brodie, you're so—"

"Look, Cait, I know what I know. I'm sorry as hell Duran and his bunch got their hands on Mackenzie. I'm sorry I didn't do my job and make contact with him and Gallagher days ago. But there's not a damn thing I can do about that now."

"We can help her go after Mackenzie."

"Help her? Help her face down Duran and God knows how many of his goons? I don't like the odds, Cait."

"The odds may be better than you think. You heard what Leigh said. Sarah Gallagher is special. She may be the one."

"In a year or two she may be the one. Maybe even in six months. But right now, she's a very tired and confused lady *with new psychic abilities she doesn't understand and can't control worth a damn."*

"Maybe, but—"

"Cait, Brodie's right. Sarah's at a very vulnerable stage right now. She needs help to make the transition, and time to make it at her own pace. If she pushes herself too hard, we could lose her. It's . . . happened once before. About a year ago, before you joined. Brodie remembers."

"Christ, yes, I remember. And I'll do everything in my power to make sure it never happens again."

Sarah opened her eyes, and instantly the clear voices in her head became the distant murmur coming from downstairs. She lay there for a moment or two, staring at the ceiling while questions and thoughts went round and round in her head.

Finally, she threw back the blanket covering her and got out of bed. The clock on the nightstand told her it was after four in the afternoon; she had slept for hours. She washed her face in the bathroom adjoining the bedroom and finger-combed her hair, mostly ignoring the reflection in the mirror that told her she was too pale and still hollow-eyed with weariness.

Without pausing or hesitating, she went downstairs and into Leigh Munroe's living room.

Three people were sitting there, and as soon as Sarah walked in, the man rose to his feet. He was a big man, physically powerful enough to give one pause, and very good looking in a dark, brooding way. He made Sarah think of a soldier; something about the way he stood, about his sharp sentry eyes and spring-coiled stillness, spoke of danger and the readiness for danger.

"I'm John Brodie," he said to Sarah.

"I know." She looked at the woman sitting beside Leigh on the couch, a younger woman with dark gold hair and friendly gray eyes in yet another face she had encountered along the way, and said, "You're Cait."

"Yes. Cait Desmond." She looked pleased, but whether it was because Sarah recognized her or just knew her name was hard to say.

Sarah nodded. "I . . . heard you all talking. When I woke up. So I listened."

Brodie glanced at Leigh. "Did you—"

Leigh shook her head. "No. I had no idea she was even awake. Remarkable."

"Who are you?" Sarah asked Brodie.

"If you were listening to us," he replied, "you must know."

"I know what I heard. I don't know what it means."

"We're the good guys," Cait said, in the tone of someone who'd wanted to say that for a long time.

Brodie looked at her and then, dryly, said, "We left our white hats at home this morning."

Sarah ignored that byplay, still a bit suspicious and too anxious about Tucker to feel much humor. Looking at Brodie, she said, "You—the two of you—have been following us."

"Until Chicago," he agreed. "When you traded cars, we lost you."

"Sit down, Sarah," Leigh invited, gesturing toward the chair beside Brodie's.

She did, slowly, trying to think. To Brodie, she said, "The bug. The tracking device. It was yours?"

He nodded, sitting down. In answer to her obvious confusion, he said, "The other side doesn't use electronic tracking devices, so far anyway. We don't know why."

Sarah thought it was interesting that he used the same phrase to describe their enemy that she and Tucker used. It was a fleeting thought, however. "But they were able to track us. They were there in Cleveland. And they got Tucker here in Portland when we'd been here hardly more than twelve hours."

Grimly, Brodie said, "They're very, very good. And they seem to be all over the place, certainly in every major city."

Sarah was still trying to think clearly. "If they were with us all the way, why didn't they move? Why didn't they try to get me?"

It was Leigh who asked, "Why do you think they didn't?"

"Tucker said . . . he thought it was because I could sense them near me. He said they'd only move against us in the middle of the night, while I was sleeping and unaware of them. And only then if they could do it without attracting attention. That was why we stayed in large hotels and kept moving in the daytime."

Leigh nodded. "Very wise."

"And they did move at night, last night while I was asleep. But I don't understand how they were able to get

Tucker. I know they weren't in the room and I know he wouldn't have left me alone."

"Not in his right mind," Leigh murmured.

Sarah stared at her. "You mean they . . . did something to him?"

It was Brodie who answered that. "Probably. One of the things we know about them is that they have some psychics under their control who are sometimes able to influence the minds of others."

"Neil Mason tried to influence my mind," Sarah said. "But I was able to . . . keep him out."

Leigh nodded, unsurprised by the information. "We know of him. One of their tools, or was."

"Was?"

"Gone," Brodie said unemotionally. "We checked on him periodically; as of this morning, his house was empty and the neighbors have no idea when he left or where he went."

"They don't like failure," Sarah murmured, chilled.

Leigh nodded. "And he failed. You were getting stronger by then, and when he failed, they knew they had missed their chance to convert you that way."

"Why didn't they try earlier? When I was still so confused and didn't know how to resist them?"

"As nearly as we can figure," Brodie said, "they use their psychics very sparingly, always trying more . . . conventional means first. We think it may be because when a psychic touches another psychic's mind, it's like opening a corridor between them, leaving both vulnerable. They seem to avoid that whenever possible, though we aren't sure why. It may be another reason why they decided to tap into Mackenzie's mind instead of yours."

"Think. Seem. May." Sarah heard the frustration in her own voice. "You don't know much for certain, do you?"

"No, we don't." Brodie met her gaze steadily. "Can you tell us more?"

Her eyes fell. "No."

Gently, Leigh said, "Not yet, anyway. But, Sarah, we believe you may be able to tell us a great deal about them. One day. When your abilities have had the time to develop properly."

"And until then—what? Hide me away somewhere?"

"No," Brodie said. "Hiding isn't the best idea."

Cait spoke up finally. "And in another week or two, you'll be much safer from them."

Sarah remembered the conversation she had overheard. "Six months since I woke up a psychic. Why six months?"

"Another thing we don't know," Brodie replied. "But it always holds true for the psychics like you, the ones who aren't born with it but suffer head injuries or some other kind of trauma later in life."

Leigh said, "In the life of every psychic, there comes a moment when full potential is realized. Control may be lacking, knowledge almost always is, but the ability is there. For a new psychic, a person who becomes psychic abruptly when all the other faculties are fully mature, the threshold seems to occur around the six-month mark. From the evidence we've seen so far, it appears that once that threshold is crossed, the other side finds it difficult—if not impossible—to convert a psychic. Whatever it is they want of us, we apparently become useless to them."

"You become a threat to them," Brodie corrected.

"We don't know that," Leigh argued. "Not for certain."

Brodie let out a short laugh and looked at Sarah. "It's another assumption of ours, based on the fact that we're sure they continue to keep tabs on psychics long after they seemingly give up trying to take them, and because there have been several disappearances, possibly even deaths, of psychics we thought were safe."

"Nothing was ever proven," Leigh said.

"Nothing ever is," Brodie retorted. "But there are some assumptions we'd damned well better make to keep our people safe."

"I don't believe we're of any use to them once the threshold is crossed," Leigh argued. "Those disappearances all involved psychics who were having trouble adjusting to their new lives; they probably just wanted to drop out of sight and did just that."

"It would be nice to think so, Leigh—but I don't. Whatever these bastards want with psychics, it doesn't just end when you cross that threshold of yours. They've got something else in mind for you, I can feel it in my gut." He laughed shortly. "I may not be psychic, but I know what I know. Taking new and inexperienced psychics is just step one of their plan. Step two involves the rest of you."

Leigh seemed unwillingly impressed by his certainty,

but shook her head a little. "I don't feel that. And none of the others has felt it."

"Maybe all of you are too close. Maybe it takes some-body *without* psychic abilities to see it."

"Maybe."

Sarah probably should have been disturbed by this lack of consensus among people who had fought the other side much longer than she and Tucker had, but instead it gave her an odd feeling of comfort. This entire thing was so bizarre, so inexplicable, that it felt wonder-fully normal to watch and listen to people who couldn't agree on the details—but were very clear on what the problem was.

"What about people like you?" she asked Leigh. "You've been psychic from birth, right? Why are you safe from them?"

"She isn't," Brodie said. "She just thinks she is."

Leigh smiled at him briefly, then looked at Sarah. "Like many born psychics, I had nonpsychic parents who tried their best to make me—at least seem—normal. I was always encouraged to hide what I could do, to keep to myself the things I saw. I learned secrecy at a very young age."

"So the other side wasn't aware of you?"

"So we believe. When I finally did go public, so to speak, it was with my full potential realized. They never even tried to take me."

But they had, Sarah knew, taken plenty of her friends through the years. That was why Leigh Munroe was involved in this. Not out of fear for herself, but out of fear for others.

Brodie leaned forward, resting his elbows on his knees as he looked intently at Sarah. "They outnumber us, Sarah, but we're growing. In strength and numbers. We're getting organized, even if it's loosely, and we're fighting back."

"How?"

"Marshaling our own strength. Gathering what few facts and little information we can lay our hands on, so that we may be able to expose them some day. Finding and protecting psychics, keeping them away from Duran and his goons."

"Duran?"

Brodie nodded. "The head goon."

Cait murmured, "Well, he isn't really a goon."

Brodie glanced at her, then looked back at Sarah with a wry expression. "Crocodile. Shark. Smiling villain. Whatever the hell you want to call him, he's obviously in charge, at least of their field operations."

"Field operations? You make it sound . . . military."

"Maybe it is. Or maybe it isn't. Until we get strong enough as an organization, or find a single psychic who's strong enough, we have no way of knowing. They don't leave evidence behind them, not so far."

Sarah thought about it. "So that's what you meant when you all were talking earlier? That I might be the one?"

Leigh replied to that, this time obviously in agreement

with Brodie. "We're convinced that a strong enough psychic will be able to find a way past their mental shields and give us the information we need to fight them."

"What makes you believe I might be that one?"

"I can feel it in you. The strength. The potential." Leigh smiled. "And I gave you a little test, Sarah."

"What test?"

"Earlier today, when you looked into my mind. Remember?"

"How could I forget. You opened a door and showed me . . . everything inside you."

Leigh shook her head slightly. "You opened that door, Sarah. Something not one in a hundred psychics could have done. The door was not only closed, it was locked— and I've spent a lifetime learning how to make those locks strong. But they didn't stop you. You didn't force your way past them, you didn't hurt me. You just opened the door as if it were no barrier at all."

Sarah didn't know what to say to that.

"You're the one, Sarah," Leigh said. "You're the key to our future."

———

"Well?"

"She's made contact with Munroe."

"And?"

"Brodie's there. And the girl."

"Then we can assume they're making plans."

"Yes."

"Good. That's good."

It was unsettling, to be told she was so important in a cause she hadn't even been aware of a week before, and Sarah wasn't sure what she felt about it. All she knew was that a weight of responsibility was settling on her shoulders, and it was heavy.

After a short silence, it was Brodie who spoke, his voice matter-of-fact. "Until we know who they really are and why they're taking psychics, all we can do is fight a holding action. They don't win—but neither do we. And all the while, for every psychic we get to in time, we lose half a dozen more."

Sarah shook her head. "I never realized there were so many people with psychic abilities." She saw Brodie, Cait, and Leigh exchange glances, and added immediately, "There's something weird about that, isn't there?"

With a slight smile, Leigh said, "Never use the word *weird* in the presence of people with psychic abilities, especially a born psychic; we've heard it entirely too many times in our lives."

"Tell me," Sarah insisted, ignoring the wry humor. "I'm tired of being in the dark, and I have a right to know."

"It's all supposition, Sarah," Brodie said.

"All of this is supposition, according to you. So? What is this about the number of psychics?"

Brodie leaned back and gestured slightly toward Leigh, who spoke slowly.

"We don't know what's causing it or what it means,

Sarah. All we know is that the number of people with psychic abilities is increasing, not only generation by generation, but year by year. More are born. And more are, for want of a better word, made. Created. Changed from latent to active. Twenty-five years ago, there might have been one or two people who became psychic in a given year due to a head injury or some other kind of trauma; this year, so far, you are one of fifteen."

"What?"

Leigh nodded. "Fifteen that we know of."

"How many did you get to in time?"

"Three. Not counting you."

"The others . . . they were taken?"

Leigh nodded again. "One of them was snatched almost under Brodie's nose. He wasn't happy."

With a grunt, Brodie said, "I hate to lose."

"It wasn't your fault," Cait told him loyally. "The guy couldn't bring himself to believe he could be involved in something so bizarre. He just didn't believe in the threat against him."

"We lose some because of that," Brodie agreed. "Psychic abilities vary; sometimes the people we're trying to help have no way of knowing the truth of what we try to tell them. They don't know they can trust us. So they run. Right into one of Duran's traps." He looked at Sarah. "That's why we had to be so careful with you, why we held back the couple of times we got close enough to make contact. It was my decision, and I've learned never to approach a wary psychic in the dark. Makes a bad first impression."

Sarah smiled slightly. "Yes, it would have."

He nodded. "But we're here now. You do know you can trust us, or at least you're giving us the benefit of the doubt. And you do know what we're up against."

Softly, Cait said, "And you know, now, how valuable you are."

Sarah drew a deep breath. "If all this was intended to persuade me not to go after Tucker—it failed."

"Sarah, you can't fight them." Brodie's voice was steady.

"I can try."

"You'll lose. They'll take you and kill Mackenzie. They're just waiting for you to come after him. You know that. He's bait."

She stared at him for a moment, then shifted her gaze to Leigh. "I came here hoping you could tell me some way to fight them. Teach me how to use my abilities against them."

"I don't know how, Sarah. I'm sorry. I can help you learn to use your abilities, but that will take time. It's a matter of concentration, of focus. Of learning how to tap into those places deep inside you—and outside you."

"The crossroads. I already found it."

For the first time, Leigh was obviously surprised. "The crossroads?"

A bit impatiently, Sarah said, "That place we all pass through, the—the junction of past, present, and future."

"You tapped into that?"

"Yes. Tucker needed to know something and . . . and I just reached out to find it for him." For the first time, she realized that each time she had found a new use for her abilities, it was because Tucker had asked it of her or needed it of her.

"And you found it? Something . . . from the past?"

Sarah nodded. "Someone he knew a long time ago. I had to find out what had happened to her."

Brodie turned his frowning gaze to Leigh. "That doesn't sound like what I'd expect from a precognitive psychic."

"No," Leigh said slowly, still staring at Sarah. "It isn't. Sarah, can you tap into that place at will?"

"I don't know. I don't really know how I found it the first time. It was . . . for Tucker."

"You're in love with Tucker."

It wasn't a question, but Sarah found herself nodding even as she felt the shock of awareness. *Yes. I'm in love with him.*

"You two are lovers?"

Cait, a bit uncomfortably, murmured, "Surely that isn't important?"

Leigh didn't even look at her. "It's vital. Sarah?"

Again, she nodded. "But just . . . one night. Last night. Before they got to him."

"I wonder if that was by accident or design," Leigh murmured.

Brodie was still looking at her. "Why's it important?"

"It's important because unless I miss my guess, there's now an unbreakable link between Sarah and Tucker. Sarah, can you sense him right now?"

"Yes. Just faintly, on the edge of my awareness. He's

sleeping now, or unconscious. He woke up once, briefly. It was cold and dark, and somebody was watching him." She shivered, remembering.

"Could you sense him like this before last night?"

"No. Though I did . . . hear . . . him thinking about me last night before we . . . before we became lovers."

After a moment, Leigh looked at Brodie. "We don't have a choice. If we want to save Sarah, we have to save Tucker as well."

"Why?" He glanced at Sarah. "I don't mean to sound cruel, but my job is to protect you—not Mackenzie."

"He's single-minded," Cait murmured.

"I didn't ask you to protect me," Sarah reminded him. "If it comes to that, you haven't been—Tucker has. So *he's* been doing your job."

"He's been dragging your ass all over the country is what he's been doing, bouncing around like a tennis ball. He should have sat tight in Richmond and made so much noise the other side wouldn't have dared to move against you."

"We didn't know who we could trust," Sarah snapped, not bothering to explain that their ultimate destination had been decided by her own budding but then inexplicable instincts. "And hindsight is twenty-twenty."

"You two stop arguing." Leigh's voice was mild. "Brodie, we have to go after Tucker. If Sarah doesn't take the bait and come after him, they'll kill him, right?"

Brodie nodded. "Not much doubt about that. They don't leave anybody alive who could testify to illegal acts such as kidnapping."

Leigh glanced at Sarah, then looked back at Brodie. "If they kill him, they'll sever the tie between him and Sarah. From what Sarah's been telling us, I believe that the tie is deeper than you can imagine and now is absolutely vital to her existence."

Brodie stared at her. "He dies . . . she dies. That's what you're saying."

"That's what I'm saying."

It should have shocked Sarah, but instead she felt only a faintly unsettled but unquestioning certainty that Leigh was right. She had never thought much about the term *soul mates*, but she knew now that that was what she and Tucker were. They were connected, mated at the soul, and neither of them would be able to survive now without the other.

Whatever else destiny intended for them, it was clear they were meant to be together.

Somewhat grimly, Brodie said, "I've seen a lot of strange stuff since getting involved in this, but I've never seen two people bound together because of a psychic link. Not to the death."

"If they kill Tucker," Leigh said quietly, "there'll be evidence enough to convince even you."

After a moment, he leaned back in his chair and, morosely, said, "Shit."

"There is a plus side to this," Leigh told him.

"Oh, yeah? I'd love to hear it."

"Sarah will have his strength as well as her own to draw on."

Sarah frowned. "That makes me sound . . . like a parasite."

Leigh shook her head. "Hardly that. The connection between you and Tucker runs both ways; eventually, he'll be able to tap into your abilities as easily as you do."

"A remote-controlled psychic," Brodie muttered.

"More or less," Leigh agreed. "Sarah, you two are a team. Two halves of a very powerful whole. And that might just give us an unexpected edge over the other side."

It was Cait who said, "But if they used a psychic to control Tucker's mind, won't that person be aware of the connection?"

"I doubt it. I wasn't aware of it, even after Sarah looked into my mind. It's too deep to be seen or sensed, and so rare that no one would think to look for it."

"What about when they use it?" Brodie asked, intent now and not so dour about the situation. "Won't it be obvious then? To another psychic, I mean."

"It might well be obvious even to a nonpsychic." Leigh frowned and shook her head. "The problem is knowing how all that power will . . . manifest itself. Sarah isn't the usual sort of precognitive psychic, and her ability to tap into that place she calls the crossroads makes her unique."

"It does?" Sarah asked.

"It definitely does. Sarah, in all these years, I've never known another psychic able to do that. We've theorized that such a place exists, but to my knowledge, no one has ever found it. Besides which, psychics tend to . . . specialize. I'm a telepath, as unable to see the future as Brodie or Cait is. I read thoughts, period. A precognitive psychic sees the future. An empathic psychic senses emotions, often through physical contact or objects. A telekinetic psychic is able to move or influence objects. And so on. But you . . ."

"I've seen the future."

"Yes. But you're also a telepath, a strong one. I believe you're able to send as easily as you receive. And if you are able to tap into this 'crossroads' you describe, then all of time is open to you. It may take you a lifetime to learn how to use the ability, but once you do . . ."

"Interesting possibilities," Brodie drawled.

Sarah decided not to think about the possibilities. Not now. There was already too much to take in, to understand; she focused on the most important thing in her life, and held him before her like a lodestar.

"I don't care about that. All I care about is getting Tucker away from those people."

"Which opens up a whole new set of possibilities," Brodie said, not drawling now. "Most of them unpleasant."

"I'm not asking you to help me," Sarah told him. "This is not your problem, so don't worry about it. It's not your fight."

Brodie linked his fingers together over his middle and looked at her expressionlessly. "Not my fight. Why don't you take a quick look inside me, psychic. Then say that again."

Sarah didn't intend to do it, but by now it really was like using another of her senses, like turning her head to listen or moving her eyes to watch: virtually automatic and without conscious effort.

What she saw was like scenes of a movie flickering past rapidly, scenes with abrupt cuts and odd angles, sometimes with sound and sometimes without—but always with tearing emotions. As she had with Leigh, she saw violence and danger and lost friends, but Brodie had lost much more than that. He had lost part of himself, and it had left him filled with rage and grief and a deadly, implacable determination to defeat the other side.

Sarah pulled herself out of the dark fury of his mind, more shaken than she had ever been before. She opened her eyes slowly and looked at him, at that handsome, expressionless face and those sentry eyes, and wondered how he could keep going when he was carrying around with him such a terrible burden of pain.

"Because I have to," he said softly. Then he looked at Leigh, and added in a more normal voice, "You're right. She's damned powerful. And she can send. Her voice was so clear in my mind it was as if I heard it out loud."

Sarah looked away from him, still shaken and conscious once more of what looking into another mind had taken out of her. She found Cait watching her and, even weary and not much interested, she saw a flicker of jealousy in the younger woman's eyes.

She didn't like me in Brodie's mind. I wonder if he knows . . .

She kept those thoughts to herself, wondering for the first time whether it was even possible for her, now, to shut off that other sense.

"Sarah, you need to eat something. We all do." Leigh looked at her watch. "It's suppertime anyway. You stay here and rest a bit, and we'll get something started in the kitchen. Then we'll talk about what we're going to do. All right?"

Sarah nodded. "Brodie?"

He looked at her as he rose to his feet. "Yeah?"

"I'm sorry."

He smiled slightly. "Don't worry about it."

He and the others went into the kitchen and very soon were working together to prepare the meal. Brodie gathered the ingredients for a salad and began chopping vegetables, and when he spoke to Leigh, it was in a low voice.

"That took a lot out of her. And I was wide open, not fighting at all. What happens when somebody fights her?"

"I don't know."

"Is she strong enough for this?"

Leigh shook her head. "I just don't know. If she can borrow some of Tucker's strength . . . if she gets mad enough, or scared enough . . . if she finally believes that she can change the future she saw for herself . . . then maybe."

Brodie grunted. "We'd better come up with a hell of a plan."

"Is Murphy close by?"

"Close enough. Figure we'll need her?"

"Her. And an army, if we can raise one."

FIFTEEN

Cait felt very much like the new kid on the block. Brodie and Leigh had worked together before and were comfortable despite their differing beliefs on some topics; they didn't consciously shut her out, it was just that they were long accustomed to discussing things between themselves.

And Cait was conscious of her own inexperience, her lack of history in this. She was a new recruit, actively involved for only the last six months; her brother had been one of those people who became psychic because of head injuries in the last year or so, and it had been Brodie who had contacted him and made sure the other side didn't get their hands on him.

During those dangerous and exciting weeks, Cait had decided that she wanted to work with these people. Brodie

had been reluctant, telling her she was too young and
should finish college before deciding what to do with her
life, but she had been determined—and he'd had to admit
they could not afford to turn down anyone who wanted to
help. Besides, there was someone else Brodie reported to,
someone who made certain decisions, and that person had
decided that Cait could be of use.

She didn't know who that was. Truth to tell, she knew
blessed little about how this loosely organized group of
people operated. According to Brodie, the number of
people who knew most of the details could be counted
on the fingers of one hand. As for the rest, they knew
what they needed to know, and not a single detail more
than that.

Which was fine for Brodie; unless Cait missed her
guess, he was one of those few who knew everything.
And his history with the group went back several years,
possibly as many as ten. Cait wasn't sure about that, but
she knew he'd been involved in this for a long time. And
though he didn't talk about it—to her, at least—she had
guessed that he was in this because something bad had
happened to somebody he'd loved.

Of course, Sarah knew all about that. She had looked
into his mind minutes ago, accepting his open invitation
to do so, and she had seen all his pain. It had been on her
face when she was done, a reflection of great anguish,
and in her peculiarly dark eyes had been sadness and
compassion and understanding.

Cait wanted that understanding, and it really bugged
her that Sarah had gotten it—on a silver platter, so to

speak. Hard as she'd tried in the last months, Cait hadn't been able to get past Brodie's guards, and he had sure as hell never thrown himself open to her in any way. Not that she was in the least psychic, but still. He treated her rather like a baby sister—when he wasn't coming down on her like a ton of bricks for carelessness or forgetting some rule or other—and as far as she could tell, that was exactly the way he saw her. As a troublesome kid.

It was very annoying. And annoying to be working her ass off in the kitchen while he and Leigh discussed other people she didn't know and tried to decide between themselves who they could call on for help.

"We probably don't have much time," Leigh was saying as she checked on potatoes fast-baking in the microwave. "Sarah isn't going to be willing to wait much longer."

"I know," Brodie said. "And that limits our options. If we figure tonight is a wash—and I sure as hell don't like the idea of moving against them at night—and that we move early tomorrow, that gives us only a few hours to make whatever preparations we can. Murphy can get here by morning. Maybe Nick and Tim. Nobody else I can think of."

Leigh said casually, "How about Josh? He could get here in time. He could raise an army in time."

Brodie shook his head. "No way. Duran's too close, and I don't want him to get so much as a whiff of Josh. No, this time it's just us. And that isn't much of an army, Leigh."

"No, it's not. On the other hand, we don't know what

we're facing. When Sarah's rested and eaten, we'll see if she can give us some idea of where they're holding Tucker, and maybe even the number of people holding him. Surely Duran wouldn't commit more than half a dozen of his people to this. He has other irons in the fire, and I would be very surprised if he really knows Sarah's potential value to him."

Brodie frowned. "Now that I think about it, it's not really like Duran to use bait to get a psychic to come to him. He tends to favor sending his goons in the dead of night to quietly remove people. Or to arrange some kind of convenient *accident* for them."

"Maybe he's feeling the pressure."

"Maybe." Brodie shrugged. "But if the bastard is anything, he's deliberate; I've never known him to rush into anything."

"The steaks are almost done," Cait announced.

"The plates are in that cabinet over there, Cait. Brodie, what about weapons?"

"Compared to the other side, we're seriously underarmed. Always have been. And we're hamstrung by the fact that we don't have any kind of official status or authority. We can't just rush in and start blasting, as good as that might feel to some of us. Plus, we don't want the kind of violence that makes headlines any more than Duran does. The only defense we have if bodies start turning up is not going to be believed, and our credibility is shot once we start talking about some vast conspiracy we can't prove exists." He shook his head. "No, we have to be very, very careful. In any kind of a showdown with Duran and his goons, we are critically handicapped."

Cait tuned them out, feeling even more frustrated. She had nothing to contribute, that was the problem. She was still learning how to handle weapons, and she didn't have the first idea how to plan for some kind of dramatic confrontation with the bad guys.

In fact, she felt incredibly useless.

They wouldn't let her help clean up after the meal, and since by then much of her energy and all of her anxiety had returned, Sarah found herself moving restlessly around the living room while they worked in the kitchen.

The need to find Tucker was nearly overpowering now, and with it came the niggling awareness of something else that was . . . wrong. She didn't know what it was, but somewhere, sometime, she had missed something she should have paid attention to. Information or an observation . . . something. Whatever it was, it seemed to be out of reach now; whenever she tried to concentrate on it, all she got was increasing uneasiness and the urge to look back over her shoulder.

Watching. Somebody's watching. But is it me, or Tucker? The uneasiness he felt about that went with him into his dreams . . .

That was part of her apprehension, she knew. That skin-crawling sensation of being watched had been uppermost in Tucker's consciousness just before his keepers had knocked him out once again, and even now his sleeping mind was giving him nightmares with that theme. Eyes watching him. Creatures watching him.

Sarah wasn't exactly caught up in the nightmares with Tucker; it was more like listening to the dim and distant sound of a television in the next room and being aware of what was going on there. She could push the faint sounds out of her conscious mind by concentrating on something else, but they were always there just under the surface, contributing to her uneasiness.

"Sarah?"

She turned to look at them as Brodie, Leigh, and Cait returned to the living room. "There isn't much time."

"Why not?" Leigh asked quietly. "The trap is baited and ready for you; won't they just wait for you to come?"

"I . . . don't know. I don't think so. There's a feeling of urgency."

"Maybe that's just you," Brodie suggested. "Your need to get to Mackenzie."

She shook her head. "No, this is something else. Somebody's anxious, worried about time passing. I'm sure of it."

Leigh looked at her for a moment, then said, "Let's sit down. Sarah, do you think you can sense where Tucker is being kept?"

"If he was awake, I know I could. But he's still asleep. Dreaming."

Leigh waited until they were all sitting down before suggesting, "Try anyway. Try to concentrate on his physical sensations rather than his emotions. You may be able to shut out his dreams that way."

Sarah was hesitant, wary of his nightmares, but she closed her eyes and tentatively reached out toward Tucker. Instantly, gooseflesh rose sharply along her arms and she shivered in a wave of coldness. It was very cold here, and very damp; there was water dripping somewhere. And another sound, very faint. Breathing. Someone's breathing.

She was lying on her side on something not quite as hard as the floor, and it was dark when she opened her eyes. It should have been too dark to see, but she thought she could anyway, though more with another sense than with her eyes. She got up cautiously, vaguely aware of leaving something behind her and hating that, but intensely aware that she had to see what she could of this place.

She moved soundlessly several feet and then stopped, abruptly. Someone was right beside her. She couldn't see him, but she felt him. She almost touched him.

Shadows.

Gooseflesh spread all over her now, and she found herself flinching to the side, drawing into herself. He hadn't touched her, didn't know she was there, and she had to make sure not to betray her presence. She didn't know how she knew, but she was convinced that if he knew she was there, he would instantly kill Tucker.

Cautiously, moving with exquisite slowness, she eased past the shadow in the dark. There was a doorway she went through, and it puzzled her a bit because she was almost sure the door had been closed. And locked.

She had the overpowering sense of space around her,

above her, cavernous and empty. No, she realized. Not empty.

Shadows.

They were all around, though not close. Watching, she realized. Waiting. Waiting for her to come. Whispering among themselves . . .

Sarah moved slowly through the darkness, listening intently and trying to get a sense of her surroundings—and avoid those lurking shadows. There were other doorways, and stone or concrete walls and old, old timbers. The air was musty and damp, the dripping of water somewhere an incessant sound.

She was so cold.

With fingers that were slowly going numb, she reached out to touch the walls around her. After several minutes, she touched a ledge or narrow table and upon it found rows of pillar candles connected with the wispy, sticky threads of cobwebs.

She jerked her hand back, wiping it fastidiously against her thigh, and for a moment had to stand perfectly still and breathe evenly. It was all right. Nothing here could hurt her. Because she wasn't really here, was she? She was . . . well, she was somewhere else. So nothing in this place could hurt her.

But it could scare the hell out of her.

She forced herself to go on, searching the darkness with every sense except sight. The cavernous sensation had diminished as she had grown accustomed to the dark, and she was aware now of a roof of some kind not many feet above her head. In one small room, she found stacks of old furniture, the wood splintered and smelling of rot. In another, she found the tattered remains of some kind of cloth in moldy piles against the cold earthen walls. In still another, she found shelves and cabinets containing dusty, rusted objects she tentatively identified by touch.

She kept going, and after she passed through what she thought was the back of a closet, she found herself in a low-ceilinged corridor that felt like a tunnel. It was leading her away from the rooms and the place where she had gotten up from the floor, and though the air around her lightened and she was aware of climbing as though out of a pit, it disturbed her to get so far away from what she had left behind.

It was important, though, so she kept going. Until, finally, she pushed her way through heavy brush and found herself standing only a few yards from a rocky shore. The ocean, she realized, watching waves lapping against the rocks. She turned to look back at the tunnel's entrance, finding that it was cut into almost solid rock with a cliff rearing steeply above it.

She lifted her gaze beyond the tunnel, beyond the cliff. And in the twilight, etched sharply against the sky, she could see a cross.

Behind her, something tugged sharply.

———

"I don't like this."

"Neither do I."

"Then bring her out of it, dammit."

"She has to find her own way back. If we disturb her now, she could lose the connection."

"Look at her. Her skin's like ice, she's barely got a pulse—and she's been like this for nearly an hour. What the hell is going on?"

"I told you. She's out of body."

"Christ. I thought she was just going to reach out to Mackenzie, not go visit him."

"She did reach out. And since he was unconscious, it seems this was the only way she could find out where he is. By going there."

"There must be a better way."

"I don't think so. My God, Brodie—she is the one!"

"She's going to be the dead one if we don't get her back soon. Sarah? Sarah!"

"Brodie—"

"Sarah!"

"What?" She opened her eyes, abruptly and completely awake and aware, and found three pairs of eyes staring at her. Their expressions varied from Cait's half-fearful fascination to Leigh's excited interest. Brodie just looked relieved.

"Jesus. Don't do that again."

Sarah shifted a bit in her chair and found herself a little stiff, but curiously refreshed and no more tired than she'd been before. Either this was getting easier, or she had borrowed some of Tucker's strength. Or else this new thing required much less energy. But her hands were very, very cold. She rubbed them together. "How long was I gone?"

"You realize you *were* gone?" Leigh asked.

"Sure," Sarah replied, absently stretching her arms out before her to ease the stiffness. "How long?"

Brodie glanced at his watch. "Since you closed your eyes, an hour and five minutes. You became a zombie about ten minutes into the procedure."

She smiled at him. "A zombie?"

"Soulless," he explained frankly. "A body with a beating heart. Creepy as hell."

Rather to her surprise, Sarah found that his honest aversion didn't make her feel like a freak. Or maybe she was just getting so accustomed to this that acceptance had built its own armor. "Sorry I creeped you out."

"Oh, don't mention it. I find this sort of thing happening with alarming frequency these days. You'd think I'd get used to it."

Leigh cut in impatiently. "Sarah, were you there? With Tucker?"

She nodded. "It was dark; that's why it took me so long. I had to feel my way around until I found the way out."

Bewildered, Cait said, "I thought the way out was back through Tucker. Leigh said that's how you got there, and—"

Sarah didn't blame her for being confused. "I got there through Tucker, and I came back through him, but I was looking for a physical way out. One we could use when we actually—I mean physically—go there."

There was a part of Sarah that couldn't believe she was discussing this so calmly and matter-of-factly. Yet to another part of her, it seemed perfectly normal and nothing to get upset or excited about.

"A way out," Brodie said. "As opposed to a way in?"

Sarah looked at him. "They believe there's only one way in, and they're all around it—that's the trap they've set. I go in, and no matter what happens inside, I can't get out, because they close the way behind me. But I found a back door we can use, an entrance they know nothing about. How we use it depends on the plan we decide on."

"Where is this place?"

"It's an old, abandoned church right on the coast. Outside the city, but not too far away. Tucker is being held in the cellar, and it's a big one. Lots of rooms and a rabbit warren of narrow corridors. And there are tunnels spreading out from the church; I think they were built and used for storage, and to get to other buildings when the weather was bad. Most of the tunnels are probably caved in now, but one leads through the rock and out to the beach. At that point, in that place, no one paying attention to the church would see us go in."

Brodie frowned. "Do you know how many of them are there?"

Sarah felt herself shiver and looked down to watch gooseflesh rise on her arms. "I . . . couldn't count them. Couldn't . . . differentiate between them somehow. Just shadows lurking around me, and above me in the church. But I know there are several of them, at least. Maybe half a dozen. And one very close to Tucker, keeping watch."

"Did they know you were there?" Leigh asked.

"No." Sarah looked at her. "I was very careful not to

touch any of them. I knew it was vital that they not find out I was there. Because if they had, they would have killed Tucker immediately."

"Why?" Cait asked, still baffled.

Softly, Leigh said, "They would have known how she got there. They would have understood that she was already lost to them, her potential fully realized. Worse, they would have known that she was able to move among them, unseen. Find out things about them. They would have had to destroy her. Killing him would be the quickest, easiest way to do that."

"If they aren't psychic," Cait said, "could they have known she was there?"

Leigh looked at Sarah questioningly.

Slowly, Sarah nodded. "If I had touched any one of them . . . they would have known. They may not be psychic, but they—somehow—instantly recognize the paranormal when it comes into contact with them, I'm sure of that. If they had touched my . . . my spirit, the energy of me that was there, they would have sensed and recognized me. And if any one of them touches me physically, they'll know I'm connected to Tucker."

This time, Leigh looked at Brodie. "There's something new, something we didn't know. We can recognize them by touch—and they can recognize us."

Brodie was still frowning, though he didn't seem bewildered, just thoughtful. "I'll make a note—for future reference. So . . . we have to get in there and get to Mackenzie before any of them touch you. What about him? I assume they've touched him already."

"He isn't a strong enough psychic for them to sense," Sarah said slowly. "And he doesn't yet realize he can tap into my abilities. As long as he doesn't know that, doesn't do that, they can touch him without sensing the connection. But . . ."

"But?"

"They've got him drugged. But if the drug wears off and he becomes conscious, he'll reach out to me."

"You're sure of that?" Leigh asked.

Sarah nodded. "Positive. When he became briefly conscious hours ago, I reached out to him. If I'd realized . . . but I didn't. I just wanted to touch him, to make sure he was all right. And just before they drugged him again, he realized what was happening. When he can think clearly again, he'll try to reach me. And I can't close that door." *I wouldn't even if I could.*

"So they'll know about the connection if they touch him when he's conscious."

"Yes."

"And will immediately kill him."

"Yes."

Brodie raked the fingers of one hand through his hair. "Great. Just great. We have to get past their guards without any of them touching you in any way, get our hands on Mackenzie, get him and you out of there without any of them grabbing or even touching either of you, and get away with our hides intact. And all that's assuming we can sneak in and out and that Mackenzie doesn't wake up and give away the show."

"That's what we have to do."

Cait said, "But if you're such a threat to them, won't they just keep coming after you? I mean, even if we can get Tucker away from them, it won't be over, will it?"

"No," Brodie said.

"Duran always backs off once he's missed his chance," Leigh disagreed. "Sarah will have to be careful, of course, because we do know they tend to keep tabs on us. Every time I participate in one of the psychic fairs in the area, or meet some reporter for an interview, I can feel one of them nearby. But I haven't had to look over my shoulder in years."

"And I think that's a mistake," Brodie said flatly.

Leigh smiled at him. "You worry too much."

"It's my job to worry." He looked at Sarah. "I'm plenty worried now. Even with a back door they don't know about, finding Mackenzie sounds like finding the center of a maze in pitch darkness—without touching any of the walls."

Sarah looked at him with a certain amount of sympathy but said reassuringly, "I have an idea. I think."

He eyed her. "Glad to hear it. Because I'm fresh out."

"Do you think you could get your hands on a few pairs of those infrared glasses I've seen soldiers wear in the movies? The kind that let you see in the dark?"

His brows rose, but Brodie said, "Given a few hours, I think I might be able to do that."

"Good. I don't know how many we'll need—enough for all of you." Almost absently, she added, "They like the dark, and they can see in it better than we can. I guess they have the glasses too, or something like them."

Brodie shook his head slightly but brought her back to the point. "Enough glasses for all of us. Okay. What about you? Please don't tell me you're planning to just walk into the trap?"

"I'm afraid so."

"Goddammit, Sarah—"

"It's the only way, Brodie. All their attention has to be on me, or you won't be able to get to Tucker. But don't worry, I don't have a death wish." She glanced at Leigh, who was smiling. "Not anymore."

"If that's supposed to make sense," Brodie said, "it doesn't."

"That's okay. It makes sense to me." Sarah began to lean forward to tell them all what she had in mind, but when her hand came to rest on her thigh, she felt something peculiar. She looked down and, as she lifted her hand slowly, saw the sticky white threads clinging to her fingers and to the denim covering her thigh.

It was just where she had wiped her hand in the cellar of the church.

Where she had not physically been.

"Sarah? What is it?" Brodie asked.

"Cobwebs," she murmured. She looked at him and the others, saw their puzzlement, and said slowly, "I think I have another plan."

———

Cait slipped out of the house through the patio door and felt rather than heard Brodie glide up beside her. "My turn to stand watch," she said in a low voice. "It's nearly three." She paused, looking up at him as her eyes adjusted to the dark, then said, "But I don't know why we're doing this. You said nobody's been watching Leigh."

"As far as we know, that's true." His voice was as low as hers. "But they've been on Sarah ever since she left Richmond, so it's at least possible they know she's here. And I wouldn't put it past Duran to make his move tonight while we're trying to get rested and ready for tomorrow. So stay alert, Cait. Keep your gun handy, and don't hesitate to raise the alarm if you even suspect something is wrong. If there's one thing they hate, it's attention, but it's something we can deal with; explaining a few gunshots to the police is a small price to pay for caution, and it's a hell of a lot better than having another psychic taken from under our noses."

Cait nodded. "Don't worry, I know the drill."

"I know you do." Still, he sounded restless, and unease was reflected in his next words when he said, "I think I'll take one more walk around the area, just to be sure—"

"Go to bed, Brodie." She stared up at his shadowy face and wished she had the nerve to suggest she join him there. "You haven't slept more than two or three hours a night since we got on to Sarah, and you'll need to be rested when we go after Tucker tomorrow. I can handle this."

He hesitated a moment longer, but finally nodded. "Yeah, I'm beat."

The admission surprised Cait, but she had the sense not to say so. "See you in the morning."

"Right."

When she was alone outside, Cait automatically adjusted the pistol stuck inside her belt at the small of her back and started to walk the perimeter—Leigh's front and back yard. There was no moon, but there were numerous streetlights in the neighborhood, and they lent the area enough light for her to see fairly well.

Either there were no dogs nearby or else they were no more disturbed by Cait's almost silent movements than they had been Brodie's, because no barking greeted her as she made her cautious way around the property. In fact, she heard no sounds at all, other than the usual peaceful night sounds.

She didn't think too much, just did what she'd been taught to do. Move slowly and quietly, watch everything, and stay alert. But as time passed, inevitably, she grew a little bored and found her mind wandering even as she completed yet another walk around the house.

Which was why she nearly jumped out of her skin when a man stepped out of the tall shrubs in front of her not two feet from Leigh's front walkway.

"Shit!"

He chuckled. "Sorry—I thought you saw me coming. You're Cait, right?"

Her hand on the pistol's grip relaxed. "Yeah. And you're—Nick? Tim? I knew Brodie called in reinforcements, but we weren't expecting you until morning."

"Traffic was light." He stepped closer, his smile a slash of white in the darkness.

There was absolutely no indication that anything was

wrong, but in her head, suddenly, Cait heard Brodie's implacable words.

Never trust anybody who comes to you in the dark.

She tried to pull her gun, but it never even cleared her belt.

———

Sarah woke suddenly, her heart pounding. She had no idea what was wrong, but something was, something was terribly wrong: There had been a scream in her mind. She threw back the covers and got out of bed, not bothering to find her shoes or put anything on over the white sleep shirt. And she didn't turn on the light.

She wasn't trying to be quiet, so it wasn't surprising that she woke Brodie hurrying past his door; she heard a sleepy curse from inside the room but still didn't pause, and she was at the bottom of the stairs by the time he reached the top of them.

"What the— Sarah?"

"Something's wrong," she flung back over her shoulder, struggling with the front door's lock.

"Don't go out there! Goddammit, Sarah—!"

She could have told him that whatever danger there had been was past, but Sarah didn't waste the effort or the breath. Instead, she got the door unlocked and flung open before he could reach her and rushed out of the house with no clear idea of where she was going.

She tripped over something that lay in the shadows of shrubs near the house and went down hard, bruising her knees. But she barely felt that pain, because her hands were in something warm and sticky, and a wave of terrible revulsion swept over her.

"Oh, God," she whispered.

"Sarah?" He was coming through the door toward her.

She wanted to warn him, to say something, but the only sound Sarah heard escape her throat was a kind of moan.

Then the flashlight in Brodie's hand came on, spearing stark white light through the darkness. The light fell on her shaking hands, held out in front of her, and she stared numbly at the blood dripping.

She heard a sound come from Brodie, saw the light jerk away from her hands . . . and fall on Cait's white face and staring eyes.

And the gaping wound that opened her throat almost to her spine.

———

The sun was well up when Brodie came into the kitchen, where Sarah and Leigh sat in silence with coffee cups before them. He poured himself a cup, his hands steady, but his voice was stony when he said, "Nick isn't here yet."

"What about Murphy?" Leigh's voice was calm.

He nodded. "Gathering some supplies. We should be ready to move in another couple of hours."

Sarah looked at him incredulously. She could still feel Cait's blood on her hands despite a hot shower and lots of soap, yet this man who had been her partner stood there talking as if nothing had happened. Before she could say anything, however, Leigh spoke gently.

"We'll grieve later, Sarah. Cait would understand."

"Would she? I'm not so sure I do. You both act as if nothing happened. What about—what about her body?"

Brodie's jaw tightened. "We've cleaned up the walkway so there's no visible evidence anything happened. Tim's taking her back to New York. It's where she's from. I'll talk to her brother after this is finished, though he probably knows already. And . . . simple enough to arrange to have the body found so it'll look like one more victim of senseless violence."

Sarah moved slightly, not realizing how clearly her feelings showed on her face until Brodie spoke again, harshly this time.

"There's nothing else we can do. We can't afford to call in the police, Sarah. We don't have any answers they'd believe, and no time to even try convincing them."

"But . . . just to dump her somewhere . . . How can you?"

He drew a breath and let it out slowly. "Listen to me. We don't have a choice. Bodies require explanations. Serious explanations to serious people in authority. And people in authority frown on murder. They look for likely suspects—and they don't believe in ghostly conspiracies involving psychics and shadowy merciless bad guys. So who do you think they'd suspect?"

"Not us," Sarah objected. "Surely—"

"Of course us. We found one of Leigh's kitchen knives out there. The murder weapon. With her prints on it—or mine, or yours. Sarah, the other side doesn't generally leave bodies lying around just to show they can."

"What do you mean?"

"I mean they always have a reason, a purpose. Cait was meant to be a murder victim, and we were meant to be suspects."

It was Leigh who said slowly, "But, why? They have a baited trap waiting for Sarah. Why this . . . diversion?"

"I don't know why." Brodie, his face still gray and older than his years, stared at his coffee with a frown. "It's a stupid, senseless waste of a life. A young life. I never should have taken her on as my partner, never. She was too young, too reckless."

"Brodie, it isn't your fault," Leigh said quietly.

He shot her a look but, instead of arguing, said, "The only thing I can think of is that they're trying to delay us and figured a murder would do it. If Sarah hadn't awakened knowing something was wrong, the first person to . . . see Cait would have been that neighbor of yours across the street, Leigh. The one who goes to work so early. When he came out his front door, he would have seen your front walk clearly. And seen her body."

"And raised the alarm," Leigh agreed.

Brodie nodded. "Even at best, we'd have been kept tied up with the cops all day. At worst, one or more of us would have ended up in jail."

Sarah shook her head a little, trying to make her mind work as logically as these two seemed able to. "I just don't understand why they would want to delay us."

"Neither do I," Brodie said. "Stalling for time. But why?" He looked sharply at Sarah. "What's going on with Mackenzie?"

By now, Sarah didn't even have to close her eyes and concentrate. All she had to do was pay attention.

"He's . . ." She stared at Brodie. "The drug's wearing off. He's beginning to come out of it."

"Then," Brodie said grimly, "we're out of time."

SIXTEEN

Astrid kept her eyes closed, concentrating intensely, her nimble mind feeling its way. Varden watched her, every bit as intent and glancing more than once at his watch.

"Faster is better," he said finally, impatient.

She opened her eyes with a sigh and stared at him. "Not in this. Look, do you want me to do this, or not? Because if you do, peace and quiet will help me do it."

There was little Varden could do but accept that, but he made a mental note to teach this one a lesson or two in obedience in the near future. "All right. Just do it."

Astrid closed her eyes again, and for a good five minutes there was utter silence. Then she frowned, her head tilting to one side in a considering pose. A moment later she opened her eyes and looked at Varden. "I don't think you want me to do this. He—"

"Of course I want you to do it. Do you know how to follow orders, Astrid?"

"Yes, but—"

"Then do it. Just do it."

Astrid opened her mouth for further protest, then closed it. A faint smile curved her mouth, and her eyes glittered briefly. "Okay. You want it, you've got it."

"That's better," Varden said, satisfied.

Astrid closed her eyes again.

————

The drug they used made his head pound. That was Tucker's first clear realization. His head pounded, and his mouth was dry, and as sensation slowly returned to his body, he ached all over. And he was cold.

As before, it took him several minutes—he thought—to get his eyes to open. And, as before, all he saw was a lot of dark. *But I'm not blind. It's just fucking dark in here.*

He was sure of that. He wanted to be sure of that.

But there was one difference between this time and last. He wasn't absolutely positive, but he thought he was no longer being watched. Those eyes that had followed him into nightmares were gone now. There was no sense of anyone nearby sharing this darkness with him.

Or was that just another thing he wanted to be sure of?

No. No, he was alone here. His jailer had apparently left him alone, for some reason he couldn't fathom or simply because he'd not been expected to recover from the drug so quickly.

He wanted to try moving and test that theory but

forced himself to remain still because he had the dim idea that it had been some involuntary movement last time that had caused his jailer to jab him with a needle and knock him back out for God knows how long.

How long?

He didn't really have a sense of time passing, but a hollow, queasy feeling told him he hadn't eaten in at least twenty-four hours, so there was that. He was so damned stiff, he doubted he'd moved or been moved for at least that long. But was it longer?

Sarah . . .

Even as her name rose in his mind, he remembered that just before he had blacked out, he'd felt a whisper of her touch in his mind. Just a whisper, unfamiliar yet certainly her and real, not his imagination. For a brief moment, Sarah had been with him.

Could he reach her? He didn't have the faintest idea how to do it, but he'd urged Sarah to try too often not to demand the same thing of himself now. If he just concentrated . . .

Shhhh.

He didn't realize he'd closed his eyes until they opened suddenly and he peered warily into the darkness surrounding him. And even then, he wasn't sure he hadn't actually heard her until she spoke in his mind again.

Shhhh. Don't let them touch you. Whatever happens, don't let any of them touch you.

Sarah?

Do I sound so different this way?

It's . . . I'm not used to hearing you this way.

No. It's . . . strange. Her thought was almost apologetic.

Not strange. Just different.

We'll argue about it later. She seemed amused, he thought, but something else as well. Tired. And shocked, deeply shocked, because of something that had happened . . .

No. Don't go there.

But what's happened?

Never mind. Time enough to talk about that when we get you out of there.

We?

You were right; we aren't alone in this. I've found some . . . comrades. We're going to get you out.

Out of where? Where the hell am I?

In the cellar of a deserted church. Listen to me. Can you pick a lock? Open a locked door?

Cautiously, he flexed fingers that felt stiff, numb, and wondered whether he could. But he answered with confidence. *I learned how to pick locks to research a book.*

I thought you might have. Again, he felt a flicker of amusement in Sarah, but whether it was because of his stated confidence or the actual uncertainty she surely must have felt in him, he didn't know.

I don't have anything to use for a tool, he admitted. *And I was being watched.*

But not now.

No.

All right. We have to get you out of there, and soon. If this is going to work, you can't be where they think you are.

I want you to get out of that room as soon as possible. When you get the door open, turn immediately to the right and move a dozen paces. There's a door on the left. A storage room. Go in there, close the door behind you and wait.

But

Tucker, it's too dark for you to help us in any way except to put yourself out of their reach. That's vitally important. If any of them touches you now, they'll kill you. And me.

That was enough of a threat to gain his obedience. *All right. But I may not be able to find a tool in here to pick the lock—*

You'll find one. Close by. Don't waste any time, Tucker. If this doesn't work—

It will.

But I want you to know—

Shhhh. I'm going to leave you now. Try not to reach out to me; it distracts me and I need to concentrate.

He felt her easing away, and it took all his willpower not to try to follow her. Instead, he concentrated on flexing his fingers again, trying to ease the stiffness and cold numbness. To be ready.

———

"It's very simple," Duran said patiently.

The boy looked at him, amazed. "Simple? My head's gonna hurt for a week—"

"There will be . . . rewards if you're successful."

"And all you want me to do is take it from her, the way I gave her the cobwebs?"

"Exactly."

The boy sighed, and made himself comfortable. "All right. I'll try."

Softly, Duran said, "Rewards for success, Jeremy. Punishment for failure."

Jeremy looked at him and briefly chewed his bottom lip, then shifted a bit on the couch. "All right, all right."

Duran didn't say anything further. He just waited. And watched.

———

It seemed to Tucker that he had waited an awfully long time, flexing his fingers and blowing on them, before much feeling returned to them. He put his hand down, finally, touching the stone floor as he prepared to try to push himself up. And his fingers were still so chilled that he nearly missed it.

Even when he managed to pick it up, it took him several minutes to convince himself that the thin, flexible lockpick was real.

———

Sarah opened her eyes and drew a deep breath.

"Well?" Brodie asked.

Her right hand was clenched shut in her lap. Sarah held it out palm up and slowly uncurled the fingers. It was empty. Not ten minutes before, it had held a small tool designed to pick a lock.

"Son of a bitch," Brodie said quietly.

———

Sarah slowed the Jeep as she neared the old church. It was very old, constructed of stone and timbers that had weathered brutal Atlantic storms for probably a hundred years or more. Yet the cross atop the steeple was still straight, even if most of the windows were gone and vegetation had encroached on the building.

It looked deserted, an appearance Sarah knew was deceptive. There were no other buildings close by, though piles of stones here and there indicated where there might have been other structures once, and a forest of tall trees reared on one side of the property so that the church stood facing the woods with its back to the sea.

Isolated by miles from the nearest habitation, it was a perfect spot for clandestine activities; a bomb could go off here and the widely scattered neighbors in the surrounding countryside would probably not even notice.

It looked bleak. And lonely. And with every sense Sarah could lay claim to, it reeked of decay.

Shadows.

She could feel them all around the place, feel their attention, their eyes on her. Feel them like the certain knowledge of something twisted and dark hiding among the rocks. And terror crawled over her flesh like the cold touch of a dead hand.

She actually stopped the Jeep and sat there for several minutes gripping the wheel. Trying to breathe evenly, to get control of her fear. Being here physically felt radically different from being here in spirit had felt, the threat to her more direct and far more deadly.

All her instincts were urging her to run, to get away. If it had been anybody but Tucker inside, she thought she would have.

Sarah drew a deep breath and, steadily, sent the Jeep forward once again. No matter what, she couldn't allow any of them to touch her. Or Tucker. Even Brodie conceded that if they could get Tucker out of there and escape themselves, the other side would back off at least for the moment, but if Duran even guessed what Sarah was capable of, she and Tucker were dead.

The raw memory of Cait's blood staining her hands was proof enough of an enemy that wouldn't hesitate to kill.

She guided the Jeep to a level place near the church where a parking area might once have been and cut the engine. She got out, trying not to look too conscious of being watched. Not that it really mattered. They had to assume she knew it was a trap, particularly since she had been bluntly invited to come after Tucker. If they were as good as Brodie said they were, they would be looking past her even now, searching for the others they had to assume would be following.

It was a classical tactical move, Brodie had told her. She went in, seemingly alone, and when the enemy closed in behind her to seal the entrance of the trap, her backup would close in behind *them*—catching them in their own snare.

Of course, they would expect the tactic. So they were going to get it.

Sarah opened the hatch to get out the kerosene lamp she'd brought with her, then brushed her cold hands down her thighs one at a time, took a deep breath, and concentrated on enclosing her mind with the strongest walls she could build. Then she walked steadily into the church.

———

There was nothing easy about picking a door lock in pitch darkness, even with a lockpick. In fact, it was difficult as hell, especially with chilled, nearly numb fingers. Tucker had the feeling it was taking him too damned long to do it, but he gritted his teeth and kept working on it.

He was conscious of Sarah on the edge of his awareness, a spot of warmth he wanted to pull around him like a blanket, but kept his attention fiercely on what he was trying to do. He had no clear idea what Sarah had been through since he had left their bed at the hotel, but that brief glimpse into her mind told him that it had been rough for her, and he wasn't about to add to her burdens.

So he had to get his ass out of this room before somebody came back here to check on him, and he had to make damned sure none of those bastards got their hands on him.

Simple enough.

But the reality made the odds against those simple goals rather high. He was still fighting his way out of the drug-induced haze, for one thing, so concentrating or even thinking clearly was a problem. He was also stiff from lying immobile for such a long time, and strength was only slowly returning to his muscles.

Dexterity was also a problem; he dropped the lockpick twice and had to feel around on the cold stone floor for it. It occurred to him that if he lost the thing he'd really be up a creek, so he tried to be more careful.

He didn't realize what a strain the physical and mental effort was until the door finally opened and he had to hang on to the knob and just breathe for a few minutes.

It was as dark outside the room as in, though he could faintly discern a glow maybe two shades lighter than the darkness way down the corridor that stretched out straight ahead. The temptation to move toward the light was strong, but Tucker remembered his instructions and, after he'd closed and relocked the door behind him, turned right and plunged into more darkness instead.

He found the storage room on the left just where Sarah had said it would be, and for the first time wondered how on earth she knew that. Of course, she seemed to know a hell of a lot about many things, more with every day that passed, but he still wondered.

Life with Sarah was going to be very interesting.

He slipped into the room, his senses flaring out in an attempt to get some idea of what was in here with him, and closed the door softly behind him only when he was reasonably sure he was alone. From the door, he began moving very slowly along the wall clockwise. It was distinctly unsettling to be feeling his way around in pitch darkness, but it was better than just standing or sitting and waiting with no idea of what was around him.

He found out quickly enough that most of what was around him was boxes and trunks, and numerous piles of rotting furniture and apparently scrap wood.

The furniture was easy enough to identify by touch, and it cost him only one splinter and a bruise on his shin. It was much harder to make himself reach into trunks and boxes when he couldn't see what he was about to touch, but he steeled himself and did it.

He had no intention of making things harder for Sarah, but he was also not used to feeling helpless—and he'd been helpless too long. If he could find anything that might help him get himself and Sarah out of here in one piece, then he intended to find it.

Most of the stuff in the boxes and trunks was unidentifiable; a couple of sharp, metallic edges made him glad his tetanus boosters were up to date, and he once encountered some squishy stuff he didn't even want to think about, but mostly it seemed to be household objects and the like that might once have been packed away down here as charity contributions no one had been able to use.

Tucker agreed that most of the stuff was useless, to him anyway, and he was feeling very frustrated when he pried open a smaller box, earning himself another splinter and a jab from an undoubtedly rusty nail, and this time found bottles. Several of them.

It took him only a moment or two to realize what he'd found, and when he did, he knew he had two-thirds of a dandy weapon. If he could only find the other, necessary, third.

"My kingdom for a match," he muttered.

"I think I can oblige," said a voice out of the darkness.

———————

The inside of the church was dim and dusty and very quiet. Sarah paused only a moment among the few remaining pews, then made her way to the back where she knew the stairs would be. She found them easily enough, the door waiting open for her, and again it took more courage than she thought she had to make herself walk down into that black maw.

She paused only long enough to light the kerosene lamp. It had been chosen with care, because it would give off plenty of soft light all around her rather than a beam of brilliance as a flashlight would. Even so, it threw as much shadow as light as she went down the narrow stairway, and those shadows made her skin crawl once more.

Shadows. You're here. Close. But she thought there was only one or two of them beneath the church, which surprised her for only a moment. *Of course I can't get out of the trap. So two—one to grab me, and one to guard Tucker. And all the rest guarding the door.*

The smells of musty age closed around her, damp and moldy and dank, and she found herself breathing through her mouth rather than her nose. It got colder with every step she took, and despite her warm sweater and jeans, she was chilled before she reached the bottom. At the bottom of the stairs, she found herself in the large, square room that was the original cellar of the church, her lamp showing her what she had felt her way through before. Numerous doorways and halls opened off this central room, some of them cut into the rock the building sat upon while others tunneled through earth.

Sarah made her way immediately across the central room to the narrow table holding all the pillar candles. Without so much as a glance toward any of the rooms or corridors around her, she set her lamp on the table, reached into her pocket for matches, and began lighting the cobwebbed candles.

She was nearly done when a gust of air from somewhere nearby caused the flames to waver wildly, then blew half the candles out. She dropped the match, and it sputtered out on the stone floor.

"Waauur."

Sarah nearly jumped out of her skin, and stared incredulously at the large black cat that had leaped onto the far end of the table and sat watching her with a slowly lashing tail.

"Pendragon?" Surely, it couldn't be . . .

"Waauur."

Despite her amazement, she didn't have much doubt that this was the cat she had left behind in Richmond. He was just too distinctive looking, those eyes too blue and collar too individual for her to be mistaken. What she couldn't begin to imagine was what he was doing here. And how he'd traveled so far.

Another brief gust of air made the candles waver again. Pendragon hissed softly, then leaped from the table and vanished into the shadows near the stairs. Before Sarah could do more than stare after him, a voice spoke mockingly no more than three feet away from her.

"Don't like the dark, I see."

She turned quickly and for an instant thought her eyes were playing tricks on her, because all she saw was a huge, hideous shadow looming toward her. But when she blinked, it was only a man.

A very average man. Average height and weight, average brown hair, and average blue eyes. Wearing a very average business suit.

Somehow, that made it worse.

"Who are you?" she demanded. "Not Duran."

That surprised him. "No. I'm Varden."

"So this was your game." She wasn't really thinking about what she was saying, just talking to stall for time.

"It was."

"Bucking for a promotion?"

He smiled thinly. "If so, you'll help me get it, Sarah."

"Pass. Where's Tucker?"

"Safe. I just sent one of my men to . . . watch him. We'll let him go, of course, as soon as you leave with me."

She smiled. "Sure you will."

Varden shrugged carelessly. "He's of no interest to us."

"But I am. Want to tell me why?"

"Don't you know?"

"I know it's because I'm psychic. I don't know how you mean to use that."

"Come with me and find out."

Sarah stared at him almost curiously. "It'd be a feather in your cap if I did, wouldn't it? Why is a willing psychic better for you?"

His mouth tightened. "We're wasting time. It's over, Sarah. It's time to go."

Even though she had been expecting it, Sarah jumped just as he did when, high above their heads in the rotting building, the old church bells began a jangling, discordant song, accompanied by the sharp reports of gunfire.

"Your backup, I presume," Varden drawled, his face calm even as his hand dived inside his jacket and produced a businesslike black automatic. "We were expecting them, Sarah."

————

"You're a very good shot," Leigh said, looking admiringly toward the church and its swaying bells.

Murphy swore and aimed a shot at one of the broken windows, where a head had momentarily appeared. "I'd rather hit some of them instead of the damned bells. Just one, at least. Come on, Leigh—"

"No bodies, Murphy. We can't afford them."

"We can't afford to leave our own here, either," Murphy snapped. "Dammit, Leigh, will you get down? One lucky shot and—"

Leigh obeyed, ducking for a moment behind the pile of old lumber they were using for cover. When there was a lull in the gunfire coming from the church, she got off a few shots of her own. She hardly knew one end of a gun from the other, but the illusion of an army was needed, so periodically she aimed her pistol at the largest expanse of wood she could find on the church and fired.

"You're a menace," Murphy noted as what was left of a stained-glass window shattered under one of Leigh's bullets.

Leigh winced. "Now, if that isn't bad luck, I don't know what is."

"We make our own luck," Murphy told her flatly.

"Um. Maybe so, but I think I'll circle around and check on Nick. There's less glass on his side. And I've got to take care of step two."

"I wish you'd let me handle that," Murphy said.

"You're a much better shot than I am. You and Nick are needed for this."

"Will you, for Christ's sake, be careful?"

"You bet."

———

"We were expecting them, Sarah."

"Were you? Damn."

His eyes narrowed at her mild tone. "What have you done?"

"Read my mind." She knew that taunting him was a bad idea, but she couldn't help herself. She had been getting angry for a long time, and Cait's senseless death the night before had turned anger into rage.

He cocked the pistol and leveled it at her. "We're going upstairs, Sarah. Now."

The bells jangled above them, along with gunshots and, now, a crackling, whispery sound.

"I don't think so," she said.

"Varden! Get out of there!" The voice came echoing down the stairs, urgent and more than a little panicked. *"They're burning the place!"*

Sarah had counted on a moment of surprise, and she got one as Varden's gaze lifted instinctively toward the burning church above them. She moved instantly, leaping away from him and the light and toward the protection of a jumble of wooden crates.

A bullet splintered wood a heartbeat behind her, accompanied by a snarl from Varden.

Sarah didn't waste a moment, moving as swiftly as she could toward the corridor she knew would lead her to the escape tunnel. She tried to keep the boxes and junk of the cellar between her and him, but she had to circle widely to pass by him. She counted on Varden to head toward the stairs and his own escape.

For once, her instincts and senses failed her.

He was there, in front of her, gun leveled and face savage, blocking her way to the tunnel. "Bitch. Where do you think you're going? I haven't come this far to let you get away now."

For an instant, staring down the barrel of that gun and listening to the whispery "voices" of the fire spreading above them, Sarah felt an urge to just accept the inevitable.

I'm going to die here. The vision's coming true.
Destiny.

But the rage bubbling inside her was, finally, stronger. "I want my life back," she snarled right back at him. "You can't have it, you son of a bitch. You can't have anything I am."

Whatever he saw in her face, it was clear that Varden recognized a point of no return. And his own defeat. But his failure was mixed with thwarted fury. His free hand lifted, a walkie-talkie in it, and he snapped, "Braun! Kill Mackenzie!"

———

Murphy tried to keep Leigh in sight as the older woman put step two of their plan into action and torched the building. It was supposed to be a fairly simple action: toss a couple of incendiaries against the back of the church and set that end on fire, driving those inside out the front door.

Murphy had argued for a good, old-fashioned turkey shoot but was overruled. So it was with utter disgust and an itchy trigger finger that she watched several men stumble from the burning church within minutes and pile into two waiting long black cars.

The gunfire over, she eased the hammer back on her pistol but remained wary until the men had fled the scene.

"Not very loyal, are they?" Nick noted as he joined her. "They left at least two of their own behind."

"They're bastards, every last one," Murphy said, more or less automatically. Her gaze was directed toward the church. Through one of the glassless windows, she could see inside the church. See flames and falling pieces of timber. And . . .

"Jesus. Is that—?"

Nick followed her gaze, and his thin face tightened. Very quietly, he said, "Oh, my God."

"Braun! Kill Mackenzie!"

Sarah's heart stopped for an instant. But then a voice she recognized as well as her own erupted from the walkie-talkie in a cheerful response.

"Sorry to be the one to break it to you, but Braun sort of fell down on the job."

On the last syllable, a Molotov cocktail crashed against the wall just a few feet from Varden, and he flinched away from it instinctively, his gun hand lifting to shield his face from the heat.

Sarah wanted to kick him where it would hurt the most but still didn't dare touch him, and it was with immense satisfaction that she saw Brodie step from the doorway behind Varden and bring a bottle of something crashing against the back of his head.

Varden dropped like a stone.

"Aw, gee, did that hurt?" Brodie stared down at him pitilessly.

Tucker came through the doorway to stand beside him and said reflectively, "Terrible waste of thirty-year-old scotch."

"You wasted the first bottle," Brodie reminded him.

Sarah threw herself into Tucker's arms.

"Not wasted," Tucker said a bit thickly, his arms tight around her. "Hey, let's get the hell out of here. This place is on fire."

Brodie set an unused Molotov cocktail aside with a sigh. "You two go on. I'll drag him along. Guess we can't leave him down here to roast, much as I'd love to."

Sarah avoided the spreading fire and darted over to grab the kerosene lamp to light their way back through the tunnel; the two men had infrared goggles hanging around their necks, but she didn't feel much like plunging back into the darkness.

There was a crash from above and the floor of the church shuddered beneath the weight of whatever had fallen, so they didn't waste any more time. Sarah and Tucker led the way swiftly, while Brodie followed with an unconscious Varden slung over one shoulder.

"Where's the other one?" Sarah asked breathlessly as they hurried along the tunnel. "The one Varden wanted to kill Tucker?"

"I found him long before he heard that order," Brodie replied. "Knocked him cold and dragged him to the mouth of the tunnel. Any sign of Duran?"

"No. Varden said this was his game."

Brodie grunted. "That explains a few things."

"Like what?" Tucker demanded as they emerged from the tunnel and into bright daylight.

"Like why he baited a trap. Not Duran's style." Brodie dumped Varden unceremoniously just outside the tunnel and looked around with a frown. "Now, where the hell—"

"No need to clean up the mess, Brodie. I'll do that."

It was a deep, pleasant voice, cool and oddly resonant, and Sarah knew who he was even before she jerked around to find him standing only a few feet away.

Duran.

SEVENTEEN

Not an average man.

He was tall, athletic; physical power was obvious even though he wore a dark trench coat open over a sober business suit. He was dark, his hair the true black of a raven's wing, and strikingly pale and almost iridescent greenish eyes looked out of an extraordinarily handsome face.

Sarah was vaguely aware that both Brodie and Tucker had drawn guns and leveled them at the man, but he was looking at her. And she recognized him.

"I've seen your face," she said slowly. "I've seen you. In my visions."

He didn't look surprised, merely nodding, and he stood relaxed and apparently at ease despite the guns pointed at him.

Brodie said, "I've been waiting for you to turn up, Duran."

Those pale eyes flickered toward him, then returned to Sarah's face. "My apologies, Miss Gallagher."

"Why?" she asked blankly.

"This has been badly handled from the beginning. There was no need for so much . . . trauma."

"I suppose my dying in the house fire would have been much less traumatic for everybody involved?"

He smiled. "Exactly."

She knew it wasn't wise to try, but she let her senses reach out anyway, very carefully.

Immediately, she felt he was a dangerous man, yet that was only an intuitive judgment rather than something definite. She sensed no threat from him. In fact, she sensed . . . nothing. Not even shadows.

It was as if whatever made him the man he was—his personality, his spirit, his soul—were encased in something she simply could not penetrate.

Not, at least, without touching him.

Tucker said, "If you think you're going to get your slimy hands on her now, think again."

Duran glanced at him, then shrugged wide shoulders. "With a small army protecting her, I imagine you're correct, Mr. Mackenzie."

Tucker looked a bit surprised, and distinctly unbelieving, but since it wasn't the moment to bring him up to date on what they knew and had surmised, Sarah merely said, "I won't stop looking back over my shoulder. Just so you know."

Duran smiled again, and there seemed to be a flicker of honest amusement in his pale eyes. "Noted."

They could hear, faintly, the sounds of sirens approaching, and Duran added dryly, "It seems the local officials have finally taken note of the fire. Your people have pulled out; I suggest you do the same."

"And just leave you standing here?" Brodie demanded. "Why the hell shouldn't I drop you now and save myself a lot of trouble down the road?"

Duran looked at him and, pleasantly, said, "I have a mess to clean up. And we both know you aren't going to shoot me, Brodie. The only man you could kill in cold blood would be the man who killed your wife—a crime you know I'm not guilty of."

"What about Cait?" Brodie demanded harshly, not reacting in any visible way to the mention of a dead wife.

Duran shook his head slightly. "None of my people killed her."

"Do you expect me to believe that?"

"I don't care what you believe." Duran's voice remained pleasant. "But if I were you, I'd look inside my own house. For a traitor."

Brodie's finger tightened on the trigger for an instant, and his face was stone. But then he swore and said to Sarah and Tucker, "Let's get out of here. Now."

They left Duran standing there, and when Sarah glanced back, it was to see him looking down at Varden's unconscious body with a singular lack of expression.

———

The rendezvous point was about two miles away, and when Sarah, Tucker, and Brodie arrived at the clearing not far off the road, they found another Jeep waiting for them.

Murphy was sitting on the hood. A tall and very athletic woman with short, spiky blond hair and fierce green eyes, she looked like somebody the Navy SEALs might have trained, especially since she was wearing fatigues.

Sarah had met her only briefly and Tucker hadn't met her at all, so introductions were in order. As seemed to be her nature, Murphy was taciturn, merely nodding at Tucker, but then she said something that stopped them in their tracks.

"We've lost Leigh."

"What are you talking about?" Brodie demanded.

Murphy's voice was flat, hard. "She started the fire, as planned. And then—I don't know what happened. All I know is that I saw her inside the church, just as the roof started to cave in. Nick and I checked it out, but there was so much heat and smoke . . . He stayed back there to lurk in the woods and see what the cops find."

Brodie stood very still, his body rigid. His face was gray, his eyes hollow. "We have to look for her," he said mechanically. "Something else could have happened to her." He looked at Sarah. "Tell me something else happened to her."

She had closed her mind so tightly in order to get into the church that opening it widely now required an effort. But as soon as Sarah made that effort, she felt an icy wave sweep over her, shaking her badly and leaving behind it nothing but an empty ache.

She was holding Tucker's hand and was grateful for his strength and the solid warmth of him beside her. He hadn't known Leigh, but he felt Sarah's pain and loss, and his mind reached out instinctively to offer her compassion. It was a light but comforting touch she needed.

She put her other hand on Brodie's arm. "I don't . . . I don't think so. She's gone, Brodie. I can't sense her at all."

He drew a deep breath. "Christ." He looked suddenly much older than his years. First Cait and now Leigh. This time, the price had been high indeed.

Tucker asked quietly, "Why would she have gone in there?"

It was Murphy who answered him, her voice still hard but beginning to crack around the edges. "She might have seen one of them still trapped in there. She would have gone in."

"Even for one of them?" Tucker asked.

"Even for one of them."

———

It was decided not to return to Leigh's house. Murphy vanished for a few minutes and then returned to lead the way to what she called a safe house in Portland. Nick would meet them there later, and Murphy and Nick would remain with the others for the night, then go their separate ways in the morning while Brodie took Tucker and Sarah back to Richmond.

The first part went according to plan, but once they reached the house in Portland, one last surprise awaited them.

It was Sarah who realized that there was a faint sound coming from Tucker's computer case (which she had packed up and brought with her after he'd been taken from the hotel), but before anyone could panic, she said, "It sounds like e-mail again."

Brodie and Murphy looked at each other, and it was she who said, "Even if the machine is on, this shouldn't be happening. This place is a dead zone for wireless, I made sure of that."

Tucker sat down in the living room and got the computer from its case, placing it on the coffee table. It continued to beep quietly, regularly.

It was not on.

Tucker hesitated before turning it on, looking at the others and saying, "This is almost as creepy as finding them in my head."

"Sure it isn't a low battery?" Murphy asked, but not as if she considered that a possibility.

"When it's off? No. But it was on battery power when I left it at the hotel the other night. I'd be surprised if it has any power at all."

But it had power.

Power enough, anyway, to bring up a blank screen instead of the program manager, a black screen.

Words appeared on the screen as if they were being written as they watched, bright white against the black background, and the voice behind the words was so evident that they could almost hear it, low, pleasant, incongruously courteous.

Duran.

> You disappointed me, Brodie.
> I was rather hoping you would finish off Varden
> in the cellar and save me the trouble.
> But . . . what will be, will be.
> Isn't that right, Sarah?
> Until next time.
> Oh, and by the way—
> Leigh says hello.

Brodie sat down heavily in a chair across from Tucker, his face white and his eyes filled with a terrible awareness. "Jesus Christ. It was Leigh he was after all along. This whole thing . . . just to get Leigh."

"Then she's alive," Tucker said.

Sarah, with a good idea of what it would cost Leigh to survive, shook her head numbly. "She would have preferred to die in the fire. Believe me."

It was Murphy who said, "I bet when Nick gets here, he'll tell us the cops found a body in the church. A woman's body, burned beyond recognition. If Duran's been planning this all along, he would have been prepared."

Brodie slammed his hand down on the arm of the chair with a force that made them all jump, then shot to his feet and left the house.

"He needs some time to himself," Murphy told the others.

"He hates to lose," Sarah murmured.

It was much later that evening when Tucker had a chance to sit down and really talk to Brodie. The other man had returned to the house nearly an hour after his departure with a calm face and little to say, but when he and Tucker were alone—Sarah was in the shower, while Murphy stood guard outside the house and waited for Nick to join them—he was entirely willing to fill Tucker in on the details he had missed.

"Why can't we go public with this story?" Tucker asked after he heard it. "Break it wide open." He had his own opinions on the subject but wanted to hear Brodie's.

"Think about it. Conspiracy theories run amok in our society these days. If it isn't about Kennedy's assassination or Watergate, it's aliens or the space program or Vietnam or the mess in the Middle East—or just the government trying to pull something over on us. The very mention of a conspiracy theory makes people shake their heads and smile—and the idea isn't taken seriously. And that's at best. At worst, we're labeled nuts. So, we wait."

"Wait for what?"

"Hard evidence. Proof. Enough proof to go public. Enough proof to convince even people who don't believe in psychic phenomena *or* conspiracy theories that the threat is real. And growing." He shook his head. "We wait, and we watch, and we listen. Look for evidence. Try to get to and protect the people we know are in immediate danger. And build our network of people who do believe—and want to fight."

"In case you never find enough proof?"

"It's a possibility." His smile was both faintly amused and more than a little weary. "When the shit finally hits the fan, we may be the only thing standing between the bad guys and the future."

"I've never thought of myself as a revolutionary," Tucker said slowly.

"Maybe you'd better start. You have a personal stake in the fight now. And we need all the help we can get."

"What can I do? I'm a writer, not a soldier."

"I'm a lawyer," Brodie said dryly. "Cait was . . . was a waitress putting herself through school. Nick's a builder. I couldn't tell you what Murphy is or was, except hard as nails. Among the others I know personally in this thing, there's a truck driver, an architect, an engineer, two doctors, several nurses, a Nobel Prize–winning scientist, a very young student, a country-western star, and a billionaire. They aren't psychics. They aren't soldiers either. We don't need soldiers, Tucker. We just need people who believe in the fight and want to help."

After a moment, Tucker silently held out his hand, and the two men shook firmly.

"What about this 'traitor in your own house' business? Or do you think Duran was lying?"

Brodie frowned. "As much as I hate to admit it, I'm afraid he might have been telling the truth. It's not his style to kill without reason, and Cait's murder was utterly senseless. And even though we're reasonably sure it was Varden's plan to set a trap for Sarah—whether he was a red herring in Duran's plan to get Leigh or not—killing Cait doesn't seem to figure into that either. It just doesn't make sense."

"Unless it was done by somebody bent on weakening your group? Taking out a link of the chain and, worse, spreading suspicion and mistrust among you?"

"That could be it. We're still so scattered, so dependent on one another for information and support, that taking out a single link throws all the rest into confusion. Losing both Cait and Leigh means we'll be cutting and rerouting lines of communication for weeks. Maybe months. And we'll have to move some people, some of Leigh's contacts."

"Because you don't know what she'll tell the other side?"

Grim, Brodie nodded. "Exactly. That's why we're so careful, why so few of us know the complete setup of the group. The more who know it all, the greater the risk of the other side getting the information."

"What would they do with the information?"

"What they've done in the past. Destroy some of our outposts or safe houses—and infiltrate the group. Our psychics can spot most of them, but they use tools—like that cop back in Richmond—and the tools aren't always so easy to spot, even for psychics."

"But that's someone from the other side. What if

Duran was telling the truth? Have you ever had to fight a traitor among you?"

"No."

"Are you sure there's never been one?"

"As sure as we can be. But if Duran was telling the truth . . . then we're all going to have to be a lot more careful."

After a moment, Tucker nodded. "What's next for Sarah and me?"

"First," Brodie replied, emphasizing the word only slightly, "we find the safest place possible for Sarah. Richmond is okay for the time being; they'll avoid the place for a while after the fire, that cop's murder, and all the publicity. But we'll have to get another psychic in the picture to help Sarah learn how to use her abilities." He looked steadily at Tucker. "She's pretty incredible already, as I told you. Until we learn the limits of her abilities, we don't know how she'll be able to use them—but you can bet they're the best weapons she can have against the other side."

"She'll always be a target, won't she?"

Brodie didn't sugarcoat it. "Yes. Leigh was left untouched for years, but when Duran saw his chance, he took it. And her." He shook that off with an obvious effort. "But the news isn't all bad. We've found through trial and error—costly error—that total secrecy is the worst possible tactic we can use to protect our psychics. The answer isn't to hide Sarah away. It's to make her as visible as possible. The more people who are aware of her existence and abilities, the less likely she is to . . . disappear. Or have an accident."

Tucker's jaw tightened. Grimly, he said, "I know one way of alerting a few million people to her existence and abilities. I'll write a book about her."

Brodie smiled. "Already thinking like a soldier, I see. Good. Just don't mention our nutty conspiracy theory, okay? Not until we're ready to go public."

"No problem."

"In the meantime, we'll work up a plan of where and how best to . . . position her."

"She's going to hate this," Tucker said.

Brodie nodded sympathetically. "Most of them do, at first. The instinct is to hide, to pretend not to have dangerous abilities, certainly not to stand in a spotlight. But it's the only way. As far as Sarah's concerned, I think she'll find out she's more of a fighter than she ever suspected. I think she already has."

"I think you're right," Tucker said.

––––––––––

"I nearly decked him when he spoke to me suddenly out of the dark," Tucker said much later as he and Sarah lay in bed together catching up. "But since he had the goggles and I couldn't see a damned thing, he was able to dodge me until he could convince me he wasn't one of them."

Sarah didn't ask how Brodie had managed to do that. "I was very glad to see the two of you appear behind Varden, I can tell you that. He wasn't behaving as I'd expected. Most people have the sense to try to escape a burning building—especially if they believe there's only one way out."

Tucker's arms tightened around her. "He was too obsessed with getting his hands on you."

"And unless Duran was lying in that message to us, it probably got Varden killed."

"Brodie said he was pretty sure Duran had been running the show, at least as far as the lake, because he saw him there. But somewhere between there and Portland, whether in a setup Duran planned or on his own, Varden must have set his plans in motion."

"And grabbed you." Sarah moved a bit closer.

"I had no idea they could get inside my mind like that. I didn't even realize what was happening until it was too late."

"It wasn't your fault, Tucker. Um . . . you do realize, don't you, that we sort of have a thing between us?"

"A thing? Well, I guess that's one word for it."

"I'm serious. This connection."

"Yes, I noticed it."

"Does it bother you?"

"Don't you know?"

"Dammit, I'm trying to be courteous and not pry into your thoughts."

He chuckled. "I appreciate the effort."

"Well?"

"No, it doesn't bother me. You don't believe that yet, of course, but you will. Eventually."

She lifted her head from his shoulder to stare at him.

"Brodie told you some of the stuff I've been doing the last day or so, right?"

"He did."

"And none of that bothers you? Not the telepathy, or the out-of-body thing, or the lockpick I was able to send to you?"

"No. Although I'd like to try the out-of-body thing when I'm not drugged. Brodie said the consensus seems to be that you can only do it through our connection— to wander around where I am if we're separated, or wander around near your own body."

She eyed him in fascination. "That was the consensus, yes. Because I tried to go somewhere on my own and couldn't. I had to—to use you as a doorway."

"We'll have to experiment."

"Tucker, this really doesn't bother you?"

"Well, no. I love you, you know. That would probably account for it."

Slowly, she began to smile. "This is very sudden."

"Yes, it was. At first sight, I think."

"You know I love you too."

"This connection is a wonderful thing."

"I guess we'll never be able to say we don't understand each other, huh?"

"Not with a straight face."

Sarah's smile widened as he pulled her over on top of him. "It's going to be interesting, isn't it?"

"Oh, yeah," Tucker said. "That's one word for it."

The plan to leave for Richmond in the morning was delayed somewhat when Sarah announced at breakfast that they had to go to Holcomb first.

Tucker had more or less forgotten about that, so he was surprised. And since Sarah was staying very quiet and still on her side of their connection, he had no idea why it was so important to her.

Brodie was distinctly unhappy.

"What's in Holcomb?" he demanded.

Vaguely, Sarah said, "Something I have to do. It won't take long. And it's important, Brodie."

"We've been heading toward Holcomb since we left Richmond," Tucker said, and shrugged when Brodie frowned at him. "It was always her goal."

"Have you two checked out the weather? It's getting very cold out there, and it looks like we may be in for early snow. Heading farther north, even for a little while, is probably not a good idea."

"It's important," Sarah repeated.

That was all Brodie could get out of her, and since Tucker would only shrug and smile, he was no help at all. Finally giving in, Brodie consulted briefly with Murphy and Nick, and the group split into two, with the Jeeps heading in different directions.

Brodie had been right about the weather. It was extremely cold for the second day of October, and they ran into some snow flurries as well as a bit of sleet. But the drive to Holcomb was fairly short, and when Brodie parked the Jeep in a one-hour parking place on Main Street, the worst of the weather was still holding off.

"Now what?" he asked Sarah.

"Do you mind waiting here? This is something Tucker and I have to do."

Brodie frowned, but even the most suspicious glance around this extremely small and peaceful town could discern no threat whatsoever; it was a postcard-perfect image of small-town America.

"Don't be long," he requested.

Sarah led the way, walking beside Tucker along the sidewalk toward the edge of town.

"Where are we going?" he finally asked her. They were walking up a slight hill, and the only thing he could see in this direction was a pretty little church at the top of the hill. "If you mean to make an honest man out of me, I think we need blood tests and a license first."

"Not much farther."

"Sarah, why is it that you have to be here?"

She didn't answer until they stood before the small church. Then she stopped and looked up at him gravely. "We didn't come here for me, Tucker. We came for you."

Even then, he didn't understand. Not until she took his hand and led him around the church and into the neat graveyard behind it.

Then he understood.

He almost turned around and retreated then. But she did know him better than he knew himself, because Sarah never hesitated. She led him through the graveyard to the very back, where a big oak tree stood bare-limbed in the cold October air.

There were two headstones placed where they would

be shaded in the summer. Side by side. One was the standard size for a headstone. The other one was . . . very small.

Sarah had been right. Here was where something had ended.

She left him there by the graves, slipping away silently so he could be alone to say his good-byes to Lydia.

And the son she had named after him.

———

Sarah stood on the sidewalk in front of the church and looked vaguely down on the small town of Holcomb. It was still early, but the town was awake, people moving along the sidewalks, in and out of stores and the small café and the bank.

She wasn't really aware of time passing but thought it was probably at least an hour later when Tucker came up behind her. He slipped his arms around her, and she relaxed back against him.

"All right?" she asked.

"Yes. Finally." His cheek rubbed against her hair. "Thank you."

She felt his inner sense of peace, the relief of a burden long carried finally lifted from him, so Sarah didn't have to ask anything more. Instead, looking down on the town, she said, "Look at them. Going about their business as if nothing has changed. As if nothing is different."

"For them," Tucker said, "nothing is. Not yet, at least." He took her hand, and they walked back down the hill together.

EPILOGUE

Miranda Bishop closed the folder and returned it to her husband. "Are you sure this is something we need to monitor?"

"Aren't you?"

She hesitated, then swore beneath her breath. "None of our people have been touched by this. None of the Haven operatives. Maybe because we're too visible as and to law enforcement?"

"That's one of the unanswered questions. I don't like unanswered questions."

"Just what you've found out so far . . . there are some damned powerful psychics out there. We don't have any agents or operatives who can do what Sarah Gallagher can do. If they manage to teach her better control, who knows what she's truly capable of."

Bishop nodded. "And we have no way of knowing—yet—how many others are out there with powerful abilities. Within this . . . network, or on the other side, being somehow used. More unanswered questions."

Miranda was frowning. "I know you let yourself be seen this time, and I know why, but I think we need to be very careful. A psychic they assumed to be safe turned out to be a target; we can't make the same assumption about our people. Or about us."

"Especially," Bishop agreed, "if they really do have a traitor in their midst. We both know how damaging just the suspicion of a traitor can be when our lives depend on the teammates we expect to be watching our backs. The stakes are just as high for them. Maybe higher."

"So . . . we wait and watch. Gather information when we can, as quietly as we can. Keep our own people close. And don't stick our noses in unless and until we know what's really going on. Or know we can help the network somehow."

"It seems the best way to handle this, at least for now, and unless something changes."

"You trust Murphy."

Slowly, Bishop said, "I think Murphy has more secrets than her allies know about, her contact with me being one of them. But is she a traitor to their cause? I'd be surprised if she turned out to be that. On the other hand, I wouldn't be surprised to find out she has her own agenda."

"Another unanswered question?"

"Another piece of the puzzle, at least. We just have to

figure out where the pieces go. What the big picture really is."

"Oh, is that all?" His wife's tone was dry.

"Another challenge," Bishop noted with a faint smile. "Whatever the truth is, whatever that big picture turns out to be, we'll be ready when the time comes."

"I don't doubt that," Miranda responded. "We'll be ready. I'm just not sure the rest of the world will be."

"No," Bishop said. "Neither am I." He tapped the edge of the folder against his hand and repeated slowly, "Neither am I."

Another nightmare, in the woods this time.
Different: She was running. Trying to escape.
But the same ending. Always the same ending.
Another dead girl . . .

From *New York Times* Bestselling Author

KAY HOOPER

HAVEN

A BISHOP/SPECIAL CRIMES UNIT NOVEL

Emma Rayburn was born and raised in Baron Hollow, North Carolina. It was a quiet life, then came the accident . . . and the nightmares—each filled with unshakable visions of darkness, blind panic, and desperate women chased toward inevitable death. With no reports of local women missing or found dead, Emma has written it off to troubled imaginings—night after dreaded night, until her sister arrives to wrestle her own demons. As the two begin to face the past, a long-dormant secret threatens to emerge . . . one people would kill to keep.

facebook.com/BishopPage
facebook.com/TheCrimeSceneBooks
penguin.com